THE
GETBACKS
OF
MOTHER
SUPERIOR

THE GETBACKS OF MOTHER SUPERIOR

OF

MOTHER SUPERIOR

B Y

Dennis Lehman

ARBOR HOUSE

NEW YORK

Designed by Robert Bull
Manufactured in the United States of America

10 9 8 7 6 5 4 3 2 1

Library of Congress Cataloging in Publication Data

Lehman, Dennis.
    The getbacks of Mother Superior.

    I. Title.
PS3562.E4282G4   1987   813'.54   87-921
ISBN: 0-87795-888-2

*In loving memory of Leo F. Lehman
and in honor of Dorothy M. Lehman,
my parents.*

I'm fishing. An unopened telegram waits confidently in my lap, caution yellow clinging to Levi's worn icy blue by excessive but loving care. A breeze tickles the flap of the envelope, and my fingers begin to tingle. Pandora had fingers like mine.

Woman would say I'm ambivalent about opening the wire, a feeling she communicated when she dropped the telegram in my palm and fled, her heels clicking out "yourdecision, yourdecision, yourdecision" on the newly planked dock. Ambivalent. When I met Woman, I couldn't spell the word, let alone attempt its definition. Hers was better than Webster's: Ambivalence is watching a sworn enemy drive over a cliff in your new, uninsured automobile. I later learned a more graphic one: Ambivalence is watching a mortal antagonist being arrested for shooting your best friend.

A stronger vibration in my hands. The red-and-white Day-Glo fishing bobber is jiggling suspiciously. One more dip will force me to tug on the line in order to preserve the traditional relationship between man and fish. Funny, when I was a kid in Oklahoma, a good fishing spot was a stretch of moving water that produced rich bounties of flapping, flopping, multihued trout or sunfish. Now I prefer this quiet water, where the overfed perch don't bother you much.

This fish isn't hungry. He's bored. Nibbling forbidden fruit to put some meaning back into his life. An ounce of tension on the line reminds him the wriggling bait hides a silent, lethal hook. He nuzzles the worm a couple of more times by way of a thank you

1

and the bobber stops making distracting concentric circles on the otherwise-placid surface. I relax, straightening my legs. The movement dislodges the telegram, and I pounce as it slips toward the water: My reflex action snaps the tip of the rod skyward, jerking the line sharply toward the shore. The perch strikes, and pulls the float completely beneath the surface. He's hooked himself! Dumb fish should have known better, but maybe he thought the prize was trying to escape, or boredom made him less cautious, willing to try anything for a little excitement; whatever, he's hooked. Now custom dictates I reel him in, thereby ruining both our afternoons.

A glance back at the cottage catches Woman in a furtive return to the clothesline. She begins fluffing great cumulus puffs of sheets into a wicker basket; outwardly she's a study in contentment, yet I helped her hang those same sheets just half an hour ago. Taking down wet washing is not a good sign. Woman is worried. Me too.

I tuck the telegram into my shirt pocket, then lift the protesting perch onto the dock. The hook comes out easily, and I slide the fish into the live catch box floating in the water at my feet. He takes a couple of laps around the screened cage, yearning for the freedom he has just exchanged for a satisfied impulse. Finally, he stops, lazily finning the water as he stares sadly out through the mesh. I drop the tattered remains of the worm in front of his nose; the fish snaps up the tidbit and begins munching, quickly consuming the cause of his downfall as though it were suddenly good for him, something he really needed after all. As he begins sniffing the waters of his new home I know he's surrendered. A quick jump would easily put him over the top of the box. Certain escape is but a tail flick away. Oddly, he doesn't look upward for relief; up is a new dimension, and his eyes and thoughts are locked on his old ways and neighborhood. He can't change. Fish are like that. Sharks or salmon, piranha or perch, no matter how badly they might want freedom, fish are the perfect captives, natural prisoners, who require only an occasional feeding; yet, when one dies on land, its head is invariably pointing toward water and a freedom squandered but not forgotten. Dumb fish. From a dark and murky pool at the far edge of memory, the phrases *new fish* and *fish tank* make the swim from past to present, bringing a shiver of understanding and a dull ache near my heart.

My fingers have recaptured the telegram, and it slips readily out of my shirt pocket. I give the envelope the careful inspection it deserves and my anxiety demands. Not much glue on the flap, for instance. Some bright young man at Western Union must have figured using spots of adhesive instead of covering the whole flap would save considerable money and the customers would not notice the difference. Smart. Most folks attack a wire like a bear going after a honey-bee tree. Not me. Not this telegram.

I ease the envelope open a fraction, the senior surviving member of a World War II bomb squad.

I already know what's inside. Woman does, too; a time bomb she's been dreading for nearly three years. I haven't been worried about it, just waiting, like Word Dog, Noid Benny, and the others.

My fingers are telling my neck it's time to bend the head, focus the eyes, and read the message. I can't think of another stall for the life of me.

FLAT STORE:
3-J-5 PROJECT REQUIRES YOUR TALENTS.
CALL YESTERDAY.
NOID BENNY

Woman is whistling. A little ditty called "Camptown Races." Funny, after all this time together, I didn't even know she could whistle. She catches me staring in her direction and begins re-hanging the damp sheets.

Decision time. When I make up my mind about something, I want all the facts in front of me. A lesson I learned the hard way, like nearly everything else in my life. With the telegram tucked securely beneath my chin, I tug my wallet out of a too-tight pocket and remove a clear plastic packet I've been carrying around, waiting for just this moment. When the contents of the bag are spread upon the dock and weighted with grey, slug-shaped lead sinkers, I inventory the lot.

Four items: a police report, a newspaper clipping, a two-dollar win ticket from Longacres Racecourse, and a scrap of ordinary notebook paper folded into a chubby cube and taped shut. I rearrange the articles into a predetermined order and hunker down on my heels, a shaman studying chicken bones.

Aside from the lead pressing them to the dock, each of the items has a different weight that must be balanced now, past against the present, present against the future, and the sums versus the unfixed values of things like friendship and loyalty. I will need to put my mind in another time and place . . . when I was a vastly different me. Sounds crazy as I think of it, but there are places on this earth, even right here in the good old U.S.A., where insane is normal, truth is a fiction that is continually being improved upon, and wars are waged with raccoons as deadly weapons . . . and in this same time and place I learned a vital fact: At the outset of any conflict, the first casualty is the truth.

The flat, dry language of the police report does not hide the humor of the story it tells. A hint of a grin is lifting the corners of my mouth as I begin my journey back into the past. I've read this report and the companion news article a dozen or more times, usually when I was down and needed a quick lift. It was a wild caper for sure. . . . Little did I know the first time I read it I was seeing a blueprint for the madness to follow:

DEFENSE EXHIBIT B
FALL CITY POLICE
FALL CITY, IDAHO
****Interdepartmental report felony crime****

Officer: Arnold Boakes   *Type of Crime:* Armed Bank Robbery
Crime Scene: 111 Pioneer Ave., Main Office, Fall City National Bank

At approximately 1900 hours on 12-7-75, I was making a routine check of the alleyway between the Fall City National Bank and Sherman's Hardware Store. Upon entering the alley from the east, I observed two white males sitting in the snow, their backs resting

against the south wall of the bank. I recognized the subjects as Ed
Waterman and Frank Pierce, individuals known by me to be security guards for the subject bank. Both men are former Fall City
Police patrolmen with good reputations for reliability and obser-
vational skills. On closer inspection, I found they were emitting
an odor I have been trained to recognize as PCP. Both men
claimed they had been assaulted by a giant penguin using crutches
made out of shotguns.

I radioed for an ambulance and backup units, then comforted
the officers until Patrolman Pete Dolan and Auxiliary Patrolman
Si Kummert arrived on the scene.

I left Kummert with the subjects and Patrolman Dolan and
myself proceeded to the front entrance of the Fall City Bank. We
observed that all of the lights were on, the lobby was deserted, and
the door to the president's office was ajar. We then entered the
building following standard backup procedures and found all
other exits to be closed and locked. The structure appeared to be
empty.

Patrolman Dolan called my attention to the fact that the main
vault door had a red circle drawn upon its face. Upon closer examination, the circle appeared to contain a full thumbprint. As we
were examining the print, I heard a muffled shout or scream from
inside the vault. I directed Patrolman Dolan to draw his service
revolver and assume a backup position. I began to articulate the
wheel on the face of the vault to see if the door would open. It
was unlocked, and swung open easily. At the moment of opening,
I shined my service flashlight inside and observed the following:

1. Everett Stonemann, the bank's president, was blindfolded and
   tied spread-eagled on the floor.
2. An estimated three hundred garden snakes were crawling over
   his body.
3. Several of the snakes had what appeared to be baby rattles attached to their tails.
4. Mr. Stonemann appeared to be in some emotional distress.
5. A considerable amount of fluid of unknown origin had soaked
   subject's lower torso.
6. There was no sign of currency in the vault.

Patrolman Dolan remained in position while I went inside
and freed the subject. Mr. Stonemann jumped to his feet and im-

mediately fled the scene. I was unable to overtake him after a four-block chase, and returned to the bank to help secure the crime scene until Detective Albert Stonemann and fingerprint expert James Stonemann arrived in the company of an unknown federal agent.

Report ends.
By Arnold Boakes, patrolman.

****This report is adjudged to be Freedom of Information Act exempt.****

My eyes jump eagerly to the news article before the police report is back in the bag. The by-line catches my eye. Cynthia Evans. The name still causes a chill to gallop down my spine. I want to pause and relive the days when my life was turned upside down, but her words are leaping up at me. I remember the Giant didn't care for chocolate and he disliked cookies; still, he was hooked on chocolate-chip cookies. That's me with danger and suspense. I begin to read, even though I can feel Woman's eyes burning the back of my neck.

The perch in the live box makes a feeble slapping sound with its tail. A downward glance leaves me with the haunting impression of sad eyes staring *upward;* this discovery and its accompanying twinge of guilt are pushed aside in my rush to read the article one more time.

MOTHER SUPERIOR'S MOTIVES ULTERIOR

By: Cynthia Evans, *Seattle Times* staff

The daring, single-handed robbery of the Fall City National Bank took on an added, mysterious twist this afternoon. Sources close to the FBI field office charged with the investigation revealed today that the robber who disguised himself as a nun had apparently made an appointment with Mr. Everett H. Stonemann for the exact time the crime was committed. Internal bank memos clearly indicate the president of the oldest lending institution in the state deliberately kept the bank's vault open well past the normal closing time.

Officials on the bank's board of directors refused to comment on how this new information might affect the bank's insurance coverage. A spokesman at the Seattle offices of the Prudential would only admit that the matter is under consideration at this time. Thus far, no payments have been made to the bank. Officials at the Federal Deposit Insurance Corporation, which underwrites primary insurers in bank matters, also declined comment.

An anonymous source inside the bank confirms the bank's president did in fact receive a call from a Sister Carrie, who identified herself as the mother superior of the Sisters of Janus convent. Apparently, the "sister" informed Mr. Stonemann that she had found some $780,000 in the convent's poor box and was seeking investment advice. My source speculates that Mr. Stonemann invited the robber to bring the money in after the normal closing hour. His rationale for this arrangement remains a mystery.

A check with Monsignor Hennessey of the Spokane, Washington, archdiocese reveals that there is no order of the Sisters of Janus within the Catholic faith.

Janus, the Monsignor noted, was in fact the ancient Roman god of duplicity, always represented with two faces.

The red-circled fingerprint left on the face of the vault has proven to be a problem to investigators on the case, first leading to a suspect who fled the country just as he was being cleared and then to a man who could not possibly fit the physical description of the robber. Despite this apparent confusion, Detective Division Chief Albert Stonemann predicts an arrest within 24 hours.

Sources near the FBI's investigators relate a less-rosy scenario. In fact, the FBI is considering pulling out of the investigation. A hint of political pressure may be the reason, according to the source. The bank's president, Everett H. Stonemann, is the nephew of United States Senator William Obert Stonemann of Idaho.

A final note to this growing mystery: All of the bank's loan records are reported missing in the robbery.

A local wag confided that, based upon the fact that the vault was virtually cleaned out, the good sister's full name must certainly be Carrie Itaway. At this point in this bizarre story your reporter would be somewhat disappointed if it were not.

The clipping slips back into the bag. The two-dollar win ticket is next. "The seventh race at Longacres" is still visible on its face, but the date is rubbed to a blur from countless fondlings. No matter; I know the numbers by heart: 9/8/77, a single evening out of my life when I came to know more about sacrifice, loyalty, and courage than most men have when their caskets are filled with twenty-four-hour days.

I also learned there are real heroes on this earth—me, Flat Store, the homegrown cynic who had never once before believed in Superman, John Wayne . . . or himself.

The win ticket gets tucked inside the folded note. I've been told not to read the note unless or until I have to decide whether or not I want to help a friend. I'm going to read it, of course, but not now, I'm thinking as I slide it back into the packet. And besides, I argue with myself, my fingers seem to have lost their lust for exploring. Time to stop and think.

My legs register a couple of complaints, so I stand and push my back into the rough but somehow comforting support of the fir piling. The wind adds a flutter to the tips of my moustache, and I become aware of the smell of salt air blown over the fresh water of my little pond. For me, it's the perfect combination, nature's mental Jacuzzi. The fresh breeze is the main reason I bought this place. I turn toward our gingerbread house and find Woman is still doing local weather summaries with the sheets, and her clouds are becoming larger and puffier. I hate to see her worried. We've had enough difficulties. Briars was supposed to be a place to lay all our troubles to rest; now maybe even Briars is at risk . . . along with my freedom.

Our home is really a part of a tract once advertised as "Estate Condominiums." According to the brochure, we live in a quiet country atmosphere near a lake teeming with fish; a bastion of rustic elegance without surrendering the cultural amenities of metropolitan Tacoma, Washington. Briars is the optimal milieu for the Young Upwardly Mobile Professional, or so the copy writer claimed. Several problems with his allegations: We aren't all that young, we're both pretty much retired, and the social amenities of metropolitan Tacoma consist of hunting for things to do and places to go where you can't smell the pulp mills. Woman came to the charitable conclusion that all ad men must live in tiny closets in New York City. Seems logical to me.

Our tract is on the bluffs overlooking a stretch of Puget Sound appropriately called the Narrows. Much of the landscaping is artificial, but the peace and quiet are the real deal. The whole package was 250K, and I remember thinking that for those prices the lawns should give foot massages. Five years ago, I had no idea what the *K* stood for. . . . That was when I was still out on McNeil Island. A flex of my toes and I can see the island from where I'm standing. Not the whole thing, of course, just the northern portion, where the prison is located. McNeil Island prison. The name causes me to take a deep gulp of air; I have to force myself to continue my study of the island.

A large flock of gulls, at this distance no more than flashes of eyebrows, now frowning, now surprised, glide by one of the prison's more-infamous features, an obscene, two-hundred-foot smokestack. I know from long experience that a rain of sea-gull droppings is pouring down over the buildings and grounds of the prison. According to legend, a prisoner could not make parole unless one of those paddle-footed alimentary canals dumped its load on him.

I never did get a chance to test the parole theory, because I never got my parole load. . . . What hit me was a full-blown, life-shattering, character-breaking shit storm.

The visual recharge of my memory banks sends electric ripples down my spine, part fear mixed with a few apprehension-charged electrons and a high-voltage dose of anticipation. I *need* to experience those days on McNeil once more, bit by bit, slice by slice. Maybe this time I can put it all back together and make some sense out of the Alice in Wonderland world I once called home.

Inside my head, old phrases and phrasings are bouncing around with frightening familiarity. Speech and thought patterns shed with my prison clothes and convict mentality click back as easily as any bad habit. Habits. The building blocks of prison. Bad habits, which become both the prison's regulations and the convicts' way of life.

I want to return to the day of the murder. When a violent death touches your daily routine, the date is fixed in your memory along with the most trivial details relating to what you were doing at the time. Ask anyone over thirty what he was doing when John Kennedy was assassinated.... Life in prison is not much different than the rest of the world except it's more intense and one hell of a lot less gratifying.

Of course, it's a lot easier to get killed there, too.

My eyes blink open, and for a second I can't get a handle on where I am. . . . Happens every morning; the mind doesn't want to admit it has tricked the body back into the joint. A sleepy glance confirms my first impression. Three/four cell house, McNeil Island penitentiary; and this concrete momma is an ugly mother to wake up to.

2 From the outside the cellblock resembles any bombblasted German railway station you may have seen in a Holocaust film. Most of the windows are broken out from the last outpouring of rage that ripped through the cellblocks. Of course, the warden isn't about to replace them until the middle of next summer.

Inside you could be looking at a huge barn with stacks of cages piled five high in two neat rows. The cells are built back to back down the center of the floor and remind me of a high-rise kennel with barred fronts and screened walkways. The pens are twelve feet by eighteen feet, and eight feet from floor to ceiling. Cozy, since into this small area the Bureau of Prisons crams as many as ten convicts; some clean, some not so clean, and some so greasy you could set them afire with a flashlight.

As always, it was the smell that woke me up; a combination of smells is closer to the truth. The acrid bite of fumes from the Tacoma Paper Company, overlaid with the thousand and one individual odors of the men who lock in three/four house. I pay an additional penalty for being a nonsmoker when the nose detects an extra delight to kick off the day. The island's sewage-treatment plant is suffering one of its breakdowns. Combined with the mill and two thousand perspiring feet the result is what Word Dog has called "a bouquet of remarkable robustness when considering the nascent, precadet cask life of the vintage." Whatever all that means, the joint smells like King Kong's armpits. In ten minutes a bad situation is going to be one hell of a lot worse.

Each of the ten-man cells has a single toilet and washbasin. The sink is cleverly mounted directly over the toilet, and since damn few people are comfortable with being perched on the commode while some big hairy sucker is brushing his teeth over the back of their neck, the arrangement makes for at least one argument in each cell during the rush to make the 7:45 A.M. work call. Our bunch has an agreement that allows the most pressing calls to be answered first, sorta backward from an airline ticket office or AT&T.

Prison stinks; it's ugly, miserable, frightening, uncomfortable. And every day I'm here something happens to get me more agitated and pissed off than a woodpecker with chapped lips. Since this is my third time down I'm starting to wonder what the attraction is.

I remind myself to avoid the philosophical bullshit and get on with the day. The task of wriggling my size eights into a pair of stockings made for a three-toed aborigine with heels where his ankles ought to be provides a clean break from my musings of the morning. This particular pair of stockings is a pathetic mismatch, and I can't help thinking the BOP would get a better product from a factory not managed by an ex-warden and that was working from a drawing of a human foot. The Messicans in the cell next door are chattering something about *"pinchi concertinas,"* and it ain't necessary to know Spanish to tell they're having the same problems. Getting these suckers over your toes is a bit like trying to slide your feet into a baby accordion.

A pitter-pat on the tier and News Boy hustles by. His short, link-sausage legs are pumping, but he is about to run out of gas. "Creech is on the range," he wheezes, and scurries on to spread the word. Bad news. Creech, *Lieutenant* Creech if you're talking to him and don't want to go to the hole, isn't the type of person who would climb five flights of stairs to tell a prisoner he's made parole. He would only make the trip for the pleasure of giving some con a running start on a very bad day. Creech before six A.M. is like the red phone in the White House. Disaster messages is all it delivers before the sun is properly up.

Creech has raised the image of a sadistic asshole to an art form. Even his body, sloppy-fat and double-ugly, announces the fact that he's mean by profession. Most truly evil people have a few redeeming qualities—their kids love them, they keep a flower garden, or do work for the Boy Scouts—a smattering of normal human attributes to balance their makeup. Not Creech. He sports a personality like fingernails down a blackboard, and rumor has it he holds the Guinness record for a man being bitten by his own dog.

He rolls to a stop in front of my cell. 3-J-5. I live here with seven other guys, but they're still asleep, and Creech is grinning at *me*. The longer he holds the smile, the thinner the line of his mouth becomes. By the time his lips have shrunken to reptile size the focus of his attention has become the empty bunk over my head. I remember the Giant took his batch of homemade wine out of the ticking last night. That's a comfort. The bother is I replaced the booze with a pair of contraband bull cutters about four feet long.

Creech tightens the smile another notch. Now his head is bobbing up and down like a salivating cobra, and I know there isn't a mongoose within a thousand miles. This is some serious trouble.

A rusty rendition of a military left-face, then Creech is slithering away. Over his shoulder he hisses a chilling postscript to the silent message he has delivered. "Have a nice day, Flat Store."

Flat Store. My joint handle. I don't like the moniker, but with Humbert James Barker on my birth certificate, FBI rap sheet, and commitment papers, I got a world-class problem. If I attempt to wear an uppity tag like Humbert around the joint, some hard-rock con is going to try and hang a dress on me. At five ten and one fifty, a monk with a name like Humbert is open to a wide variety of dangers. There is another reason I'm stuck with Flat Store. All of the regulars have joint handles, a regular being a person who has been in and out of jail since his stuff began to get hard. Since the dude has grown up behind bars, everyone in the penitentiary knows his life history ... and all of his dark corners. If he's done some telling somewhere down the line, he doesn't get honored with the handle. Not having a joint handle makes it real rough in prison. Stool pigeons, suspected rats, or just plain squares don't have it very easy in Slam City. At worst they get killed, and at best their laundry never comes back.

Since Creech hasn't spoken to me in three years but has made a point of remembering my handle, I know something damn serious is up. The question is, what? I slip what information I have into the upstairs sorting machine and come up with a string of zeros, which is unusual. I have a genuine talent for patching together bits of information and arriving at a logical prediction. The cons say, "Flat Store can sort dry bullshit from loose straw in the middle of a tornado." Probably not, but I can spot a lie better than most.

Creech's whole act was a lie. Of course, with BOP employees, nailing a lie is simple. When they lie, their lips move. Cons are a little tougher to catch. They have deception in their bones, while the cops need to have it trained into them. As these thoughts are zinging around in my head it occurs to me that wives and sweethearts are the best liars of all. Oftentimes a con will bring me a letter to scan, and it takes very little work not only to be able to tell him that his old lady is screwing around on him, but to provide a ball-park figure about when the Dear John letter will arrive. The secret of a number of my successes with letters is that many of them are written only to deliver the P.S. ... "Joe came over and fixed the washer. He was real nice to help out, doncha think?" is a fairly typical giveaway.

I still don't have my own mind straight when the Word Dog announces the start of his day with a rumbling fart. The incredible volume forces me to look up and across the cell to his bunk just as Dog sits up and dangles his feet over the side of his rack.

He's a sourpuss gargoyle right off an old French church, and his bandy legs are swinging a pair of hairy feet that would normally generate wisecracks, were it not for the fact that the rest of his furry self is perfectly designed to swat the airplanes away from the Empire State Building. He is an imposing monster, with a great shaggy head sprouting blond-streaked hair that runs into a beard as rich, blood-red, and kinky as a thousand years of his Viking heritage; he also keeps a few drying artifacts from last week's menu around his mouth to provide a historical reference. Dog's beady-eyed melon is wagging back and forth over his short, powerful arms and drum-taut stomach as he makes ritualized adjustments of his issue boxer shorts and the misdirected ear hairs that plague him in the dark and earlies. Even with his two hundred eighty spread over a six-foot frame, his short, stubby arms and barrel chest make it impossible not to envision an overfed English bulldog, particularly if you've ever seen him in a fight. He is pure terror, all growls, surrounded by fleeing antagonists.

Dog would be a good nickname. Word Dog is the perfect one. He knows pronunciations, spellings, and meanings of words most folks have never heard of, and if you ever want to challenge him, he carries a Roget's *Thesaurus* and Webster's *New Collegiate* around as faithfully as any joint Bible thumper with the Old and New Testaments. This monk knows enough words to strangle a word processor and is strong enough to throttle a buffalo. You are never sure just what he is going to come with next . . . the soul-filling tones of Stratford Willie or the "fill yer hand" growl of Billy the Kid.

Ninety-five percent of the prison's population thinks he's just throwing words and sounds around for the hell of it, but I have the feeling he might actually be bright. I get a message from the hair on the back of my neck saying I'm not about to witness a demonstration of Dog's brain power today. His beady green eyes are fixed on the lump in the mattress just above my head, and anger is twisting his face into hard lines and sharp angles. I figure I'm about to hear some west Texas as opposed to some *New Collegiate*.

"Whut the fuck is that?" Dog grunts.

Odds, a compulsive gambler from Gardena, California, is also awake. "What is what?" he replies, deliberately avoiding my eyes, the clippers, and Dog's accusing finger.

"Whatever it is you're fuckin' scared to look at when I point," Dog snaps. His eyes grab me again. "Well?"

I remember from school that a good mumble will sometimes work in place of the right answer, but "bull cutters," hops out of my mouth, and I blow the opportunity to test the evasion on Word Dog.

Dog is out of the bunk and across the cell before I can get the rest of my sock on. He's making an obvious effort to regain control of his vocal cords, and finally succeeds. "Flat Store? Does my penchant for stunning insights once again obviate the need for contiguous interrogatory effort? Have you not, in a stellar fulmination of idiocy, involved the unwashed denizens indigenous to this comely hovel in an act of homicide, the ignoble sin of Cain?"

From his expression, I know there's an accusation in there somewhere, so I explain. "Me and Odds promised Greasy Dannie we'd take the fence cutters back to the metal shop before the foreman comes in to do the morning tool count," I whisper, looking to Odds for some support. The sleazy little bastard has put me on the shine. He's busily cleaning the rust from the eyelets of his army surplus boondocker boots. Just like him to bail out at the first sign of trouble.

Word Dog is back on the attack. "Do I, then, now abide in the metal shop? Have I lingered under the apparently erroneous impression this diminutive cube is actually a portion of the warren of incarcerated souls the warden himself believes is a cell? And finally, have you forgotten it is the policy of our captors to demand the equal shouldering of guilt and punishment in matters of this sensitive genre?"

I don't know what he said, but I know what he expects. "Me and Odds will get the cutters out first thing."

Word Dog is mad, but he's all convict. "No. Better this instrument of someone's pending destruction be returned by the Giant and myself. The Ogre has the length of limb to conceal the odious tool." He pauses, massaging a grimace and two HiHo cracker crumbs from the corner of his mouth. "When is the murder, by the way? Or has Greasy Dannie, in his rush to orgasm, once again neglected to provide the masses with programs?"

Dog has a way of giving you the velvet needle, which leaves no room for a comeback. In a few words he's sketched a damn accurate picture of Greasy Dannie: too: a stupid, sadistic killer who profits by his reputation of offing cons and getting away with the crime. For the most part, his victims are the weaker, outcast types, but he also does an occasional contract if the target isn't too tough and the money is right. He might be getting ready to kill anybody. Shit.

I was sucked into his latest scheme because he is, despite his character flaws, a stand-up convict who never ratted on anybody, so when he asked for help in an escape attempt I felt obligated. I figured from the jump that the escape scam was a story, but have a habit of allowing the chaplains and caseworkers to make the moral judgments about bald-faced lies. Hell, it's their field. A quick check of the Dog's expression tells me the escape line has as much chance of being accepted as a budget cut at the Pentagon.

I have to say something, and I can't argue fear, because even Greasy Dannie wouldn't take on a whole crew like 3-J-5. Too risky. Dog has me pinned down. His green and beadies are turning into lasers, and all I can do is work my mouth in and out of different-sized circles like the constantly ovulating guppy we keep in a pickle jar over the sink. "I ain't all the way sold this is a hit. Greasy told me personally some of his *pissanos* wanted to beat the perimeter fence and needed the tool. I don't think he—"

Word Dog is on my bullshit like a half-starved June bug. "Greasy and his ilk would not abscond on a three-dollar bail," he says softly. "What they have done is cut the walkway safety screen, concealed the marks of their nefarious effort with liquid solder from the cable factory, and now await the opportunity to lure the intended victim near the aperture of his demise. A quick

push, undoubtedly preceded by boisterous expressions of false camaraderie and a lead pipe or two to the base of the skull, and they
have upgraded their reputations to the point where an inundation
of ice creams and boxes of HiHo crackers will enlaurel their noble
brows in a sickening display of life-insurance premiums disguised
as friendly gifts." He sighs, and a glimmer of sadness scoots across
his mug. "Flat Store, if only your reflexes were as slow as the syn-
aptic junctions and transfer mechanisms of your brain." He turns
and shuffles to the sink, adding his scratches, rumblings, and
groans to the growing morning hum of three/four cell house; a
stirring of sounds that will soon become the animal roar of a zoo
at feeding time.

Our whispering has tickled Noid Benny's antennae. He is up
on one elbow, his eyes clicking back and forth like two Messican
jumping beans. These syncopated tics are one of the elements the
cons considered in selecting his joint handle, but there were other
factors, the first being that Noid Benny *is* paranoid. If me and the
Dog had been yelling back and forth he'd have slept right
through breakfast, but Noid knows shouts are bluff and it is the
softly spoken conversations that are dangerous.

"What's happening?" His voice is feather-soft as his feet slap
the floor after the drop from his upper. Ordinarily, a hundred
forty pounds of nervous tissue wouldn't make much noise, but at
the south end of his five-foot-eleven frame is a set of ground pads
flatter than a Johnny Cash high note.

Now Odds wants into the conversation. "Flat Store has been
up all night figuring out a cinch way to get everybody in 3-J-5 a
life sentence."

I need to object. The little shit was right there with me when
I made the commitment to help Greasy. Now he is trying to shift
all the weight onto me. Noid beats me to the punch. "Can the
cute shit, Odds. Have we got troubles or what?"

Nobody says a word. I'm too mad, Dog is off on some mental
voyage, and Odds knows if he says another word I'll break his
scrawny neck. The silence is driving Noid nuts. He's hopping
around like a Messican hairless on a cold linoleum floor. Born a

nervous wreck, Noid's life has been a downhill slide of worry followed by disaster ever since. A touch of implied trouble is not Noid's favorite way to begin the day, particularly since major difficulties always mean the loss of your parole date, a feat Noid has managed three times in the previous ten years. As I watch him spinning around on one foot like a freshly sprayed cockroach, I can't help grinning, not over his current upset, which is both real and consuming, but because of his last episode at the prison's honor camp, where an act of revenge backfired and completed the hat trick of his blown parole dates.

McNeil Island is a Federal Game Preserve as well as a prison. This means that no animal, fish, crab, or clam can be caught, killed, or otherwise removed from the island without generating more paper work than Eisenhower needed for the invasion of Normandy. These regulations caused an overabundance of everything that lives by the seashore, and the potential tickled the warden's greed one day. He made an arrangement with the local Puyallup Indians, which both met their needs and set the scene for Noid's final fall from grace.

By virtue of their fishing treaties, the Puyallups could sell shellfish the year round, unbound by season or bag limit. The warden figured the game department wouldn't miss a few clams, so he set the minimum-security cons to digging the suckers up when low tides and darkness coincided. Noid was assigned to the clam detail. Within a week, he hated the predawn clam patrol, the clams, the Indians, and, most of all, he hated Warden Stonemann. One day when the Puyallups came over to pick up a load of clams, Noid was standing on the dock, pissing on the burlap sacks that held the bounty of the previous evening. When the Indians asked him what the fuck he was doing, Noid told them the warden had *ordered* him to piss on the clams, since the con who ordinarily performed that task was out with kidney stones. While the Indians' jaws were still bouncing off their chests, he added: "The warden told me it was okay. He says you blanket-assed Puyallups are too stupid to tell piss from clam juice, and besides, the extra salt makes them taste fresher. He told me that's *very* important, because he throws in the dead butter clams that wash up during the night on the high tides."

When Warden Stonemann came down to get paid for the clams, the Puyallups beat the dog shit out of him, tied him up, stuffed him in one of the empty burlaps, and began a war dance around the wriggling lump in the middle of the dock. Periodically, one of the Indians would relieve himself on the warden. Noid swears they told him it was a ritual called "Fixing a Smart-assed White Eyes," but Noid lies a little now and then.

The Indians left with the clams, promising to sell them to a Russian processing boat. Noid left the warden where he was, later explaining to the Institutional Disciplinary Committee that he was prevented from freeing the warden by the Indians' admonition and threat of death should he interfere with the warden's "absorption of Indian wisdom." The story earned him a badly hidden grin from Mr. Wheeler, the cable factory manager, who chaired the committee, plus the loss of his parole date and sixty days in the hole. He came out more paranoid than ever.

Noid's growing anger isn't dampened by the silly grin I'm sporting. "If one of you monks doesn't tell me what the hell is going on, I'm going to wake up the Giant and tell him you gave his wine stash to the Messicans next door." He shoots his eyes to the mountainous, seven-foot-long lump in the adjoining bunk. "When he goes into his act you'll wish . . ."

The warden himself is in front of the cell. Noid's jaw drops open, and me, Dog, and Odds freeze. The warden isn't saying a word, and you can't tell from the expression on his face whether or not he even sees us. He has those flat, dead eyes you'd expect to find on a witch doctor's helper or the night ticket salesman at the Amtrak station. Stonemann is a slick piece of paper, never giving up a hint as to what he's thinking. Word has it he never swears, shouts, or otherwise loses his temper. Employee gossip says he drinks, gambles like a horny Chinaman, and carries a pistol around inside the prison, all violations that would get any other warden fired. Despite his bad habits, Stonemann has never been in the slightest trouble with his boss, Delbert Allen, head of the

BOP. Rumor has it he gets his juice by virtue of being a big war hero. There's a running argument among the cons as to whether he won the Silver Star or the Medal of Honor, was in WWII or Korea, led a charge or defended a position, saved the life of a congressman or a senator. I couldn't look at him and tell which *side* he fought on. Since he's got me slammed down tighter than frog pussy and it's waterproof, I can't see why I should give a shit what he did; I'm spending my energy on trying to figure out what he's going to do *next*. One thing's for sure: He has a bulge under his coat that verifies a part of the story about him. It's a pistol, all right.

Whatever, this polished-up, scaled-down, three-piece-suit-wearing version of Lieutenant Creech is in front of the cell at six in the morning, and the hair is standing up on the back of my neck, doing the Watusi. He looks like he's taking an inventory. Not much to see—a ramshackle card table, two broken chairs, several mounds of war-surplus clothing left over from arctic wars we never fought, and us, four pieces of shocked statuary.

His eyes linger a couple of beats on Noid, then whip to the empty bunk over my head. The examination is followed by another sweep of the disorder, mess, and refuse that have led Creech to refer to 3-J-5 as "the Wallows" in his weekly inspection reports. His only-ever attempt at humor.

The warden checks the empty once more, gives us an approving nod, and strolls out of sight. I'm dumbfounded, but I know as sure as Governor Ronnie Reagan is a Miss Clairol junkie, 3-J-5 is into some very deep shit.

"Jesus," whispers the Dog, "the head Philistine. Could it be he has garnered advance knowledge of our mutual-assistance pact with Greasy and his band of emotional troglodytes?"

We shrug. When the Word Dog gets up with a fresh supply of words he's too much to track. Fast Eddie, a black drugstore burglar from Alhambra, California, kicks out of his lower and stands up, yawning. "You white folks got no sense of social justice," he begins, showing flashes of sparkling enamel. "Don't you know it's inhumane to wake a nigger up before nine A.M.? You gonna keep fuckin' 'round and destroy every racial myth you got left." Fast is into his act, unmindful of the tension in the cell. "A nigger got to res' and dress, man. That's what life be all about." He shoots his eyes toward the ceiling and falls to his knees. "Oh, Massah Allen, who ain't in hebbin' but be mighty close as boss of the BOP, why you done made up a rule there got to be a nigger in every cell? These white folks got no 'preciation, and this good old Tom nigger be needin' him a cell change." Fast pauses, awaiting the good-humored response his Richard Pryor routine usually earns. When he doesn't get paid, his eyes cut across the room to Word Dog. Dog's expression is an explanation in itself. "Oh, oh," Fast whispers, "We got us some bank-robbery-sized troubles."

The rest of us are waiting for Dog to give Fast the bad news, but instead he shuffles to the commode and plops down like it was a barstool.

Fast Eddie's temper blazes in the manner that got him his handle. "What are we playing? Don't give a lame the game? What the fuck is going down?"

Fast's angry voice rolls the Giant over, and he's up; his size fifteens hit the floor, raising little puffs of dust, and he's off, chasing an enormous hard-on in the general direction of the toilet. His eyes are half-closed, but Dog's are wide open, the size of Ping-Pong balls. A quick spin just as the Giant arrives saves the Dog from a shower, but the Giant's shorts are down and he's nearly settled into Dog's lap. The Dog growls, "Cease and desist, odoriferous ogre."

The Giant stands back up, but I can see he's confused, not fully awake. His eyes are all bloodshot, and he's wearing a face longer than an abandoned mule's. The vision triggers a realization. The Giant downed the whole wine stash to make room for the cutters, and there is a worse thought tagging right along behind. The Giant doesn't have a wake-up drink to handle a world-class hangover. Now he can't go to the bathroom, either.

Trouble.

Wrong.

The Giant and Dog trade places without a word, and Dog goes over to the bookcase and starts leafing through one of the hundred and fifty western novels we keep on display as proof of our wealth. I really wasn't worried about Giant and Dog's getting into it. Giant has a reputation for being a peacemaker around the joint, Fast says he's the nice-guy type who even steps out of the shower to pee, and besides, Dog wouldn't tangle with him anyway.

All the commotion has left Fast and Noid without an explanation, so I motion them to the front of the cell to fill them in; besides, I want to get far away from the toilet, because some of the Giant's postwine orgy trips to the john have been known to generate fumes that set off the smoke alarms.

Neither one of them is aware of the favor I promised Greasy Dannie, and their reaction doesn't figure to be much more enthusiastic than the Dog's, but I run the story down to them. Fast gives me a cold stare and mutters, "What happened to all of your natural, down-home prejudices? Jesus Christ, Flat Store, Dannie is a fucking greaseball!"

Fast and Noid turn away shaking their heads, and I'm starting to feel about as welcome as Herpes II in a hot tub. Jesus, what the hell else can go wrong before breakfast?

I know what this situation needs. First, to solve the mystery of why the prison's brass is playing us so close. Then we need a plan to deal with them. Simple. Next we will require some strong direction, a plan, instead of the usual badly choreographed, knee-jerk reflex actions we generally operate with in tough spots. I give myself the bad news in a single jolt: All 3-J-5 has to work with in the think-tank and operations departments are me, Noid, Fast Eddie, Giant, Odds, Dog, and two bearded, glue-sniffing hippies we call the Smith Brothers. If 3-J-5 has a single leader, it's Dog, but we rarely know what he's thinking, even after he tells us. Christ, you couldn't put a crew like this together again if you hit every Skid Row from the Bowery to the Tenderloin armed with butterfly nets and animal collars.

Fortunately, the Smith Brothers aren't awake yet, a condition that greatly improves our chances of figuring something out and hatching a workable plan. For the last three years the Smiths have been working in the hobby shop on a model airplane project. Thus far they've made a couple of items that look a great deal like the little umbrellas some bars put in the drinks instead of the proper amount of booze. All the rest of their glue has gone up their nostrils, reducing their remaining brain cells to a mismatched pair apiece. On a good day they can barely outwit one Pet Rock between them, and they have the combined attention span of a strobe light.

"What do you think our next move should be?" I ask no one in particular.

"Get the damn cutter back to the metal shop, keep our mouths shut, and put a watch on you so you don't get us into any more shit," Fast offers.

Every head in the cell nods in agreement, even the Giant's. He's found a few ounces of wine in an old honey bottle and seems to be ready to face the coming day. Myself, I'd just as soon skip over to tomorrow.

The P.A. system scratches to life, ending my mental agony. "Three and four house officers rack I and J ranges for the morning feeding." The door of our pen slides open and we're up and moving.

At least we're first out for chow, I'm thinking; the day can't be all bad . . . but the hair is standing up on the back of my neck like a rutting porcupine, and I know I've just told myself a government-class, Bureau of Prisons–sized lie. Sure as Sophia Loren's kids got stretch marks on their mugs from breast feeding, this day is going to be a pure bitch.

Life's a bitch, and then you die. At least that's what's in store for Murray, the snitch who lives at the head of my tier. And I'm in the murder up to my butt. Damn me and my reflexes. I should have told Greasy to take care of his own business.

I got the bad news about the killing from Fred Parker first thing this morning. Fred's knowing about the murder means the administration knows about it too. A quick check around the cell house tells me if they do know, they aren't going to try to prevent it; it's 3:40, time for the crowds of work crews to come in from the shops and factories, perfect setting for the hit, and not a cop in sight. Maybe their snitch has outlived his usefulness and they don't want to bother with trying to protect him any longer. Happens a lot, so I'm not surprised.

Fred Parker works in the lieutenant's office. Most guys avoid him like the plague, but since I know he's a sure-enough rat, I stay careful and mine information out of him from time to time. Fred's a good source because the Feds have never woken up to a simple fact: All of their informants are two-way radios.

Most snitches are lonely people who just like to talk, but Fred has another strike against him. He's a child molester. The military police picked him up on Fort Lewis with a boy scout in the car. Fred claimed he was just trying to brush some spilled ice cream out of the kid's lap when the cops drove up on them. The judge didn't go for the story, and nobody else has since, but Fred keeps on telling the tale like it was gospel.

25

I caught Fred as he was coming out of the minimum-security dorm, heading for work. He was walking down the corridor, one shoulder against the wall and his head twisting nervously from side to side as he slid along. Fred knows the early bird gets the worm, and his conscience has him on the lookout for birds.

I had a new interrogation system I learned from reading the Watergate-related biographies and I'd been dying to try it out. Fred looked perfect for a test run.

"What's happening, Fred?"

"Nuttin'," he mumbled, and tried to slip past. I grabbed his arm but was careful to flash him the double-nonchalant, don't-give-two-hoots-in-hell expression I usually wear to court for sentencing. His eyes were zipping around like lights in an Atari game on speed, and I could see he was scared even to be seen with me. This wasn't going to be any ordinary information-mining expedition. I figured I'd have to fake him out with a lie, buddy up close, and then pump him dry, a trick I learned from reading Spiro Agnew's biography.

"Come on, Fred. You're the only person on the compound who can tell me what the warden and Creech were doing sniffing around my cell this morning. Give it up for old time's sake."

He kept shaking his head, so I switched to Haldeman's biography and added, "You're the last, most valuable friend I have right now. Come on, Fred, be one of the boys." It worked on Nixon, but I came up dry with Fred. "Okay, maybe we haven't been all that tight, but this is your big chance to be one of the fellas. Let old Flat Store in on the real deal." Hard to believe that kind of rap worked in the White House, but it did. Worked on Fred, too, a little.

"Warden and Creech had a meeting. You're getting a new man in your cell," he whispered, tugging to get away.

"That's it? Nothing else?" I was dumbfounded. The warden and Creech never get involved with cell assignments.

"They didn't mention the hit that's coming down on Murray, if that's what you're asking. Please, let me go." He tilted his head at the corridor officer. I checked, and the monk wasn't paying us no more attention than Martin pays Lewis.

Fred was *too* anxious to get away, so I borrowed a page out of
G. Gordon Liddy. "Talk, you little commie-homo-pinko, or I'll
beat your goddamn brains out."

"All I could overhear was Stonemann telling Creech he'd
done a good job. 3-J-5 was the perfect spot for the new man." Fred
froze up again, and I was running out of Nixon aides. I tried a
John Mitchell. "You know there's going to be a killing, maybe
today. If someone does get whacked out, your ass will fry for conspiracy."

"Honest, Flat Store, I don't know nuttin' else." His eyes were
pleading, and I knew he was telling me the truth. I gave him a Jeb
Magruder. "Give me a pack of smokes and I'll keep my mouth
shut about your role in this leak." He handed over a pack of
Camels and I tucked them away, gave him a Colson/Erlichman
"God bless you," and left before I was tempted to scare him into a
John Dean protective-custody move.

I'd gotten damn little out of Fred. He'd told me everything
and I still didn't know shit. I decided a trip to the yard might give
my sorting machine some air to work it out.

It was raining when I hit the yard. No big surprise—McNeil
only has two seasons, August and the monsoon. I tugged my
raincoat up around my ears and set out to take a lap around the
track while I tried to figure out why in hell Creech and the warden had this sudden desire to move someone specific into our cell.
Of course, they could just be trying to make the new man look
like a rat, let us figure that out as being too obvious to believe,
and take him in with open arms. If he was an informant, he'd
then be perfectly planted. Complex, but Creech and Stonemann
are so twisted they'll have to be screwed into the ground when
they die, so I didn't rule out the possibility.

I killed the day sitting on the bleachers staring at Mount
Rainier. I didn't come up with a single answer. Maybe I can get
some help from Word Dog after count time. The sweat is stinging my eyes when I reach the top landing, but I figure I got at
least a couple of minutes to slip past the cut Dannie made in the
screen and get down to 3-J-5 at the end of the tier. I can't even
trot, the first thing Creech will ask his informants is if they saw

anyone running around the time of the killing—so I'm walking fast and staring straight ahead, trying to ignore the burning feeling in my gut. If I could ever be halfway honest with myself I'd admit I'm sick for getting hooked up in Dannie's shit so easily. It's not the presence of death that has me upset; I've seen people dusted before. But this time I have a role in the murder of a human being. New experience, and a damn sickening one. I don't like the feeling, either, and right now, I don't even like me very much.

The crew from 3-J-5 is gathered along the railing, staring down at the chain of new fish who just drove up. Good Ears Kelly says the marshals who brought them over on the ferry are from Utah. This means everybody on the transport is from Utah, Idaho, or eastern Washington. Not earthshaking news, but something to mull over while trying to avoid the eyes of my cellies. The Giant tries to make me welcome with: "No sweat, Flat Store, me and Dog got them clippers back slick as a gut." Dog nudges him in the ribs, and Giant actually blushes. "Ooops, can't keep muh mouth shut."

I lean against the safety screen and inspect the new arrivals as they are uncuffed and lined up, waiting to be strip-searched and issued their red coveralls. We call this sideshow "Creech's Follies." It's the first and most degrading thing to happen when you arrive. In front of half the cell house you strip, bend over, and spread your cheeks. If Creech is feeling particularly sadistic, he has the physician's assistant shove his finger up your ass in a senseless search for contraband. Dr. Cold-Finger is another instrument of Creech's various perversions. He's flashing a middle digit at least seven inches long and wears an eager glow in his eyes. He's tall, Ichabod Crane skinny, and has a face so ugly it could make a freight train turn off onto a dirt road. Worse, he's actually caressing the rubber finger sheath he's slipped over the bony, yet certainly not magical, wand.

This joint sure puts its best foot forward. Most of the cops who work here, about ninety percent, are regular working joes. They do their jobs, don't cause anyone any extra upset, and go home to their wives and kids. The new fish are going to meet the other ten percent. The ones who actually run the place.

The fish are schooled up in a tight little knot, staring out through the wire mesh of the receiving cage at Mt. Rainier, a symbol of the freedom they've exchanged for a satisfied impulse. They'll miss chow waiting to be screened for general population, so they're digging into their sack lunches, munching on the bologna sandwiches as though they were something they really needed. Something good for them. Dumb fish.

Range Bull moves into the group and separates two from the rest, a sign we'll probably never see them in population. They figure to go to P.C., protective custody. Since I want to share my conversation with Fred in private with the Dog, I've got some time to kill, and I give the pair another read.

One is a big, good-looking sucker with an FBI agent's haircut and a physical presence that announces he's ready for whatever comes next. Beside him is a slender youngster with long red hair, limpid eyes, weak wrists, and the kind of complexion you expect to find on the cover of *Health* magazine. If Creech doesn't lock the kid down—and he might not, just for the pleasure of seeing what happens—the kid is going to be instant trouble. Sissies in the cell house are like dynamite at a marshmallow roast, and when their complex love affairs begin to blow up, it's a cinch there'll be a bloodbath.

"Hey, Miss Fine! Will you be mine?" is the first of many catcalls from the cons who are now streaming in from work.

"Turn around, girl, and let me see the whole *thang.*"

The next voice I recognize, the Booty Bandit's. "Don't let these crude bastards bug you, kid. I'll be down right after the count clears and keep them off you." Booty Bandit leans over the stairwell and shouts for the whole building to hear. "Anybody gives the kid troubles, he's got troubles with me."

Booty Bandit means every syllable of the threat. His game is to protect a new fish like this kid. If no one else makes a move on the sissy's ass, Booty Bandit sends in a couple of his buddies, they threaten a rape, and then Booty Bandit runs them off, emerging as the kid's sole chance to survive. Once the kid is in debt, the Bandit explains that he needs a few "favors," just to take the pressure off. From the moment of their first sexual encounter, the Bandit's in love. If someone tries to move in, the Bandit will do whatever is necessary to keep his property secure and happy. The Booty Bandit is hooked on asshole as badly as any heroin addict on junk, and he'll kill to keep his habit going. But he's a stand-up con, hates cops, and don't bother me, so I don't do any more moralizing over this rape that's coming down if the kid doesn't eventually give up the rim out of gratitude.

The FBI haircut is pinning the Bandit with a stare as cold as a parole officer's heart. I upgrade him from a P.C. case to dumb square. Nobody burns Bandit like this monk is doing without a lot of prepaid insurance or a total ignorance of how little a life means in the penitentiary.

"Another sister of sodom." The Dog sighs at my elbow. "The latest court-ordered offering to the altar of colonic fertility."

"I'm scoping the copper-looking monk," Noid whispers.

Odds moves in closer and asks, "Why? Six to five he's a square. First-timer for sure."

"Maybe, but we got two empty bunks," Noid reminds him.

"Aw, Noid. You're just bein' 'noid." The Giant is grinning mischievously. "For sure no clean-looking chumps like them would move in with us; even if they got told to move in, they'd move right out 'cause of . . ." He frowns, concentrating, then turns to the Dog. "Whut was that you said whut keeps squares from stayin' with us?"

"A negative screening process of amazing consistency that assures us an uninterrupted amaranthinity of our rudimentary lifestyle," the Dog answers without missing a beat.

"See?" The Giant's smile quickly becomes a frown. The Dog takes pity on all of us. "Even if we get a citizen, he won't live in this mess. He'll wake up the first morning and beat feet to the desk for a cell change. Just like all the others."

The Giant is grinning again. "Tole you so; we got nothin' to worry—"

A loud burst of laughter from the other end of the tier cuts the Giant off. Heads turn as if they were welded together.

Greasy Dannie and Murray, the guy Fred identified as the target, are yucking it up and pointing down at Fish Row. What the target doesn't see is Frog and Squid creeping around the corner with their coats on and their arms a little too stiff. It's a slow-motion film: The pipes slip out of their sleeves and, during the following frames, swing in wide arcs to crunch into the base of Murray's skull. Bits of hair and bone explode from the impact. Bright red blood soaks the corpse's shoes before his knees begin to buckle. Greasy shoves him against the gaffed screen, and the body somersaults through. Were it not for the rag-doll fluttering of his arms and legs, the snitch might have been a platform diver spinning through the air to a pool sixty-five feet below. With each revolution, the body leaves a vertical stripe of crimson down the outer wall of the cell house; dotted splotches punctuate the lines as a bloody shoe strikes the concrete with each turn. It flashes through my mind that the passage of a human life should leave a more meaningful mark than a string of bloody exclamation points down a prison wall.

Somehow, I've locked eyes with the FBI haircut. The body hits right at his feet. The force of the impact showers him, Lieutenant Creech, and the fish with bits and pieces of flesh and blood. The FBI haircut doesn't even flinch. I spot a bit of sadness, maybe resignation, in his eyes, and then nothing. He's flat, dead calm.

What follows is like the silences in antinuclear-war films where they set off an atomic bomb in the first few seconds but don't feed in the sound until the blast hits the camera. . . . The joint explodes. Creech is trying to yell and puke at the same time. He's screaming for a lock-down, cons are scuffling to get out of sight, and over it all the earsplitting whistle of the personal alarms the officers carry. In a matter of seconds, everything else is drowned out by the rolling thunder of the goon squad rumbling down the main corridor, heading for three/four house.

The P.A. system roars to life. "Lock-down! Lock-down! All inmates to your cells immediately. Lock-down! Lock-down! Cellhouse officers rack open your doors for incoming traffic only. Stand by for head count."

The rest of the men are easing their way into the crib, but I'm fascinated by the FBI haircut. He steps over what's left of the snitch and leads the kid off to one side. The kid's mug is as white as the congregation of a Baptist church in a Dallas suburb, and even from here I can see he's wet his pants. He's sobbing into the haircut's shoulder, and maybe, I think, the haircut's got a couple of extra sexual gears himself. It doesn't figure that he can watch a body come apart on his shoes without a show of emotion, yet still feel some compassion for an obvious homo, unless he's gay too. I shrug. Whatever else is happening, I got to get in the cell. Range Bull is giving me hard looks and jiggling the doors.

Inside it's so quiet you could hear a mosquito pissing on a bale of cotton. Everyone is listening for cells being racked open after the lock-down. Doors opening now can signify a shakedown, somebody wanting to snitch, or an arrest, all items of importance to us, since I've managed to involve the entire cell in the murder. I'm not really worried about there being much of an investigation. I figure from Fred's rap the cops wanted this one, too, but I'm damn close to upchucking, so I don't say anything.

Except for the Smith Brothers' giggling as they stuff their mugs into their glue rags, the silence continues for the next five minutes.

Range Bull pulls up in front of the cell and does his head count. He's a nice-enough guy, one of the ninety percent. A huge, funny-built critter who is so bulky from the waist down, if he had to haul ass anywhere, he'd need to make two trips. He has a big, deep voice and no volume control. When he's talking at you, he sounds like he's trying to call a frog out of a well three counties away. "Soon as the investigation is over and Lieutenant Creech clears the new fish, you guys get a new man. They want him in the corner, right over you, Flat Store."

That grabs our attention; even the Smith Brothers manage a glassy-eyed stare.

"Not my decision, fellas. See Lieutenant Creech if you have any questions."

I put on my tough-guy face and say, "We ain't taking no fruiters. Last one you sent us was doing time for sucking the chrome off trailer hitches on a federal reservation. First words outa his mouth were that he'd crawl forty miles through broken glass on his hands and knees to make out with a doorknob. We ain't taking no more trash like that in 3-J-5, and Creech has let his hummingbird brain overload his alligator mouth if he thinks we will."

"Don't worry about the gay; you're getting the warden's special," Range Bull says.

"Who?" Noid asks. "The dude in the FBI haircut?"

"That's your man. His name's Conroy, and you lugs keep this in mind: I won't tolerate any trouble on *my* shift." With the warning, he's off down the range and out of sight.

Noid nods to the empty over my head. "Solves one mystery."

"The warden's special. I got that message. They're trying to put 3-J-5 out of business," Odds says, and looks around for some support for his theory.

Fast snorts. "What business? Flat Store rolls joints for the Mexicans for three cartons a week. Giant grabs off a couple more boxes selling leftover wine. I cop thirty-five packs a week with my clothes-pressing hustle, plus whatever Dog brings in for doing legal work. That's it. A hundred packs a week average. Sure no business the warden would be interested in; it's food-stamp city."

"What about the twenty-five packs I make running sports tickets for the dago clique?" Odds is miffed. "Must count for something."

"It counts for shit, Odds," I put in. "You blow three times that right back into the book."

"I win a little," he whines.

"At the end of every season we have to pay off your debts to keep the wops from killing your ass. You keep 3-J-5 so broke we could qualify for adoption by boat people."

"Ain't true, and you know it. Shit. If I can't run the tickets because of some stoolie moving in, I might as well take a job in prison industries."

Word Dog explodes. "You mention somebody from 3-J-5 taking a j-o-b one more time in my presence and I'm going to stomp a mudhole in your ass. We live by our wits in this cell."

Much as I'd like to see Odds get it, I'd rather we spent the time sorting out this problem. "Why in hell would Creech and Stonemann waste a plant in this cell? Why not one of the Mafioso cribs on I range?"

"Simple," Noid answers. "Odds has a line on every bit of illegal gambling going on in the prison, plus he stands point for the sex orgies over in four house." He throws up a hand to ward off Odds's lying objection. "The Giant knows where every wine stash is. Flat Store has the scoop on the drug traffic from his association with the Messicans. Fast Eddie gets the joint gossip from the pimps and players down at the laundry, and I can tell you where every knife in the joint is stashed. On top of that, the Dog knows weeks in advance if anyone is going to sue the joint and why." Noid pauses, watching the lights go on in our eyes. "Now, if you were running the prison and wanted to put an informer in a spot where you could keep tabs on everything going on, where would he land?"

The chorus takes a collective breath and sighs, "3-J-5."

If I could believe the conversation I just left, I'd have another murder to worry about, but I know there isn't a real killer in 3-J-5.

I'm through the door as soon as they unlock for chow, off to try and get some drawings on Conroy, the dude in the FBI haircut. I'm glad to be out of the cell. When I left, Giant was pouring his new batch of wine down the toilet. His neck was blown up like a congressman's expense account and redder than a Fonda's politics. "Sumbitch stoolpigeon mother-fucker's not gonna stay here 'n' fuck up muh wine business," were the last words I heard. The rest of the crew put me in mind of a Democratic convention, not one good idea on the table and stuck with a square they couldn't get rid of. Two hours of arguing over whether or not this Conroy is an informant, getting my ass chewed by everyone for talking with Fred Parker, and watching a group of men paralyzed by fear of the unknown just about wore me out. Much as I relish a good argument, it didn't take long before I felt like the tomcat who, while fucking the skunk, discovered he'd enjoyed about all he could stand. I know this, though: If we don't do something about this guy and he is in fact a plant, we'll be the laughingstocks of the prison . . . or worse.

As I turn the corner leading past the mess hall and out to the yard I hear Range Bull trying to console Creech. "Not your fault, Lieutenant. With less than a half-dozen guards on shift trying to watch a cell house with a thousand cons, it's a wonder they don't sneak in a tank. Those fence cutters weren't really all that—"

35

Creech cuts him off. "No big deal. The cons had quit talking to him anyway. The warden decided this morning he was an asset turned liability."

I scoot past Creech and Range Bull and hit the yard. Force of habit causes me to pause at the top of Cardiac Hill and check for potential danger. The recreational yard is about average for a prison. A three-eighths-mile track circles a grassy oval of flat ground divided into football, baseball, and softball fields. The west side has handball courts, a basketball court, and the weight pile. The east end holds the clubhouse and showers, built blind to the gun towers so the men can have sex or commit murders after the games. Surrounding the entire section, and the prison itself, is an abundance of gun towers, high fences, and razor wire that would do any Nazi concentration camp proud. Missing is the skinny SS Oberführer in a long black leather coat holding the leashes of a bunch of German shepherds and Dobermans. We have Creech instead.

The sun outmaneuvers several puffs of clouds as I reach the handball courts. High on the back wall, a piece of new graffito stands out among the initials of all the secret members of the prison's ethnic gangs.

CHICKEN LITTLE WAS RIGHT!

The fresh paint of the message is spattered by several near misses from the Mormon Air Force, a term we gave the gulls after a visiting Mormon preacher explained how, in 1866 or there-abouts, the gulls ate the locusts who were devouring all the grain in Utah, and thereby saved the new religious community from starvation. He said the Mormons built a statue right downtown honoring them. I dodge a couple of poorly aimed parole loads and make my way to the bleachers. Mount Rainier is just peeping above a scattering of high clouds; reminds me of a big pile of Frosty Freeze that somebody has taken a bite out of, leaving the imprint of their choppers in the form of three separate peaks. Mount Rainier is obviously the boss mountain of the chain, with a few others like Mount Saint Helen's in the gang who obviously aren't going to amount to much. I like this spot, and I do some damn good thinking here. Waves are slapping the shore like a pimp hitting a whore he ain't really mad at, and the gulls, graceful critters in the air if they aren't squawking over a dead clam or trying to shit on your head, are circling around like lazy shoppers hunting a place to park.

A couple of hours pass quickly enough as I'm running our problem through my sorting works and coming up with zeros. As the cons fill the yard after evening chow, I see them shooting knowing glances in my direction. The story about the FBI haircut's being assigned to 3-J-5 is all over the prison now, and they're waiting to see how we'll handle the situation. I'm a little more than curious myself.

Fast Eddie comes out with the Smith Brothers. It's really my turn to watch them, but I forgot. They wander off to one corner of the yard like a pair of bonkers bedouins with glue rags covering their faces. The rest of the crew heads for me.

They straggle up the bleachers, and Word Dog gives me a summary of their findings. "Nary a soul has heard of our most recent foundling. He is a veritable enigma, even to the men who came over on the chain with him."

"I say we whup his ass and tell him to move," the Giant votes.

"I think we should just push him through the hole Dannie cut," Odds says, trying to sound tough. "Every con in the joint expects it."

"Every con in the joint don't have to do the life sentence," Fast reminds him. "I think we should just ease back up and question him. If he is a rat, we'll make him split. Ray Charles could see offing him's a dumb-assed move."

The argument goes back and forth for another half hour, and it begins to rain. The yard empties quickly, but I know everyone in the joint is inside, picking out a seat to watch our little melodrama play through. "I'll get the Smith Brothers," I say to end the misery. "Then we'll go see for ourselves what we've got in the house." At least my suggestion offers some action, and we're up and moving without an idea in our heads on how to handle the situation. Typical 3-J-5 knee-jerk reaction.

A large crowd has gathered, awaiting our return. Every range lizard in the prison is standing with his back flush to the bricks and one foot propped against the wall, the time-honored stance of the regular. Most are wearing badly hidden grins—vultures waiting to see something else die. A joint gossip flutters out of the flock and greets me with: "Hey, Flat Store, hear you got a new cellie."

"Wouldn't know, Blabbermouth. Been outside, minding my own business." I get some appreciative nods from the range lizards as they lean closer, wanting to hear where I'm going to take this turkey. "By the way, did you ever make up your mind whether you wanted me to buy you a Taco Bell or a Dairy Queen?"

He goes for it like O. J. Simpson going for a goal line. "Why would you want to do that?"

"So you'll have a little business of your own to mind." The corridor explodes in laughter as my target tries to disappear into his field jacket. Out of the corner of my eye, I see the Giant breaking for the cell house. I nod to Word Dog, and he takes off after him. The last person we want alone in the cell with the haircut is the Giant. If he goes off, he doesn't know his own strength, and the loss of his wine has him plumb homicidal.

Just inside the door to three/four house, Word Dog has the Giant pushed up against the wall, talking to him. Greasy Dannie and I arrive about the same time. "Hi, Dog. Heard you monks might be in need of my services."

"No, thanks, Greasy. We've decided to help the new man escape." The reference to the lie he told me so I'd help with the cutters puts a wrinkle of anger on Greasy's mug, but right now I don't care.

"Well, if you change your mind—"

Dog cuts him off. "If he changes his mind, we'll make sure you get the trade-in. There ain't nothin' happening in 3-J-5 a dip-shit like you could handle anyways." Greasy takes the hint and sidles off, throwing murderous glances back over his shoulder.

"Your Texas is showing a lot tonight, Dog," I tell him as we lead the crew up the stairwell.

"Stress," Dog mumbles.

As I make the turn onto our range, I glance down at the cell-house desk. Creech is talking to the night cell-house officer. It's almost nine P.M., and Creech has been away from home for fifteen hours straight. His dog must be happy as hell. I check the other runs and don't spot a single cop above the flats. If this isn't a raw setup for us to kill this Conroy monk, then there ain't a hot dog in Disneyland. I nod to the Dog, and he follows my pan of the cell house, shrugs, and motions me on toward the cell. By the time we arrive, I still don't have a handle on what to expect, but one look at this Conroy character erases all my doubts.

He's the big, good-looking sucker in the FBI haircut, all right. A too-pretty, movie-star face; brown, wavy hair; and the kind of build you can hang a flour sack on and it will turn into a Hickey Freeman brushed silk. He's parked his six-two, two-ten by my bunk as he puts the finishing touches on his own. It's made up like the one in the picture they show army privates just before inspection. Neat, envelope-folded corners, flat pillow, and the blanket is so tight a quarter would ricochet off and *into* the concrete ceiling . . . even if tossed there gently.

All the hair is standing up on the back of my neck and trying to rhumba to the top, where there's getting to be more room. Most of the time when you meet a new man in a prison setting, he's harder to figure out than Chinese arithmetic. Not this one. If he isn't a fallen federal agent or a joint-planted rat for the BOP, then there ain't a moustache in Mexico. Right away I'm as interested in having this monk in the cell as a low rider is in owning a seat cushion.

The Giant sums the picture up perfectly. "This damn sure ain't no convict."

"Could be a square," I offer, and I'm not sure of myself again. I wish to hell I could make up my mind. I once spent three months arguing with myself over whether or not Dolly Parton sleeps on her stomach. The Giant brings me back to the problem at hand. "This shit right here is some heavy trouble, and I mean trouble with a capital P, and that rhymes with *punk.*"

Giant's been listening to the *Music Man* tapes up in education, is the only thought in my head. For the third time in as many minutes, I make my final decision. We're looking at the blueprint model of the eternal enemy. A citizen.

While these various evaluations are taking place, Conroy doesn't give us a nod. By now the whole 3-J-5 crew has arrived, along with fifteen or twenty neighbors who just dropped by to witness the murder. The new dude must see a hippie lynch mob: beady eyes, scraggly beards, drooping moustaches framed by greasy, stringy hair over faces being worked into caricatures of every comic-book tough guy they've ever seen; a reunion of Turkish army rape squads that should make Conroy's skin crawl.

Giant's whisper is deliberately loud. "Let's drag his ass outa there and toss him over the side." The Dog places a restraining hand on the Giant's arm, but the Giant shakes him right off. "At least I gotta tell this punk to go lock up in protective custody." A seven-foot blur and Giant is in the cell with Conroy.

As the Giant swoops in, Conroy does a quick inventory of the room; then he's in the Giant's shade, but he doesn't blink, even as the Giant begins to shout. "Creech sent us a message we ain't supposed to bother you none. Yuh got any ideas on why he might say some shit like that?" The Giant is hot. Murder is staring out of one eye; mayhem is peepin' out of the other.

Conroy has a calm, radio-announcer's voice. "My guess? Lieutenant Creech wants to create the impression I'm some sort of informant. His motivation may be unclear to you, but he appears to have been successful." A warm, friendly smile to the audience says this settles the matter. Not for the Giant; he's glancing at the commode, which recently swallowed his tomorrow's happiness.

"Damn right! Creech has everybody plumb convinced." He waves his arm toward the rest of us, but his eyes continue to burn Conroy.

On that cue we start hunching our shoulders, trying to look even tougher. Lots of beefs get settled in prison by a show of force, sort of a miniature arms race, so we're all balled fists and evil eyes, giving it everything we have. Even Ass For Gas, a dingbat sissy, is posing mean. Right then, Ass For Gas is a stone-cold killer, not an easy acting job for a punk everybody knows can do more tricks on a six-inch dick than a monkey can do on sixty feet of jungle vine.

As a group, we're damn impressive, but we're gaming the wrong mark. Conroy's expression is vintage Clint Eastwood. My ass takes a big bite out of my shorts, and I get a feeling the Frenchies call day-ja-voo. I *know* the next word out of Conroy's mouth is going to be *friend*.

"Friend," he says to the Giant, "your eyes tell me you are about to make a very bad mistake. Relax. We can sort this out." He offers his mitt. "Name's Conroy. Donald Conroy."

I want to tell the Giant to take his hand before he gets it in the mouth. I didn't watch every movie Clint Eastwood made without learning what a really bad son of a bitch is going to do in this situation.

The Giant ain't been watching the same movies. He grabs Conroy's hand, all right, but he spins him around and twists it up between his shoulder blades. He's got him! Problem is, Conroy is still smiling.

Giant's on him like a cold sweat, talking into his ear. "I don't give a shit if your name is Godzilla, you punk. I seen you holdin' hands with that sissy on the flats today, and you're gonna go down to the cell-house desk right now and tell the officer you're a homo and need a cell change. We got no room here for—"

The Giant has Conroy wrapped up tighter'n a store-trussed turkey when Conroy sorta flips forward and plants both his heels square in the Giant's chest. Suddenly, the Giant is on the floor, with pain twisting his mouth and sweat popping out of his forehead. Conroy is forty kinds of quick or Muhammed Ali was a no-boxing sissy, take your pick.

Conroy is over him, offering his hand, and I'm hoping the

Giant takes it before he changes his mind. "Look, friend," Conroy says softly, "let's put it to bed. Anyone can make a mistake, and you have made a pair of beauties. First, I'm not an informant, and second, you may be quick with your hands, but I think I'm just a bit quicker. And one other thing"—he grins at the very subdued group of ex-tough guys—"please call off your . . . gang." He chuckles. "I came here to do my time, not provide entertainment for half the prison." Now his smile is down-home friendly, warm, and toothy.

The Giant ain't made a move to shake. Me? I'd take that paw and shake all the nails off it. Right now if Mr. Conroy told me a mouse could pull a house I'd be off harness hunting.

The Giant isn't sold. He rolls to his feet, and without missing a beat, he's trying to light Mr. Conroy up with a flurry of lefts and rights. Mr. Conroy slips most of the punches, but every third or fourth one lands with tooth-rattling force. They're body and arm punches, mostly; Mr. Conroy ducks everything coming at his head. Then the Giant tries to swarm him, not giving him any breathing room; now Mr. Conroy's grin has returned, only stingier, and not showing any teeth over the front porch, either. He starts dancing, slipping every single punch and goading the Giant with that smile. "Fight fair, sumbitch"—the Giant pants—"or I'm gonna get something and stick it in yer ass."

Mr. Conroy frowns, and backs near his bunk. He dodges a roomful of lefts and rights, sweeps his arm under the pillow, and comes out with a rolled-up newspaper. "I'm forced to believe you, friend," he grunts. Then he snaps the paper up-side the Giant's temple. Giant goes down like a poleaxed mule.

The Giant is flat on his back, doing the tuna: His baby-blues are white now, all rolled up in his head. Mr. Conroy drops the paper and grins. "Power of the press."

"Where in *hell* did you learn that?" Noid asks, almost to himself.

"Indiana," Mr. Conroy explains as if he's answered the question. "Where does this one sleep?"

Odds points to the Giant's upper. Mr. Conroy scoops up the

fallen Giant and tosses him into the bunk like he was flipping a flapjack. He rolls the Giant's eyelids back, studies each one carefully, and says, "He'll be okay. Now, is that it?"

I'm shell-shocked. So is everyone else. The strongest man in the prison just got took out by a newspaper! I've been around the world three times, worked every county fair and midway in America, and even pimped belly dancers in downtown L.A., and I ain't *never* seen no shit like what just went down.

Mr. Conroy takes the stunned silence for acceptance and returns to the corner of the cell, hops up into the bunk without using his hands, lays back, and closes his eyes! He looks so calm I'd swear he's gone to sleep, but he's tricked me again. "Good night, *gentlemen.*"

The Smith Brothers stagger into the cell, and Fast, Noid, and Odds follow. The audience leaves, and I know this story will be around the joint in a New York minute. I turn to the Word Dog. "Well?"

"Well, what?" Dog says.

"Ain't we going to do anything?"

"Like what? You saw this double-tough mother-fucker in action. You want to jump his ass?"

I have to give him a shrug.

"Me neither. Let's just wait and see."

"Wait and see? He just coldcocked our best friend."

"You heard him. Giant's going to be all right."

I'm tired of fucking with this cover-up for our cowardice. I spin and head into the cell, shaking my head. I'm two idols down for the day now, and I'm afraid to look at my autographed picture of Rocky Marciano; surely he'll have traded his boxing shorts for a pair of panties.

They lock us down, count one more time, and Creech slips by, peers in, and walks away, shaking his head. He obviously didn't expect to see everyone on his bunk, staring at the ceiling.

Lights out. Arkie Davis gives us his loud, usual "Come and get me, copper," and draws a few chuckles from the recent admissions.

From the cell at the head of our tier, the Poet comes with one of his occasional nightcaps. A clear, perfectly modulated voice floats through the darkness: "Something to think about, fellas.

The vilest deeds, like poison weeds,
Bloom well in prison air,
It is only what is good in man
That wastes and withers there."

Like most of us, Poet is better at stealing than he is at creating. I read that on the wall of the court tank at the King County Jail. By Oscar Wilde, if I remember correctly, *The Ballad of Reading Gaol.*

Well, I ain't going to waste and wither here, regardless of what Mr. Conroy turns out to be. I'm going to come out of here with something, even if it's only my good name.

The little voice of mine I used to call a conscience returns from a five-year vacation and says, *Bullshit, Flat Store, you're a professional loser, and you love it.*

This pair of socks is unbelievable. Straight tubes of material lacking a hint of top, bottom, toe, or heel. I can put them on and prance around like a ballerina, or rough it; for the second day in a row the feet hit the shoes as naked as the day I was born.

A check of Mr. Conroy's bunk reveals he's up and gone, silent as a passing thought . . . as usual. Every day he's out at the six A.M. rack, disappearing into the prison for the balance of the workday. Weird. The last three weeks have been weird.

Mr. Conroy hasn't spoken a word to any of us since the fight with the Giant. The cons on the yard don't talk to us unless they have to, because they figure we got a rat in the cell and they don't want to take any chances on information leaking back to the administration. Odds lost his position with the dago sports ticket, took a job in prison industries at the cable factory, and now Word Dog won't speak to him. The Messicans fired me off the weed-rolling gig and everybody is taking their legal work to Word Dog's competitors. The Giant quit making wine and went on a health kick. He's hardly talking to anybody, and every time Mr. Conroy's name comes up he walks off with the tight-assed little shuffle you'd expect to see on a person who's had the misfortune to contract diarrhea and a bad cough at the same time.

Me and Dog are speaking again. The Giant told me he'd instructed the Dog to stay out of the fight, just before we all went up to the cell that night, so I forgave him; hell, Churchill pulled out of Dunkirk when he saw it was no win, and my favorite, General Lee, left Gettysburg in a bit of a rush. Besides, I'd finally checked my Rocky Marciano picture and found him in a proper set of trunks. My faith in the crew has been restored, but the rest of the prison thinks we've become bad news. 3-J-5 is slowly going bankrupt from the damage this Mr. Conroy bastard has done to our reputations.

I inventory my Camel stash. Since I don't smoke, I'm doing fairly well, but cigarettes are the coin of the realm in a slam, and since everything costs, including decent stockings, the stash is shrinking rapidly. I'm not quite broke, but 3-J-5 without hustles is Colombia without coffee or cocaine. No wonder those beaners put pot in as a third crop.

Today is the day I've set aside to cold-trail Mr. Conroy around the joint and see what he's up to. He's taken the job as institution mail runner, a bit of information that pulled every face in 3-J-5 longer than the temporary deficit of 1776. It's a job that clearly identifies him as a trusted inmate, because he gets a permanent pass to go to every part of the institution, delivering the memos that control the daily operation of the place. Various cons have reported that he's all over the prison, sticking his nose into every corner like one of the raccoons that infest McNeil Island. Some of the older cons take him for a man who is looking for a way out, but most of the joint has put him down as a rat and let it go at that.

I hustle out of the cell, leaving my worries on hold. I've got a wire that Mr. Conroy makes his first stop of the day at the electronics-equipment factory, where they make the secure telephones for the FBI, CIA, and the National Security Agency. His next stop will be the electronic-cable factory, where Odds is working now in quality control. I figure to take a quick run past the weight pile, where Word Dog and Giant have been going every morning, then shoot over to the factory area and catch Mr. Conroy on his job.

I bump into Fast Eddie as I'm heading down Cardiac Hill to the yard. "You're out early," I note.

"No shit, Dick Tracy."

"Hey, Fast, no need to get shitty."

"There isn't? Well excuuuuse me! I figured with all you white folks so busy ignoring that rat in our cell a poor old field hand might be able to get away with some uppity talk."

"What's buggin' you?"

"I'll tell you what's bugging me. Cadillac Brown just canceled his pressing contract, Sweet Mac Washington hired another nigger to do his piss-cutter fatigue pants, and Young Blood just stiffed me on last week's work." He sighs, staring down at the ground. "Now *you* want to know what's wrong? We got a rat in the cell and we ain't doing shit about it; that's what's wrong. You white folks kill my ass. When a nigger has a wart on his butt he whips out a razor and cuts the mother-fucker off. If Mr. Conroy was black, you can bet your ass I'd have run him off long ago. You monks ought to jump him or put on mini-skirts; in a couple of more weeks, folks are going to be trying to fuck you." Fast wanders off, shaking his head and mumbling.

When I reach the weight pile, Dog and Giant are off into their routines, huffing and puffing, two perverts at a peep show, so I don't bother them, and head off for the factory area.

Odds is outside the cable factory, taking a smoke break. "You seen Conroy this morning?"

"He just left. Got run off, is more like it," Odds replies.

"What happened?"

"Wheeler, the factory manager, caught him screwing around with the test equipment again."

"Test equipment?"

"Yeah, the wiretap tester. Yesterday he caught him messing with the Multimeters."

"What the hell is he up to?" I ask.

"Who the hell can tell? I make him for a curious monk who ain't got enough sense to leave shit alone he ain't supposed to be messing with. Even money he's going to blow that job, screwing around."

"If you make it even money, it must be ten to one. You're the worst gambler in the world."

"You think so, listen up tonight. I got a cinch-domino way to make a hell of a score with horse races."

"Horse races! Jesus, what next? Anything for a bet, huh? Christ, Odds, you'd bet the Mormon Air Force was constipated if you had sea-gull shit dripping off your hat."

"Bullshit. A stomp-down gambler like me don't bet on nature. I make smart bets, Flat Store, not shit bets. You don't think so, listen real close tonight. I got it all down pat. Don't bet a gray horse in the mud, skip the second favorite, and don't go for anything six to five."

"Sounds great. Try and remember we got no money to back you up anymore."

"I'm a working man, Flat Store; I got money of my own."

"Don't mention that in front of the Dog."

"You just pay attention tonight when I run this down to Noid. Might want to get in yourself."

"Sure, and if I get confused, I'll get the Smith Brothers to explain it to me. See you later, Odds."

I spend the next few hours trying to catch up with Mr. Conroy. He's into every office, nook, and cranny in the joint; real familiar with all the cops on his stops, too. There is no question in my mind anymore. The guy is a rat in the perfect spot. He could be dropping off his reports to the warden at any one of several different stops.

Three P.M. and I'm back in the cell. The Smith Brothers are up, staring up at the rack above my head as though it were some sort of spaceship.

"New man," I tell them. "Moved in about three weeks ago."

I can't tell if they're nodding their heads in agreement with my evaluation or are just on the nod. They take a couple of hits off their glue rags and hop into bed, clothes and all. If I was to be all the way honest with myself, I'd have to say I'm tempted to take a few hits and hop right in beside them; life in 3-J-5 has ceased to be the predictable, manageable world I have become so accustomed to.

Mr. Conroy comes in from work, crosses the cell without a

word, and does his no-hands leap up on the bunk. He opens a thick, university-looking book on his first bounce, and I notice the cover is loaded with electrons zipping around a clump of unripened grapes, so I make it for another evening of science for our unwanted guest.

The rest of the crew straggles in, Range Bull counts, and we all take a nap. It's pouring rain on the yard, the gym is closed for repairs, and the mess hall is having liver for the third time this week. Beats me how a cow can produce enough liver for three meals a week and only enough hamburger for one. Long ago I concluded the cows the joint buys to slaughter must all have serious drinking problems and I quit eating the shit. So I'm in for the night with nothing to do, until I remember Odds is going to run some new gambling scam past Noid. Figures to be a chuckle, so when Odds starts laying out his paper work and shooting glances at Noid, I swing my feet to the floor and pay some close attention.

Odds is all fired up over this new wrinkle he's discovered. He probably lifted it out of the *Gambler's Gazette,* but I promise myself not to front him off; getting charitable, I suppose.

Odds cranks up his spiel, and right off I can see he's trying to suck Noid into putting up some capital. Noid makes the scam, too, but he's playing dumb, forcing Odds to give him an education on how the pari-mutuel pools operate. He keeps him rapping for nearly two hours.

As Odds is explaining, I notice Mr. Conroy; he's stretched out, one elbow cocked, and resting his head on his hand; his eyes are closed, but he's on the conversation like a wet T-shirt. First time since the fight he's shown the slightest interest in what's going on in the cell.

Odds lays out the whole process for the third time, and Noid is still asking questions: "I don't see the difference between shooting craps in Vegas and betting at the track. You lay the money down, and the houseman picks it up."

"Look." Odds is unaware of the change in his voice when he speaks of gambling, but the rest of us aren't. By the time Odds's voice turns husky and breathless, a trick discussing prices with a hooker, we're all paying close attention. "Let me take it from the top. Gambling in itself is not chance; it's mathematics and odds. You put a two-dollar bet down on any game in Vegas or Atlantic City and you are wagering against a *fixed* set of odds. A predetermined mathematical probability. When you win, the payoff is also a set amount, right?"

"Agreed. *If* you win." Noid is easing in the needle. "And right there is the part of gambling you don't have any experience with."

Odds is so wired into the subject he overlooks the cut. "The difference with a bet at the track is the way the odds are computed. At the racetrack you are betting into a pool of money put up by other players. The track management doesn't care who wins or who goes home talking to themselves, because they take their eighteen percent right off the top. . . . The balance is divided up among the holders of the winning tickets."

"So what? I still don't see the difference." Noid's face is the picture of innocence. I glance up; Conroy is a study of concentration.

Odds throws up his hands. He is about to give up on Noid. I check Mr. Conroy again, and damn me if he doesn't look like he's going to jump into the conversation if Noid fades out!

But Odds is a gambler to the bone. As long as there is a hint of a gambling audience, he's going to keep talking gambling. "The difference, Noid, is the odds at the track have no relationship whatsoever to the probable outcome. Track odds reflect the crowd's belief about which horse will win, not the actual chances of its winning. A horse who is ten to one, for example, might very well be the fastest animal in the race."

Noid has him now. "How often?"

Odds is ready for him. "The favorite at Longacres only wins twenty-eight percent of the time."

The lights go on in Noid's eyes. "You mean to tell me the person who does his homework, studies the *Racing Forms,* and keeps the best records has a huge edge?"

"You got it!" Odds shouts.

"Then the smarter bettor, the one with the heavy brains and best research, should be taking home most of the money?" Noid shoots back, sounding more excited than Odds.

"Right! Oh, Noid, you've got it down cold."

"And since they divide the money up among the winners, only the smart bettors share in the pools?"

"Exactly!"

"Then you ought to leave the racetrack all the way alone, Odds."

Odds is so dumbfounded by the switch, he goes for the bait. "Why?"

This is too good to pass up, so I jump in. "Because of your habit. Odds, when you get a chance to lay a bet, you're worse than a priest getting ready to lay his first broad. You rod gets harder than Superman's kneecaps and all your brains fall down in your *jockey* shorts."

The Dog breaks his month-long dummy of Odds with: "Marvelous piece of Freudian insight, Flat Store."

"What the fuck is that supposed to mean?" Odds growls.

"Means your dick is wired to your gambling habit, Odds," Dog explains patiently. "Probably a side effect of working that suck-ass j-o-b in prison industries."

Everyone in the cell cracks up. Dog has laid a perfect getback on him, and by the time Odds wakes up to how expertly Noid and Word Dog got him, the cell is humming with the closest thing to normal chatter I've heard in some time.

I check Mr. Conroy. A hint of a smile is playing with the corners of his mouth as he settles back into his pillow. He puts his book aside, and for the next half hour he's still, except for patting himself on the stomach with his fingers; they're drumming out a rhythm I feel I should know but can't get a handle on—it's from a snappy little song, but I can't land on a title, so I let it go, roll over, and give some serious thought to chokin' my chicken tonight after the lights go out.

Since Mr. Conroy moved in I could qualify for admission to

an abbey. I'm so horny the crack of dawn isn't safe around me. I'm hormone-stuffed; an orgasmic accident looking for an excuse to happen.

It's damn difficult to masturbate when you're double-bunked in a ten-man cell. There are certain conditions to meet and steps to follow, or things simply do not work out. First, there is the problem of mood, recalling the warmth of a woman. Lately, I've been craving the gentle touch of someone soft and feminine from the class of sweet, loving, and caring females I have absolutely no experience with; I've always gone for the bimbos, the gum-popping, thigh-flashing type with the off-red, colorfast, back-teased hair, who wears electric-orange pedal pushers and pulls them up so tight in the crotch her pussy looks like two sixteen-ounce boxing gloves jammed together. The Dog maintains I have "an affinity for the fallen flowers of womanhood that engenders a continuous search for the fair Guinevere beneath the scaly hide of sundry lounge lizards." I haven't argued the point. Most of my conquests are the bathed-in-lilac-water, knock-around, sleep-around types who have a pussy longer than a dead jackrabbit. The most memorable of these, and the object of my evening's lust, rolled over when we finished, scratched a notch on the bedpost between the faded Double-Bubble and the graying Juicy Fruit, and said, "My, that was quick." What the hell, I'm thinking, it was free, and the doctor only charged me thirty-five dollars. With Zelda thus firmly in mind, I'm ready for the mechanical portion of the process.

The second phase of the warm-up is to program the fantasy and the motion it generates for maximum control. If the situation gets out of hand, so to speak, and the bed approaches mid–Richter Scale, your bunkie has license to roll over and shout, "Quit lopin' yer mule," or "Don't pull the turtleneck sweater off'n yer one-eyed skivvie snake," or a whole raft of other timeworn sayings, to announce to the rest of the cell that you have sweat on your forehead, a grin on your mug, and a jailhouse sock wrapped around your cock. I don't think Mr. Conroy would say anything, but sometimes when I get into the short rows, one of the others does.

I remind myself of the Dog's suggestion. "Proceed in the manner of the fornicating porcupine . . . carefully, very carefully."

I'm all set, when the lights flicker and Arkie Davis yells, "Come and get me, copper! I got something for your ass . . . a rod-on that looks like a baby's arm with an apple in its fist, and it's all pumped up to ransack your turd locker." I never should have given him the line, because the laughter rattles the remaining windows in the cell house and puts women and sex further from my mind than William F. Buckley, Jr., is from communism, common sense, or humility.

"Hey, Odds," Noid whispers.

"What?" Odds grumps back through the darkness.

"You sure your system will work?"

"*I'm* not going to pass it up; it's the best system I ever thought of. No way I could turn this opportunity down."

I can't stay out. "When it comes to gambling, Odds, you don't turn down anything but your collar." Not quite as good as an orgasm, but I do get some satisfaction.

Odds chuckles and ruins my getback. "Screw you, Flat Store. I'm sitting on a gold mine and getting my ass up with the chickens to work it."

"A stunning, graphic, and word-perfect mixture of clichés," Dog grunts.

"You talking about yourself or Ass For Gas?" I ask Odds innocently.

"Couldn't be Ass For Gas," Fast Eddie chips in. "He damn sure knows where the gold mine is he's sitting on. Even a fruiter knows the difference between his butt and his think tank."

"Agggggggg," the Smith Brothers groan.

"We need to do something for those monks," Fast whispers.

"What?" I ask. "Poor bastards are so gone they think Peter Pan is a hospital utensil."

Mr. Conroy sighs, and I can't help wondering if that was meant as a comment on the conversation. Fuck him, I decide. We were doing pretty respectable before he came; when he goes, things will get back to normal. I hear the Giant panting in his bunk as he goes through his nightly routine of five hundred sit-ups. If I have the Giant figured right, he's getting ready to give Mr. Conroy another shot at his country ass.

Funny duck, Conroy. When Odds was into the gambling I was *sure* he was going to join in. . . . What the hell; at least the rest of us are talking to each other again . . . sorta.

I'm out on the track, keeping an eye on Mr. Conroy. Across the oval from where I'm standing, he's having an intense discussion with Ass For Gas and the new homo everyone is calling the Kid. Booty Bandit's Kid, by now. He moved in on him as soon as the Kid was out of Mr. Conroy's shade in the fish tank. Booty Bandit laid his protection game down just like I'd figured. Wasn't no big-time prediction. Booty Bandit's made exactly the same move on so many people, it's like reading yesterday's newspaper.

Ass For Gas and the Kid have "sister'd up." The twisted sisters of the prison set always run in pairs, with the older one serving as the psychologist, concerned family member, and, occasionally, pimp. What a pair. Ass For Gas is a "joint turn-out," but the Kid is a true homosexual, and now Ass For Gas is his adviser. Life sure gets out of focus in a hurry in prison.

Poor Ass For Gas. I can't help feeling sorry for the punk. Soon as the Booty Bandit ran the lifesaver game past him, he dropped him for another new arrival. Humped and dumped, Ass For Gas turned to sniffing the chemical used in the cable factory to shrink rubber cable jackets. It gets you loaded by numbing the brain. The cons call it "gas." As soon as the factory manager found out Ass For Gas was sniffing up his precious chemicals, he fired him, cutting off the Gasser's supply. He took to trading his sexual favors to all comers for tiny cans of the gas that made his life bearable. An endless cycle and the source of the "Ass For Gas" handle. He *says* he's been off dick and gas now for some time, but

55

he can't shake the name. Don't think he wants to, actually. He once told me it was a reminder to keep his fears to himself.

All the while I'm ruminating, Mr. Conroy is walking backward, obviously explaining something to the two of them. They're laughing, but I don't want to get much closer, so the conversation is another Conroy mystery. I hear my name called and turn to see Blabbermouth hustling down Cardiac Hill. When he pulls up all out of breath, I can hardly understand him. "Your boy Conroy ain't no pigeon, Flat Store. You guys ought to lay off him."

This is one of the numb-nuts who was trying to goad us into murdering Mr. Conroy when he first drove up, I'm thinking as I allow him some time to get his breath back. "What the hell do you mean—all of a sudden he's *not* an informer?"

"Well, if he is, the staff don't give a big rat's ass about him. Fred Parker just told me the warden chewed Creech up one side and down the other just this morning because nothing serious has happened to Conroy."

"Jesus." I whistle. "Is this straight skinny?"

"Fred dropped it like it was solid gold," Blabbermouth assures me. I leave him puffing and panting and trot to the weight pile, where the Dog and the Giant are talking a self-taught class in the only rehabilitative program Delbert Allen, the director of the BOP, allows. Part of his enlightened corrections philosophy. The course is called "Lifting Heavy Objects," good training for safe thieves, car strippers, and truck hijackers.

I try to call them away from the weights to share Blabbermouth's news, but the Giant won't move. He keeps slamming a bar full of weights up and down on his chest, until the Dog makes him cool it. He glares at me for a full ten seconds, then puts the weights on the rack and follows us up Cardiac Hill. At the top, I spot the Booty Bandit. He's hot-eyeing Mr. Conroy and the two fruiters. I nudge the Dog. "Trouble down the line for sure."

Dog gives me an affirmative nod and we go inside. I call Fast out of the laundry and send the Giant down to the factory to tell

Odds to scam out early. We need a meeting before Mr. Conroy returns for the four P.M. head count.

By three-thirty, we're all together, and I give them the news. After ten paranoid questions from Noid Benny, we agree to give Mr. Conroy some slack. Everyone but the Giant. He isn't saying a word, and he's looking poorly, too; I take it for wounded pride. Getting a licking like he did from Mr. Conroy is embarrassing enough, but getting caught out in public with your mouth over-loading your ass can be downright debilitating. Gave Nixon clots in his legs, if I remember correctly.

The Smith Brothers' vote is *"aaaagggggghhhhhh,"* from their corner bunks, so Dog outlines the plan for our reconciliation with Mr. Conroy. "We tender our heartfelt apologies while explaining away our frigid demeanor as the outgrowth of . . . no, an accumulation of . . . better yet, a massive infusion of erroneous empirical information."

"Does that mean he's off the dummy?" Noid asks.

"Try this one." Fast is frowning. "It was Mr. Conroy who put *us* on the silent treatment."

"Three to one—no, make that five to one—if we cop a plea with him he's going to give us a hard look, roll over, and dive back into one of those books he's always reading."

All eyes turn to me for the next wild guess. "I figure him to accept."

Fast Eddie isn't completely convinced. "It sure would be a put-down if we apologize and he does leave the freeze on."

Mr. Conroy puts an end to the conversation as he strolls in, ignores the red-faced group of amateur plotters, and does his no-hands leap into the upper bunk. He lies back and closes his eyes, and I'm waiting for someone to take charge and put the plan into action. . . . Nothing. The only sound until Range Bull comes by, counting, is one of the Dog's earth shakers, which doesn't in itself set the stage for much talking.

As soon as Range Bull passes, Giant is down from his bunk, heading in Mr. Conroy's direction. He's going to jump him while he's napping, is my first thought, but no, that's not the Giant's style. He sure looks strange. Now he's standing in the middle of the floor, with his hand on his chest, rubbing it in little circles. Then he starts chafing his left elbow like it's gone to sleep. He starts toward Mr. Conroy again, and his knees buckle a little. Giant hasn't got a drop of evil in his face; matter of fact, he looks scared. He wavers for a moment, then falls over like a crashing redwood.

Mr. Conroy must have had an eye on the Giant. He's off the bunk in one jump, checking the Giant's eyes, pulse, and breathing in a practiced sequence.

"Man down, 3-J-5." Dog sends the time-honored distress signal.

Mr. Conroy is working clockwise around the Giant now, straightening his legs and stretching him out flat. He gestures for my pillow and I slip it under the back of the Giant's neck. Mr. Conroy puts both hands to the sides of Giant's throat and frowns.

Range Bull waddles up just then, takes one look, and yells at Mr. Conroy. "Get away from the body."

Mr. Conroy ignores the command. "You," he said instead. "Get your ass on the radio. Call the hospital and tell them to send a gurney to 3-J-5, then prepare to triage—test a myocardial infarction for transport to the mainland."

The doors rack open amid a ground swell of the sounds of tragedy in the cell house. Range Bull is in the cell, trying to get Mr. Conroy's message across to the hospital. He's stumbling over the words, though. He finally puts the radio down to Mr. Conroy's mouth and holds down the "talk" button.

"Hospital?" Mr. Conroy asks.

The radio scratches for a second, then answers, "Hospital, by." I recognize the voice. At least it's not Cold Finger.

"We have a myocardial accident in 3-J-5. We need a gurney fast, and I suggest you set up for an M.C.I."

"I'll have to call the doctor. What does it look like?" The voice is squeaky, up-tight.

By contrast, Mr. Conroy's voice is smooth, professional, and filled with medical terminology I'd have expected only from a doctor making rounds in a teaching hospital. "Presumptive myocardial infarction. Migrating chest pain, apparent circulatory interruption, causing left arm and elbow distress. Evidence developing of rapid-onset cyanosis, with loss of consciousness. Patient is currently in cardiac fibrillation. I intend to terminate the hypertachycardia by instantaneous radical sternal compression, and will follow up with standard CPR procedures. Beginning now. Will advise. Out."

The voice on the radio sounds calmer. "Roger. I'll make the call to the physician and stand by."

Mr. Conroy strips off his wristwatch and tosses it to the Dog. "Watch the sweep second hand and sound off the seconds in groups of five. Flat Store? Each time the Dog says 'five,' you pull the Giant's head back like this, push down on his chin and blow into his mouth." He gives me a quick demonstration that has me searching the cell for a substitute. I can hear the stories already about how Creech busted me kissing a dead man.

Mr. Conroy isn't going for my stall. "Do it, goddamn you. We can save him."

I drop down and do like the man says. When the Dog says "five," I blow the Giant's lungs full and get out of his mouth as fast as I can. It's cold. He feels dead to me. While I'm worrying about my dumb-assed reputation, Mr. Conroy straddles the Giant, locks his hands together, and slams them into the center of the Giant's chest. The force of the impact blows *my* lungs full. Mr. Conroy has his ear to the Giant's chest. He has a half-smile on his face as he motions for the radio. "Sternal blow has terminated the fibrillations. Am commencing external cardiac massage. Any word on the doctor or the gurney?"

"The gurney is on the way. Still waiting for the doctor's return on my call to his answering service." The voice is starting to waver again.

Mr. Conroy is speaking softly, half to himself. "We've stopped the ripple beat; now we need to set and maintain a steady rhythm." He locks his hands together again and I flinch, but this

time he places them in the middle of the Giant's breastbone and
rocks forward, making gentle, even compressions.

The doors rack open again and the cell fills up with cops. Out
of the corner of my eye I see Range Bull motioning to them to
leave us alone. Mr. Conroy is pumping steadily, the Dog is
counting, and I'm puffin' the Giant's lungs up; at least that's
what I hope I'm doing. Some of the air is escaping through the
Giant's nose. Mr. Conroy hears it and reminds me, "Clamp your
hand over his nostrils when you breathe for him, Flat Store." I try
that and it does the trick, but this huffing and puffing is wearing
me out. Seems like the Giant feels warmer, though.

"Hospital to 3-J-5."

"3-J-5, by," Mr. Conroy answers as Range Bull and Creech
lock eyes.

"The doctor is on the mainland. I've sent the patrol boat to
the Steilacoom dock. His answering service will send him there
when they locate him. Looks like we're on our own." The voice
has a tone of concern half a note away from panic. Mr. Conroy has
picked up on it too.

"Okay. We'll get along just fine for the time being. Want
some notes on what to do until the doctor comes?" His voice is
chipper, almost joking, but his face is plenty concerned. Through
all this talking, I notice, he hasn't missed a beat on the Giant,
either.

The physician's assistant responds to Mr. Conroy's bantering
tone. "I read that book, but sure, and thanks."

"Okay, here we go. Get your cardiac tray and call out the inmate EKG technician. His name is Wilson. Lives in two cell
house."

I notice something. Mr. Conroy's been talking to more people
around here than Ass For Gas, and he's cataloged where they stay,
too.

The radio hisses; then the PA is back on. "Okay with the
EKG man, but we don't have a cardiac tray set up." The panic is
back in his voice, even stronger.

"Swell—gives us a chance to set up a good one for the doctor,
right? Got a note pad?"

I can't believe this: He has sweat running down his forehead, he's working like a coolie, and his voice is announcing bus departures at the Greyhound station; if it wasn't, I guess I'd be scared as the PA. As it is, everything here looks better and better. The Giant's face has lost the blue tinge and his mouth is definitely getting warmer. Now I've got to worry about his tongue coming back to life before his brain wakes up.

"Okay, here's what you'll need for the cardiac-tray setup. First, the lab section: four red-topped vacuutainers for the CPK, SGOT, SGPT, and LDH. Better plan on doing fractions one, three, and five for the lactic dehydrogenase. One five-mil lavender top for the prothrombin time baseline, and you're set. For the heart meds you'll need lidocaine, sodium bicarb, digitalis, and epinephrine. Hang one thousand mils of D5W ... no, make that Ringer's lactate for the extra potassium, crack the IV sets, and you're ready for anything."

"Got it. ... Good news! The launch is on the marine-band radio, says the doctor is at the Steilacoom dock. They'll have him here in ten minutes."

"Great! ... and thanks. It's nice to work with a professional." Mr. Conroy is still stroking him, but it ain't necessary; dude sounds calm now.

"You're welcome," the radio says. "How's the patient?"

"Doing well," Mr. Conroy answers, and he isn't stretching it. The Giant has all of his color back and I feel him trying to breathe on his own. Mr. Conroy drops down and ears Giant's chest; a grin is the prognosis.

"You can stop now," he says, and right then I realize how tense I've been. My arms and hands ache from prying the Giant's mug open and I'm panting like a fat puppy.

The Dog says, "Whew!" and starts nodding his head, grinning. First time in my life I ever saw him at a loss for words. Might have something to do with the glistening I detect in his eyes ... or is it in mine? Jesus, I'm thinking, what an experience. I'm glowing. Doctors get some nice psychological fixes, I decide, and I can imagine how proud Mr. Conroy must feel.

"Just make sure everybody knows I didn't enjoy rooting

around in Giant's mouth," I say, turning to Noid Benny. "And he never was awake, not for a second."

Mr. Conroy is staring at me, puzzled, but my statement is perfectly sensible. I'm watching Creech whispering to the head of the goon squad and I know we're going to the hole for this barbaric act we've just committed.

The head gooner is right on cue. "All right. Conroy goes to C-seg for assault with intent to commit murder, impersonating a doctor, and unauthorized use of an institution radio. Flat Store gets a shot for osculating a fellow inmate."

I knew it was going to happen! A new joint handle is next. James the Giant Kisser, or some equally dumb shit. I check the gooner to see if I'm going to seg or will wait out the I.D.C. hearing in population. I'd prefer seg. The cons are going to rib me to death over this one. The gooner is smiling at me through a set of choppers he could use to eat corn off the cob through a picket fence if the gaps between his teeth hadn't been plugged up with chewing tobacco. I wonder where they find guys like this. . . . Must go out at night with a light and turn over lots of stuff. His face tells the story. I'm going to have to stay in the cell and face the consequences.

The gooner who is cuffing Mr. Conroy up is whispering. "That was a slick piece of work, mister. Where'd you study medicine?"

"Mississippi," Mr. Conroy explains.

The Giant's eyes flutter open, and he asks, "Whut happened? Felt like an elephant waz standin' on muh chest."

"Heart attack," Odds blabs. "You were stone dead until Mr. Conroy snatched you back."

The Giant rolls his eyes up to Mr. Conroy and manages a weak smile. "I still owes yuh a whuppin'."

"Don't worry, you'll be back for another shot." Mr. Conroy's voice is as warm and soft as the rest of his face. "And believe me, I'm not looking forward to the rematch, either. You're the toughest man I ever faced. Next time I might not get lucky."

The Giant lights up and rolls his eyes around the cell. "Yuh see? I tole you monks." He relaxes and smiles contentedly.

"Make way for the gurney!" a voice on the tier shouts, and the crew of the wheeled stretcher swoops in and scoops the Giant up without dangling an arm.

One of the gooners who has been rummaging around in the cell comes up with a glue-sniffing rag in each hand. Creech walks over, pokes the Smith Brothers with a stubby finger, and tells the gooner to take them along to the slam. Off they go, Mr. Conroy leading the procession, the metallic jingle of his waist chain and handcuffs providing the march music.

The fastest way for the administration to turn a suspect rat into a hero is to chain him up and trundle him off to the hole. This case is even more interesting to the cons because Mr. Conroy has saved the life of a former adversary. Good stuff, right out of a Louis L'Amour western, primary role-model manual of most convicts.

News like this travels faster than crotch crickets in a submarine, and the whole population has turned out for the show. They're lining the screened walkways, throwing cups of what the gooners *hope* is warm water down through the screens on the vanguard of Mr. Conroy's escort. One con leans around the safety screen at the end of the tier and hits Creech up-side his head with a wet Bull Durham sack of carefully hoarded sea-gull droppings. The bag explodes on impact, and Creech yells, *"Shit!"*

"Precisely," the Dog shouts back, and the applause, hooting, and hollering continue until Mr. Conroy and the Smith Brothers are out of sight.

The next couple of hours are a tough wait, but we finally get word from the con on the gurney crew that the Giant is listed as stable. The doctor had asked to have him sent to Tacoma General Hospital for a bypass evaluation, but the warden, ever conservative with the budget, decided to gamble with the Giant's life instead of wasting government money.

By the time lights out rolls around, I've discovered there is a lot to be thankful for. The Giant is going to make it, Conroy might get roughed up in C-seg but he won't be killed, Creech forgot to come back and write the shot, and no one has razzed me for my role in saving the Giant's life.

Light's out. Arkie Davis yells, "Come and get me, copper."
Then the Poet ruins my whole day:

> They hauled away the Giant
> on the gurney's cold gray pad.
> Left our poor old Flat Store
> feeling blue and looking sad.
> He's concerned about tomorrow
> and his tonsil tennis set.
> The Giant is his partner
> and he can't get up just yet.

Laughter might be the best medicine, but it's damn tough to
take. Best to put this fire out quick, so I break an old rule, think
before speaking, and come back with, "The Poet writes fairy
tales." We're starting to enjoy the ripple of chuckles for my wit
when a voice out of the darkness shouts, "Yeah, but Flat Store
lives them."

"Even the simple fish might avoid the vicissitudes of life by
keeping his lips compressed," the Dog advises out of the murk.

"I wish to hell there'd been another way to save Giant," I
whine.

Word Dog is ready with some thoughts on the subject:
"Truly, life is a hand job, and the hand is filled with stinging net-
tles. One gets an enormous amount of pain in exchange for the
brief, frothing moments of pleasure."

I can't argue with that.

A cold, clammy little hand caresses my face, rousing me out of the half-stupor I'm in. I'm not really asleep; my name is still getting kicked around by cell-house smart-asses, so I went into autopilot to turn off the noise. I check the watch. Two A.M. Wait a minute. That hand! A quick glance over the edge of my bunk reveals a baby raccoon sitting there staring hopefully up at me. I check the front of the cell. Sure enough, his mother is standing out there, waiting for her kid to wiggle back through the bars with a handout. I get up, shake out a few HiHo crackers, and he scarfs them up. As he's eating, I notice several other raccoons trooping by on nightly begging rounds, babies clutching mothers' fur as they make their nocturnal tours of three/four cell house. They pass 3-J-5 by; I'm staked-out territory, with a baby in the cell and the mother riding a very convincing shotgun just outside the bars.

Funny, this baby is learning to bum food from the cons just as generations have before him, clear back to the time when the joint opened, just before the Civil War. Kids in the animal world seem to learn everything from their mothers. Not me. I ran away from home at sixteen and started working carnies. My poor old mom wouldn't know a flat store from a skin game. All of this early A.M. mental meandering tells me man has a better shot at improving himself than any other animal; he's not locked into set patterns of behavior from the jump, and can be whatever he wants to be, because inbred mental and biological dependence is absent. But that line of reasoning doesn't explain me . . . or convicts.

Noid is talking in his sleep. His mumbling blanks out the conclusion I'm heading for with, "But we still don't know who that masked man was, do we?"

I take Noid's unanswered question and my own, tuck them next to some bittersweet memories of a smiling face and graying hair, and bury my face in the pillow until the sun comes up.

The mess hall is packed at breakfast. Everyone is out and around, buzzing about how *our* Mr. Conroy has turned out to be an okay dude, even if he is still a bit of a question mark in the prison's glossary. I'm a little more than embarrassed by all the attention my relationship with the Giant is suddenly getting, and use the excuse to head back up to the cell early.

On the way up to the house, Cowboy stops me with a report on the Giant.

"He's doing okay, Flat Store. Dr. Hart stayed here all night keeping an eye on him." Cowboy is nodding. "Dr. Hart has heart."

Cowboy ain't lying. When Doc Hart went to the BOP training school at Glenco, Georgia, the staff there told him the cons only go to the hospital for three reasons: Get out of work, steal the drugs, or screw the nurses. Doc didn't go for it for a second. His method has been professional: Give good examinations, keep the drugs locked up, and hire ugly nurses. The only hole in his plan is that he doesn't know a convict will fuck a rattlesnake if someone else holds its head. Cowboy is getting down with at least two of the nurses on the night shift, where he works as an orderly.

All in all, Doc Hart is damn good for a prison doctor. I think he'll pull the Giant through just fine.

I thank Cowboy for the info and make the hike back to the cell without further interruptions.

News Boy is waiting at the cell door. I invite him in, and by the time I give him a cup of coffee, the rest of the crew is back from chow. News Boy obviously has some hot flash burning a hole in his cheeks, and he's holding a fat folder of newspaper clippings, but he slurps his way through half the cup before he cracks. "I got *big-time* news. Your boy Conroy is famous!" He nods into the cup while our eyebrows are doing McDonald's imitations. News Boy smacks his lips. "You haven't got one of them dough-nuts layin' around here, have you?"

"I have, in interminable quantities, something less delicate than the pastry you seek," the Dog mutters through clenched teeth. "A right-fucking-hook, for instance. What do you mean, Mr. Conroy is famous?"

"He's a world-famous ass-hole." Creech ends his stealthy approach with a roar. He pushes into the cell and spins my official incident report onto the table. "The paper work regarding your world-class *lovemaking*," he sneers.

"You know that's a bunk shot, Lieutenant. . . . What's the real deal?"

"The real deal is, you keep bad company. I suspected you guys had enough nuts to have a rat like Conroy on his way home by now."

Now it's out on Front Street. Creech is so desperate he isn't even trying to put any shade on his intentions. By every rule of what Dog calls "the mores of the deviant subculture in which we abide," I'm supposed to keep my mouth shut in this spot; but it's already hanging open, and besides, I don't have a comfortable place for my foot. "Lieutenant Creech, with all *due* respect, that move is three days older than dirt."

Creech hisses, "I made you for more brains. What side of Stu-pid City are you from, anyway?"

Fuck it. I'm in this deep. "The old-school side, where the cons don't do the cops' dirty work."

Creech spins and hits the door, doing about forty.

"You got major-league problems now, Flat Store," News Boy says. "Word is all over the joint that Creech was supposed to set Conroy up as a personal favor to Stonemann. Send him home with a tag on his toe, Stonemann . . ." The lights in News Boy's eyes are flashing like a high-speed Xerox machine. "Stonemann. God! Don't anybody move; I'll be right back." He's gone faster than Creech.

Noid has been leaning into the conversation. He falls forward on the table, beating his fists in mock despair. Odds is scratching his head like he's come up one short of a pair, and I'm facing the rest of the staring eyeballs with a blank look. I don't know what set News Boy off, but the hair on the back of my neck is galloping around like an oversexed caterpillar that woke up in a toothbrush factory.

News Boy only lives three cells down, and he's back before we get our questions properly arranged.

"You guys came close to the fuck-up of the century."

Blank stares and held breath. Noid asks, "How?"

"Your boy Conroy was on the Most Wanted list, for one."

A chorus. "You sure?"

"Got it right here," News Boy says, patting a second fat envelope.

"Sit down." Odds is holding a chair. "One of you monks get News Boy a couple of chocolate doughnuts." He looks dead at me, and I kiss good-by the two I've been saving for Thanksgiving, next month.

News Boy is down on the table, rooting through a mound of clippings and muttering to himself. "Conroy is the dude who pulled the biggest bank robbery in the history of the Northwest." He flops a stack of clippings out on the table and grins.

"You mean the silly-sister score?" Noid asks, collapsing into a chair that I happen to be already occupying.

"The very same. Look! Big headlines, four-inch columns, a three-page spread in the Sunday supplement." He's whipping the articles around the table like a berserk blackjack dealer; the incriminating articles are falling face up. Now he's reading the highlights. "Donald R. Conroy of Spokane, Washington, wanted by FBI for major bank robbery." The articles keep coming, and I'm thinking, Jesus, we hung a rat jacket on the slickest bank robber since John Dillinger.

Noid is furious. "Why didn't you hip somebody to this?"

"The day he drove up I went to the slam for keeping too many papers in my house. I just got out this morning," News Boy complains.

He's telling the truth. News is a sexual thing with News Boy, and a couple of times a year they raid him, make him reduce the morgue by several tons, and give him a few days in the hole to make everything official. Fortunately, News Boy saved the right clippings. "You want me to tell you the story?" His eyes are pleading; he gets off on doing imitations of old newscasters.

"Sure, go ahead," I tell him.

"It happened out west, in Fall City, Idaho. A sleepy little town, one bank, four mom-and-pop stores, and school kids in the clean, well-pressed everyday clothes typical of any farming community. Of course, our quiet little village has one very unique feature . . ."

"Jesus fucking Christ, News Boy, will you just get to it?" Fast Eddie is hopping around on one foot and then the other.

News Boy looks hurt, shuffles the papers, and continues. "The Fall City National Bank handles the mine payrolls for Brighton Industries. One of the largest cash payrolls left in America." He smiles, warming up to the tone and pace. "On the fateful afternoon, the president of the bank receives a call from the mother superior of the Sisters of Janus convent. The banker has never heard of the institution, but, being a Mormon, doesn't want to admit to the deficiency. He sounds delighted as they discuss mundane things, and she sounds even more so, punctuating the conversation with ill-suppressed giggles. There are three important items unknown to the banker. The convent they are discussing doesn't exist, the woman he is talking to is really a man, and Janus is the Roman god of duplicity."

"Janus was the master's stroke," Dog allows.

"Downright devious." I can't conceal my admiration.

"Now our entrepeneur put in the hook. He . . . or is it she? . . . the good mother tells the banker there is approximately eight hundred thousand dollars sitting in her poor box. The gift of an anonymous donor. She is asking for guidance as to what to do with the money . . ."

This is too beautiful to pass unnoticed. "God, what a hook. The banker would have to give away fifty gross of pop-up toasters and a handful of trips to Disney World to develop an equal amount in new deposits."

". . . and the story now moves to its mysterious and devious end. The banker convinces the sister to brave the wintry roads and transport the money to the safety of his impregnable vaults. . . . Ahh, but there is a small problem, the sister confides; she is nearly incapacitated and on crutches, none of the other sisters are allowed outside the cloister, and the distance is too great to make it before closing time. Sooooooo, he tells her, 'I'll keep the vault open until you arrive.' Now, this banker is not stupid. He knows the robbery insurance is void after closing, but on the other hand, he figures he and two armed security guards can certainly handle one old nun on crutches if she starts getting out of line. Beyond this point in the story, we have no more reports from the banker. He claims to have amnesia after the phone call."

"He wants to forget losing the eight hundred thou. Even money his amnesia is *still* bothering him," Odds notes.

"The story goes on, nevertheless. Police later found the two security guards in an alley near the back of the bank. They had been rendered ineffective by PCP or a mixture of other chemicals *and* PCP. The president was found in the vault, bound, gagged, and wearing a blindfold fashioned out of a potato sack. He was covered with a writhing mound of harmless garden snakes, many of which had baby rattles tied to their tails."

"Some sort of a getback?" Noid asks.

"Don't know. But get this. The president of the bank is named Stonemann. Everett H. Stonemann." He reads from an article. "Ironically, his brother is the warden of McNeil Island penitentiary, where the perpetrator, Mr. Donald R. Conroy, was sent to serve his twenty-five-year sentence."

"Jesus H. Christ."

"That's the fellow you need, Flat Store. Warden Stonemann is into some *blood-feud getbacks* of his own." He pauses and adds, "There's some local news, also."

"Huh?" Noid is on the statement like a cheap suit.

"Your cellie got his joint handle."

"How? I mean what?"

"They found a thumbprint on the vault. The robber had drawn a red circle around it, and before the local police finally made the identification, the FBI spokesman slipped during an interview with Cynthia Evans of the *Seattle Times*. He said the prints would identify the mother when captured. Everyone on the compound is calling your man 'Mother Superior' . . . Mother, for short."

"Yeah, swell, and when this double-tough, triple-bad mother-*fucker* gets out of the hole, which one of us is going to lay that shit on him to his face?" Noid has very clearly identified a problem.

"Won't matter where it comes from first, you guys know that. *Mother* is down for his joint handle, and it'll stick like ugly on an ape."

"That's my line," I complain.

"No, that's your mother."

Noid is quiet. I check and see the questions forming. I have some myself. "But why the snakes?"

"That's one you'd better ask Mother about," News Boy suggests. "Say, you got any more of those doughnuts?"

I'm sick to death of getting ribbed about hanging a rat jacket on Mother and even sicker of being called James the Giant Kisser. Three weeks since News Boy spread the word around, and the cons have been having tons of fun with all the possible scenarios of what Mother will do when he gets out of the slam. Calling a Dillinger-class robber a stoolie has been known to generate a lot of excitement in the past.

As I'm heading up toward the cell to wait for lunch call, Fat Poncho adds his bit to the load I'm already carrying. "Hey, when's that killer you hung the jacket on getting out?"

Bastard blew me out of my joint-rolling job and now he wants to get cute. "Soon as we find something out for him."

"What?"

"Maybe you can help. How come they don't have drivers' training and sex education on the same day in Messican schools?"

"Hell, I don't know. Why?"

"Too hard on the donkey!" He had that coming for killing my action with the other Messicans when all the bullshit started about Mother.

"Hey, gringo, *mi amigo,* why all the bad vibes?"

"Hard to keep your spirits up when you've been done out of your hustle by a bum rumor. I been starving to death."

"You want the weed-rolling job back?"

"Is there a fifty-seven Chevy in East Los Angeles?"

"You got it, gringo. Start tomorrow?"

"First thing."

I leave Fat Poncho standing on the flats and scoot up to the
cell.

Loyalties sure swing easily in prison, I'm thinking.

"Hi, Flat Store," one of the Smith Brothers chirps up as I go inside.

"What's happening, old folks?" the shorter one asks. I check,
don't see any disrespect on his mug, so I answer. "Nothing much.
Did you get a chance to talk to Mother while you were in C-seg?"
A double blank. Maybe they're off into the glue already.

"Who's Mother?" they ask in chorus.

"Mr. Conroy. Mother's his joint handle." Their faces go test
pattern again, but I haven't got the energy to explain things to a
couple of glue-heads.

"Have we got any glue left in here?" the big one asks.

"Not a smear," Noid Benny says as he comes in. "Bet you're
glad to be home."

The little one is pressing it. "You sure there's no glue?"

"Nope on the dope," Fast tells him.

"Good," they chime, beaming at us. Then the big one adds,
"We'd better go on down to the hobby shop." They hustle out,
and Noid turns to me and grunts, "How come they said 'good'
when we told them the glue was gone?"

"Stuff in the hobby shop is probably fresher" I surmise.

"Shit's worse than heroin," Fast mutters, and the conversation
dies.

I got a little time to kill before chow, so I break out a note
pad and try to sketch out a profile of Mother by making lists of
knowns and unknowns, figuring the hard copy might help the
upstairs sorter kick back into operation. I end up with more questions than answers for the umpteenth time in a row. The hard
facts are few. He's from Spokane, robs banks real slick in Idaho,
knocks folks out with newspapers from Seattle, and says he
learned the trick in Indiana, then does a perfect Dr. Kildare number he says he picked up in Mississippi. He's a carnival itinerant,

that's what he is. When I feed in his good looks and the handle "Mother," my upstairs sorting machine turns the whole job over to my fingers, occasionally interrupting their attempts to strangle a number-four soft-tip pencil by feeding in a burst of unintelligible doodles. I give the scribblings another scan. . . . *Whistles a ditty* . . . William Tell *Overture? . . . check cartridge belts for silver bullets.* . . . That's where I leave it.

The Smith Brothers return, alerting my Mother-fogged brain that the afternoon has gone by and count time is approaching. Damn, I missed lunch, and they're probably having liver for dinner again.

"Look what I made," the little one says. I glance up and he's holding a perfect model of a Fokker Bidekker, the double wing.

"And me." The big one is trying to get my attention. He's buzzing my head with a beautiful red-and-black Tridekker, the triple-winged pursuit von Richthofen flew to his death. The detail and workmanship on both models are perfect.

"A picture of logical form and function." The larger one beams.

"You put these together in four hours?" I reply.

"We had the parts all cut out, a prerequisite to ordering the glue," the little one informs me. "A simple matter of the not-illogical progression of fit and paste after that."

Noid is thoroughly confused. "How come you wasted all the glue on your models?"

"We've quit sniffing. For good," the big Smith answers proudly. "It was not a logical pursuit."

"Very illogical," Little Smith agrees.

"Good!" Noid grins, then frowns. "But why? I mean, what rolled you over? That was a four-year habit, wasn't it?"

"Mr. Conroy showed us it was illogical," the shorter one explains.

"Lacked logic." The big one is nodding.

"I was under the impression the vehicle of your combined, and much belated, rehabilitation was Dr. French, the psychiatrist.

He's been doing considerable self-aggrandizing over his success with you two." I shoot Dog an inquisitive look. " 'Tis news of the over-the-mush variety," he explains. "Cowboy told me the tale at lunch."

"Doc Flinch is a quack," the small Smith puts in, grimacing. "He's completely wrapped up in his own sexual problems. One of those twisted shrinks who tries to solve his own sexual hang-ups under the guise of treating a patient. You can't believe how strung out he is on other people's fantasies. Not only illogical, downright cruel."

Big Smith is nodding his agreement. "If you are reluctant to discuss the first time you ogled your sister's rear end, he threatens you with his handy-dandy chemical straitjackets. We were working up a getback on him with Mother when we were released."

I'm having a tough time adjusting to this conversation. Here are two monosyllabic minds laying out logical thought processes framed in the appropriate language. I come to the realization that I have absolutely no idea what these two are capable of. Noid is having problems too.

"How did you get the drawings down on Doc Flinch so cold?"

The little Smith chuckles. "Mother made him for a fraud during his initial psychiatric interview. Since then, he's been taking Flinch on some bizarre trips to avoid the Thorazine. He gave us the system—not at all illogical, by the way—and it's worked out just fine."

"True," the big Smith says. "We've got Doc Flinch hooked on us!"

"What else did Mother tell you?" Noid asks innocently. I can see he's trying to find out if Mother has any plans for a getback on us when he gets out.

"We talked about lots of things," the little Smith replies evasively. "Logic, reason . . ." He turns to his partner, receives a warning eyebrow, and continues. "Well, we did a lot of talking about our next project."

"More cutting and gluing?"

"No. Logic. We've signed up for home-study computer courses," the big Smith answers.

"Model airplanes to computers?" Noid's jaw is hanging open. "Why computers?"

"We can't say," Big Smith reminds his partner with a pointed look.

Fast Eddie is up off the bunk and glaring at the both of them. "Hold it right there, white folks. You quit glue because Mother told you it was illogical. You're taking computer courses because Mother told you to, and now your cellies, the monks who have led you around this mother-fucking shit heap for the last few years, don't have an answer coming? You'd better check your bullshit–Mr. Spock logical/illogical systems." Fast is steaming now. Right up in the big Smith's face. "Let me 'splain somethin' to you, Big Smith, and this goes for you, too, Little. You're still living in 3-J-5, where people take care of each other and don't hold nothin' back when it comes to serious shit. There's something funny happenin' here, and it's not going to get past my black ass without an explanation." He pauses, then flashes a disarming smile, two neat rows of Chiclets. "Now, from the top. Run it."

"Sorry," Big Smith says, standing his ground. "Mother said he wanted to explain the whole operation to everyone at the same time. We gave him our word. We can't discuss the project until he is released from C-seg."

"Operation? Project? Computers?" Noid is right behind Fast Eddie, barking up into Big Smith's face. "Look, I don't give a fuck what you promised; I'm with Fast. Either you give it up or we're going to have some serious—"

The Dog is on his feet, glowering and pushing his way between Fast, Noid, and the Smiths. "Do you imply it is a valid part of this process, the program of turning vegetables into convicts, to encourage that they repay Mother for their newly found sensibilities by breaking an oath stoutly given? Would we reshape these fledgling members of the 3-J-5 crew in the image of Fred Parker? Stay your lips and errant curiosities, comrades. It might become upsetting to Mother to learn we have undone his fine work of psychological legerdemain."

"What?" Noid yells.

"Lay off, assholes. Allow Mother's nature to work its wonders," Word Dog growls.

I'm thinking a gentler tone right here might prove more effective. "Why computers?" I get paid with a glare from the Dog.

Big Smith looks at Little Smith, and I see messages pass between them. I know before Little cracks his mug I'm going to get something as watered down as mess-hall omelets. "Mother believes we have a talent for thinking in abstract terms," Little replies guardedly. "He encouraged us to develop the skill, since we are going to be able to enjoy more waking moments." He punctuates the statement with a sheepish grin.

I nod my acceptance, ready to follow Dog's wise advice, but poor old Noid *can't* let go. "What does your quitting glue, learning computers, and holding out information got to do with the rest of us?"

"Can't say," they chorus.

Noid gives up. "Mother damn well better come out of the slam with a face full of answers. How long does he have left?"

"Creech gave him an extra thirty days for fat-mouthing. Puts him out the tenth of next month," Little answers quickly.

"Who did Mother fat-mouth?" Noid says softly.

"Doc Flinch. Mother has problems with people who make their living off the skinned-up asses of the ignorant and helpless," Big answers. "Flinch's chemical intimidation got to him. . . . Not logical for Mother to blow, but he is human, you know."

"Besides, he knew we were going to run the getback on Flinch soon anyway," Little adds.

Noid is warming up to dig into this new wrinkle when the Giant appears at the door. "Howdy," he grins.

"Noble beast!" Dog exclaims, and is up and hugging the Giant before he remembers his condition. "Sorry. Forget about the ticker bone."

"Nuttin' to worry about. Doc says if I take it easy for a while and watch muh diet, I should be okay. He's still tryin' to get me over to Tacoma General fer some overpass surgery."

"Bypass," Dog corrects. "Did you hear about Mother?"

"Who didn't?" He puffs up a little. "Got whupped by a pretty tough sucker, didn't I? Remember whut he said about gettin' lucky with me? Cowboy and Pills began tellin' thut story to all the nurses. Plum embarrassin'."

I catch the Smith Brothers exchanging eyebrow messages again but don't call them on it. I get busy with the makings of the traditional coming-out party, break out the stinger, do a safety check on its component two mess-hall spoons separated by a Popsicle stick, separate the bare wires soldered to the ends of the handles, and plug them right into the wall receptacle. It doesn't blow the circuit breaker at the end of the tier, and I've got a gallon of boiling water in twenty seconds. I'm about to unwrap three giant Hersheys for the hot chocolate when Dr. Flinch appears at the door.

He isn't interested in me; he's grinning at the Smith Brothers, a junkie peeping a spoon. They're off their bunks and at the door like the Welcome Wagon. Messages are flashing between them, ships going into battle formation.

"Hi, Doc Flinch," they trill.

"Hi yourselves, fellas." He smiles, a shy kid on the street corner who is trying to be one of the gang.

"We missed you." Big Smith takes over the conversation. "We were afraid our release would mess up the appointment with you." Big Smith is too warm, too friendly. Puts me in mind of a carny pitchman working a mark. "Have old Range Bull rack the doors open and come on in. We can have our session right here. The gang won't mind, will you, fellas?"

We follow Big Smith's lead; return to our bunks and start looking disinterested. Flinch motions down to the end of the tier and Range Bull eases the door open, then closes it quickly as Dr. Flinch steps inside. Flinch trots over to the Smiths' side of the cell and asks, "How's it going today?"

Little Smith is wearing a strange, terrified expression. "Bugs! Ladybugs!"

"Where? What are they doing?" Flinch asks, already oblivious to the rest of us.

Little Smith lowers his eyes; his voice becomes that of a confessing three-year-old. "Fucking," he whispers.

"Where?" Flinch asks, and I'd swear he was *really* looking for bugs.

"There are two on your lapel," Big Smith says, his eyes turning to huge, amazed discs. "God, look at them hump!"

Flinch is scanning his collar, doing a more-than-adequate imitation of Noid Benny in the process.

"Aw, don't worry, Doc," Big Smith says. "I know these two. It isn't anything personal. Little critters will fuck on any pile of shit they happen to land on."

Flinch is so glassy-eyed he doesn't know he's been had. Both Smiths are staring at the wall now, ignoring him, their heads bobbing up and down like a pair of teenagers watching an X-rated movie. Flinch is getting red in the face, and he's two deep breaths away from panting. He must have seen this movie before! "Please, tell me what you can see." He's beside himself, the kid with the pimples who can't get to the knothole to see into the girls' locker room. He *has* to see what's happening. "Come on, guys, share."

Big Smith turns to him with an evil grin on his otherwise-innocent face. Mother should have worked more on his stage presence. "Fuck you, Doc. You want a blow-by-blow, call Howard Cosell. You want to get a real blow job, call Ass For Gas. You want some answers for your own perverted shit, call Jesus Christ. This is *our* picture."

Flinch is fingering a crucifix and eyeballing for wolfbane, but he's had patients turn on him before; he slips the insults with studied professionalism. "Is He in there too?"

"Who? Howard Cosell, or Jesus Christ?"

"Either . . . both?" He's the rejected kid again.

"Neither. They all went off with Reverend Jimmy to Oshkosh, Wisconsin, for the International Evangelical Money-Raising Championships."

"What are they doing there?" Flinch is spinning the crucifix between his fingers.

"Standard evangelical work. Taking money out of older women and putting it into the younger ones."

"So much religion and *sex* in your hallucinations." He goes for his handkerchief at the mention of sex.

"This is no hallucination, Doc. This is *real!*" Big Smith is panting.

"If it is real, why don't you tell me what you see?... Please... you know, so I can ... enjoy the pictures with you."

"Think we should, Little?"

"He may have read *Oedipus*, Big. This one is not strong in the brain. Could be dangerous. What did you want to see, Doc? Specifically." Big's voice is soft, innocent.

Flinch is so turned on he's missing every shot they take at him. I've never seen compulsion at work before. This is a solid introduction.

"Can we start with who is having sex? ... you know, descriptions and, of course ... what they are doing to each other ... *exactly* what they're doing."

Little eyes Big, then answers. "This big, hairy mountain gorilla is off up into a broad's ass with fifteen inches of big, blue-veined thumper!"

"What is the little tramp doing?" Flinch is breathless.

"Wriggling her ass, rubbing his nuts, and screaming for more."

"The slut! Are there any ... ahh, juices?" Flinch pants.

"She's foaming!"

"God. What does she look like?"

"You know her!"

"*Who? God, I have to know!*" I can't see the handkerchief now. "Please! Who?"

"*Your mother!*" They scream.

Flinch drops like he was hit with an ax. He's on the floor, knees together, feet splayed to the sides, sitting on his ankles. In a pleated skirt he'd look just like a teenage girl, sobbing up at her parents. He's mumbling something, and I move a little closer. "Mother ... I always knew you were bad ... making me go to church with one man so you could have another . . . but why a *gorilla* instead of me? . . . You wouldn't even take me to the zoo because the monkeys masturbate all of the time . . . and now . . . a gorilla . . . oh, God." His voice has dropped, and I can't hear the rest. I don't think I could stomach it; not only is this poor fucker pathetic, he's the staff member who does the psychological evaluations for the parole board so the BOP doesn't let any undesirables out into the community.

Fast Eddie clears his throat, and I look up. Range Bull is at the door with another guard. I tap my temple. "He just blew." I shrug. "One minute he was *talking* like a psychiatrist, and the next he was *acting* like one."

The door slides open and Range Bull comes in, helps Dr. Flinch to his feet, and leads him away. The other guard looks at the Smith Brothers and says, "Pack it up."

"Anything you want us to tell Mother?" the Smith Brothers ask around pan-sized grins.

"Tell him I owes him one"—the Giant is grinning—"'n' make damn sure he understands we didn't have nuttin' to do with hanging that 'Mother' handle on him."

The Smith Brothers get cuffed up and led away, chuckling like a couple of kids off to the ball game. Maybe they are. I am about ready to take a dive to C-seg myself, just to find out what is happening to this well-ordered world we used to live in at 3-J-5.

I can smell something strong as hell on the wind, and it isn't the paper mill, either. . . . It's change.

I have everything laid out; been running around like a newlywed giving her first Tupperware party. Mother and the Smith Brothers are getting out right after the four P.M. count clears, and we intend to make the traditional "getting-out party" one to remember: five giant Hersheys to melt down for hot chocolate, three full boxes of HiHo crackers, two jars of peanut butter, and some strawberry jam Giant got from his old storeroom connection. The door racks open as soon as the count clears, and a bedraggled-looking trio troops in, tosses their property on their bunks, and stares at the rest of us. By agreement, we're acting like there's nothing special going on. We give the three of them a few nods and return to our magazines. I notice the Giant has his upside down, and Mother pins it, too, along with the fact that there's been some obvious effort to clean up the cell; at least Dog and the Giant threw out some empty cracker boxes.

Odds can't hold his mud. He grins, runs over, and starts pumping Mother's hand. The dam breaks. What the hell; I hustle over and get in line myself. Feels nice and warm around Mother, for some reason. By the time the Giant has apologized enough times to settle a major border dispute between Russia and China, and been forgiven with a half-dozen nods, Mother tries to put an end to it. "Look, Giant. I should be apologizing to you. I feel responsible for your heart attack."

"Doc says that didn't have nuttin' to do with it."

"Nevertheless, I kicked you too hard in the chest. Hell, you had me scared to death. I thought you were going to take me apart one brick at a time."

"Aw, shucks, Mother. Wuz ya really scairt?"

"For sure! I woke up every morning in seg worrying about facing you again. Truce?" Mother sticks out his mitt.

This time the Giant is on it like a rubber glove, and we all relax. What's good for the Giant, we figure.

"Lest this mutual-admiration society take an unwanted, less-than-manly turn, might it be possible to interpose a number of vexing questions?"

"Sure, Dog," say Mother. "I suppose some areas might need clarification. . . . But keep in mind that in a search for truth there must be one to speak, another to hear, and both to understand." I *think* I read something close to that in *The Prophet* when I was memorizing Kahlil Gibran so I could get in this hippie chick's drawers. God, I wonder, is Mother a Muslim on top of everything else? I have painful memories of the embarrassment it caused us when Fast first moved in; he was out on the range every morning, facing Mount Rainier and whoppin' his head up and down on the concrete for hours at a time.

Noid puts an end to my self-inflicted punishment with: "Why did you go to so much trouble to scare the banker? Rounding up all those snakes seems like a lot of hassle for nothing."

"*I* didn't scare anyone," Mother replies pointedly. "Someone certainly did, though. Could have been any number of people; the entire community hated him."

"Why?"

"He had gobbled up most of the better farmland in the county and ruined a number of lives in the process. The snakes were probably a getback for his adderlike methods."

"Did he scam you, too?"

Mother's eyes pair anger to a misty look. He clears his throat and answers. "No. But he defrauded my aunt and uncle; Stone-mann was very smooth about it, too. He would keep an eye open for a family farm in financial difficulty, then make them a loan with terms so stringent several years of perfect harvests would be needed to pay it off. These terms were as oppressive as the law allowed—even more so, in my opinion. Once he'd signed the farmer up on an unpayable contract, he would wait for a bad crop, move in, and take the land for next to nothing."

"Greedy, cold-blooded son-of-a-bitch," Fast whispers.

"Ah, but this ambience of greed in the Shylock's heart was also the heart of the confidence scheme and robbery, which divested him of his ill-gotten and unconscionable gains. The getback was a work of art." Dog is beaming.

"I couldn't have said it better myself. Have you ever considered becoming a writer? You seem to have the talent with words."

The Dog actually blushes! "I have given the vocation some consideration."

"Everyone has a talent; you should develop yours. Remind me and we'll discuss the matter another time."

Now the hairs on the back of my neck are rubbing together like a herd of oversexed crickets. The Smiths, Giant, and now the Dog. One by one, Mother is co-opting us. He's most definitely up to something, and I need a breather to figure it out. I'll break one of the oldest rules in prison and put him on the defensive at the same time. "What happened to the money?"

It's a low blow, but Mother fields the jab as though I weren't one bit out of line. "The robber eventually returned it to the bank," he replies matter-of-factly.

"Returned? How? My God, Mother . . . why?" Noid is back in form. Shooting triples at him.

"The money was mailed to the chairman of the board of the bank's parent company," he explains, as though discussing a postcard.

Fast Eddie is near tears. "God, Mother, you can't be serious."

"The money really wasn't worth much. Money in itself is only paper and ink. This particular sum had been somewhat modified to make it even less valuable." I can feel my jaw trying to spring open. For the first time in my life I know exactly what a bass is thinking when the plug hits the water right in front of his nose.

Giant beats me and Noid to the question. "How come this-here money weren't worth nuttin'?"

"All of the bills had been burned, the ashes mixed with mule manure, and stuffed into the same Fall City National Bank money bags the robber used to remove the money."

"Shit!" Dog exclaims.

"No, a logical existential symbol." Big Smith corrects Word Dog in a role switch that has my melon spinning.

"Huh?"

"Ashes to signify the burn of the loan, animal dung to symbolize the fertility of the stolen soil, and the money bags to represent the banker's greed," Little Smith explains for the masses.

Dog is eyeballing the Smith Brothers. Existential interpretations from them come as a challenge. "An ancillary goal of the theft was the displacement of the banker from his position of oft-abused power?"

"True. Someone obviously wanted him fired," Mother concedes.

"You infused the wealth of Mammon with the body wastes of a common draft animal and deny our kudos?"

Mother just nods.

Dog blows it. "You going to sit there like a damn chessy cat and tell me this weren't no world-shakin' getback?"

"It was because of your aunt and uncle, wasn't it?" Noid is back on his job.

Mother shrugs.

"Had to be some white mother. No brother in his right mind would blow three-quarters of a mil for a getback." Fast is still ten questions behind.

"Those were the motives the detectives dwelt upon," Mother allows.

"Mother, you got to straighten this out, please." Noid is reduced to this, I'm thinking. This conversation has gone too far and got nowhere. "It was a getback, wasn't it? But why waste so much of the money?"

"The obvious and apparent motive of the robber was revenge.

Maybe he felt there are situations when the *cost* of poetic justice is
not a consideration. But"—he sighs—"not being the robber . . ."
He shrugs and looks out at Mount Rainier, but I know his mind
is somewhere over the horizon.

Now that he has us convinced he's the robber, I expect him
to change the subject. Mother stands, wincing from the effects of
the rehabilitative techniques used in C-seg, and walks to his
locker. A minute of rummaging and he extracts a newspaper clipping, then tosses it onto the table.

Noid Benny is on the paper like Maybelline on a bimbo.
Under threat of mob action, he shares the article.

> Everett Horton Stonemann, former president of the Fall City Na-
> tional Bank in nearby Fall City, Idaho, was arrested today as he
> attempted to place five boxes of dynamite in the poor box of the
> Holy Name convent, which is located on the outskirts of Spo-
> kane, Washington.
>
> Relatives of the subject told this reporter he had been "out of
> sorts" since the spectacular robbery of his bank some six months
> ago. The money from this robbery was never recovered, and Mr.
> Stonemann told the arresting officers he was certain the stolen
> funds were hidden within the walls of the convent. He is quoted
> as saying, "I have it on the word of God. My money is in there."
> By way of support, he offered a document from the Oral Roberts
> organization that maintains the Lord once said, "The more money
> you place in my chapel, the greater shall be your wealth." (*Seattle
> Times* researchers were unable to find this passage in the King
> James version of the Bible, but the Reverend Zackary "Sweet
> Words" Washington, of the Take Stock in the Kingdom of God
> Church, assures staff investigators this is a valid interpretation of a
> passage from the Gospel of Mark.)
>
> Everett Horton Stonemann further advised the arresting offi-
> cers that his belief was supported by undeniable logic: the robber
> *was* a nun, and not Donald R. Conroy, the man serving a twenty-
> five-year sentence for the robbery. According to Mr. Stonemann,
> since the robber was a nun, the Holy Name convent would be the
> perfect place for the robber to stash the loot and disappear into
> the crowd.

THE GETBACKS OF MOTHER SUPERIOR   **87**

Officers Reilly and Fuccinado took the subject to the state mental hospital at Medical Lake, where he was promptly admitted.

We are staring at Mother in open admiration. The perfect cap to this flawless getback. I get a flash of Doc Flinch's face as Mother slips the clipping back into his locker. "That should clear everything up for you. Even the victim no longer believes I'm the robber."

"Boy, Mother, yuh got some mountain-sized troubles with the warden, though; he's gotta be plumb convinced you wuz the guy whut fucked up his brother's whole world," Giant says.

Anger streaks across Mother's face and disappears into a smile I saw once on a concentration-camp guard in a movie. "I've got trouble? I don't think so. Warden Stonemann took his best shot and missed. Now it's *my* turn."

The statement, or maybe it was the tone, stills the cell, the first tick of the bomb.

"All that money." Fast Eddie's whisper is a gunshot. "Up in smoke. Shit."

Mother is scanning the cell, the head inspector on a potato-grading line. "I have been giving some thought to our financial situation in conjunction with a project I have in mind. What I would like to do is . . ."

I'm waiting for Mother to continue, when I pin his eyes. I turn, and all thoughts are ripped away by a screaming danger signal rocketing through my mind. Booty Bandit is standing in front of the cell, wearing an evil scowl and a jacket with too-long sleeves. The fact that he resembles Bluto from "Popeye" doesn't help much.

"Hey, Mother." Booty Bandit's voice is smoking like acid dropped on thin cellophane. Not his normal tone; I make it for some serious acting. Trouble smells like garlic when you've whiffed enough of it, and right now the cell is reeking. "You and me. We need to talk. Now."

"Sure." Mother smiles. "Come on in."

Good thinking, Mother. He's not going to get out of line in a crowd, and sure as the Russians got atomic submarines, Booty Bandit is packing a shank sharper than a sackful of razors.

Bandit does a quick head count. "Uh-uh. Out here. Just me and you."

I shoot Mother a warning glance. He might be a double-tough monk, but this time he's up against a vicious killer. Out on the range he'll be in a spot where we can't get involved when the shit comes down. Before I can get within reaching distance, Mother is out in front of the cell. "What can I do for you?" he asks, calm as you please.

"What you can do for me, Mother-*fucker,* is leave *my* kid alone." Bandit opens the conversation at the top of his voice, try-ing to intimidate Mother.

"Kid?" Mother replies puzzled.

"Yeah, James O'Learly. The Kid . . . *my fucking kid."*

Noid is out of the cell and around the end of the tier without the Bandit's seeing him. Now, I'm thinking, we'll have some heavy weapons if we need to jump in.

Mother makes a very bad mistake. He's talking softly. Almost sounds like he's about to give in, or something. No, he's trying to put the Bandit to sleep with soft words, so he can whip a move on him like he laid on the Giant. "I'm not quite sure I understand. Are you saying you don't want me even talking to him?"

I recognize *that* tone of voice. The Giant does too. The frown leaves his face and is replaced by a sly grin. He nudges the Dog and winks at me.

"I don't want you even *looking* at him, asshole. That kid is mine."

"You mean you own him?"

"You bet your ass I own him."

"Gee," Mother says softly, "I certainly didn't mean to im-pinge on your rights as the Kid's owner. Sure, I'll leave him alone. Haven't spoken with him in weeks anyway. No problem."

"You're a lying mother-fucker, Mother." Bandit's voice is reaching the upper limits of his vocal scale, where the triggers to his madness are. "I saw you rappin' with him on the way up from C-seg. Little bitch was down there waiting for you to get out." Booty Bandit is emphasizing his words by jabbing Mother in the chest with his finger. His other hand has disappeared up his coat sleeve.

"Where in hell is Noid with our artillery?" I whisper to Dog.

Mother backs away from the probing finger with a note of ir-ritation in his voice. "I really wish you wouldn't poke at me like that. It is *very* annoying."

"Annoying?" The Bandit laughs. "Annoying? Listen, you overrated shit-head. You may have got a lucky shot in on the Giant, and you might be some superslick bank robber, but you know what? I think you're chicken shit!" He slaps Mother with his open hand.

Here it comes!

Mother's hand goes to his cheek, and he's staring at the Ban-dit, horror-stricken. "Why did you strike me?" His voice is high and trembling. "I said I'd leave the Kid alone. There's no need for this violence."

Bandit is leering at a cellful of blood-drained faces. "Some tough mother-fucker you got here. Mother Superior for sure. This here piece of shit is pure *bitch*." He laughs and tweaks Mother's cheek. "When you guys get done fuckin' him, send him on down to me." He spins and leaves, chuckling to himself and waving triumphantly to the crowd that has gathered on the tier.

Mother is still standing there with his hand to his cheek. I have to turn to the wall. I can't believe it! No way would the weakest punk in the prison take this. I feel like Superman just jumped out of a phone booth and said, "Anyone for tennis?"

The Giant pulls Mother off the tier and grabs him by the front of his shirt, lifting him to face level. "You just can't swaller that shit, Mother. He'll blow the story all over the joint, and every punk sumbitch in the population will be takin' pot shots at you. Come on, we got to go and jump his lyin' ass."

Mother pries the Giant's fingers off his shirtfront and begins massaging the bright-red finger marks on his face. "No, let it be."

"The Giant's estimation of the incident and prognostication of the future are unerringly accurate, Mother. Once this sort of confrontation has been effected, it must be dealt with in the strongest possible terms or everyone in the prison will judge you a coward."

Mother turns and moves toward his bunk. "You think I care what these animals think of me?"

"But we can't have a monk with a chicken-shit jacket living in 3-J-5," Fast complains. "Think of our reputations."

"You want me to risk my life for your *reputations?*" Mother is openly sarcastic. "Not very likely."

"If you're fuckin' scared, say so." Fast is up in Mother's face. "Let's quit pussy-footin' around with the perfectly obvious. If you want to lay him out, we're ready." Noid comes through the door and opens his jacket, revealing the handles of several knives he's tucked into his belt. "But," Fast continues, "if you're afraid and want to keep backin' up every day for the rest of your time, you're all the way off on your own."

I want to come to Mother's defense. I can see the Giant does, too, but the problem is, Mother is dead wrong. I feel like the hero's best friend in an old RKO western; whatever I do, I'm going to make matters worse.

Mother ends my worries. "Look, I'm not going to get myself or any of you involved with this madman. Whether you like that or not is your problem." He does his no-hands leap up to his bunk, picks up a book, and turns to face the wall.

The Giant has never looked sadder, the Dog more perturbed, or Fast Eddie more angry. Me, Noid, Odds, and the Smith Brothers stare at one another and shrug. Mother's afraid of the Bandit, and there's no two ways about it.

Now I'm thinking, maybe the only reason he fought the Giant was because he had no choice.

And maybe he really didn't rob the bank.

And maybe he is, and maybe he isn't.

I'm back to square one.

My right foot goes through the sole of the stocking like it was made of wet Kleenex. Ditto the left. At least I got a matched pair this time. More than I can say for my attempts to figure out Mr. Conroy; he doesn't match up to anything or anyone. Every day I wake up to a whole new world with this monk around. The deal

10

with the Booty Bandit has just about turned me upside down again. I can't really say I blame Mr. Conroy for not wanting to fight the Bandit—I'd rather run through a lion's den in a pork-chop overcoat than tangle with him myself—but now that he's "Mr. Conroy" around the joint again, all of us are suffering. In the three weeks since Booty Bandit made him punk out, none of us have spoken to him, and for the most part, the men in the joint have quit talking to us. In all fairness, I guess we started the silent treatment on Mr. Conroy and he just slipped back into his old ways of ignoring us, walking around with his lips pressed together tighter than a nun's knees at a penguin orgy.

We've let it be known we're not having anything to do with him, too. Might not be all the way fair, but there was also a story going around that his cellies didn't back him up right. We couldn't set the matter straight, so we just slanted it in our direction.

Since Mr. Conroy went back on the rat mail-delivering job, has been made for being a coward, and has the whole prison on the dummy, the hustles are suffering again. I still do an occasional job for the Messicans, but I have to work in the rec shack. Nobody wants their business exposed in 3-J-5.

I'm off to the yard to meet Fat Poncho at first rack.

Two hours pass, and not a sign of Fat Poncho. I'm watching a couple of gulls fighting over a clam when I hear a shotgun go off.

Blam! Blam Blam! One shot, then two close together. I follow the direction of the sound out to the end of the repair dock, just outside the fence. Fred Parker and Warden Stonemann are out for their weekly shooting session. Fred is throwing up the clay pigeons and Stonemann is shooting at them. A target sails up into the sky and Stonemann looses off three more rounds from the Browning automatic shotgun he's shouldering. Three more misses. That's unusual, so I start paying closer attention.

Stonemann is swearing at Fred now, wavering from side to side as he berates him for throwing the targets too high and fast. Jesus. Stonemann's drunk. I can hear him yelling from here.

I'm about to give up on this sick shit and go back to the cell when I notice Stonemann's kid pushing his bicycle down in the direction of the dock. The rear wheel is flat and off the rim; it's about all the little guy can do to push it along. He stops at the end of the dock, leans the bike against the door of his father's pickup, and starts out onto the dock. Warden Stonemann has seen him now, and he's stomping up the planking when I hear this godawful screeching sound. The bike has started to slide down the door of the pickup, its handlebar scratching a deep gouge through the paint. Stonemann gets to the kid, picks him up, and shakes him so hard his neck is whipping back and forth like a cornstalk in a rain squall. He plops the poor little sucker down on the dock and hustles over to his precious government truck to inspect the damage. He shoots the little tyke a withering glance, motions for Fred Parker to hop into the back, and drives off. For the next few minutes I'm watching the little guy struggling to get his bike back up the hill. I hope to hell God saw what I just saw.

Blabbermouth breaks into my thoughts uninvited.

"Your man Conroy is having hisself a visit, Flat Store."

"Why should that interest me?"

"It's that Cynthia Evans broad who does the investigative reporting for the *Seattle Times*."

My gut rolls over with the news, but I play it off to keep Blabbermouth confused. "Really? I wonder what she's up to now."

"So does everybody else. Rap around the joint is she's going to do another exposé on sex, drugs, and violence here on the island." Blabbermouth attempts to lend credence to what is probably a bald-faced lie by bobbing his head and pinching his eyebrows into sincere, concerned furrows. I can see this is the half-baked story he is going to spread as soon as he finds a single fact to mix with all the yeast he has on hand. I'd better check this out for myself. "How do you know she's visiting?"

"Saw her on the outside yard. Figured she'd be here to see Conroy, since she was the reporter who covered his trial. I checked at the desk. Conroy, all right. He's on his way out right now."

There is an outside chance we can slip up to the fence near the visiting area and scope them out without getting caught. "Let's go check it out." We're off up the hill.

The sun is making an appearance, so the visiting area is crowded with families waiting for the men to get through the shakedown, orifice search, and identification process the prison uses to make sure you aren't smuggling anything *out* of the prison and won't enjoy your visit too much. Little children in faded jumpers and hand-me-down dresses are cavorting about under the eyes of teenaged mothers loaded down with diaper bags, prison-hobby-shop purses, and the tired faces of women twice their age. A scattering of older women serves as the nucleus for clusters of too-tight jeans and low-cut blouses that have Blabbermouth jabbing my ribs and pointing. He sees women, tits and ass. All I notice is misery, and the wreckage of families sharing equally in the punishment of the husbands and fathers.

"Here they come." Blabbermouth points. He's up on his tiptoes, and I have to pull him to the ground before he attracts the attention of the yard officer. The area we're in is a couple of blades of grass away from being out of bounds, and we won't last if a cop spots us here.

Whatever else she might be, Cynthia Evans is a knockout lady. Long brown hair, perfectly clipped and combed, bounces comfortably from the shoulders of a woman's business suit. The masculine cut of the pinstripe does little to conceal a stunning figure. She's tall. About five eight, I figure from where her head comes to on Mr. Conroy. Pretty kisser, too, the heart-shaped, model variety. Except for the obvious arm-waving, finger-shaking argument and Mr. Conroy's prison khakis, they could pass for a couple in a travel ad.

She whips out a long yellow legal pad and begins waving it under Mr. Conroy's nose. Each time he speaks, she shakes her head, leafs through the pad, flips out a specific section, and makes him read it. Whatever they're beefing about, she seems to be winning, point by point. She puts me in mind of a detective, and if she's trying to pump something out of him, she's close to success. Mr. Conroy is definitely on the defensive.

"What do you think, Blabbermouth?" I'm just talking to myself, not expecting anything very original, when he comes right back with: "Foxy lady, but all copper. I'd let her sit on my face and knit an overcoat for an elephant, but I wouldn't put her to stand point while I told a lie on a pay phone."

I'm impressed. My evaluation down to the comma and period.

"Okay, ass-holes, show's over." The yard officer's voice blasts in my unsuspecting ear.

Blabbermouth has a lie ready for him. "Sorry, boss. I heard my sis was up here visiting Flat Face Marty again. Just wanted to be sure it was a bum wire."

I catch a final glimpse of Mr. Conroy's face as we leave. He's glowering, and damn me if the Cynthia broad don't look like she's about to bust out cryin'. I wish I'd had some audio for this soap opera.

I hit the track to kill time till chow, trying to sort out this latest upset. Goddamn Conroy, he ain't begun to live down his coward jacket from the Booty Bandit incident, and now he's working on building up his rat jacket again.

Dumb son of a bitch hasn't got enough sense to pour piss out of his boots if he had the directions written on the heel.

What a day.

All I need now is to see liver on the menu again.

Fast Eddie is stabbing a metallic green slab of liver with his fork. His eyes are stabbing me. "Story about Mr. Conroy and Cynthia Evans working together on a new investigation is all over the joint. Seems like even a black mother-fucker should be able to get the news from his cell partner instead of having to hear it from Blabbermouth."

11

Sometimes the truth has a bit of space left over for some improvement. When I answer, I take that option. "I was waiting to see what other information I could shake out of the guys who were on the scene. All I came up with is that Mr. Conroy and Miss Evans kept pretty much to themselves."

"Brilliant piece of investigative work," Dog comments dryly.

"Well, if you want me to bring home raw information, I can give you all kinds of watered-down or yeasted-up stories. Red on the Head said she was a fox with legs that reached all the way up to a Pillsbury Doughboy ass, and Jew Manny told me she was an ex–test pilot from a broom factory. You want that kind of news, I got a pocketful." True statement. Cynthia Evans made an impression on everyone who saw her. Jew Manny is into dudes, so I discount his evaluation and go on what I saw myself. A showstopper copper. "My impression was she's a hard-nosed, uninformed beat cop type slipping around in a lady reporter's underlovelies. Beauty with your bust."

Little Smith wanders into the mess hall, pins us clustered up in the corner, and meanders over, doing a very bad job of acting like he was in no rush to get there. "Here comes Little. Looks excited."

"Might be. Conroy's had Big and Little up in the cell for over an hour now," Odds tells me.

"Doing what?"

"Probably got them back on the logic kick."

Little is at the table. "Mother would like to talk to everybody on the Flats. Card-table area. Mother says—"

Fast cuts him off. "Joint handles are for convicts, Little. Better just call him Mr. Conroy, like it says on his government ID card."

Little shrugs. "Whatever. I think we should go. It's important or I wouldn't be in here bothering this brain trust."

"Kindly inform the chameleon personality for whom you bear invitations laced with logic that we will consider his offer of a parley at our leisure. In the interim, I would suggest he insert his indexing digit into the nether world of his anal aperture and await our reply." Dog smiles disarmingly. "In the event this response is not to his liking, you might add that I said he could go fuck himself."

"I think you should all come. Now." Little's response is surprisingly sharp.

"When we're mother-fuckin' good and ready. Why don't you just get in the wind and let us make our own decisions?" Fast is ready to boil over.

Conroy is being high-handed, but the hairs on the back of my neck are screaming for me to go and see what's up; if I don't, they'll be plaiting themselves into corn rows in a couple of seconds. "I think we should check it out."

I'm up and moving. Fast is still arguing, but the voices aren't growing any weaker, so I know they're following my lead.

The card tables and BS area on the Flats have the usual liver-night crowd. Twenty tables ringed by cons playing cards, kibitzing, and generally bitching about the fact that the prison buys thousands of pounds of beef each month yet hasn't fed us a steak in five years.

As we pass Booty Bandit's cell I notice there's a blanket up over the front and Ass For Gas is on point for the man. "Think maybe Mr. Conroy figures to make peace with Bandit after he's all fucked out?" Noid whispers.

"I don't know what he has in mind," I reply just to shut him up. I'm paranoid enough on my own. I don't need the assistance of an expert.

Mr. Conroy and the Smith Brothers are waiting for us at the end of the line of tables. They've pulled a pair of the rickety, war-surplus cardboard leftovers together to give us some privacy. We rate a lot of hot eyes and poorly disguised giggles as we pass the other cons. I spot Blabbermouth smiling and give him a killer stare. He learns a painful lesson from that: You can't hide a grin behind your hand and smoke a cigarette at the same time.

We straggle into the last row of tables, and Mr. Conroy waves us to chairs. When we're all seated, he begins without acknowledging the three-week-old noncommunicative nature of our relationships. "I called you down here because we have some very important business to dispose of; I'm not insensitive to what this will do to your reputations, but we have matters to resolve that dictate we meet. Thank you for coming."

"Can the hearts and flowers," Fast Eddie says. "Speak your piece so we can get out of here before somebody thinks we're enjoying ourselves."

"I know there's a lot of confusion about me; what I am, what I stand for, et cetera. Some of you feel I just fell off a banana boat . . . a dumb square . . . or I'm an informant and a coward . . . or"—he grins easily—"all of the above. I can't say I blame you for being confused. It's taken me a while to figure prison out, but there are some points I'm going to make right now. One, I'm not stupid. Two, I'm not an informant. Three, I'm not a coward. Now, if—"

"How about you can the lies and just get to the point?" Fast isn't giving Mr. Conroy any air. "It's damn embarrassin' to be seen out in public with you. Do you understand me?"

"First, I want to explain about the incident with the Booty Bandit." Mr. Conroy takes off like Fast hasn't said a word. He draws a chair from under the table, spins it around on one leg, and straddles it, facing us. "There are a number of things about the Booty Bandit you aren't aware of. I made him for the low-life

animal he is the minute I saw him. . . ." The statement is no surprise, but I'm wondering if he'd be saying that if the Booty Bandit were sitting here instead of where he is, behind the curtain and
ten inches up in the Kid's butt.

"Booty Bandit is a homosexual. I know by definition anyone
who participates in a sexual act with a member of his/her own
gender is *technically* homosexual, but I'm using *your* definition."
He laid that down smooth, ignoring the shocked faces of men in a
foxhole being visited by a live grenade. "Booty Bandit is a homo
with muscles."

"Aw, sheeet, Conroy, you don't expect me to go for no shit
like that." Dog is grinding his teeth, leaning forward, tense . . .
coiled.

"You will. And before I finish, you'll also realize he's Creech's
source of information for solving major crimes in the prison.
Now, before you begin another exercise in denial, think back to
all the times Booty Bandit has raped a new fish, killed, stabbed, or
beaten anyone who tried to interfere, and yet, never once—not a
single time—has he been charged by Creech or any other officer.
Creech knows what the Bandit is, and he lets him have his fun in
exchange for information when he needs it. If any of you can give
me a better explanation, I'll be happy to listen. Anybody?"

The logic of what he just laid down has us stunned.

"How did you figure the Bandit out?" Noid asks.

"I got most of my information by observing him . . . and
Creech. The details on his homosexuality came from Ass For Gas
and the Kid." Mr. Conroy lowers his voice. "They explained how
homosexual relationships work in prison. I was amazed to discover the action is a two-way street. Like all of his kind, Bandit
eventually falls in love with his punks, and at that point, there is a
change in the balance of power within the affair. A modification
of the axiom, 'Whoever loves least controls the relationship.'
Now Booty Bandit becomes a victim of his own sexual proclivi-
ties. When Ass For Gas told me Bandit used to perform fellatio
on him, I—"

"Whut's a fellatio?" Giant asks.

"Not the small town in northern Italy you surmise, Great Beast. Cock-sucking is the local definition," Dog answers, without taking his eyes from Conroy.

"Yuh mean to tell me Booty Bandit takes them queers' peckers in his mouth?" Someone has just told Giant there is no Santa Claus.

"Right. And lately, the Kid has taken the Bandit down the garden path. The Kid now writes the scenarios. Ass For Gas says this is the cause of the bloody murders when the relationships come apart. Men like the Bandit don't want survivors of their relationships walking around."

Fast Eddie is on his feet, ready to leave. "I'm not listening to any more of your lyin' crap, Conroy. If you'd like to call the Bandit out and lay this on him to his face, I'd be happy to watch your back. But I don't believe you want that. . . . I believe you're a liar *and* a coward. Bandit has some bad habits, but he has a twenty-year-long record of being a stand-up con."

Mr. Conroy stares Eddie down for a second, then shoots his eyes to Ass For Gas. The Gasser peeps around the curtain and grins. Mr. Conroy stands up and says evenly, "I say Booty Bandit isn't a stand-up anything . . . I say he's a go-down rat." He strides to the front of the Bandit's cell and yells, "Why don't you loud-mouths dummy up for a minute?"

Fifty certified killers and a scattering of other potentially dangerous cons snap their heads in Mr. Conroy's direction. Some of them are rising to their feet. I'm looking for a riot exit. It's tomb quiet. Mr. Conroy nods. Ass For Gas pulls a string and the blanket in front of Booty Bandit's cell falls like the curtain in a cheap burlesque theater.

The inside of Bandit's cell is all done up with black-light pictures; oversized cushions are scattered on the floor around a big easy chair, all stolen from the furniture factory. The room reminds me of one of those sleazy massage parlors, except the only people in the room are men. The Kid is seated on the edge of the lower, and the Bandit is kneeling in front of him, with his hands tied behind his back by a piece of silk from the fabrics warehouse; his feet are bound together with wire from the cable factory. Bandit's eyes are squinched shut, and the Kid has his hands on Bandit's ears, desperately trying to hold on as the Bandit slobbers up and down on the Kid's throbbing red penis.

The Kid rises slowly to his feet, jamming his pelvis into the Bandit's face in sharp, rapid spasms. He eases a bathrobe off the upper bunk and slips it over his shoulders, then rips his dick from the Bandit's mouth.

For a second, the Bandit is a sightless infant, lips searching eagerly for the life-giving nipple.

The Kid is out the door and around the corner in a flash. Ass For Gas takes over; he's standing in the doorway of the cell, trousers unzipped. He's taunting the Bandit, waving his cock in his face . . . a matador with sword in hand. "Hey, Bandit. Come and get some of this, you dick-sucking, stool-pigeon mother-fucker."

The Bandit is struggling to get to his feet. He's obviously loaded on pot. After a couple of slapstick falls he's up, hopping toward Ass For Gas. The Gasser sprints across the Flats and climbs up on the bars, scattering cards, tables, and cons in the process. He scrambles up about fifteen feet, then turns and begins to yell. "Come up and get your dickey-poo, you cheese-eating chump." His penis is flopping in his hand like a partially filled Christmas stocking.

The Bandit is so enraged, he's unaware of the hundred or more hard-rock cons staring at the scene in shocked silence. He's struggling with the bonds and screaming at the Gasser.

Mother climbs up on a shaky table and begins to clap his hands, slowly at first, increasing the tempo as the other cons join in; soon the Bandit is getting the loudest cock-sucking ovation I've ever heard in three/four cell house.

Creech's body alarm screams right in my ear. The applause dies out, to be replaced by hooting and hollering as Creech hustles to the Bandit's side and begins trying to free him. The Bandit has huge tears rolling down his cheeks, and Creech is trying to calm him. Creech screams at the cell-house officer. "Get these maggots into their cells."

The P.A. system springs to life, and we're heading off. As we hustle past Creech, who is still working on the Bandit's hands, Mother says in a too-loud voice, "Birds of a feather."

Creech's head snaps around. Murder is stamped on his face in capital letters. "That tears it, Conroy."

"One would hope," Mother says, and grins.

I'm still trying to figure that one out when I hear the goon squad rolling. . . . Sounds like the drums of doom.

Mother and the Smith Brothers have gone back to the cell; the rest of us are gathered on the railing above the Flats as Booty Bandit is led away to protective custody. Already stories are floating up from those who never saw the action, and they're laced with the usual amount of prison yeast. Booty Bandit was found with a carrot up his ass, wearing a set of Frederick's of Hollywood "Catch Me, Fuck Me" panties, and he had a note to Lieutenant Creech tucked into the lacy bra he'd strapped on. By the time this story becomes legend, there's no end to the possibilities. One thing's for sure. Booty Bandit is a dead handle. "Blow and Tell" is probably his next nickname.

"Now we can get back to some serious hustling," I say, grinning. "We're back in business!"

"Mother would like to see you in the cell," Big Smith announces.

We troop down, heads hanging, ready for what we've got coming: a well-deserved, lengthy, and detailed ass-chewing.

Mother is waiting at the door, back in charge. He directs us to a circle of borrowed chairs drawn up around the table. Place looks strangely different; must be all the chairs in it. "Now, are there any questions?"

Only about four million, I'm thinking, but before I can form one of them into something that doesn't sound like a plea for mercy, Noid Benny is on his job. "How long have you known about the Bandit?"

"A couple of months," Mother answers evenly, allowing us to stew in our embarrassment.

"And you didn't tell us? You took all that shit from a rat bastard, knowing he was a rat *and* a queer, and you let us go on thinking you were chicken shit? I mean, you could have taken the Bandit that night. Right or wrong? And . . . and . . . and aw, shit, Mother, I guess we owe you another batch of apologies, right?"

I'm inspecting my shoes in the ensuing silence. Jesus Christ, Mother must think we are some really shallow bastards. *Well, Flat Store?* my little voice asks. *Well?*

"There is considerable embarrassment firmly affixed to our current state of abashment. One would hope Mother will have the forbearance and ultimate kindness not to rail upon our bared and barren souls with the tongue lashing we have clearly garnered from such unerring stupidity." Dog stands up and offers Mother his hand. "That-there was the slickest put-down/getback/cover-pullin' job this old Texas boy has ever seen."

And we're all up, laughing and trying to shake Mother's hand. Odds is last, and ends the joviality with, "Could you have taken the Bandit out bare-handed?"

"Pick up those two rulers." Mother directs him to a pair laid out next to a neat pile of notebooks and a clutch of sharpened pencils. Odds grabs them and turns to face Mother. "Now, try to stab me with either one, or both at the same time."

"I don't want to risk hurting you. I'm pretty quick. I'll just take your word for it."

Mother jabs Odds sharply in the ribs. Reflexively, Odds takes a swipe at him with one of the rulers, and misses. Mother's fist flashes up under Odds's arm, one knuckle leading the others by half an inch. A second later the ruler is clattering to the floor. Odds yelps. "Damn, that hurt." He raises the other arm in anger, and Mother does an instant replay, leaving Odds with both arms hanging at his sides and a frightened, bewildered expression on his mug. "I can't raise my arms."

"The numbness will go away in about thirty seconds," Mother assures him, "but in the interim, you're pretty much at my mercy."

Noid is right on time. "Where did you learn that one?"

"Georgia," Mother explains. "The point I wanted to make is how easy it would have been to simply disarm the Bandit and then beat him into ill health. But"—he pauses, and gives us the raised eyebrows of a college professor—"we would then have the problem of living here, with him harboring a grudge in what I'm sure is a marina-sized basin of ill will. Sooner or later there'd have been more trouble, or he would have informed on us and our projects. So I made the decision in the interest of everyone. Better to eat a bit of crow for the general population and then devise a method of getting Bandit out of our hair for all time, so I put all our eggs in one basket and set him up. . . . I hope you agree with my decision."

I ignore the two clichés in the sentence, make a mental note to give him a hand on his use of metaphors, and put my head to bobbing with the rest of the crew.

The magician is onstage and completely in control of the audience.

"So much for the values you have been living by; rather, the values of others, which have been dictating how you will run your lives. It's time for some changes, and if you will look around, you'll see the first steps have already been taken."

I loose my eyeballs to gallop around with the rest of the herd touring this, the wrong cell. It sure as hell isn't 3-J-5. All of the beds are made up with the Mother-perfect corners; the floor has been swept, mopped, waxed, and buffed. The sink and commode are TidyBowl advertisements. The clothes that usually grace the empty spots on the floor are hung in neat rows along the rear of the cell, and the water in the guppy's jar is so clean the poor little sucker is zipping around looking like Noid Benny and hunting for a place to hide.

I ease over and spin the combination on my locker and peep inside. Everything is arranged in tidy little stacks. "You burglarized my locker!"

"Mine too!" one of the other bears cries.

"Mine is all cleaned up!" the Giant says, rounding out the players. We turn and stare at Goldilocks.

"Where'd you learn burglary?" Noid asks.

"Virginia," Mother explains, lest we think it was Alaska.

A groan from the corner of the cell announces a more disastrous discovery. "Muh wine's gone. Aw, sheeet, Mother, not muh wine."

Mother nods his head. "From now on, we're neat, clean, and not an ounce of contraband in the house." I wince at the word *ounce,* since the term identifies the target perfectly.

"Why'd you go through all of this?" Noid is reaching Mach 2 on his paranoidmeter.

"Because we have a project to complete that will not work out if the goon squad is in here twice a day doing shakedowns."

"But Mother. Muh wine's muh only hustle. I got no other talent."

"No one is going to hustle anymore."

"We'll starve," Fast Eddie complains. "Shit, Mother, our bankroll—"

Mother cuts him off. "Believe me, I understand your situation. Tomorrow, no later than the day after, you'll each receive a five-hundred-dollar cashier's check in the mail. Enough to buy your commissary needs until the plan gets rolling."

"Plan? Rolling?" Noid is about to spin out.

Dog isn't doing much better. "Hold it! You arrive like an avenging Valkyrie, insinuate yourself into our humble life-style, upset our tenuous grip on this odious environment, and all for some as-yet unannounced scheme of questionable dimensions and undisclosed goals. One might hypothesize you ask a bit much."

"Not really." Mother smiles paternally. "I'm not asking you to give up anything worthwhile. You want to know what I saw when I arrived in 3-J-5? I saw a group of filthy misfits living out their lives under the mandates of such sterling examples of humanity as Greasy Dannie and the Booty Bandit; having every moment of their day controlled by the cretins who dictate the rules of your society—a society in which no normal, intelligent person would *want* to live, let alone worry about his level of acceptance. I also saw that you're good men at heart. I watched you taking care of the Smith Brothers and I sensed your willingness to protect me from the Booty Bandit. But what you don't realize is that the system you call 'doing time' is another way of saying, 'I'm a loser,' and you're not. People 'doing time' are the bottom of the barrel trying to claim it's the top. The only explanation I've ever heard for this idiotic concept of living was when Flat Store said, 'That's just the way it works.' Well, maybe that is the way prison works, but that's *not* the way we're going to work prison. We're going to become civilized."

Mother gives me a chilling stare. "You might not believe it, but right now you're all slaves to the Greasy Dannies and Booty Bandits of this world. As for me, I'd rather be free. . . . If it comes to it, I'd rather die on my feet than live on my knees."

"Shucks, Mother. We don't know nuttin' about nuttin'. What else could we have did?"

"Nothing, maybe, but that was then. Now you can change. Each of you has some talent; I want to help you put it to use. You're different from the lumps floating about in this cesspool."

Mother pauses, and although his eyes travel 3-J-5 in a second, I feel like he's reading every thought in my head. "You see, I'm not asking you to surrender your future to another being or social system. You did that long ago. The question here is whether you would prefer to live under the guidance of the Bandit and Greasy Dannie . . . or me."

It is so quiet in 3-J-5 you can hear the cockroaches stomping around behind the lockers.

Mother takes our silence for acceptance. "So, first things first." He picks up a long yellow legal pad from his bunk and begins reading, pauses, studies the layout of the cell for a moment, and, apparently satisfied, says, "Beginning tomorrow, we'll work on our vocabularies. The Dog will make up a list of five new words for each day, and we'll study them until we have them down pat. Simple words, at first; more difficult as we go along."

"Why vocabulary?" Noid asks.

"We have an immediate and also a long-range need to im-

prove our communication skills. First so we can study other subjects together, and later so we can present ourselves as intelligent
individuals in a variety of situations and settings."

"How come Dog gets to pick the words?" Noid asks. He's already in awe of the Dog's habit of blowing large words around
like they were leaves in a hurricane.

"Actually, I'll select the words, a hundred at a time. Dog will
work from that list on a daily basis. By the end of each day, I'll
expect everyone to know their meanings and pronunciations."

Dog answers our silent accusations with: "Spare this mortal
brow the pain of your accusatory visages. I myself am hearing this
for the very first time."

"Mother?" The Giant is waving his hand like a school kid.
"Why we got to go through all this-here learnin' 'n' stuff? With
your brains and our reputations 'n' stuff, we could kick back and
do some serious time-buildin' 'n' stuff."

Either the Giant isn't really into going along with Mother or
the words *study* and *learn* have brought some old ghosts out of his
mental closet. The eyes check Mother's expression and the neck
hairs do a little boogaloo, announcing that this new argument is
going to get some very rapid settlement.

"Let me lay this out one more time," Mother says, and
switches to a straight-up, stomp-down, stone-cold joint rap faster
than a Hollywood studio can change management. "You want
me to buy into this front-street sucker play you call layin' back
and buildin' time? You wanna kick back, shoot junk, put a punk
in the bunk, short hustle for peanuts like a monkey in the San
Diego Zoo? Fine, get it on, but by yourselves. You'll eventually
hit the streets with enough bucks for a rusty pistol and not
enough brains to do anything but run into a bank and say, 'Up
with your sticks, mother-handers, this is a fuck-up,' and it will be.
You'll be damn lucky if you don't shoot your own foot off. Or
you'll go out, get a job pumping gas for the minimum wage, and
work your nuts blue in the process. The first time one of your old
hard-rock 'regular' buddies drives up and says, 'Come on, we need
a wheel man for a cinch score,' you'll be off like Elizabeth Taylor's

wedding ring and behind the wheel of a car fleeing from a double murder or a drugstore heist. You want that shit? Really? No problem, cause that's where you're already headed."

He pauses, and I can almost hear him changing mental gears. "... Or you can sign on with an idea I came up with in the hole, a way to make money, a lot of money, a lot of *legal* money. And do it while we're still in here. Now ask yourself this question. Would I like to have money I can spend without looking over my shoulder?"

He's got me thinking. Truth is not only stranger than fiction. It will get your attention faster than a blister on your stuff after a night in a Subic Bay cathouse.

"How much money?" Noid asks, lowering his voice and eyebrows in equal amounts.

"I don't have sufficient data at the present time to give you a precise figure, but my estimate, my conservative estimate, is in the neighborhood of twenty-five thousand dollars a year ... apiece."

"That's a nice neighborhood," I admit, and hear something that sounds like a bass plug hitting the water.

"Twenty-five thousand apiece? A- ... fucking ... piece?" Noid is so excited he has to make two questions out of one. For myself, I can't talk; my mouth is doing the guppy routine again, and there's a thumping in my chest that feels like something in there wants to get out real bad.

"Apiece," Mother confirms as the treble hooks arrange themselves in my slavering mouth.

The Giant is on the edge of his chair now, massaging his chest, a habit he's had since he returned from the hospital. I see it, but Mother doesn't, and continues. "A minimum of twenty-five thousand a year," Mother repeats as he reels us in, "roughly two thousand dollars a month each as an average," and we're all in the net, ready to be boated. "Of course"— he pauses as though he has had an afterthought—"as it is with anything worthwhile, we will first need to make a few minor sacrifices."

"We already quit the glue," Big Smith reminds us, but burns Mother with a pointed glance.

"I'll quit feeding the raccoons," I promise.

"I'll quit gambling."

"I done lost muh wine."

The hair on the back of my neck threatens my previous record of two thousand vibrations per second, and I have to ask. "What *kind* of *minor* sacrifices?"

"Actually"—Mother switches back to his college-professor's tone—"we've already begun. Clean cell, neat storage, and absolutely no contraband. This part wasn't all that difficult. The next step in the project is to—"

"Hold, brave knight! Somewhere between the vast horizons of your thus-far articulate persuasion, I seem to have failed to assimilate a vital point. What fucking project?"

"I promise to explain the finer details once we remove a couple of more stumbling blocks." He does a quick inventory of the circle. His eyes settle on the Smith Brothers, and everyone else breathes a bit more easily. "I put both of you on the call-out sheet for the barber shop tomorrow. You'll need to get rid of the beards and have your hair cut. . . ."

"You never mentioned anything about losing our beards," Little complains, at the same time admitting to the prior conspiracy.

"Nevertheless, they have to go. Yours, too, Word Dog."

Dog is so dumbfounded, *he's* doing the guppy. Noid checks out his expression and bursts out laughing. Bad move. Mother turns to Noid and says, "Better get rid of the goatee, Noid. When you go for your job interview you should be as presentable as possible."

Dog is staggered. "My beard? My beard and a *j-o-b?*" He's hanging on to his beard like Samson should have done when that Delilah broad ran in on him with the straight razor. "No! No shave and no j-o-b. That's where I draw the line in the fuckin' dirt. Shit. My beard is *me!*"

Mother's voice is calm. "That's the problem. Your beard is you, and the old you has to go."

There is a rising hum in the cell. Either we are about to be invaded by a division of Hare Krishnas or the opposition is gathering its ammunition. "Hold it right there!" Mother stares us down one by one, until the quiet is complete. Somewhere along the way, Mother has added a glare to his repertoire that would silence a blaring radio. "Let me waltz you through the entire operation, and I'll deal with your individual objections later."

You could hear a mushroom growing in 3-J-5. Mother turns it into a mushroom cloud. "Clean up. Can the wheeling and dealing. Once those problems are out of the way, we begin the educational process. I'll teach English, Dog the vocabulary, and Odds will tutor the Smiths, Dog, and myself in the technical language of quality control so we can get jobs in the factory."

Dog raises his hand, but Mother ignores him, and starts dishing out the details. "There will be four openings in the Q.C. section next month, and we'll—"

"How do you *know* they are going to have openings?" Noid is getting desperate.

"I've been talking with the NASA/DECAS inspector who supervises and accepts finished products on all government contracts in the factories. Right now he's having a lot of trouble with the Defense Department contracts for the Hawk, Nike Zeus, Minuteman, and Trident missile firing cables. He's looking for good help to replace four guys who are being paroled next month. He's having the same problems with the secure-phones contracts for the FBI and CIA. The factory manager, Mr. Wheeler, has some sort of game going where he is able to get a lot of shoddy work past him. Mr. Shure, the NASA/DECAS man, will be very appreciative if we can do him a good job."

Now the mail runner's job is starting to make sense. Mother wasn't just wandering around; he was casing the entire joint for his project.

"Back to the point," Mother says, staring at Dog. "Under Odds's tutelage, the four of us are going to study, learn every step, procedure, and specification of quality control, then dazzle the factory manager with our knowledge while letting him know we aren't going to upset his hustle. Before he knows what we're really up to, we'll have the jobs and the backing of the NASA/DECAS inspector."

"What *are* we up to?" Noid asks. "And what makes you think you can trust those government monks with the alphabet-soup titles, and what do all those letters stand for?"

Mother sorts through the questions, rearranges them, and answers. "NASA stands for the National Aeronautics and Space Administration. They monitor all workmanship on anything destined for the upper atmospheres. DECAS is the Department of Defense Contractor Acceptance Specialist. Before the factory gets paid for work, he has to approve. His name is Shure."

"If he as good as signs the checks, he must have a lot of juice around there, huh?"

"True. As to why I think I can trust him, he has a professional air about him that separates him from the BOP types who run the factory."

"What are we doing with him?"

"When we demand standards of workmanship and quality that allow me, as the new inmate lead inspector, to create jobs for everyone in 3-J-5, Mr. Shure will be our backup."

Well, there it is. I'm going to industries, too; a quick inventory and evaluation of the faces in the circle reveals that the last line of resistance is going to be me and the Dog.

"My apologies, Mother, for this seemingly endless run of interruptions, but you have spoken in terms of overwhelming, mind-boggling sums; yet"—he winces, forming his lips to speak a sour word—"the jobs of which you speak pay a niggardly—"

Fast breaks in with, "Watch where you take this, Dog."

"My apology for the phonetic similarity between the unacceptable noun and the appropriate adjective. The labors thus far delineated will garner the poor, downtrodden workers no more than a pathetic forty-seven cents per hour. My failing is my inability to extrapolate from this near-zero starting point the Rockefellerian numbers prognosticated in your initial presentation. You paint pictures of the wealth of Solomon from the pallet of pitiful stipends."

"True." Mother clarifies the point . . . I think.

"Then whence, in this thus-far impecunious plan, is it your studied and considered expectation that the aforementioned humongous sums will so emanate?"

"Horse racing," Mother replies without a blink.

"Yeah, but where will the money come from?" Noid insists.

"Horse racing. Wagering on the outcome of horse races," Mother explains patiently to the group of gape-jawed savages who have just stumbled into the mission school. "Horse racing."

Odds croaks, then leans forward and places his face in his hands. "God! What have I done?"

Several hundred million questions on horse racing don't get answered. Creech is at the door, explaining the rising shouts of "Good job, Mother," and "Here comes the Booty Bandit's daddy!" that have been building in the last few minutes.

Creech and Mother are burning each other. Five seconds pass.

13

Ten. A minute. I'm starting to sweat; Creech is too. The contest drags on; one minute, two, five. Creech can't hold it any longer.

"I'll be back, Conroy, but worse—and I never want you to forget this—I'll always be here."

"Shucks, Lieutenant," Giant says, "yuh got rid of a pigeon and a homo; seems like yuh'd be fifty kinds of happy. We all are." He grins impishly.

"You're keeping some real bad company," Creech snaps. "Careful you don't learn any bad habits." And he's gone.

Mother turns to the Giant; his eyes are damn near glowing. "From now on, nobody in this cell ever back-talks staff. Got it?"

"Uh, sure," Giant mumbles. "I wuz jist—"

"Never mind what you were trying to do. Let me handle it. Now, where were we?"

"Horse racing," I manage to choke out.

"Yes, of course. The racing project."

Dog is back to his prior state of amazement. "You didn't, of course, mean h-o-r-s-e racing. A jest?" Mother's face clouds over, and Dog attempts to add some humor to lighten the mood. "I've misinterpreted your words, obviously. Clearly the misunderstanding is similar to the Reverend Jimmy Swaggart's proclaiming he is nondenominational to make the point he doesn't care if you send him fives, tens, or twenties?"

"No. Horse racing. Odds gave me the idea," Mother reminds us, and several sets of eyes attempt to push Odds closer to suicide. "In pari-mutuel racing, one wagers against the other bettors. We have established that the person with the best information and soundest judgment is certain to emerge the big winner. Right, Odds?"

Odds nods in agreement, but he looks ill.

"So," Mother continues matter-of-factly, "I ordered the *Chart* books on every race run in the United States for the last ten years. They contain a synopsis of each race: post position, position of the horse by quarters and the stretch, plus all of the elapsed times; also, we'll have the owners, trainers, jockeys, and the bloodlines of the horse. We should be the best-informed wagering cabal at the track."

"What are your plans to store the mountain of data our conspiratorial group will amass?"

"Good question, Dog. *Data* is the precise term. I will address the problems of storage in a few moments. What I intend for us to do, as a group, is sort through this immense number of facts and figures and isolate the reasons a certain class of horse, in a defined-conditions race, wins on one outing, and the following week runs several lengths slower and loses. The answer is either in the books and *Racing Forms* or the problem is insoluble."

"What about the difference between track condition and track surface?" Odds is fully rehooked.

"Good point. Make a note, and we'll look for it later. Now, in order to make our data base for the bets—"

"Guesses." Dog mumbles his own translation.

"We need calculators. So I paid off the clerk in the education department to fill in the gaps in your academic backgrounds. He has given you the necessary prerequisites to allow your enrollment in the Tacoma Community College geometry class. Since it is a night school, it will not interfere with our other schedules. We'll send the Giant, Flat Store, and Fast Eddie. That will give us three calculators."

"Whut's geometry?" the Giant asks, underscoring the enormity of Mother's miscalculation.

"Geometry is an advanced form of mathematics. But don't worry. I'll do the homework, and we'll devise a way to crib on the exams. The importance of this class is not the grades; it is the fact that you will be allowed to buy the calculator and keep it in the cell."

"Where'd you learn geometry?" Noid wonders out loud.

Mother explains in detail. "Oklahoma."

Giant offers his last-ditch argument. "I got no money fer no fancy addin' machine."

"You will have by mail call tomorrow. Remember?" Mother smiles.

"What's next?" Odds is breathing lustfully.

"We use the calculators to condense the numerical information from the *Chart* books and the *Daily Racing Form,* then put these data into a mathematical computer language we can feed into the memory storage."

"What computer?" Fast Eddie asks before Noid can regroup. Fast's eyes have been shining since Mother mentioned mathematics. Strange.

Mother sighs. "The computer federal prison industries is going to buy us."

"What force on earth could move those cheap bastards to buy us a computer?" I ask.

"Greed. They'll need one to reopen the cable factory after we close it down." Mother's expression is one of exasperation mixed with amazement. He can't believe we don't see the whole scam clearly by now.

Dog is close to having a terminal attack of west Texan. "We gonna close down the plant that makes the most money for the fuckin' BOP? Sheeeet, Mother. This is goin' too fuckin' far. . . . How the hell are we . . . ?"

Mother hits the end of his tolerance, struggles for control, and finally holds up his hands like I've seen the Pope do on the TV when he has a hundred thousand or more out-of-line Catlicks mumblin' in his front yard.

"Look. Get on your bunks, find a comfortable position in which you will not feel compelled to open your mouths, and lie back. If I can go on without interruptions, this should only take a couple of more hours."

By this point, we're too stunned to form another decent question, so we dutifully hop into our bunks.

And he runs it. God damn, it is something to hear. As he talks, the whole plan falls neatly together. He has worked out all the details, step by step, and he lays them on us, bit by bit, polishing each tiny facet until it sparkles in my mind with a clarity and brilliance that helps my brain cells line up in neat little rows and sort, count, store, and decide as easily as any computer. Damn thing is workin' again.

Mother finishes, scans the cell, and asks, "Well?"

One by one we raise our hands, and Mother tucks us safely into the live catch box. This is going to be the hustle of the century; win, lose or draw, convicts all over the country will be talking about it for the next two hundred years. We are about to pull off a scam that will make the creation of the Internal Revenue Service look like something legal by comparison.

It takes Noid Benny longer than usual to get his act together, but he is back on the job with, "Are you *sure* this will work?"

"Yes. But in all fairness, I didn't believe I would ever be convicted and sent to prison, either," Mother replies.

A couple of baby raccoons trundle into the cell and put the bum on me, and Mother releases me from my bargain with a grin. I stick about half a box of HiHos into the cute little buggers before the Giant gets into the act with a Snickers bar. He steals the show, the animal act, and the attention of two sixty-pound mother coons who aren't at all happy about their kids cavorting around on the Giant's upper bunk, where they can't see them. They scoot up the bars in a quick tick, issue the routine growls, and the show is over.

The lights go out. Arkie Davis yells, "Come and get me, copper! And bring an autographed picture of your star, Booty Bandit." He gets the cell houses chuckling, and then a standing-in-the-wings-of-a-Las-Vegas-supper-club voice announces: "And *now* ... from the front of J range at the beautiful not-in-town Cross Bar Hotel ... heeeeeere's ... *the poet!*"

> Your buddy's in my cell, cleaning up the broken glass.
> I made him wash the dishes, then I went up in his ass.
> 'Cause I'm a Booty Bandit, been watchin' *you* for weeks.
> I'm the Booty Bandit, I'm gonna split your cheeks.
>
> This tale made Mother angry; I know how to make him mad.
> I called him all kind of names, then went up in his lad.
> 'Cause I'm a Booty Bandit, shootin' rim shots is my game.
> The dirty Booty Bandit, breaking ass-hole for my fame.
>
> Kid tricked me in the cell house, got me ridin' on his whip.
> Before I made Mother's game, I was down with my hot lips.
> I'm the red-faced Booty Bandit; my life is gettin' rough.
> I'm the bad-assed Booty Bandit, just as queer as I am tough.
>
> I know I can't live here, though I had my game down pat.
> I need to see the captain, 'cause I'm still his super rat.
> I'm a stinkin' Booty Bandit, been fakin' all along.
> I'm a pigeon Booty Bandit; this ends my cock-suckin' song.

By the time the Poet has finished, the cons are laughing so hard the ones yelling "More!" can hardly be heard, but they are, and the Poet recites the new "Ballad of the Booty Bandit" once more ... then again .. . then again. ... Now and then he steps aside to allow an amateur to add a verse of his own.

Legends die nasty deaths in prisons. Through the whole roast of the Bandit, Mother never said a word. Me neither; I was off the island most of the time, out of Wonderland and withdrawing money from my very first bank account. And I wasn't holding no pistol, neither.

I know I'm going to sleep like a baby tonight. It's been a long day, and for some reason, the Poet's ballad doesn't really seem all that funny.

Mother is over my head, patting out the rhythm of the same little ditty on the drum of his stomach. Tonight it reminds me of a lullaby.

"Hey, Mother?" Noid whispers.

"Yes?"

"Everyone got a job to do, school, or something. How come I didn't?"

"You will."

"Damn. Doing what?"

"You're going to be our professional electronic paranoid. I believe you have a talent for the work."

"Oh."

Now what the hell is Mother up to? Never mind, it's got to be for our own good. Jesus, this has to work. For the first time in a long time, I want out. Hell, I want to live like a normal human being.

The little voice hasn't anything to add.

Gumball Slick from Philly has been married to the same woman for twenty years, doing time off and on for about the same. He got paroled about three months ago. Yesterday I got a letter from him, and he told me the only difference between twenty years with the same woman and twenty in the joint is that after twenty years, prison still sucks.

14

Serves him right for falling in love. *Love.* A four-letter word, something you fall into . . . are consumed by . . . are smitten by . . . People don't love each other; they lust each other. Hell, the symbol for love is an arrow through the heart. . . . It's a sucker's game, what else could it be? Thank God for carnies and women who don't like to get involved.

I got to get rolling.

Damn. It's seven-thirty in the morning and I still don't have my feet in this bullshit pair of stockings Greasy Dannie's partner sold me. The left one looks like it was woven over the gnarled old tree limb the raven sits on in horror movies; it's all lumps and oddball angles. The right one is perfect. Dannie's man put the good one on the outside when he made up the pair. All five rolls are the same. This was no accident. It is a reminder that any hint of squaring up isn't acceptable.

It's only been a week since Mother sold us on this cockamamie horse-racing scheme, and we've become the laughingstocks of the prison. Not because of the scam—it's under wraps; it's "the Wallows," which has suddenly become the showplace cell of the entire prison, and its inhabitants the not-very-proud owners of the weekly Superior Sanitation Award. The Dog doesn't make matters much better by calling it the "Cell-house Suck-ass Trophy."

If the last week has been tough, this morning doesn't figure to be much of an improvement. Mother has Noid Benny up and off into some secret project he's working on, and I'm waiting for him to start giving me his velvet needle about attending his fucking English class.

Mother wangled eight primary-language-skills books from the education department and strapped one of them on each of us. I wasn't more than a dozen pages into the first one before I started feeling like the village idiot, trying to remember rules and exceptions to rules I deliberately forgot long ago. The second night into the classes I said fuck it and told Mother I had to go to the gym to meet Polaroid to arrange a meeting. Mother wants to talk with the monk, but due to all of the question marks surrounding Mother from time to time, Polaroid has put him on the dummy.

Polaroid works in the photoengraving room at the print plant, and I know Mother is hot to make the connection, so I used the excuse five nights running, even though Polaroid agreed on the first visit.

Now I have to put up with the Giant correcting me every time I misuse *well* for *good* and vice versa. It's the only rule the Giant can remember, and he's getting all the mileage out of it he can.

Last night I tried an excuse to cut class that was weaker than well water, and got a pair of horseshoe-sized eyebrows from Mother, but no lecture. I would have got a doozy, but he was saving his energy for the next move in this never-ending head game we're into. He dropped the bomb at lights out.

"Just for the fun of it, I kept track of each time someone swore or used socially unacceptable language this evening." He paused without looking up from the yellow legal pad I have come to recognize as the bulletin board of my miseries. *"Fuck* leads off, with thirty-eight; *shit* is next, with thirty-five, followed by *goddamn,* with twenty-eight.... We had ... ahh ... nineteen mother-fuckers, eleven son of a bitches, and other minor aberrations totaling twenty-six." Mother looked up from the pad, expecting some comment.

"Thut *aberrations* means not normal, don't it?" Giant asked.

"Unusual, atypical, or unexpected. Well done, Noble Beast." The Dog beamed. "A word from the third list. Good memory."

"It feels pretty fuckin' *good* to know you've done *well*," Giant added.

"Fuckin' good?" Mother asked.

"Bet yer ass," Giant replied.

"Well," Mother said innocently, "it is an interesting observation. The most commonly used descriptive terms represent sexual intercourse, elimination of body wastes, oaths against a deity, and incest. The problem is, the words and their meanings have nothing to do with the point one is trying to make; nothing more than a person trying to sound tough by using obscene language."

"Best way to get a point across," I offered in defense of my obvious culpability.

"Not really," Mother replied. "Winston Churchill was fairly angry at the Germans and proud of the R.A.F. when he said, 'Never in the course of human events have so many owed so much to so few.' The speech survives as one of the most widely quoted from World War II. What if he'd said, 'We put some bad-assed mother-fuckers up against the shit-head Krauts and they kicked their goddamn nuts better than any piss-an'-vinegar bastards have ever done.' I wonder if *those* words would have been immortalized?"

The shitter and the fish tank weren't enough; now it's language cleanup, using one of my heroes as an example, too. I knew if we start sounding like some uppity English cunt, we were headed for trouble. "Let's get back to the horse-race work," I said, to end the conversation. "We can work on methods to get run out of the general population and into P.C. some other time."

"Flat Store's right, Mother," Noid agreed. "We already look like ducks; if we start walking and talking like them . . . well . . . we'd be in trouble, right?"

Mother clears his throat and brings me back to the present.

"I was thinking," he begins innocently enough, "about how you could do something more literate, more socially acceptable with the talent you have for creating similes. You are wasting a God-given talent."

This is too much. My little sayings are *me!* "Look, Mother, let's just stick to the horse racing. I've gotten my ass through forty-one years, made a lot of folks laugh, and knocked in my share of bimbos with my rap. I can take my word game to any bar in America and come out with so much eating pussy that when I wake up the following morning my mouth looks like a glazed doughnut. Why in hell would I want to tamper with a working system like that?"

"Why indeed?" he replies. "Sounds marvelous."

News Boy zips by with a Creech alarm sliding out of the corner of his mouth.

"Are we clean?" Mother asks.

"Disgustingly so. But we didn't get the *Chart* books and *Racing Forms* out yet."

"I have an authorization slip from the library to have them."

"Won't make any difference to Creech if he wants to fuck with us." I roll Fast Eddie out, give him the books and charts in a laundry bag; then I send Big Smith to put a stall on Creech if he heads our way.

"What should I do?" Mother asks.

"Get out of here. If Creech sees you he's sure to give us a roust."

"Good thinking."

"Prisons I know. It's verbs and dumb-assed English I'm weak on."

Mother and the crew leave. I find a couple of *Racing Forms* stashed under Odds's bunk and slip them behind the westerns on the bookshelf. Damn Odds. He knows we agreed to put every bit of racing material in the stash cell over in four house. He's just gotta have it, I conclude.

Creech and the gooners tear up a cell on J range and leave the cell house. Mother slides back by. "Everything okay?"

"Sure."

"Well, then, I'm off and running. There's an office I need to look over this morning while the supervisor is at the warden's conference. Make hay while the sun shines," he says, and he's gone.

Off and running . . . Make hay while the sun shines . . . Jesus Christ, he should be taking lessons from me.

Today is the first day of school, and I have a busy agenda. Education department is first. I sign a Form 24 to pay for the calculator for the geometry class; Fast Eddie and the Giant have already been by, I notice, as I add my voucher to the pile. On the way to the mess hall, I spot Greasy Dannie and Odds in an argument. It's pretty obvious Odds has let the dagos get him hooked once more. A quick mental inventory of my Camel stash tells me I can afford a few packs if it comes to bailing him out.

God damn Odds. I add compulsive gamblers to my list of most useless things in the world, right behind cold coffee, wet toilet paper, and ventilated condoms.

Back in the cell, I have to fill out my commissary list. No worry about going through it time and time again trying to decide between Dial soap and Camels. My only fears since Mother's check came is whether or not I'm going to go over the BOP's limit of seventy-five dollars per month.

The crew troops in near count time, and I take a shot at Odds. "How many cartons are you going to need this time to keep Fellatio Face from slicing you up like an Italian salami?"

Mother shoots his eyes at Odds, and I'm wondering if maybe I shouldn't put him on to Odds to cure his gambling habit. Might make him forget the fucking English classes.

Odds ignores me. The Giant speaks up. "He's down sixteen cartons. I done took over his budget; gonna see ifn I got any talent fer keepin' books. So far, I think I've done *well*." He smiles at

125

Mother. "And if Greasy don't like muh figures, I'm gonna fuck him up *good*. I put you down for twenty-five packs, Flat Store."

"Well, well, well," I say, grinning at Odds. Maybe the Giant can cure him.

"Good, good, good," the Giant says, and Mother bursts out laughing.

"Très bien," Dog adds without looking up from his commissary list. Ever since we started to improve our vocabulary, the Dog has taken to throwing French phrases into the conversation like he was scared we'd catch up with him. He might be faking; I'm going to have to check that out.

"What's on the agenda for this evening?" Mother asks Noid.

Noid has become our unofficial scribe in the budding race company. He scans his yellow legal pad. "Flat Store, Fast Eddie, and the Giant have geometry. Odds is teaching the quality-control class for Mother, Dog, and the Smith Brothers. I have to go over to four house and pick up the charts and forms. After the 9 P.M. count we have vocabulary and English review."

"How about a class in etiquette," Dog says softly, "in order that our fellow conspirator might learn how to say thank you."

"Yeah," Odds mumbles. "Thanks. This is it for me. No more gambling. I can get my fix from the racing we're going to be doing. Don't worry about ever having to bail me out again."

"Sure. You ain't never going to gamble again. Zsa Zsa Gabor ain't gonna have no more face-lifts, Oral Roberts has quit accepting money in the mail, and George Burns is off cigars and hard-bellies."

"I can quit! I already have."

I'm having too much fun to stop. "You're too compulsive. You can't stop gambling any more than I can stop eating pussy." I smile at the wince I get from the English teacher.

"All you white folks talk about is *eating* pussy," Fast notes.

"If God hadn't meant man to eat pussy, he wouldn't have made it look like a taco." I get that in slick, and everyone cracks up ... except Mother. He turns his head away, grimacing.

We're first out for chow by virtue of winning the Cell-house

Suck-ass Trophy, but since it's liver again I skip, go through the commissary, and hustle back up to the cell. I sure enjoyed the trip, no waiting, no begging, no wheeling and dealing. I just picked out what I wanted and bought it. Damn good feeling.

A quick shower and a bit of primping in case the teacher, Ms. Mary Hiller, the education call-out says, turns out to be a fox, and I'm ready for school.

Fast, me, and the Giant gather at the cell door, waiting for the school unlock. The cell is humming. The guys are humped up over their books, and terms that sound as phony as Dog's French are zippin' around the cell like the honey bees I used to catch in fruit jars when I was a kid. I can't understand much of what they're saying; I hear "multi-subject cable master," and the best picture I can get is the boss whip man in an S&M house I was in one time in Hong Kong. Finally, Odds explains that the machine is used to check wire bundles for short circuits in a cable. The explanation sounds more confusing than the machine's title, and I'm thinking I got the best deal of the bunch with geometry. Surely the teacher doesn't figure to be as ugly as Odds.

By the time we reach the second landing of the Education Building the Giant is out of breath and pale. I figure he's not looking forward to the class, and push him on up the last flight. We arrive at the classroom and hustle inside to get seats at the back, where we can crib more easily.

It's a standard joint classroom. The child-sized desks are jammed together tighter than a Greek's cheeks in a leapfrog game; the room is half the size of the office of the supervisor of education, and I can see some method to the madness. With the cons jammed in tighter than a new fruiter in a gay bathhouse, they can cheat, pass with good marks, and thereby earn the supervisor of education all sorts of "attaboy" memos from the warden and regional office. Prison education is more statistics than success.

The teacher breezes into the room in whispers of nylon, rayon, and a perfume that directs the nose to scents of femininity I haven't experienced since I was last in church. Most of the female employees at McNeil wear Brut after-shave or Moose Musk toilet water they buy from the Puyallup Indians for good man-hunting luck; Ms. Mary Hiller is, by comparison, whiffing like Miss Congeniality.

My eyes don't get shortchanged either. She's about my age, I figure. In a way she reminds me of one of those foxy-momma types in the floor-wax commercials who hops through the window, sparkles up the floor with her magic wand, and lays about ninety-six frames of Pepsodent sparkle on the audience. She's an All-American kind of good-looking, a simple skirt and blouse hiding a body that surely would draw stares instead of chuckles. Gold-flecked auburn hair pulled back into a bun is the only concession to the schoolmarm stereotype. She might be packing just a shade too much nose, but what the hell, when I get a cold in mine I'm worse off than a giraffe with a sore throat, so I give her schnoz an empathetic and sympathetic pass.

Her expression is the only thing about her I don't find immediately attractive. Cold as the ass end of an Arctic icebreaker. Might be an air of efficiency . . . or . . . someone in the room is whiffing like skunk tracks.

While I'm ruminating, some new fish is up at her desk, brown-nosing and offering to help pass out the registration forms. As he's making the circuit of the room, she begins speaking: soft, calm, and casual, like we're all old friends. "You may fill out the questionnaire anytime before the class is excused for the first break. For the present, I would like to introduce myself, give you some idea of my expectations for this quarter, and also, I'd like to get to know all of you a little better."

The Giant relaxes. All he heard her say was there isn't going to be much work this evening; meanwhile, I'm discarding my "chilly filly" theory. Her voice floats in the air like the warm, honeyed smell of roasting chestnuts. "My name is Mary Hiller, and this is my first teaching experience in a prison. I don't expect it to be terribly different than working on a campus, except that I'm told attendance will be somewhat better." She smiles sweetly and continues. "Everything here may be new to me, but not entirely foreign. I attended the Bureau of Prisons indoctrination course, but as you can see, I decided to take the job anyway."

An appreciative ripple of chuckles around the room; the course she is referring to is designed to scare the hell out of free people, on the theory that they'll not become involved with the cons on a personal basis. It's a pathetic attempt to intimidate new employees. Creech is one of the lecturers.

She just told us she isn't going to be pushed around by anyone, and put herself squarely in with the class at the same time. She got the job done in four sentences, and I catch myself smiling at her, admiring the smoothness of the mini-con she just whipped past these other suckers. She's misread my grin, because she flashes back a set of ivories prettier than cash money.

The mother's-little-helper type returns to his seat, and the teacher says, "Now, shall we get to know one another? As you know, my name is Mary Hiller, but names don't tell one much about another person, do they?" She pauses and accepts the nods of the room full of cabbages. "I took my Ph.D. in mathematics at the University of Washington, and I'm presently a part-time instructor at Tacoma Community College. Teaching, you see, is a fun hobby for me since I retired from the Hanford Atomic Plant for personal reasons"—her eyes drift to the antinuke pin on the collar of her blouse—"but I'm here now, and I want to show you how one can learn geometry and have a great deal of fun in the process.

"Now it's your turn." Her eyes wander over the room and settle on me. "Let's start with you, sir. Tell us your name and why you would like to learn geometry, if you would, please."

I stand up, but my brain remains seated. I can feel my face heating up, and the cheeks of my ass are trying to chew on my baggy drawers. I don't know why my mind and tongue stopped communicating at just this moment, but I'm in a definite brain lock, if I haven't in fact had a stroke. All I can do is mutter, "Flat Store, ma'am." What a pitiful offering for a man who has spent his entire life *talking* folks out of their money.

"Flat Store?" She's scanning the roster as I continue my futile efforts to get a couple of brain cells hooked together.

"I can't seem to find a Flat Store. Flat Store?" She's peeping at me over her horn-rims.

"It's sort of a nickname," the Giant says, trying to bail me out. "He used to work in carnivals, ya know? Pitch pennies, ring tosses, and the like. Carny folk call them flat stores, so when we found out that wuz his game, we got to callin' him Flat Store, and it stuck very *well.*" He grins, and tosses the conversation back to me.

"The name on your roll is James Barker," I snap, hoping the "Humbert" doesn't show on the roster. The wires between my brain and tongue are reconnected by a thread of anger. "I have, however, in my peripatetic meanderings over this verdant orb, developed a marked proclivity for the more colorful appellation." Damn, those vocabulary classes are great!

"Very well, Mr. Flat Store, would you share your reasons for taking this class with us?" Now her eyes are twinkling at me, and I figure to give her both barrels with the vocabulary.

Nothing. I can't seem to put a sentence together, so I immediately decide to give her a quick lie and let it go at that. Still nothing. The silence is starting to stretch out like a temporary South American dictatorship, and I'm still blank. God, this is a lousy demonstration for a man who once looked a postal inspector in the eye and told him the reason the property the Teamsters' Pension Fund had just bought was underwater in the bottom of Tampa Bay was because the Russians were messin' with the tides; and did the job so convincingly, the inspector went and checked with the CIA before he sought the grand jury indictment that got me here.

Miss Mary's eyes are flashing mischief, and the others in the class are beginning to shift around in their chairs and stare at me. It gets so bad I'm pressed into telling the truth. I shatter the tradition of a lifetime with: "I'm trying to figure out horse races."

Fast Eddie pinches my leg, and the Giant lets out a loud laugh. "Boy, teach, ain't he a pickle?"

Now I've blown the whole fucking scam just because I'm

talking to a woman and my tongue got hard. Fortunately, the entire class is laughing at the outrageous lie I just told this square teacher. Fast finishes the cover-up and destroys the last of my pride with: "You can't listen to Flat Store, Miss Mary. He has the inexpensive-Egyptian-mummy syndrome."

Miss Mary and I are both staring at Fast. She because he isn't making any sense and I because I *know* the snapper on this one. I pulled it on him two days back.

"What on earth is an inexpensive-Egyptian-mummy syndrome?"

"Means he ain't wrapped too tight," Fast says with a straight face, which he can't hold for a fifth of a second before he's damn near rolling on the floor with the rest of the class.

I'm humiliated. I want to go back three spaces and start over.

"He just can't talk to women, Miss Mary. Comes from not seeing any on that Okie farm he was raised on; he's a much better conversationalist with mules. Trust me on that one." It's Droodles O'Toole, trying to make some points off'n me.

I may be embarrassed, angry, and flustered, but there is no way I'm going to take no shit off Droodles. I trot out the heavy artillery. "I can talk to any woman in the world. Shit, Droodles, you couldn't carry on a ten-cent conversation with a two-bit hooker if you had a truckload of quarters. Telling me I don't have a rap for broads! Shit! You ain't had no pussy since pussy had you." There, I'm thinking as I begin to laugh, that should hold the punk mother-fucker.

I'm laughing all by myself, staring at a room full of mouths gaping open and of course the surprised O of Miss Mary's—the lady, I remind myself, I'm supposed to be overwhelming with my intellect.

God damn this quiet. I blew it like a thick-lipped sissy going down on a corn dog. I feel ridiculous.

"I'm Fast Eddie," Fast says, trying to come to the rescue, "but my real name is Edward McCoy. I prefer Fast Eddie 'cause I don't like the slave name. Flat Store gave me my nickname, and I've become enamored of the gift."

Enamored. That's one of the words I was looking for. Well,

shit, maybe this will blow over soon. "Mr. Flat Store? You may sit down if you wish," she says to remind me I'm standing there with my foot in my mug. "And please don't be too embarrassed by your little *faux pas*. I remember the time my brother came home from basic training and told my religious aunt to pass the blanking butter." She pauses, smiles sweetly, then says, "Please, be seated. I'm not at all offended."

Of course she isn't. She's got too much class to show it if she was. The butt hits the chair soft. It should; it has my brain for a cushion.

"Now, Mr. Fast Eddie, why are you taking geometry?"

"I have a genuine need for mathematical skills in planned future endeavors and I hope to polish up the minuscule amount of talent I have in the field."

"I see. What do you do for a living?"

"I'm in the wholesale chemical business," Fast replies without missing a beat. Well, now *he's* telling the truth. Methamphetamine sulphate, Quaaludes, and whatever other Dr. Feelgood pills he can get out of drugstores well after closing time.

"I'm thuh Giant."

"I see."

"Needs tuh polish up muh 'rithmetic 'cause I don't add well."

She is studying the Giant to see if he is putting her on, sees the sincerity in a pair of eyes that should be topping a cask of brandy on a Swiss mountain trail, and simply nods. "Well, then, shall we begin?" She turns to the blackboard and draws a large triangle. "Does everyone know what this figure is called?"

"Triangle," several of the men answer.

"Right triangle," Fast answers by himself.

Miss Mary looks up, sees it's Fast, and smiles. "Very good, Mr. Fast Eddie. The precise term is right triangle. Now, let me ask you one other thing. If I know the length of this side"—she points to the up-and-down line—"and also this length"—she's placed her finger on the bottom line—"how can I find the length of this side?" She points next to the diagonal line connecting the other two.

"Easy," Fast replies. "Take the up-and-down line, the straight-across line, and multiply each one by itself, add the sums together, and figure out in your head what number multiplied by itself will give you an identical sum, and that's how long the line is."

Everyone in the class is staring at him. I ain't got the foggiest what he just said, but from the look on Miss Mary's face he's right on the money and she's damn surprised.

"How did you learn the Pythagorean theorem? Now, this is important, so don't give me any more of the wholesale chemical business. I've read all of your files and know most of you have had the prerequisites for this class forged"—right here everyone in the class draws a deep breath—"but that's not important; we'll learn geometry anyway. Now, back to the question. I know you haven't had the formal schooling, and I'd like to know how you figured out the process without any training in advanced mathematics."

"I can just do it." Eddie is explaining to the detectives at the precinct house. Tight-lipped and stone-faced.

She stares him down for a couple of seconds; then her face softens. She opens a book, studies it for a moment, then writes groups of numbers beside two of the triangle's three sides. "Now, can you tell me the value of the hypotenuse? This diagonal line here?"

Eddie hard-eyes the board for a minute. The cons are starting to shuffle their feet, expecting him to fall on his ass. "One twenty-eight point six," Eddie says, frowning. "I don't know what all the little marks stand for."

"Feet and inches." Droodles O'Toole again. Miss Mary ignores him.

"Perfect! That was the most extraordinary demonstration of native mathematical ability I've ever seen," Miss Mary says.

"You mean native, or nigger?" Eddie asks, his eyes blinking the dots and dashes for the enamel message he's flashing. His voice is as cold and flat as the North Pole.

Miss Mary's face turns bright red, and right away I make it for anger, not embarrassment. "I meant what I *said:* native . . . intrinsic. I have never used the other word."

Now Fast Eddie's face is glowing. It's him that's ended up embarrassed. "I've been able to do a lot of figures in my head since I was a kid. I had to figure out the math to do drug-warehouse burglaries."

Miss Mary is quick enough to know that's all the apology she's going to get. "Now, if you don't mind sharing with us, I'd appreciate how you used math."

"Most warehouses are on the second floor or higher. They're freestanding buildings, mostly, so there are no nearby roofs to use to get up to them. I'd free-climb up to the floor we were going to pop, jimmy the window, and drop a line down to the alley. We'd measure the amount of line I took up, then run another one over into the dead-end part of the cross alley, and measure that. Then I'd know how much wire I needed to make a sliding pulley from the window to the blind part of the alley. Saved running whole rolls of wire up into the score. It worked every time. The cops would drive by and never see anything, because the alley always looked empty."

"You mean you'd pick an alley with a blind T to park your getaway car in, then slide the . . . aahhh . . . loot down the wire above where anyone would normally look?"

"You do second-story work before?" Fast asks, his eyes smiling. The truce is complete.

"That was very inventive. Now, lest someone think I've come to McNeil for the wrong purpose—" She's interrupted by the break bell, and I'm out of there like a shot. I know I'm in for some terrible ragging from the monks in the class. Right now I'm like the Korean honey-wagon driver with the overturned cart—I don't want to hear shit about shit.

If one of them says one fucking word to me I'll bust his ass wide open. I've never been so fucking embarrassed in my life. My solution isn't exactly vintage John Wayne. I take the only logical route out of the fix I'm in and sneak back to the cell.

On the way back something Mother said hops into my mind. We have a need to be able to converse in all kinds of situations. Even social ones, I think he said. I figured the vocabulary would fix that. Wrong. I'm just like the Dog when he gets flustered, only I revert back to Basic Guttermouth instead of Rural Texan. . . . It occurs to me Mother hasn't done any great philosophical divining here, either. It's the same with most folk: Put the pressure on them, and all the veneer of affected civilization will fall away like old polish off a hooker's fingernail. There I go again. . . . I wonder where on earth I could use that simile. Back in Hong Kong, maybe . . .

God damn, showing your ass in front of a lady is not only embarrassing, it hurts like hell, too.

Mother is seated by the door, poring over a *Daily Racing Form.* He looks up, reads my face, and says, "Home early? How'd it go?"

"Shitty. I made a goddamn fool out of myself trying to get slick with the vocabulary."

"Pretty lady, isn't she?"

16

"How'd you know?"

"I saw her out front when I picked up the afternoon mail. She was here for her indoctrination."

This dirty, low-down, farsighted, double-observant bastard has got me pinned better than a butterfly in a collection. There's nothing left to do but grin and admit I couldn't make point one with her. "I struck out bad, Mother. My rap wasn't worth two dead flies. I couldn't talk good enough to get her attention."

"I was unable to speak well enough to attract her attention," he corrects me, and the lesson begins. "I've switched you to self-study. You'll find the new book under your pillow."

While I'm trying to figure out if he is reading my mind, or worse, writing it, the hairs on my neck do their Polynesian stickleback fish imitation, and I spin to stare into the inquisitive eyes of Blabbermouth's cellie, Fred Parker.

Big Smith sees him, too, and says, "Phone's off the hook."

"What's happening, Fred?"

"Nothin'. What are you up to, Flat Store?"

"Minding my own business and trying not to help the warden mind his. And you?"

"Heard you guys finally made the store. Thought I'd drop by

136

and see if I could bum a couple of boxes of HiHo crackers until my next draw day."

"One of the vicissitudes of your clandestine profession is the quality of malapropismatic faults assimilated tympanically when the subject receptor maintains continuous proximity with the terminus of a foreign colonic tract. Given this abysmal proclivity, one can only expect you would exceed the luminal registration parameters with the excretionary refuse thus encountered."

"Huh?"

"You keep your ears close to ass-holes, so all you ever hear is shit," Word Dog explains. "The next time Creech sends you up here, have him give you some fucking rations to bring along."

"No. Honest. I just wanted to get something to eat."

"Logical. I have some leftovers," Little Smith offers.

"Leftovers?" Fred parrots hopefully.

"Leftover lefts and rights from the last heavyweight championship fight. And if you don't remove your slimy self from the front of the cell, I'm going to lay them on you one at a time until we reach the logical position: you with your good-telling ass flat on the floor," Big Smith adds to Little's threat.

"No need to get surly. I'm gone." And he is.

Mother gives the cell a quick scan. "Is there anything going on here I should know about but don't?"

He sees the innocent faces of a church choir. "Let's put some effort into this. Creech didn't send Fred up here to see what you bought in the commissary. Does anyone have any idea of why Fred should suddenly be interested in this cell?"

For a moment, we're the tidy little row of game-show contestants who have forgotten the answer the producer gave us in the warm-up; then Odds hits his head with the flat of his palm.

"Well, Odds?" Mother is patient. More patient than I could be.

"I sent away for a batch of stuff, Mother."

"How much and what kind?" I'm on him like a smoke-signal blanket. Odds has blown every bit of money Mother sent him on some gambling scam. I can read him like the Sunday funnies, and he knows it. Here comes the truth.

"I bought a winner's wheel for four hundred bucks," Odds admits.

"What does it do?" Mother asks, and he sounds truly interested. Jesus, could Mother be a closet six-to-five freak too?

Odds can't help himself. He gets a gleam in his eyes like a sailor in a notch-house line, and starts trying to sell this bunk whatever-it-is to Mother. "You put the horse's post position in one little window and the jockey's weight in the other. The track condition goes in the third opening and the class and distance in the next two. The position the horse will finish in comes up automatically in the last window." Odds is panting by this time. "It's been tested by jockeys and owners all over—"

"Hold it!" Mother is trying hard not to laugh in his face. "Odds, you are incorrigible."

"Fuckin' ignorant works, too," Dog snorts, still angered by Fred's visit.

"I think Odds is to be congratulated." I look up. Mother is pensive, a word from tonight's list.

"For what?" Noid asks.

"*Por como talle, parley vous la shoo?*" Dog says though his nose, after fixing his eyebrows in an appropriate Gallic arch.

"Gotcha!" I shout. "That makes as much sense as saying *mow de lawn* for cut the grass."

"*Mon petit chou, c'est une blague.*"

I'm thinking he's told me a joke, but don't know enough of that Frog rap to challenge him again, so he gets away.

"How in hell does Odds deserve a pat on the back?" Little Smith asks. "He blew the money on garbage without asking and brought a lot of heat on the cell. A reward is illogical."

"Odds has given us the perfect diversionary ploy—something missing from our plan of operation," Mother explains. "Each evening when we return from work, we'll have someone drag out Odds's winner's wheel and play with it right out in the open. Since Creech must know about the racing books and papers by now, the wheel will provide a logical explanation and divert his attention as we make our move to get the computer." He looks dead at me and smiles. "Every cloud has a silver lining."

He's right again, of course, but I have to say something about the cliché. "Don't count your chickens. . . . Odds will be back to betting with Greasy and the dago canines quicker than Minute Rice. Our silver will be lining their pockets again."

"No way, Flat Store. I'm off the gambling. Let me run the wheel and just act excited. I can keep the heat off the scam for sure."

Mother agrees. "It would look strange if someone else started working with Odds's machine. Okay, Odds. You're in charge of the wheel of winners."

"Winner's wheel," Odds says confidently, as if it really were.

I fiddle around with the English for the next hour or so, dreading the return of the Giant and Fast Eddie. They come through the door, looking at me like I've sprouted an extra head or something, but don't say anything about the ass I made of myself. Doesn't make any difference; the story will be all over the joint in an hour or so. I'm hoping the Poet has a sore throat. Fast Eddie slips me a note, and we trade off some puzzled looks. "From Miss Mary," he says, and winks.

I ease over to my rack while Mother is explaining the latest wrinkle in the scam. Odds keeps interrupting him and making comments like it was all part of the plan from jump street. I fight off a couple of choice put-downs and pop the note open.

Dear Mr. Flat Store (may I please call you James?),

I know this evening was a terrible embarrassment for you, and I certainly don't blame you for leaving.

I do wish you would return on Thursday and give us another try. I can tell from your SAT scores that you will not only pass the course, but enjoy yourself.

I also promise not to pry anymore.

Mary Hiller

I'm glowing, and hoping no one will notice. I must have made some sort of impression after all. I want to tuck the note away and save it, but the incident with Fred Parker has me so paranoid, I flush the note down the toilet. A private communication from a teacher would get her fired and me slammed, because it wasn't passed through staff hands. The BOP doesn't want any of the basic goodness of free people rubbing off on this year's crop of convicts.

Not only are my paranoids working overtime; they're earning their money. I don't have my hand off the flushing lever and Creech is standing in front of the cell. He nods, and the goon squad pours around the corner and into 3-J-5.

There isn't enough time to clean up; whatever contraband is in here is going to get found. Thank God we didn't bring the *Chart* books and *Racing Forms* back from the stash cell yet. They won't miss a thing; one of the gooners is holding a little mirror on a stick so he can see under everything, and another is fumbling with a metal detector. They're ready.

The gooners shuffle into the cell and strip-search us. The Smith Brothers go immediately into a Rowan and Martin routine. I want to scream at them to dummy up when I realize something. We're clean. These gooners aren't going to find a damn thing!

"Say, Little, did I ever tell you about the time my brother tried to get a job with the BOP?"

"No, but logic tells me you're about to."

"He didn't get the job. Failed the application."

"Illogical. You mean he failed the test. You can't fail an application."

"Nope. Failed the application. He wrote down that his parents were married."

A couple of the gooners are grinning. Creech sees them, and in order to get back on his good side, they rough the Smith Brothers up a bit.

"Hey!" Big Smith says. "Don't you know you're messing with a Chuck Norris type? I know fifteen or twenty deadly karate yells."

Creech is standing outside the cell, watching his pets get the worst of this battle of wits. Tough shit, I'm thinking. He shouldn't have sent them into 3-J-5 with no ammunition. "That's it," Creech says at last. The gooners stop in mid-carnage and slide out of the cell. Creech gets his duckies in a row and waddles off.

"When you're clean, you're mean," Mother says, grinning.

"Ya-fuckin'-hoo," the Giant explodes. "Thut there is the first time we ever beat them fuckers."

"We won one!" Big Smith says. "I can't believe it."

"Only the pure at heart may face the evil dragon and prevail," Dog adds, and pokes me in the ribs so hard I can barely speak.

"No doubt about it. We're in like Tampax!"

Before Mother can begin the chastisement I've just earned, Creech is back in front of the cell, holding a thick sheaf of incident-report forms. "Three of you ass-holes are out of bounds. Wrong cell. You, you, and you." He points to the Smith Brothers and Dog, then casts a critical eye on Noid. "You too." He's holding our five-by-eight identification cards in his hands while one of his henchmen is comparing the pictures to the faces leaving the cell. The assistant lines the guys up and Creech walks down the row comparing the bearded photographs to the clean-shaven faces. Finally, the light goes on for him. "Why did you ass-holes cut your hair and shave your beards?"

"We have, after much critical self-analysis, opted to mend the antisocial ways that have kept us apart from the mainstream of society for so many years. We hope now to find the means of garnering an honest wage." I admire Dog; he got it out without wincing.

"Yeah? And the head of the KGB just defected. What the fuck is going on with you ass-holes?"

"We are standing foursquare for truth, justice, and the American Way," Little Smith answers solemnly. "We are now seekers of right, the living antithesis of wrong. We have—"

"Shut the fuck up!" Creech screams, and the background hum of both cell houses dies away. "I may not know exactly what's going on in here, but I sure as fuck know who's behind it. It's you, Conroy, so save all the rehabilitation talk for the caseworkers. I know shit when I see it, and you're shit. You hear me? Shit!" He's puffing, and completely out of breath. "I got something for a

smart mother-fucker, Conroy, you remember that. No mother-fucker has ever got over on me for long."

"After such a stunning display of intelligence, why would one even try?" Mother says innocently. "Clearly your mastery of the language is enough to dissuade one from any attempt at deception."

Creech spins, and practically runs away from 3-J-5. "You're wasting time with Creech, Mother. Let me lay a little bit of carnival logic on you. No matter how hard you try, no matter how long you work, there is one thing you can never accomplish."

"Pardon?"

"You can't polish shit. Leave Creech alone."

"But when you're clean you're mean." He stares right through me. "You learn anything tonight?"

"Yeah," I admit. "I did. Creech isn't that far away from being a Booty Bandit. Now, if I could just teach you not to tickle those sidewinders, we might have a chance of getting this racing operation out of our heads and out to the track, where it belongs."

"That's where we're going. Speaking of tickling sidewinders. . . ." He turns and glares at the Smiths. "I thought I said I would do all of the back-talking to the police."

"No. You said none of us would. We were just trying to stall the Gooners to give everyone a chance to move their stashes."

"Wrong. Illogical. There weren't any. You're right, Mother. No more back-talking from us."

A few of the fellas drop by, trying to figure out how we got away with all of our contraband, and walk away shaking their heads. I can sympathize with them. Somehow, being not guilty just isn't as much fun as getting away with something.

I catch Mother making a funny-looking move and the eyeballs go automatically to high power. He's slipping something out of his shirt pocket, and I recognize the contraband at once. He had Creech's photo and print card on him when the gooners rolled in on us! The temptation is too great; I sidle up next to him and whisper, "When you're clean you're mean . . . but a little luck doesn't hurt when you're dirty. What the hell are you doing with Creech's file card?"

"I have to take it to Polaroid at the photo shop tomorrow; he's helping me with a little project."

"If Creech had found you with his card, you'd be helping yourself to six months in the slam. That's heavy-duty escape/conspiracy material you got there."

"There is no way to operate without *some* risk, and this is an important part of our insurance policy."

"Insurance? What the fuck are you talking about?"

"Why, Flat Store, getbacks, of course." He turns, hops up into his bunk, and that's the end of the conversation.

We get through the 9 P.M. count without further upset. I take a short nap. Just when I get into a dream where Miss Mary's trying to show me the values of geometric angles in the Whipped Cream Ocean, I wake up. Noid and Fast are the cause. I'm glaring at them, trying to remove the fuzzies from my brain, when the hairs at the back of my neck warn me this is no ordinary cellhouse argument. Fast is angry, and the problem is, Noid apparently doesn't notice.

"No way is God black," Noid responds to Fast's latest jab.

"And I say He is, and would have been recognized as a black man if all those Italian painters had been black men themselves."

"If God was black, I'd be black, wouldn't I?" Noid asks, a note of eagerness in his voice I've never heard before. "He created Adam in his own image, and Adam was a white man."

"Where did you pick up that racist shit?" Fast is on his feet now. "That's the kind of crap Mr. and Mrs. Roberts's little boy, Oral, puts out."

"Not *Oral* Roberts, his brother *Anal*. Broadcasts on KKK radio," I put in, trying to downgrade this coming homicide to a scuffle.

Fast shoots me a weak smile; then he's back on Noid like graham on cracker. "You've seen pictures where Adam was white, so to you he's white. I'm saying he was created in the painter's image, not God's." Fast's voice is rising again when Mother plops down from his upper.

"I wonder if Adam had a belly button," he asks casually. That stops the argument and attracts the interest of everyone in the cell. "I mean, he didn't have a mother, so he wouldn't need an umbilicus, would he? No umbilicus, no belly button. Interesting question." He's led them off their collision course so slick, they don't even hesitate, just take positions on opposite sides of this new, less explosive issue.

"God ain't got no lint trap," Noid says, "and if he created Adam in his own image, Adam wouldn't have one either, would he?"

"Bullshit," Fast replies. "God or not, there's things like heredity and genes to be considered. If Adam didn't have a belly button, neither would his kids . . . or us."

"There is something here that bothers me," Mother puts in. "Let's just suppose that the men who copied the Bible—as I understand it, they were monks in Europe—what if they were sipping their vineyard's latest and decided to do some personalized editing? Since this Bible is the source of both your positions, wouldn't it be ironic if you were working with a faulted text?"

Fast and Noid exchange glances and realize what Mother has done. They grin at each other. Fast's eyes are twinkling when he says, "I agree. God is actually a black field hand on a universal plantation system, and we're his crop."

"Some crop. Creech is growing here, too, isn't he?" Noid chuckles.

"I have to tell you the truth, Noid." Fast's voice seems serious. "I've known all my life Adam wasn't black."

"How?" Noid is back to normal.

"There wouldn't have been an Eve."

"Why?"

"Almighty God couldn't make a nigger get up off a rib . . . even for some pussy."

"Yeah," the Giant says after the laughing stops, "but what about Adam's belly button?"

"He had one," Mother explains. "The umbilicus goes from mother to child through the aperture that eventually becomes the belly button. After the child is born, the internal portion of the umbilicus begins to atrophy. Shrivel up and harden. Since the umbilicus runs right through the child's liver, the process of shriveling and hardening separates the liver, and the umbilicus becomes the suspensory ligament of the liver."

"So?" Noid asks.

"So if Adam didn't have a belly button, his liver would have fallen down."

"You're starting to become a world-class bullshitter, Mother. Keeping bad company, I suppose."

"Oh, well, at least we got all that explained," Giant says. "What's the first word on the vocabulary list for tonight?"

"Tolerance," Dog says, grinning at Mother.

I'm lying on my bunk, waiting for lights out, and am I ever ready to crash. The vocabulary lesson, the English class, and all my thoughts about Miss Mary have worn out the sorting machine. The day has been an emotional roller coaster. Mother rolls over in his bunk and hangs his head over the edge. "Tired?"

"You bet."

"Me, too, Mother," Noid adds, "but there's something bothering me. Do you really think the Bible might be all bullshit?"

"Did I say that?"

"I thought you did. Didn't you?"

"You have to be careful with impressions." Mother is switching to his "pedantic" tone again, the last word on today's list. "Is everyone familiar with the story of Moses and the Ten Commandments?"

A chorus in the affirmative.

"Everyone see the film?"

Total agreement and a couple of complimentary comments on the quality of the work.

"Well, in the Bible you'll remember Moses went up on Mount Sinai looking for God and to receive the law. He—"

"I think he went up because God told him to." Noid is correcting Mother. This has been a day of aberrations.

"Right. Thanks, Noid. Moses hurried to the top of the

mountain and stayed there for forty days and nights. Down in the valley, the people became restless, so they sent Joshua up to hunt for Moses. A logical choice; Joshua had been their scout all through their desert trek."

"Joshua is gone for about two weeks, but when he returns, he's leading Moses, and Moses is carrying the Ten Commandments, etched in stone by the fiery finger of God. Everyone agree so far?"

Total agreement, even from the Giant, who only saw the picture twice.

"So would it lessen the strength of your belief to know that Joshua must be the worst scout in history? After all, the whole of Mount Sinai is less than ten acres, and he was hunting Moses for two weeks." Mother gives us a moment to consider the evidence and continues. "Oh, yes, one more small item. Does anyone remember what Joshua's job was under the Pharaoh?"

"Son of a bitch!" Dog growls. "Stone carver!" Dog is out of his rack, all wrinkled boxer shorts and wrinkled brows. "Jesus H. Christ! The whole of our judicial system, the basis of the very laws of Western civilization, is no more than the result of a pair of charlatans on a mountain-climbing expedition who come up with a nifty way to calm down a bunch of irate sheepherders?"

Mother appears to agree. "So one could extrapolate from this that the story of Moses is pretty much malarkey?"

"Damn betcha." Giant is mad as hell, probably thinking about all the dimes he packed to Sunday school that he'd have rather invested in Cokes.

"Anyone ever read the story directly from the Bible?"

Every head wags a negative.

"Well, consider this. Nowhere in the Bible does it say our Joshua was a stone *carver* for the Egyptians. Cecil B. De Mille tossed that information into the *movie* as a joke. Joshua wasn't even born until after Moses had left Egypt. Moses was the stone carver . . . or I could have been playing off your lack of knowledge of the Biblical text, conning you."

"You're putting us on."

"No. You tricked yourselves. I selected some facts that were close to the truth and used them to lead you away from reality." Mother shares some inner thought by offering us a wry smile. "Be sure you're on strong ground before you surrender your beliefs. I was only testing you."

"Are you serious?" Noid is jumping up and down on one foot.

"How strong is your faith?" Mother replies. "Sometimes, in certain situations, faith is all you have to go on, whether it is in a religion or another person. Faith is a great human quality."

"Are you saying we should buy any religious bunk that comes down the aisle?" Noid asks.

"Let me put it this way. Suppose someone turned over the Golden Tablets Joe Smith used to found the Mormon religion and they were stamped 'Tiffany's.' Would that mean the Church of the Latter Day Saints doesn't work for its believers? No. Of course not. It is the faith that does the work. Faith like the Allies had in Patton in World War II. Faith, a pretty solid source of comfort when times are hard or your doubts are long shadows on a friendship."

"Come and get me, copper," Arkie Davis yells to remind the desk officer to kill the lights. He does, and I curl up with warm thoughts and a little rhythm being tapped out on Mother's stomach. The title damn near hits me, then disappears back into the sorter.

"Mother?"

"Yes, Noid?"

"Thanks."

"Thanks for what?"

"Just thanks."

Cramming my feet into socks with a shoehorn is especially difficult this morning. In addition to the left one's being a size six
and shaped for a cloven hoof, the right one is formed like a barbe-
cue glove. Atop these problems is an inability to manipulate my
fingers properly, a malady similar to tennis elbow, but in this case
caused by having spent the last
five weeks running endless columns of figures through a
battery-operated Mitsubishi calculator. The keys are so close to-
gether, my eyes and fingers are in constant competition to
determine the order in which they will succumb; the fingers are
usually first, with the eyeballs running a teary second by the end
of the evening. On the chance the calculator was manufactured by
the same Mitsubishi that made the Japanese fighter planes in
World War II, I have taken to calling the blinking, green-eyed
monster "Hirohito's Revenge."

We have settled on Longacres as our target track, and ever
since, I have been feeding the machine the square roots of the
elapsed times between the start, quarter mile, half mile, and top of
the home stretch on each race run at Longacres for the last ten
years. Mother says it is necessary to use the square roots of the results to minimize the margin for error on times that fall into the
2.5 percent extremes of the normal distribution curves. In the process I've learned some interesting things. First, the square root of
sixty-nine is eight something. Then I realized no matter how large
my vocabulary has become, damn few of the words are found in
scientific language; so now, in addition to studying some French

to trap the Dog, I'm learning the terminology of statistics. The other illuminating fact regards Mother: He learned his statistical-analysis techniques in California!

While attempting to tear my socks into their basic component parts of belly-button lint and thistledown, I am struck with a chilling thought. Odds has had a great deal to do with selecting Longacres as the target track. What bothers me is the glimmer of raw lust I've been seeing in Odds's eyes, particularly when he reminds us there are a scant five months remaining until the track's May first opening date. Of course, there are logical reasons to go with Longacres. It is nearby, we can get the local *Daily Racing Form* before the race date, and, since we have no way of phoning out the bets, it's handy for Dog's mother and stepfather; the Turners have agreed to move to the Tacoma area and take our bets out after they visit with Dog. There hasn't been any discussion about my next thought, but I'm sure Mother sent them some money. They haven't been able to afford a visit in two years, and now they're moving!

The hum of a hive of speeding honey bees snaps my thoughts back to 3-J-5. It's only 6:10 in the morning, and Odds is swarming over Dog, Mother, and the Smith Brothers, trying to force-feed them with more information he believes is vital to passing the quality-control examination. The test is at nine this morning, and while I'm convinced Mother has figured out a way to crib and max the exam, Odds apparently doesn't know and the others haven't figured it out yet. They believe it's down to no pass, no scam, and with our reputations and general acceptance from the other cons down the tubes with our hustles, they're thinking they'd damn well better know the information cold.

There is a tension in the air as visible as heat waves streaming from a pop-up toaster, and me, Fast, and the Giant are no better off than Noid . . . up on our tiptoes like a bevy of aging ballerinas, so as not to disturb the scholars. The situation is nerve-wracking. Noid is the first casualty. He slips off to chow even though they're having chipped something or other on toast. I decide to gather up Mary's most recent letter, a pad and pen, and light out for the yard. It's going to be a bit nippy, but the peace and quiet figure to be worth the minor discomfort, and besides, the day is clear, promising the sunrise over Mount Rainier will be something to write home about. Home? Odd thought, Flat Store. Odd.

The trek to the bleachers is an opportunity to consider what I'm going to say in the letter. It's the tenth one I've written. Funny how we got started exchanging our thoughts. The next class after I received her note, we had the opportunity to talk during recess, because the film-appreciation course was showing a skin flick, and all the guys beat feet to the next room as soon as the break bell rang.

"Mr. Barker? . . . I mean Flat Store? Could I speak with you a moment?" she'd asked.

I eased up to her desk, not knowing what to expect. "Listen, I want to apologize for the other night. I shouldn't have shot off—"

She cut me off and gave me a smile that made my chest feel as though someone were in there trying to blow up a balloon. "Nonsense. You had some feelings and you let them out. It's healthy." I couldn't speak, and the silence stretched out, until she smiled again and said, "Have a seat, James. Please?"

I slipped into the chair by her desk. "My husband"—she blushed a bit—"my *ex*-husband was like you in many ways, but . . ." She paused, and I got the impression she was going to cut the conversation off; instead, she continued. "He lacked one quality that you have. The ability to demonstrate his feelings." She paused again and stared straight at me. "He started drinking to hide his feelings; then he started hiding his drinking to avoid hurting mine."

She was in such obvious anguish, I cut her off. "Yup. That's the way it works. When you're tryin' to keep from hurting someone you care for it's pretty easy to do something, like lie, which makes things worse . . . for both of you."

"Oh, James, if he could have been more open with his feelings . . . You know, that's the problem with the world I live in . . . *everybody* puts up walls. I saw more real emotion in an hour here than I've ever seen in a year outside."

"One thing about convicts, Miss Mary. They've got emotions left over." I didn't know what to make of what she was saying, but I figured the move was to get out before the shimmer in her eyes turned into a waterfall. "I'm sorry to hear about your divorce. Maybe some good will eventually come of it. Life has a way of evening out, you know." There was an awkward silence as we stared at one another. I stood up to leave.

"I've been silly." She was blushing.

"No. Not at all. I feel as though I've been paid a compliment." And I did. When I left the room, she was smiling again.

I wrote her a note to help cheer her up, she answered, and before I knew it she was pumping information out of me twice a week. I wasn't pulling any punches, either. I started her out on the truth and figured if she wanted something else she'd let me know. It took a bit to convince her how dangerous the notes were. She didn't understand that the BOP didn't want any unmonitored communication between staff and inmates. If they found one of her notes, with her name on it, she'd be fired faster than a campaign manager who lost an election in Russia. After all, no telling what would happen if they exposed the cons to some basic, decent human feelings and emotions. Probably cause some rehabilitations and screw up the statistics they need to keep building more prisons.

Mary sorted my rage from the reality and agreed to be very circumspect but insisted we keep the correspondence going.

The sun peeps the horizon as I top the bleachers. By the time I have my writing tools laid out, the scene is the perfect opening for my letter. The first lines are easy:

Woman,

I'm outside, awaiting the sunrise. The first rays poking into the sky are the soft pastels of a mandarin's fan I once saw in Hong Kong. As I'm watching, the colors fade, and now a golden, regal glow has touched the glistening, treble-peaked tiara of the mountain, turning Mount Rainier into the noble, majestic regent of the other mountains in the Cascade chain. A rim of hot white light appears, and the pinnacles of the tiara dissolve in a flush of gold. I try to capture the image, but my eyes water against the power of the sun and the moment is gone. . . . Maybe I have captured a portion of it here; I don't know.

In the cold light of morning, the mountain never looked more lonely, or more free. I suppose in many ways, Mount Rainier has become a symbol of freedom to all of us, an irrefutable reminder of another world. Out There.

A world I hope will be one of simple beauty, and, like the promise of the mountain, a picture of serenity and peace. It occurs to me that all of the men I have seen sitting here over the years must have experienced these same feelings; there is something about the scene that attracts us in droves. I can't help wondering if the sight would seem as beautiful if I were not surrounded by all of the ugliness. See how you have me rambling again? There is a quality in you, Woman, that tickles thoughts and images to the surface of my mind that I'd never think of in a discussion with anyone else. Discussion!

Well, it *seems* as though I'm talking with you. Am I going bonkers? I started to answer your letter, and obviously I failed, but we must hold to our single-page rule. We have a flower growing, and as luck would have it, there are more of those who would crush it than there are who would enjoy the fragrance and move on. Now to your questions.

No, I don't know where I'll settle when I get out. I don't even know when that is. No, there is no one out there with the slightest interest in me . . . except you. Yes, I agree, sometimes life is taking what you find, where you find it. The trick is to hold your treasure close.

I'm gone . . . Man

As I'm carefully folding Mary's note for storage in my watch cap, I notice Mother is coming down Cardiac Hill. My back-of-the-neck antennae tell me his seeming nonchalance doesn't mean a thing; Mother is in a hurry, and he's heading right for me. I stand, ready to go down, but he waves me back to my seat and breaks into a ground-eating jog that puts me in mind of a military man, for some reason. He's across the field and up the steps in less than a minute.

"Morning, Mother. Through cramming?"

"I believe they assimilate the information better if I'm not sitting in. When Odds asks a question, they either wait for my answer or turn to me for affirmation when they do respond." His reply is absent, and I know this conversation isn't going much further in this direction. Mother has something on his mind.

"The factory manager, what's-his-name, Wheeler, is he still going to be the test proctor?" I ask around the lump of apprehension that is growing in my throat like a mushroom in a bullpen.

"Yes. And I'm convinced he isn't going to give us an opportunity to crib. He *wants* us to fail, so he can slip in some hand-picked people."

"Why does Wheeler go through all of this rigamarole?" I'm whispering, my throat closing with anxiety now. "Why not just assign his pets and be done with it?"

"If it weren't for Mr. Shure, the NASA/DECAS man, I'm sure he would, but the contracts dictate that the inmate inspectors be chosen by competitive examination and trained by the NASA/DECAS representative. It's something Wheeler can't manipulate; he'd be too exposed."

I'm having a tough time with one bit of information. More precisely, I can't believe I'm just now hearing it for the first time. "Do Dog and the Smith Brothers *know* they aren't going to be able to crib?"

"No," Mother replies matter-of-factly, carefully ignoring my pained, accusatory expression. "I didn't believe it was wise to worry them when Odds is dispensing information vital to their passing. I'm confident they'll do well without cheating."

"Jesus, Mother! I thought you'd have something *slick* put together!"

"I do," he answers. "They know the material inside out." He slips me one of his rare, sly grins. "Besides, Fast tells me the two of you are passing the geometry tests without cheating."

"Fast has a big mouth," I say. "But we're talking about Dog and the Smith Brothers; they're—"

"—every bit as capable as you are. Everyone in 3-J-5 has some

talent, and I think I have them married to the appropriate tasks."
He pauses, and a sad frown flits between his eyebrows, then lands
on the corners of his mouth. "Except for the Giant. He's going to
be difficult. I need something to make him feel as though he's
making a contribution." He eyes me suspiciously. I figure he's
trying to tell whether or not I've peeped his thoughts. "I may
have to invent a task he can excel in."

"Something will turn up," I say out of habit. I'm still in a depression deeper than a Republican's pockets when the United
Way is seeking donations in the neighborhood.

"I hope so," Mother says, and takes a seat beside me. He
glances up at the mountain, then back at me. "Come out here to
write Mary?"

"Yeah. I couldn't take much more of the cell. Too tense this
morning." I give him a quick scan, trying to see where this conversation might be heading.

Buddha is staring into space.

Mother clears his throat a couple of times, but his eyes never
leave the mountain, and I'm becoming as uncomfortable as the
NAACP rep at a KKK gathering. Finally he asks, "What happens
to you guys if the plan doesn't work out?"

My answer doesn't require any deep thought; we'll be in deep
shit. "We'll continue merrily along, the laughingstocks of the
prison; all of our resources—namely, our reputations—will be
gone. We'll be seen as a bunch of born-again squares. Damn dangerous in this snake pit."

I pull a quick switch on him. "Why are you putting yourself
through all of this?" I ask, and before he can recover, I pull out a
stack of evidence my subconscious has been gathering. "You obviously don't need the money; I've figured you've already spent as
much or more than you can possibly recover. You sure as hell
don't need the heat or the harassment. You have the warden's
mug flashing murder one every time he claps eyes on you, and in
general, for a person who should be trying to low-profile his way
through a bit, you've made one hell of a fuss around here, especially with those scenes with Creech and the Booty Bandit." I

pause, waiting for some facial reaction to tell me where his head is at. Nothing. "I'm serious, Mother. Just what the hell is *your* pay-off?"

He waits a couple of ticks to get his defenses together. Then a creepy little smile starts forming in the corners of his mouth, and by the time he answers, it has insinuated itself over the rest of his lips. "For the game, Flat Store, just for the game."

I don't believe that for a heartbeat. I guess he sees this in my face, 'cause he quickly, maybe a little too quickly, adds: "When the government has hidden the ball, burned the rule books, and bought off the referees, about the only thing you can do while they're holding your nose and kicking your ass is try to score some getbacks. Since I can't win playing their game, and for most government employees it *is* a game, I've learned to make them play mine."

"Jesus, you didn't lay any of that on the psychiatrist, did you?" I'm only joking, but for damn sure Mother isn't. For the first time, I see the executioner without his mask.

"You mean the same psychiatrist they carried off the island muttering something about wanting to have sex with his mother?"

Now the hair on the back of my neck does a simulated Zulu uprising and attacks the less-populated portions of my scalp. There is a blue steel light shining through this crack in Mother's shell, and behind it I see one of the most cold-blooded suckers I've ever met.

While I'm still in an advanced state of shock, Mother slips the mind wrench back on me. "So tell me, Flat Store, what is the bottom line for you? What do you expect to gain for all of your effort and sacrifice?"

"I guess if I could turn this into anything I want, I'd like to see what a Humbert James Barker could do with his life if he had one clean shot."

Mother stands up, gives my shoulder a reassuring squeeze, and says, "You'll have the chance. I'm pleased you have given some thought to what you want to do with the opportunity."

"Yeah. I got it down cold. I'll have it down better after I do these next six years."

"Nothing is written in stone, Mr. Barker," he says, and is off in a single, lithe movement that has him jogging down the steps before I can ask him what the hell he meant by his last statement, or even what he really came out here to talk to me about. I finally put it down to trying to help me get rid of my anxiety, but it's almost as though he came out here seeking justification for something. Whatever he came for, he got it, because as he trots across the field I can see an even more determined, military set to his shoulders.

Mother, I conclude, is getting ready to attack something. . . or somebody.

Jesus, what a morning, and it's only 7:30. When I went out I had my thoughts all raked up into neat little piles like the stacks of autumn leaves on the manicured lawns of suburbia I used to admire on my sorties away from the carnival to see how the other folks lived. My conversation with Mother was an emotional tornado that scattered everything over four very diverse states: namely, confusion, anxiety, fear, and ennui.

18

The inside of 3-J-5 doesn't look or sound much calmer than the inside of my head. As I come through the door, Dog is the picture of frustration, a couple of ticks away from anger. "I am unable to fathom any of this. If we are supposed to be responsible only for the finished product, why not simply attach the completed electrical cable to the cable master, turn on the electricity, and if it passes, we're done with it?"

Mother glances at Odds, then answers the question himself. "Because a cold solder joint will fall apart in the field . . . and that's the only acceptable answer to the question of the NASA soldering-specifications portion of the test. Listen up; here it is again. 'All soldering of critical connectors *must be observed* by the NASA representative or his designee.'"

Odds looks puzzled, and he's the instructor! "But that's not the way we do it now. Wheeler just has us sign off the cards."

"Right." Mother is grinning. "And that's where we'll have him when we get the jobs. He thinks he gets more done faster if he doesn't have some inspector nosing around the job. It's an even mix of greed and stupidity. A couple of weaknesses we'll use

157

as levers when they want to start the factory back up after we help Mr. Shure close it down."

"How will we close it down and how much will it lose?" Noid's nerves have him doubling up on his questions.

"The how we'll cover later. They're making about four hundred thousand bucks a month right now."

"Jesus, no wonder Wheeler wants to avoid rejections."

"If Wheeler were an efficient manager, he'd make sure the cables were built right the first time . . . and train the men as the congressional mandate demands. Production would go up right along with quality. It's a basic principle of assembly-line work."

"Where'd you learn about assembly lines?

Mother explains in considerable detail. "Eastern Michigan. Believe me, we pull this off and we'll be doing everyone a favor; most of all, the military men whose lives depend on the equipment."

"First we'd better pass the test," Odds reminds them. "Here's another sample exam." He passes out several booklets, and our budding Q.C. crew is on them like ants on aphids.

"On your bunks, chillins," Fast Eddie says as he wraps a faded bandanna around his head. "Time for ole Aunt Jemima to tidy up you younguns' livin' spaces. Me and that shiftless old Flat Store goan get ya'll one ob dem der Cell-house Suck-ass awards 'gin, sho nuff."

Fast and I are off into the cleaning chores. My first task is under my own bunk. I sweep out the dust kitties and my broom whisks out a clear plastic bag like the ones the photo shop's film comes in; inside I can see a bottle of machine oil and something that looks like a glob of Silly Putty. "Anybody belong to this?"

Mother looks up, turns red in the face, and holds out his hand.

"What the hell are you going to do with this junk?"

"Clog the wheels of industry and oil the wheels of justice," Mother replies, and ducks his head back into the examination booklet.

The work whistle blows, and Mother leads the candidates off

to the test. I'm a little concerned about Dog. He looks uneasy, the boy waiting at the schoolbus stop who hasn't done his homework.

The Giant tags along behind. Mother was right; we need to find him something to do.

The Giant is back in ten minutes. "Whut if they blow it?"

"What indeed?" I reply. That's the end of the conversation.

By the time we have the house ready for inspection, I am suffering a dilemma roughly equivalent to a young priest's discovering a pair of bikini panties tucked into the monsignor's sofa cushions. Believing in the men who are going to take the test that will decide our future has become a supreme test of faith.

Noid doesn't help much with his running commentary on the number of hours, minutes, and seconds that have elapsed and how much the crew is already over the time Odds has estimated to successfully complete the exams.

Greasy Dannie drops by, looking for Odds.

"He's down at the factory. Anything I can do for you?"

"Got business with Odds," he says through his compressed George Raft lips, and he's gone.

What a pair. Odds is the product of a typical middle-class family, and Greasy is right out of Little Italy, where he's learned that the value of a human life and of a pushcart full of canteloupes is roughly about the same. Odds has probably lost another football bet, and now Greasy Dannie wants to introduce him to their cultural differences. Jesus, I'd better go and count my Camels.

Another hour goes by and Noid is out on the range, peering over the edge with his hand mirror. Ten minutes later he's up on his bunk with a towel wrapped around his eyes.

Another half hour goes by and Noid gets up, has another cup of coffee, then goes to the commode, sits down, and pees in his pants. "The sample test only took forty-five minutes," he moans.

"Here. Have some more coffee," I offer, pointedly ignoring the darkening shades of his trousers. "Settle down."

"Coffee! Settle down! Shit, I've had ten cups in the last three hours, and it's a wonder my bladder ..." His eyes register the enormity of the error his sphincter's made. "What the hell, maybe I'll just go and take a shower." He begins to strip off his clothes as I inspect the bars for potential dust accumulations.

While Noid is in the shower, the crew comes in without fanfare. Big Smith is in the lead, pushing thirty-two gleaming exclamation points in front of him. "We maxed it, Flat Store! Mother missed a question, of course, but the rest of us blazed right on through."

Their expressions confirm the news. Little Smith is as proud as a bucktoothed girl in an apple bobbing contest, and Mother has just been told his herpes test is negative. Odds and Big Smith are puffed up like the glands on an Italian actress, and Word Dog has a country grin that would melt an iceberg in three seconds flat.

I haven't realized it till just now, but I think I may have broken the Guinness record for holding your breath. Problem is, I can't remember when I started.

What a worrywart I am. One minute I had us out like the king of Greece, and the next I figure we're in like a military-budget increase.

Character deficiency, my little voice tells me.

We took the celebration to the mess hall, only to discover the food-service administrator had broken prison tradition and served liver for lunch. We made the lap through the mess hall, then joined the group of cons in the hallway, bitching about the food and trying to pump a little life back into our dying celebration.

I'm hearing some serious grumbling about a food strike or work stoppage. Be just my luck. Now that the first phase of the scam is accomplished, some malcontent wants to have a sixty-five-day lock-down and screw up the works. Giant reminds me I made the same suggestion a few months back, when the storeroom ran completely out of socks. Funny how rapidly my perceptions have changed.

"Don't worry about a lock-down," Mother tells the Giant. "Mr. Shure and I were talking, and he tells me the factory is so far behind on its orders they've been discussing working evenings and Saturdays. It is highly unlikely Stonemann will shut the prison down; he'd look too bad with the director and the rest of the BOP staff in Washington, D.C."

"So we're cool?" Noid asks.

"Better than that," Mother assures him. "In addition to the intrinsic greed that is always pushing them, the factory staff will be worrying about losing the contracts to another prison if they can't produce."

Picks Monahan slides by Mother's shoulder and whispers, "I got your stuff together. You want me to bring it by the cell?"

"I'd rather pick it up tonight, if it wouldn't be too much trouble. 3-J-5 is due for another shakedown."

"Done," Picks mutters, and eases off into the crowd.

Little Smith beats Noid to the punch. "What you got going with Picks? That's not a very logical association."

Little has surprised me. Phil Donahue wouldn't be dumb enough to ask that question, and he goes to beekeepers for brain transplants.

"What can't you take to the cell now?" Noid asks angrily. "Our deal was *no contraband,* wasn't it?"

"I remember," Mother replies. "You heard what I told him."

Creech and Warden Stonemann pass, burning us the way people do when they're talking about you. I tug on Mother's sleeve, and he does something incredibly stupid. He waves, and shouts, "Good afternoon, Warden. Out walking your lieutenant?"

Creech's and Stonemann's jaws start working like a pair of piranhas in a perch pond, but their lips are jammed together so tight you couldn't drive a flax seed into their mouths with a pile driver.

Dog is pulling Mother toward the cell house. "Mother! You have to learn some respect for the sidewinders. Creech is never going to forgive you for the Bandit. . . ." The conversation fades as Dog leads Mother away.

"I still can't believe the relationship between Creech and the Bandit. Illogical," Little says.

"The colonel's lady and Rosie O'Grady are sisters under the skin," Big Smith says softly.

"Don't be puttin' no sisters in the same conversation with Creech," Fast says. "Lay off the Kipling and get back to the clichés. Remember Mother told Creech something about birds of a feather? Not all homos got weak wrists. Maybe Mother struck a nerve with Creech."

When we get back to the cell, Mother is sitting at the card table, with a folded bath towel between his hands. He motions us to gather around the table, and when we're all in place he flips open the towel and we're looking at a stainless-steel shank about eighteen inches long, a state-of-the-art people killer. "Anyone?"

Frantic, negative nods.

"Then we've been planted." He is staring at the knife, rubbing his jaw. "Okay. From now on, first man in the cell shakes it down. If several of us arrive together, one man goes inside and clears the cell . . . goes over it with a fine-tooth comb. Agreed?"

This is some serious shit, so I give him a pass on the cliché. Possession of a weapon is another five-year court sentence, and if they can't hang the case on an individual, everyone in the cell gets the nickel.

"Better give that to me." Noid's fright motor is turning about seven thousand RPM. "The inspection team is due any second." He grabs the knife, tucks it under his shirt, and is off, down the tier and out of sight. The inspectors are at the door a couple of seconds later. Noid must have walked right past them. We nod to the inspection team and walk out onto the tier.

While we're outside, wiping off the sweat and waiting for the inspectors to finish the microscopic inspection they're giving 3-J-5, I notice they're not digging into things. If the shank was a setup, the inspection team was not designated to find it. They walk out, give us a nod, and the head inspector says, "3-J-5 . . . perfect score. Good job, men." I hear the Word Dog suck in his breath; getting a compliment from a cop isn't his favorite way to cap off an otherwise great day.

Odds comes back with an armload of *Chart* books and *Forms*.

"Hey, man. We aren't supposed to bring that stuff into the cell house during working hours," I remind him.

"No sense wasting the afternoon," Odds answers. He's already looking lustful, and Mother doesn't object, so I drop it and go inside with the rest of the crew.

We spread out the work, and I'm through worrying about who may have planted us, when a voice behind me rekindles the fear and solves the mystery at the same time.

"Here they are, Warden. My own, personal grouped set of supersanitary ass-holes."

Stonemann has enough class to wince at Creech's language, but the observation doesn't raise him a single notch in my estimation. People tend to hire their alter egos, I remember from a class I attended once at the unemployment office.

"Yessir," Creech hisses. "These pieces of shit have just about everyone convinced they're trying to rehabilitate themselves."

Stonemann and Mother have locked eyeballs, and Stonemann says softly, "Is that right, Mr. Conroy? Has 3-J-5 become your private rehabilitation project?"

"Guilty, Your Honor." Mother responds pleasantly, but his eyes are colder than a well digger's ass. "We have decided to mend our ways and work to *get back* into the mainsteam of middle-class America."

It takes a couple of ticks for the "getback" crack to sink in, but when it does, Stonemann is doing Creech's cobra imitation. Mother has enough sense to quit this time; he's got to know Stonemann understands enough convict to decipher "getback." I'm just starting to let the air out when Mother gives him another shot. "We've become sort of a family, you see. Looking out for one another. You know how it is with family; there is a very strong motivation to be protective and helpful. This is particularly true when they're all working to get back . . . to society, that is. Yes, we watch out for one another . . . like brothers are supposed to."

That's all Stonemann can take. His hand moves toward the bulge in his jacket. Creech's face turns the color of pancake dough. He throws Mother a wild glance, grabs Stonemann's elbow, and propels him down the tier and out of sight.

"Mother! Quit acting like a goddamn fool!" Dog warns.

Creech is back at the door. "I've seen stupid, dumb shits in my life, Conroy, but you win the fur-lined piss pot and the trip to Alaska." Before Mother can respond or I can write that one on paper, Creech is off down the range again, his size thirteens slapping the concrete, sounding like cannon shots.

"Better put the *Chart* books and *Forms* back in four house," Fast Eddie suggests. "Creech isn't going to let Stonemann down. He'll retaliate." Fast sounds disgusted, and Mother picks up on his tone. For the first time since he moved into 3-J-5, I see a flash of panic—maybe some inner-directed anger? Whatever, Mother is looking pretty damn ashamed of himself.

"Making them play your game?" I ask uncharitably.

"No. I lost my temper. You're right; worse, Creech was right. That wasn't very bright on my part." The insincere tone slips past everyone in the cell but me.

Mother scans the stacks of *Forms* and *Chart* books, then asks, "What do the rest of you think? Should we get this out of here? Myself, I go along with Fast."

Odds wants to get to work, Noid wants it out, and the rest of the committee has to express opinions somewhere in between. I remember God made all of the animals himself, except for two he assigned to a committee of angels. They came up with the platypus and the giraffe. We came up with enough wasted time to get caught in a shakedown.

Creech and the goon squad are at the door. Creech is grinning like a punk in a pickle factory. He can't believe his good fortune. "My, my, my, just look at all the lovely contraband. Must be enough gambling paraphernalia to start booking horses." He nods, and the gooners roll into action like a well-drilled gun crew.

From the jump I can tell this is not going to be any ordinary shakedown. 3-J-5 is going to experience a bust-up. The gooners are ripping and tearing before Creech can get out his next command. I know what's coming, and have my shirt halfway off.

"Okay, my supersanitary ass-holes, strip. I want you outside this door like the day you were born."

We shed the togs like a bevy of starlets at a casting cell.

Mother doesn't seem at all perturbed; matter of fact, he has this half-assed grin on his mug that is irritating me almost as much as it is Creech. By the time I get to the buff, Creech has the rest of the crew down at the end of the tier. They're broke open like a row of sixteen-gauge shotguns; hands spreading cheeks, and teeth biting lips. I take a spot at the end of the line, bend, and spread; I'm looking right down at the Flats and a crowd that is starting to gather. The gooner checks my ass-hole for any hidden escape rafts and tells me to stand up. Now the crowd below is growing larger and larger. Something about watching a group of cons get their house torn up and their asses jacked open brings out the comedian in them.

"Oweeee, *mama!* Check the cheeks on that chicken."

"What a shitter on that critter!"

"Hey, Flat Store. What you doin' with that swizzle stick between your legs?"

"My, we certainly named the Giant properly, didn't we, girls?"

"I deeeeeeclare. Mother isn't a Mother after all!"

I hear glass breaking in the cell, and make a mental note to buy myself a new jar of Taster's Choice coffee next Thursday. When I hear a second one break, I scrub my plans for bumming from Noid until then. The crash of a falling locker explodes through the cell house, and the Dog yells, "Cease and desist from this mayhem, foul dolts."

A voice from the Flats brings a roar of laughter with: "Show them your Cell-house Suck-ass Award, Dog; maybe they'll lay off."

The laughter is pinched off sharply when a photo album comes sailing out of the cell, trailing a streamer of photographs. Even the insensitive bastards on the Flats know this is a no-no, including the gooners. I recognize the hand-tooled leather jacket of the album. It's the Giant's.

"Them's pictures of muh family," he roars, and starts down the tier toward the cell. As he approaches, Creech puts his hand to his belt, locates his body alarm, then deliberately steps on several loose pictures, grinding them into the concrete with his heel.

"That's enough of this-here shit," the Giant growls, and charges. Mother is on him like body odor, hugging him around the waist and lifting his feet clear of the ground to keep the Giant from getting any closer to Creech. The humor of two naked men wrestling on the range isn't lost on the wits and half-wits below; worse, Mother has grabbed the Giant from behind.

"That's it, Mother. Take a quick trip up his Hershey High-way."

"Put him down and see if he'll let *you* kiss him."

"Better get a grip on his snake, Mother, 'fore it whips around and bites ya!"

Now Creech wants into the act. "Well, well, well. What have we here? A little homosexual activity, perhaps? I don't want to interrupt, but I'm afraid you girls will have to wait until after the shakedown is completed."

"Mother-fucker, you're messin' with muh pictures!"

"I don't see any mother-fucker around here," Creech says innocently, "only a group of officers doing their duty and two convicts in a very suggestive embrace." He turns to the head gooner and says, "Write it up just like that, will you? A very suggestive embrace."

The Giant is so angry he's turned blue, but Mother doesn't notice, because he's spun him around and is pushing him back down the tier to where we're standing. A gooner comes out of the cell with an armload of *Chart* books and *Racing Forms*. "Found a bunch of the shit you said to look for, Lieutenant Creech, but there weren't no knife. We tore this mother-fucker up good, though; these stupid shit-heads will be workin' till midnight trying to get their Suck-ass trophy back. I mean we done tore this mother-fucker up! Not one fuckin' breakable thing unbroke. This mother-fucking cell is wrecked!"

The gooner is such a pathetic dummy, even Creech looks uncomfortable. Mother is on him. "Stunning display of intellect," he says dryly. "Train him yourself?"

"I trained him to know gambling material when he sees it. I assume you have a property slip from the education department authorizing these publications?"

"I had one in my locker," Mother replies, smiling evenly, "but it undoubtedly became lost during your search."

Creech looks to the head gooner for confirmation. "Gone," he mutters.

"Well." Creech is smiling now. "Since you don't have the slip, I'll have to put this in the warden's evidence safe until the investigation is complete. You won't lose a page, so don't worry. Should get your things back in . . . oh . . . say, six months?"

"Man down on J range," a voice screams right in my ear.

The Giant is sprawled on the floor, his face a dusky purple.

Mother races down the tier and bends over him, the Range Bull is on the radio, and I'm doing my part in this instant replay of the Giant's last attack. We start the resuscitation process as Creech and his gooners walk away without so much as a glancing down at the Giant.

This time the gurney crew is there in a flash, and the young doctor is with them. He and Mother exchange a few words and they hustle the Giant off to the hospital.

Mother's face is livid. His jaws are clamped up tight, and there are tears rolling down his face. "Sons of bitches are going to pay for this."

I believe him.

We're cleaning up the cell, trying to work as quietly as we can. Mother told us Doc Hart was going to insist Stonemann send the Giant over to Tacoma General for a bypass; if he won't do it, Stonemann has signed the Giant's death warrant. We're trying to work and listen for the helicopter at the same time.

Our reward has been three hours of chilling silence.

It's about ten to four, a couple of ticks before count time, when Cowboy shows up in front of the cell. He's out of breath and nervous as hell. "Doc Hart dropped this in front of me. I'm sure he wants me to tell you, but you got to keep it quiet." He takes a deep breath and continues. "Stonemann has refused permission for an airlift for the Giant. He told the doc to write him up for a transfer to the federal medical center at Springfield, Missouri, on the next transfer chain."

"Jesus fucking Christ!" Dog explodes. "That's a death sentence in itself. Every doctor in that slime hole has more suits against him than he's put in sutures."

My mind flashes back to the time John Mitchell, former attorney general of the United States, after his conviction, needed an operation routinely done at Springfield. He went to court and got a decision saying they were not equipped to do the operation properly, and sought permission to have it done in a New York hospital. And won. The court apparently forgot the hundred or more times it had ruled the other way ... of course, when good old John was still the A.G. and had a young assistant argue against any treatment for cons at an outside hospital. Shit. Giant's a dead man.

"What is the doc going to do?" Mother asks softly.

"Stay the night. Give him anticoagulants and monitor him personally. Stonemann told the doc if he kept pressing for the airlift, he'd throw him off the island and the Giant wouldn't get any treatment at all." His voice drops to a whisper. "Giant ain't going to make it, Mother. Sorry."

Mother sighs, and shakes Cowboy's hand. "Thanks for the information; you've been a big help. You'd better get back to the hospital before the count."

"No problem. Miss Willoughby, the nurse on the evening shift, will cover for me. Sorry to bring you the bad news."

"It's better we know." Mother's voice has taken on a hollow, detached tone, which tells me he's already deep off into his think tank. He shuffles to the card table and collapses into a chair, ignoring the six sets of wishful eyeballs tracking every movement he makes, right down to the tugs he's giving his left ear. Finally, he turns to me and asks, "What would it take to immediately reverse a warden's decision?"

"A phone call from the President, the attorney general or the director of the Bureau of Prisons. Maybe a United States senator could move him. Wardens don't have very many bosses, Mother."

"Any other possibilities?"

"A newspaper or television reporter might frighten Stonemann into a change of heart. The BOP is very sensitive about negative publicity," Odds offers. "Say, if you could have that Cynthia Evans broad call, she might scare Stonemann enough to make him move Giant to Tacoma General."

Mother winces when Odds calls Miss Evans a broad, but I think I see a light go on.

"Sure thing, Odds. Mother just trots down to the corner phone booth and gives her a ring. Brilliant."

"If we could get into the industry area where they store the test equipment for the tap-proof phones, I could use the tapping devices to cut into an outside line." Noid is scratching his head. "What do you think, Mother?"

"Where did you learn how to tap a phone?" I snap.

"Mother," Noid answers patiently, his eyes still on Mother. "And he learned in Virginia. What do you think, Mother?"

Fast Eddie is shaking his head and frowning. "No way can you burglarize industries at night. Wheeler has assigned inmate fire watches that make Fred Barker look like the Sphinx. Those monks would drop a dime on their mothers."

Mother nods in agreement, then goes back to scowling and rubbing his chin. "There might be another option. I've been planning a raid on the warden's office for some time now, and the logistics are already in place. Listen to my plan of operations and see if you detect a flaw."

Noid asks the question that has popped into everyone's mind. "Why have you been scheming on the warden's office?"

"Intelligence-gathering mission," Mother explains. "Now, listen carefully. It's dark by five-fifty, and by six-thirty everyone is out of the mess hall. But the yard is closed, right?" He accepts our nods of agreement and continues. "As soon as everyone is out and moving around, I'll get the set of lockpicks I had Picks Monahan make for me, slip down to the back of the auditorium to Short Mort's janitor closet, and pick the window lock. This will get me out on the compound. I'll go behind the hospital to the power-house, cut the electrical lead that brings the power over from the mainland, and plug the fuel lines to the backup generators. With the lights out I can run over the roof from the powerhouse, across Education and two house, then up onto the roof of the Ad Build-ing. I'll go down through the skylight in the warden's office, then out to the switchboard, take it off automatic, and make my call to Cynthia. She can take it from there."

He checks the circle of gaping jaws, smiles, and adds, "While I'm there, I'll open Stonemann's evidence safe, recover our notes and enough of the *Chart* books and *Racing Forms* to finish our work, and then I'll hustle back here. The whole operation should terminate by twenty-thirty hours." He notes the confused stares and corrects himself. "Say, eight-thirty P.M. Any questions?"

Fast Eddie is the only one of the crew who wasn't rendered speechless by the audacity and detail of Mother's invasion plans. When I hear what he has to say, I put it down for professional interest. "Better take me along to open the box."

"The safe is no problem: a Mosler square-door walk-in. I can open it in twenty seconds."

"Where'd you learn safecracking?" Noid asks.

"North Carolina. Any other problems?"

"About fifty." I manage to squeak out the words. "First, as soon as the lights go out they'll lock this place down tighter than a bull's ass at fly time. Within a few minutes, they'll be running the ranges taking a count. You'll be busted before you get to the warden's office, Mother. When those lights go, every cop on the island is going to be thinking 'escape.' "

Dog shouts in my ear before I can get on to the next problem. "Cowboy!"

"Cowboy?" Mother asks.

"Sure. He said he could get Miss Willoughby to cover for him at the hospital. That would leave him free to slide up here and make the count in your bunk. As soon as the count clears, we can get him back by . . ." And the lights go out in Dog's eyes, but he's given me an idea.

"The clothing and linen cart with the weekend supplies for the hospital is still parked in the hospital tunnel. It's supposed to be picked up at seven-thirty by whoever has extra duty that night. I could stash Cowboy under the sheets, and if Fast can get the black guard at the hospital gate into a game of chess, I could roll the cart right past him."

"That nigger can't play dead," Fast complains, but he's grinning. "No problem. I taught him the game, but he didn't learn a damn thing. He thinks a strong chess move is to go to the john, open a *Playboy's* magazine, then flog his bishop. If I can convince him he's actually beating me, you could roll the *Queen Mary* past and he wouldn't tip over a pawn."

Mother is definitely interested, but he's frowning. "Sounds

great, but I'm a little concerned about involving Miss Willoughby. Why would she want to risk being fired to help Cowboy?"

"I understand the concern, Mother. You have never gazed upon the moonscaped countenance of Miss Willoughby, or considered the heroic proportions of her *derrière*. Miss Willoughby could flaunt her naked virginity through the length of the Mongol hordes and not get a tumble. Cowboy, on the other hand, has the noble yet vulnerable good looks of a Johnny Carson, who, as you know, keeps countless millions of middle-aged *hausfraus* across the width and breadth of this fair nation glued to their television sets, giggling and whacking their chubby little thighs as they languish in veritable oceans of unrequited estrogen while awaiting the unwanted return of the four-wheel-drive, three-baths-a-week, too-tired-every-night machos they married. In short—"

"Please—"

"—Miss Willoughby would kill for a pat on the ass from Cowboy."

Mother turns to me and says, "What else?"

"As soon as the lights go out, Creech will send three, maybe four men out to the yard. They'll be frightened, nervous, and alert, thinking there might be some convict out there with a length of pipe in his hand and escape on the brain. One of them is sure to spot you."

Mother puts on the smile da Vinci made all the bucks off of, and replies, "If I cannot successfully evade a four-man patrol behind my own lines, I deserve to be captured. Anything else?"

It is 6:30 exactly when the lights go out. The P.A. system is screaming for an immediate lock-down. I double-check Mother's bunk to make sure no recognizable portion of Cowboy is sticking out from under the blankets; then I relax.

"So far, so good," Odds whispers.

It flashes through my mind that this is the sort of thing a parachutist might say while falling to the ten-thousand-foot level after having discovered he's left his chute in the plane. The evening officer comes by, flashes the cell with his nine-battery phallic symbol, and leaves, the light never quivering when it passes Mother's bunk.

The count is cleared within an hour. Miss Willoughby has something coming from Cowboy, and whatever it is, she must be grinning like a fool, because Cowboy is damn near tears and won't tell us what little service he has to perform for her.

Now there is nothing to do but wait.

And wait.

And while I'm waiting, I get this nagging thought in the back corridors of my sorting machine. Every scam I know for sure Mother has been involved with has had some bad spin-offs. The Kid and Ass For Gas were shipped to Lompoc after the Booty Bandit incident. But to be honest, maybe that isn't too bad—Lompoc is in California and therefore full of fruiters—still, they did get shipped. Now I'm thinking, if Mother hadn't been so intent on pissing Stonemann off, maybe the shakedown that brought on the Giant's heart attack wouldn't have been so bad. What the hell, the other side of my melon argues, the Giant's ticker bone would have given out sooner or later. Good arguments, but I don't have to be a professional gambler to know if Mother keeps betting everything each time he gets into a poker pot with Stonemann, sooner or later he is going to lose, and when he does, *our* hopes and dreams go down the tubes with him. Maybe the dream has already become a nightmare, I'm thinking, when the whop-whop-whoosh of the chopper's rotor blades blow away all of my doubts.

He did it! I'm thinking.

"We did it!" Odds shouts before Dog can get a fat paw all the way over the little bastard's mouth.

We're all on our feet now, silently cheering for the Giant; arms raised, clenched fists mutely signifying our victory as we watch the red, green, and white flashing lights of the chopper as it settles to the helipad just outside the rear gate. We're still giggling, whispering, and poking each other in the ribs when the cell-house lights come back on.

Mother had this figured down to a gnat's ass. As soon as the doors rack open I hustle Cowboy off to meet his fate at the hands, or whatevers, of Miss Willoughby. Poor Cowboy. I once overheard her asking another nurse if she knew the difference between sensual and kinky. The other didn't know, so Miss Willoughby said, "Sensual is when you use a feather. Kinky is when you use the whole chicken." Well, at least he's taking it like a man.

By the time I get Cowboy loaded into the hospital linen cart and down the tunnel to the hospital gate, Fast has the hospital officer hooked up good in a chess game. As I roll the cart safely past the chessing cats, Fast shoots me a wry grin and pockets one of his own knights. This cop must be a real turkey if Fast has to steal his own pieces off the board to keep the game going.

I'm back in the cell, sipping some hot chocolate, when Fast returns. "God, what a mind whipping that turned out to be. He didn't have a decent move in his whole *repertoire.*" He treats Dog to an evil grin and adds, "That's French for trick bag."

"In the words of the first archbishop of Canterbury when he found himself at cross purposes with his sovereign lord, the king . . . fuck thee!"

Fast rewards Dog with a quick bow, then does a quicker inventory of the cell. "Where's Mother?"

Big Smith gives him, and reminds us of, some bad news. "He isn't back yet. It's been so long, he must have got busted."

That realization has stricken everyone in the cell before Big is able to vocalize it. I'm looking at six faces long enough to be ushers at a million-dollar funeral.

Before we can make the situation any worse by trying to do some serious thinking on our own, Mother walks through the door. He's smiling, but his face is a mess. I don't know how he made it past the cell-house desk with all the blood he has on his kisser.

"What the hell happened?" we ask in a chorus.

"From the top, please, so I don't have to interrupt. Please?" Noid begs.

Mother chuckles, and begins sponging off the blood from several deep scratches on the side of his face and neck. As he works, he gives us a rundown. "I got out through Short Mort's 'office' just fine. Over to the powerhouse, killed the lights and sabotaged the emergency generators, then up over the roofs, up the drainpipe to the Ad Building, then rappelled down into the warden's office through the skylights. Then—"

"Where did you learn how to rappel, for Christ's sake?"

"Same place I learned basic strangulation . . . north Georgia. After I got in, things began to go to hell in a hand basket. I couldn't reach Cynthia at home, her answering service couldn't raise her on the pager, and I ran out of places to check. I—"

"But the chopper—how did you . . . ?"

"I took Flat Store's advice and had a United States senator call Stonemann."

"How? Jesus Christ, who?" I gesture to Dog, and he slaps his hand over Noid's mouth.

"I called Stonemann's home, figuring if he answered I'd pass myself off as a new guard and tell him Lieutenant Creech had talked to some senator he was supposed to call; then I'd give him a false number with a 202 area code. As it worked out, Stonemann's wife answered, mistook me for Mr. Wheeler—that was strange, by the way—then I gave her the number. When Stonemann got out of the shower, he called the number I'd left, but got me at the switchboard; he thought he'd reached the office of a United States senator at ten P.M. Washington, D.C. time and found him waiting in the office. This gave me some extra leverage. Senators don't answer their own phones and they seldom hang around the office waiting for a call from a prison warden unless the matter is high priority." He pauses, dabs at another scratch on his chin, winces, and continues. "I told Stonemann I had received a call about an inmate he was apparently allowing to die in the prison hospital. Of course Stonemann denied everything, tried to shift the responsibility on to Dr. Hart. He said he'd check immediately, and if the man needed medical treatment, he'd get him to Tacoma General Hospital at once. I told him to get on it and be ready to give me a full report when he called back on

Monday, with a written copy to the Director of the BOP. Then I hung up on him."

"That's beautiful," Dog says, laughing so hard the tears are streaming down his face. He stops in mid-chuckle and notes, "Stonemann is going to think the doc told on him."

"Not when he calls Senator Magnuson's office on Monday and makes a fool out of himself before he discovers the call he got tonight was a fake. And it will be too late to stop the Giant's operation. Stonemann won't have any idea who did him in, either."

"A fix, protection for the innocents, and a getback! A tidy finale for a world-class caper." In his awe, Dog lets his hand slip from Noid's mouth.

"But what happened to your face?"

"Short Mort's raccoon, Killer. He thought I was a cop invading Mort's territory when I slipped back through the window. Mort got him right off me, but he's a vicious little critter . . . well trained, though, because when some cops came to investigate the disturbance, Mort had Killer go into an act that put them into an immediate retreat."

"Where's the forms, notes, and stuff?" Odds is bouncing around, looking for all the world like a little kid who wants to pee and go ride the merry-go-round at the same time. "Did you find them?"

"Yes. But I was unable to figure out a way to bring them back. Too great a volume. I put them in envelopes and mailed them down to Mr. Shure's office via institutional mail. All we have to do is slip in and pick them up Monday afternoon."

Noid is wearing a pained expression, and I can tell something is really bothering him. Finally he blurts it out. "But why were you planning a break-in even before we needed one?"

Mother frowns, takes a ten-beat break, which I assume is for the purpose of doing some editing, then replies. "Ever wonder why we eat so much liver and hamburger?"

Heads are bobbing like sunflowers in a summer breeze.

"Me too. I did some checking around and discovered all of our beef comes in from the slaughterhouse at the minimum-security camp. The food administrator buys our meat on the hoof from local cattle auctions and sends it to the camp to be processed. One day when I was delivering the mail to the accounting office I took a peek at the payment vouchers and realized they were buying a lot better grade of beef than we were eating. . . ."

"You saying the food administrator is knocking down a little for himself on those purchases?" Noid is fuming. Me too.

"Knocking down a lot!" Mother corrects him. "And it followed that Stonemann had to be in on it. I figured if that was true, there had to be another set of books. The logical place for them to be kept was the evidence safe in the warden's office."

"Right," Dog agrees. "When these Philistines wish to prosecute one of our brethren, the courts require a clear chain of possession of the evidence; no more than one person may have access to wherever the evidence is stored."

"I'd appreciate it if you armchair penologists would allow Mother to tell the story." Little Smith is dancing around as though he's contracted Noid's disease. "What the hell did you find?"

Mother pauses, scans the eager faces of seven children who are waiting breathlessly to see if Superman can get away from the Kryptonite before he loses his powers. His mouth twists into a tight, sardonic smile. "Records. I found Stonemann's records. Detailed entries showing how the food administrator buys Standard and Good grades of cattle at the Auburn sales yard, pays for them with the vouchers Stonemann signs and gives him, then trucks the animals over to the Renton sales yard and sells them for cash. According to the entries, he goes back to Auburn the following day and buys an equal weight in Canner- and Cutter-grade cattle, mostly old milk cows, for which he pays twenty-five cents a pound less. These are the animals he sends to the slaughterhouse at the camp. The butchers out there process them, Stonemann and the food service administrator split the profit, and we eat all the evidence!"

"Son of a bitch!" Big Smith groans. "They're making a bundle."

"And it isn't enough for Stonemann." Mother is grinning broadly now. "He's up to his ears in debt, serious financial trouble."

"To who?" Noid is beside himself; his eyes are flashing revenge.

Mother corrects him. "To *whom.* Several people. Not your average, run-of-the-mill citizens, either. Stonemann is a compulsive record keeper and an even more compulsive gambler."

"The poor mother-fucker," Odds whispers with considerable authority.

"*Poor* isn't an adequate word, Odds. Stonemann is close to bankruptcy. He owes over forty thousand dollars to bookies for bets he placed last year on Longacres horses."

"You're telling me Stonemann is a fucking *horseplayer?*" I'm doubled up with laughter. "Jesus, what a stupid bastard." I wish I hadn't said that; I'm working my ass off to *become* a horseplayer.

"And an extremely poor one. He once lost twenty-five consecutive bets. Every bit of the money he makes from the clam scam and the meat swindle is going to pay off his debts . . . so's most of his salary."

"Hot fucking damn," Noid says. "And we have enough on him to put him right next door, don't we?"

"Yes, but no." Mother says with a grunt. "I have no intention of turning any of this over to the Department of Justice."

"You mean you just left all of that good getback ammunition where it was?" I ask, unable to believe my ears.

"No. It was too much to bring back with me, yet I wanted Stonemann to know *someone* was on to him, so I took the files and hid them."

"Where? For God's sake, where?" Noid shouts.

"Shhhh. Behind the paneling in Lieutenant Creech's office."

"So Monday, Stonemann will know someone has stolen his little secret," Little Smith notes. "But he won't know *who*. Logical getback. Brilliant."

Mother flashes us a Marquis de Sade smile. "Sometimes worrying about being exposed is worse than actually being exposed

. . . and"—he bears down on the sadistic smile—"the anguish lasts longer."

All of this is moving way too fast for my upstairs sorting machine. Bits and pieces of information are falling out of the input slots, and sure enough, some of them end up in my mouth. "Hold everything!" I find myself saying. "There's a batch of loose ends here I need to get straightened out, and damn quick. First, all those 'accidental' discoveries I've been making: the Silly Putty, Creech's personnel card, your trips to the photoengraving shop, and that little bottle of machine oil. You planted that stuff, or led me to it, Mother, and I want to know why, and what it all means, and what you used it for, and . . . and—"

"Why, Flat Store," Mother says innocently, "for a getback, of course."

I'm not going to buy another brush-off, and I'm just opening my mouth to lay into Mother, when Cowboy runs into the room, gasping for breath.

"I only have a couple of seconds before lock-down, so listen up." He takes a deep breath, and everything comes out in a rush. "The surgeon over at Tacoma General was just on the phone to the doc. He's prepping the Giant for a triple bypass. He thinks he's young and strong enough to make it."

"That's it?"

"Jesus, Noid, what do you want?" Fast asks. "The Giant is going to live!"

Dog explodes and gives a chilling rebel yell for some counterpoint. "Yahooo!"

I know I'm the only one in the cell who noticed the tear in Mother's eye.

Cowboy sprints out of the cell, apparently now in a hurry to pay off his debt to Miss Willoughby, and 3-J-5 falls into a whooping, back-slapping celebration that lasts until lights out. When we're all in bed, I remember Mother got away from me again. I decide to sneak up on him with a quick question.

"Mother?"

"Yes?"

"Why are you always going so far out of your way to anger Creech and Stonemann? I know there has to be some very good reason, but I never have been able to get a handle on it."

"Simple," he answers, and now I hear the ring of truth I'm looking for. "When a person is angry, he tends to make poor decisions. Everything we're planning is predicated on the staff's seeing red every time my name comes up. Anger enhances the basic flaws in any person."

"Well said," Dog rumbles.

"And now to one other question." I'm speaking quickly, trying to take advantage of the mood Mother is in. "Just what in the hell are you *really* doing with those odds and ends I asked you about earlier?"

"Nothing. I'm finished with them."

"What *were* you doing, then?"

"Fixing things. Buying insurance. Please. Have some faith. Trust me."

Why the hell not? my little voice asks.

There are few sounds in the cell house at 4 A.M. The tick-ticking of a pair of raccoons' claws on cold concrete as they hustle down the range and past the cell, noses bent to the floor in search of a last tidbit to carry back to the warmth and security of their dens; an occasional hacking cough from someone who read the Marl-

boro man ads and believed them; and a faint whispering from one of the cells down below that announces the beginning of another day of hustling and con-

niving either to get ahead or simply stay alive. Six weeks ago I would have been deeply curious about the muttering drifting up from B range; this morning I can't seem to get interested.

When my head hit the pillow last night I had no intention of staying awake until sunup, but I haven't been able to unplug the thinker. Between sorting and re-sorting through the turmoil of the last few weeks and trying to organize what promises to be an eventful and gratifying day, I haven't relaxed enough to lower the lids, let alone doze off. Mother kicks off Operation Reject today, and I'm going down to industries to watch; but the primary reason I'm wired up like a Jap TV and humming like a four-dollar electric razor is that I have finally sold Mary on a scheme to give us a few minutes alone together after this evening's class.

If I were to label my condition right now, I'd put myself somewhere between a kid waiting to play his first game of post office and a Saudi sheikh at an arms sale.

The phone at the cell-house desk chatters, and I wait, watching in my mind's eye as the guard lets it ring a few extra times to

awaken the light sleepers. An increase in the stirrings and cough-
ing satisfies him, and the jangling ceases. The incursion of the
telephone into my thoughts has one positive effect: For the first
time tonight, I realize that the problem with my sorting machine
is the extra oil of emotion that thoughts of Mary pour over the
works. What I need to do is separate my emotional/personal relationship from the rest of the events of the past month.

Okay, Flat Store, first things first, as Mother would say.

Mary, of course.

I slip the sorter into past/reference and begin.

Mary has been a real princess to the Giant. She's visited the
hospital every day, and with the exception of the two-week
Christmas break in our classes, she's been keeping me apprised of
his progress both by the notes she attaches to my test papers and
on those rare occasions when we have a few seconds to talk during
recess. Those precious moments have become the high point of
each week. Since I worked up the nerve to tell her exactly how I
felt about her-me-us and discovered she welcomed my feelings,
we've been a couple of teenagers, blushing, exchanging sly
glances, and generally acting like a pair of love-sick idiots. It's a
nice sort of "going to Disneyland, then coming home to a comfortable house" kind of feeling. A mixture of emotions I've concluded I can live with for a long, long time.

Telling Mary wasn't easy. First there was the paranoid's question of why in hell I went for her, and worse, what in God's name
could she possibly see in me? I was wondering if I'd run into one
of those Catherine the Great types, women who like to diddle
around with the common folk every now and then. You see a lot
of that among female employees in prison. I didn't know what
else to do, so I asked her what she saw in me, and she wasn't two
seconds off into her response when I knew damn well she wasn't
some broad pushing her pelvis around to put a little danger and
adventure in her life.

Mary said she liked me because I was real, funny, vulnerable,
honest, and attractive. I figure her last reason to be as close to a
bald-faced lie as she'll ever come, but give her a pass in exchange

for the warm pitter-pat she put into my ticker-bone. My final thought on the subject was to promise myself to quit drinking out of Noid Benny's cup and settle back to enjoy being in love.

The single negative wrinkle in our relationship came when I got angry with her for sending me a letter through the mail during the Christmas vacation. I was terrified, because I was convinced someone in the mailroom had read the letter and we would be finished. In my panic to preserve the relationship I overreacted, and came down so hard on her I brought tears to her eyes. I didn't believe she understood just how precarious our day-to-day situation really was. As it turned out, the mailroom was so busy during the Christmas rush, they must have missed it.

Mary was bright enough to understand I was being overprotective, and classy enough not to mention my lack of tact. This upset aside, her letter did wonders for the morale of the rest of the 3-J-5 crew; in particular, an item she shared from a conversation she'd had with the chief of surgery, who had elected to handle the Giant's case personally. It seems he had received a call from Stonemann on the Monday after the Giant's attack. Stonemann wanted him to ship the Giant back to McNeil, regardless of his condition. The surgeon refused, because he'd already had a long conversation with Mary about the prison in general and the staff in particular. He told her he was going to keep the Giant through his convalescence instead of returning him after he was out of the Intensive Care Unit.

Two days later, Stonemann arrived at the hospital with Creech and a pair of guards to take the Giant back. They argued until the surgeon called the Tacoma police and had the warden removed for causing a disturbance. All Stonemann got for his troubles was a call from a friend of the surgeon, Senator Warren Magnuson! Of course, Stonemann believed the call was another hoax, and said some very unkind things to the senator. Magnuson then wrote a letter to the director of the Bureau of Prisons, asking why a person of Stonemann's obvious mental instability was running a prison.

The Monday after the Giant's air-evac must have been a rough one for Stonemann. Not an hour after his first rebuff from the surgeon, Stonemann discovered his safe had been broken into. Around 10:30 A.M. all hell broke loose. Shakedowns, rip-ups, and then the telling factor. Stonemann had the fingerprint specialist from Receiving and Discharge go out to his office and lift some prints. Mother dumped another cliché into my memory with his "I'm as pleased as punch."

I assumed Mother wasn't worried about the prints being his. Didn't figure he'd be dumb enough to get busted again for leaving his prints on a safe door.

The next few weeks were as good for the 3-J-5 crew as they were bad for Creech, Stonemann, and company. Mother, Dog, and the Smith Brothers joined Odds in the quality-control department of the cable factory, and night before last, Mother decided to launch Operation Reject. His plan was deceptively simple, and came to us in the form of a memorandum:

Subject: Operation Reject
Distribution: "Eyes Only" 3-J-5 Strike Group

From: Conroy, O.I.C.

According to the intent of the congressional enabling act, Federal Prison Industries (hereafter UNICOR) exists for the following reasons:
1. Provide low-cost, high-quality goods to the United States armed forces and other governmental agencies
2. Provide the inmates with an opportunity to learn good work habits and job skills, to enable them to compete in the labor market upon release.

Functionally, this program does not exist in the UNICOR division at McNeil Island. The deficiencies are listed below:
1. While the subject factories do provide low-cost equipment to the above-listed entities, the quality of the material is without question substandard. This is a result of having "key" inmates hand-build a single cable for each contract run, insure it is up to specifications, then present this same cable over and over to the NASA/DECAS representative for acceptance, even if the

contract run numbers as high as several hundred or thousand cables.
2. Virtually no concurrent training program exists at the present time.

The function of Operation Reject will be to correct the above deficiencies with the support of the NASA/DECAS representative.

Mother laid that one on us at a cell meeting, and after we'd studied it closely, he explained the details of the project to us. UNICOR was in trouble. While turning to the prison system for cheaper parts, the military had discovered it wasn't saving much money because it had to buy three replacement cables to get one good one. Since the factory was paid as soon as Mr. Shure, the NASA/DECAS representative, signed for a cable, Wheeler, the factory manager, didn't care. He had the inmate inspectors in his pocket, and they were helping him beat Mr. Shure.

The basic problem at UNICOR was unskilled, unmotivated workmen, but Wheeler couldn't see it. Every time he wanted to cut corners to increase profits, the inmates lost something else. The final blow was the cessation of the training programs. Since the men had limited skills, they would sit at a table soldering pin A to connector B for five years, never learning anything else. Instead of being able to get a job in a civilian electronics factory when released, they didn't have a wide enough range of skills to blow a slightly trained chimpanzee off a soldering line at an electronics company in Taiwan.

In short, Mother told us, UNICOR was a rip-off. A rip-off to the taxpayers, the servicemen who depended upon the materials, and the convicts, for whom the entire plan had been conceived.

Our job was to shut the factory down, and reopen it with Mother running quality control and the rest of us working for him. The key to the success of the plant closing was Operation Reject, and to get it off the ground, Mother needed the cooperation of the inmate inspectors and the men on the soldering lines. We decided the first order of business was co-opting the inspectors, and Mother scheduled a meeting to take care of the problem. He set the meeting for yesterday to give him an opportunity to work out some details with Mr. Shure. Shure was in on the operation, for sure; he just didn't know some of the finer points, like the actual goal—a computer so we could go horse racing! . . . at least I *think* that's our goal.

We went down to the factory early, slipped into the dusty classroom, and sat down to wait. At first Mother had been against the idea of having everyone from the cell attending, since he wanted us to keep a low profile until he hired us. I reminded him how the North Koreans stationed armed guards behind their side of the negotiations table during the United Nations peace talks. I won the argument on historical grounds.

The inspectors trooped in, looked around, checked the glowering faces of the crew from 3-J-5, and nervously settled into their seats. "Where's Mr. Shure?" a con named Kramer asked.

"He won't be sitting in this morning," Mother replied smoothly. "For the present, just consider me his representative." I saw Kramer's eyebrows go up; he's the inmate acting lead inspector.

Mother didn't give him a chance to question his authority. "The reason we're here is fairly simple. We're going to correct some problems in the factory that have been having a considerable negative effect on the UNICOR image and ripping off the convicts in the process."

"Yeah? Like how? I'm doin' pretty good, myself." Kramer again. A big, fat slob from Los Angeles doing time for peddling pornography through the mails.

Mother turned the blue lasers on and burned him until Kramer was shifting uncomfortably in his chair. "Yes, I suppose *you* are. But what about Howser, there?" He nodded to a thin, weasel-faced man at Kramer's elbow. "He must be having a tough time sleeping at night."

"Me?" Howser grinned nervously. "I'm fine."

"You have a son in the army, don't you?"

"How'd you know that?" Howser sat straight up in his chair.

"I checked," Mother replied curtly. I noticed the first glimmer of respect in the eyes of the other inspectors. "Your son is with the First Armored Division at Fort Hood, Texas. Scout platoon. Matter of fact, he's driving a Jeep that mounts the antitank missile we build the firing harness for on the 12D360 job."

Howser's mouth was hanging open. Mine too. Mother continued. "Let's suppose your son's outfit is called to Cambodia tomorrow. Would you be comfortable with his life depending upon that weapons system?"

Howser shifted uncomfortably in his seat. Kramer said, "Don't let him con you, man. He's up to something."

"Right, I am. But I didn't get an answer to my question."

"No," Howser answered. "I wouldn't be comfortable."

"Why?"

"Because the damn thing can't possibly work. Hell, we made one good one and been running it past Mr. Shure ever since. Some of the cons on the lines are putting glue on the connectors, instead of solder, and covering up the work with the cable jackets." He paused, then started speaking, his words tumbling out like he was in a confessional. "It's a game, Mr. Conroy. The factory manager lets us screw off as long as we don't snitch to Mr. Shure about what's going down out on the work lines."

"And what is going on?" Mother must have known already. He just wanted it out in the open.

"That list is a mile long. Half the shit we make falls apart when we're trying to put it in the boxes."

"That's bullshit. It ain't nearly that bad," Kramer snapped. "If it was, everything we make would be coming back, and it ain't."

"Bad argument," Mother snapped back. "We make replacement parts. Often the servicemen don't know the part is faulty until they need to use a lot of them for repairs . . . like during a battle."

"Suppose I'm not patriotic?" Kramer was sneering . . . until he saw Noid Benny's hand go under his coat.

"Then I'll assume you're not stupid," Mother told him.

"There's another side to this. Since you guys aren't doing any inspecting, UNICOR doesn't have to provide the training Congress mandated. It allows Wheeler and his foremen to leave a man soldering on the same job forever, never learning anything. If a man isn't learning a trade and is only making forty cents an hour, that's slave labor. If I were to tell those poor bastards out there on the lines that's all your fault, Kramer, you might find yourself in a position worse than Booty Bandit did. True?"

"That's *if* I let this fat, greasy bastard out of this classroom," Fast Eddie said.

"We'll all end up in the hole." Kramer was sniveling. "Stonemann has an investment in UNICOR, too. . . . It provides the money to pay the cons on jobs around the prison. He loses that money, he'll have a work strike."

"If Stonemann and Wheeler go so far as to put us in the hole for living up to the contract requirements regarding quality, I have a big surprise for them. We'd be out in an hour. That's a promise."

"Okay," Howser said.

"Kramer?"

"I'm in," he replied, glancing nervously at the 3-J-5 negotiators.

"What do you want us to do?" Howser asked.

"Just do your job. Inspect everything, down to the last nut, bolt, and solder joint. If you can't find anything wrong, bring the article to me." Mother paused, then added, "You're doing the right thing, men. It's going to work out just fine."

"When does this scam kick off?" Howser asked.

"Right now." Mother smiled. "Operation Reject is a go."

As we were walking out of the classroom, I asked Mother how he'd come up with the name for the scam.

"Mr. Shure," he answered, and I knew I hadn't given Mother enough credit . . . again.

I left the industries area with the knowledge that Mother was about to do some serious sidewinder tickling.

The cell-house lights come on and snap me back to the present. I still don't have my thoughts of the past few weeks separated from the cold reality of morning, when a pair of brand-new socks slides over the edge of the upper bunk and hits me square in the mouth. A second later, Mother's smiling face appears, over the side of the upper. "Big day today. I thought you'd want to get off to a running start with a brand-new pair of stockings—you know, get off on the right foot?" He has an impish gleam in his eyes. Maybe he really does drop those clichés on me on purpose, I'm thinking.

I grunt a thank you for the socks, slip them on, and scoot down to breakfast, another of Mother's modifications in our life-styles. A few more weeks of this and I'll have every bad habit of a nine-to-five, brown-bag-totin' citizen.

The breakfast is perfectly coordinated with the morning, cold and gray, and there is a hint of something odoriferous and foul lurking in the murk. Halfway through the meal, the hairs on the back of my neck start standing up for no reason. No reason? That's never happened before.

Creepy.

Back in the cell I'm getting ready for work, dodging the cleanup crew working to earn the Cell-house Sanitation Award. Since Mother told us it pisses Creech and Stonemann off to see us win, we've been hard at it, trying to cinch up the award each and every week. Angry people make mistakes.

The work whistle blows, and I'm off with the rest of 3-J-5 to watch Mother, Odds, Dog, and the Smith Brothers in action. When we hit the Flats the cell-house officer yells, "Conroy! Barker! Step over here."

"What's the problem, Boss?" I ask.

"No problem. You and Conroy got a media visit from . . . ahh . . . Miss Cynthia Evans."

Mother and I exchange questioning glances; then he turns and tells Dog, "Put the operation on hold. We might not be finished in time to start today."

We go back up, change into the mandatory khakis, grab our visiting-room passes at the cell-house desk, and we're out of there like Puffed Oats. I have this sinking feeling in the pit of my stomach as I hurry to the visiting room. I'm not sure what's coming down, but I'm close to throwing up. The hairs on the back of my neck are standing up, saying, "We told you so!"

We zip through the previsit search and aperture inspection, are declared free of any sort of gift you might want to pull out of your ass-hole and give to a friend, then are buzzed through the solid oak door into the visiting room.

It's like stepping into another world. A world of color, scents, and familiar yet strange sounds. The visiting room is small, only thirty feet by forty feet, and it's already packed with all of the diverse forms and essences of humanity you can imagine. The air is thick, loaded with the hopes, dreams, frustrations, fears, happiness and sadness, love and anger that normal relationships spread over a week or more. Here everything must be experienced or dealt with in a few short hours. I see faces strained with tension, flushed with lust, and pinched with anger. It is a whirlpool of bright colors, sharp words, stolen embraces, and the shrill cries of children competing with their parents' hormones for the attention of a once-a-week or twice-a-month father.

I spot Cynthia Evans standing in a quiet eddy in this sensory torrent. She certainly doesn't appear much like the stiff, proper lady-reporter type I saw last time. She is all done up in soft shades of pink and has a silky diaphanous scarf looped about her slender neck, which further enhances the appearance of elegant femininity. Her hair is brushed to a burnished bronze tone, and her makeup is absolutely perfect. She smiles and waves, and I feel Mother stiffen at my elbow; he's as taken aback by her change of appearance as I am. Miss Cynthia Evans of the *Seattle Times* sure as hell isn't dressed for work.

The flood of emotions, sights, and sounds is swirled together in a mixture so heady it nearly makes my knees buckle.

We hurry through the crowd, and Mother introduces me as we arrive. "Miss Evans."

"Cynthia," she corrects him with a warm smile, and offers her hand.

"I would like you to meet Mr. Barker."

"Flat Store," I correct him, and take her hand. It's softer than a piece of thistledown as it rests lightly in mine.

"James," she says, correcting me. Her eyes, warm and loving when she was looking at Mother, suddenly become distant, sad. "I have some bad news," she says softly, her voice reaffirming the message written across her face. She reaches into her bag and brings out a note. "From Mary." She presses it into my hand. "She asked me to deliver it for her."

My knees are weaker than a sissy's in a sausage factory. Anticipation is mixed in equal parts with an understanding of the enormity of what the note represents. Mary isn't coming out tonight!

I squeeze the note into my fist, walk woodenly to the corner of the visiting room, and plop into a chair. The note smells of Mary when I pass it beneath my nose and take a couple of deep breaths. Mary. Jesus. Maybe she's sick . . . cancer, or something. . . . I tear into the note.

> My darling James,
>   How can I put a good face on this? There is good news and there is bad news, as you might say. As I'm sure you would insist, the bad news first. Warden Stonemann saw me visiting with your friend the Giant yesterday evening, and he told me I cannot come back to work on the island.

My eyes blur, and I drop the note into my lap while I try to figure out a way to remove the tears without anyone's seeing me. Fuck it. I swab them away with a long swipe of my shirt sleeve. Any son of a bitch doesn't like it, he can kiss my mother-fucking ass.

> Mr. Stonemann told me he really didn't want to fire me, but a certain Lieutenant Creech had read the letter I sent over Christmas and decided I was a bad influence on you. Obviously, the visiting with the Giant was simply an excuse. I was mortified. The thought of some vile person reading that letter, invading our private thoughts, engendered more anger than I should have al-

lowed. I said some unladylike things to the warden regarding the highly questionable lineage of a creature who would read another person's mail. I just couldn't help myself. His entire attitude was so patronizing yet caustic, and his insinuating smile far too much to accept gracefully. He walked away, James, but he was smiling! Oh, I hope this doesn't cause you any additional hardship.

My darling, be careful. The warden hates you and Mr. Giant and all of the other men in your cell. He muttered something about 3-J-5 under his breath as he was leaving, but I'm sorry, I didn't catch what he said. Please, my love, be careful. He is a *very* dangerous man.

On to the good news. I have to be perfectly honest with you: I feel somewhat relieved that I am not going to keep our "appointment" this evening. There is something, well, I don't know, *shabby* about sneaking around, stealing precious moments we should be sharing in a privacy of our own making. I may have to do it by letter, but now at least I can share my love with you without fear, I can write each and every day without being frightened I will accidentally identify one of us . . . and most of all, we can communicate with perfect clarity until you are out of there and we are physically together.

Until we are together, I have to ask you something that I know you will find difficult. You are going to have to trust me. Trust that I will write each day, keep you first in my thoughts, and trust that I will wait for you. Most of all, trust me not to let our dream die. That evil place may have stolen our reality in terms of touching, or even holding, each other, but only for a little while.

I'm trusting that you, too, will preserve the dream. . . . Don't let them steal our future. We have a beautiful dream, James. We must nurture, cherish, and hold it dear.

I shall wait until we can dream together, side by side.

All my love,

Mary

I check the wall clock. I've been in some sort of a trance; it's nearly the end of visiting hours. A glance toward Mother and Cynthia reveals two people staring at me as though I were a wounded animal; they're trying to decide whether or not it is safe for them to try and comfort me. I get up and walk over to them.

"Well, old son"—Mother is smiling—"looks like there are a couple of more bumps in the road to contend with." His eyes do a quick inventory of the emotions that have declared my face an open city in their warfare.

"Stonemann is going off the bumpy road onto a goat path, if I have anything to say in the matter," I mutter through teeth clenched to prevent my lips from quivering.

Mother turns to Cynthia and grins. "I told you he could handle it."

"Will you see Mary anytime soon?" I ask to avoid making Mother out a false prophet.

"She's waiting on the Steilacoom dock right now, James. Do you have a note for her?"

"Nope. Just tell her I love her, I'm not going to do anything stupid, dreaming is my long suit, and if I don't get a letter from her by the end of the week I'm going to break out of this joint."

"Deal." Cynthia gives me the prime-time Pepsodent ad. "Now you owe me one."

"Shoot."

"Take care of this hardheaded gentleman for me, please?"

I want to tell her she's asking a pissant to manage a mastadon, but don't want to change the loving warmth in her eyes as she studies Mother's blushing face. If Mary is half this stuck on me, I can do the next five years standing on my head in the treatment plant.

One of Creech's oversized pets puts an end to the visit with a reminder it's time to go back out and let them look up our asses. We're hustled out before Mother can return the hug Cynthia slipped on him. Another alteration in their business relationship, I'm thinking. Whatever that business might be, Cynthia has definitely started taking it personally.

We are through what Mother calls the "search and denigrate" portion of the visiting process before we have an opportunity to speak again. "I didn't think the two of you had come this far," we say to each other simultaneously, then burst out laughing.

"I think we were the last to know. It's hard to come out here, isn't it?"

Mother shrugs. I can see he is all business again. "It's another world. We have to go back in and deal with this one."

"And that low-life fucking Stonemann."

"Don't get so angry, Flat Store; your language regresses."

"What the fuck do you expect me to do?"

"Get back, of course, but giving free rein to negative emotions is a dangerous waste of energy."

'Well, I'm talking to the expert, so I check his eyes and see the monster peeping out again from behind the innocent blues. The sight doesn't bother me at all this time; matter of fact, I'm considering methods of feeding it when we return to the cell. Tomorrow we make our first big move on the prison, and I want the monster ready!

Me too! the little voice says.

Two cockroaches crawl up out of the hole in the floor that serves as my toilet, garbage can, and telephone service to the rest of the 3-J-5 crew. The roaches scurry over to the corner, scrabble up on top of the Gideon Bible lying on the floor, and begin to copulate. At least I hope they are; I'd like to see something—anything— getting screwed besides myself.

21 It's hard to believe, but I'm in the hole: a six-by-nine-by-seven cube in C-seg. Me, the Bible, and two orgasmic cockroaches are the only things in the cell. I'm naked, my concrete pallet is naked, and I have this naked bit of hatred which is eating a hole in my sorting machine.

I thought when Mother settled the labor dispute with the inmate inspectors by reason, logic, and a page of intimidation he borrowed from the Teamsters' *Organizing Manual* we were in for a smooth ride to success with Operation Reject.

Wrong.

The day after I got the bad news about Mary, I was up, ready to go down to the factory and watch the plan unfold. Of course I couldn't hang around the place all day, so I filled out a work application as an excuse to at least see the kickoff. It went down smoothly enough. The inspectors—Mother, Dog, Odds, and the Smith Brothers included—began working out on the lines, watching the assembly of the cables with the sort of interest one might expect from members of a board of directors. By the time Mr. Wheeler, the factory manager, noticed me hanging around, the crew had gone through a dozen bundles of the red "Reject" tags they use to mark defective pieces. Wheeler may have noticed me, but he didn't wake up to the rejection tags.

I didn't get any more feedback on the progress of the operation until the Smith Brothers burst through the door of the cell just before the 4 P.M. count.

"You should see that place, Flat Store." Big Smith was laughing so hard he could barely talk. "It looks like sale day at K-Mart. Red rejection tags everywhere."

"Yeah," Little agreed. "We're proceeding at a logical rate, but the best part is that Wheeler and his foremen are so hung over, they haven't noticed. We were damn lucky we delayed one day . . . made the timing perfect. The day after payday the foremen don't want to hear about anything that won't cure a hangover."

It took the staff a couple of days to figure out what was going on, but when they did, Wheeler and company counterattacked with a vengeance. First they called every inspector into the manager's office and interrogated him . . . one at a time. Wheeler terminated each of the interviews with the same threat. "Either those cables start moving down the lines without further interference or the whole damn bunch of you is going to be fired. Understand, now, I'm not telling you to pass any bad cables; that would be defrauding the customer and against the law. What I am saying is you'd damn well better find a way of *making* them pass. And do it quickly."

Great guy, Mr. Wheeler. There are a couple of rumors about him floating around I'd like to believe, the first being that he and the warden have two things in common: They're both drunks and they are both hot for the warden's wife. This might explain why Mrs. Stonemann thought Mother was Wheeler the night he called impersonating Senator Magnuson. The second rumor maintains that the reason Wheeler is such an evil person is related to a traumatic event from his childhood. According to the story, his dour, suspicious, slave-driving personality is the upshot of coming home from school one day at the age of seven, only to have his mother run out from beneath the porch and bite him on the leg. Could be true; he certainly has all of the other attributes of an S.O.B.

Wheeler's threats aside, the inspectors stuck with Mother to a man.

I thought Wheeler had switched tactics on the third day of the slowdown, when he circulated a memo that read:

> TO: All foremen
> FROM: D. I. Wheeler, cable factory manager
> SUBJECT: Recent increase in cable rejections
>
> There is a rumor circulating in the cable factory among the convicts that needs to be put to rest. They have been led to believe by certain disruptive elements in the factory that if they slow production to build a better cable, we will return to the old system of giving them two hours of job-related training every workday. Take whatever steps are necessary to dispel this rumor and let's get back to normal operations. Remember, a convict is dumber than a horse, in that you can lead him to water *and* make him drink.

It took me a couple of hours before I realized that *Mother* had composed the memo. The cliché nailed it for me, but no one else came to the same conclusion.

I knew the memo had produced the desired effect when Big Smith found a hastily scribbled note on the bathroom wall. It said:

> *Mr. Wheeler, you couldn't lead a sailor to a whorehouse, a June bug to a shit heap, or me out of the gate. Get this, you* horse's ass: *no training, and there won't be any cables to reject.*

For all intents and purposes, the war was over right then, only Wheeler didn't know it. With the convict inspectors, the men on the lines, and Mr. Shure on our side, Wheeler didn't have a prayer. I went down to the factory the following morning on the pretext of checking the status of my employment application, and as I was waiting outside Mr. Shure's office, I had the chance to really look the factory over for the first time. The inside of the building reminded me of an old airplane hangar—high ceilings, open rafters, and stringers holding lamps that hang down from long cables to a point about thirty-six inches over the work-benches.

On the floor of the building the worktables stretched from one end of the factory to the other, a distance of over four hundred feet. The setting was a replica of a sweatshop I once saw in an old black-and-white pro-union movie.

Something else in this setting struck me as familiar. From my vantage point on the landing in front of Mr. Shure's office I could see across to a like balcony leading into Wheeler's overstuffed haven. Looking for all the world like glowering Communist bigwigs at a May Day parade were Stonemann, Wheeler, Creech, and several foreman. Instead of reviewing endless divisions of grim-faced Russian infantry waving oceans of red flags, they watched platoons of grinning convicts hustling red-tagged cables back and forth over the factory floor.

A glance over at the shipping department revealed the shipping crew stretched out on the packing tables. There wasn't a single cable laid out for shipment. Project Reject had the UNICOR cable factory at a complete standstill.

Three more weeks passed, and by that time production at the cable factory alone had dropped to a minuscule, pathetic, two hundred dollars' worth of goods shipped. The slowdown had spread to all of the other factories, too, and they weren't doing much better.

Stonemann had become personally involved; along with Wheeler, he was offering the inmate inspectors extra good time off their sentences, raises, and more free time at work . . . if they could "solve" the problem. The bribes didn't work. Nothing did. What the staff couldn't offer the men was what Mother and Mr. Shure had already returned to them: their self-respect and a taste of dignity.

Finally, Stonemann ordered Wheeler to fire Mother, Odds, Dog, and the Smith Brothers. When Wheeler informed Mr. Shure of the warden's decision, Mr. Shure told him if the men were fired, he would walk out the minute the dismissals became effective.

Stonemann fired them anyhow, figuring to patch things up with Mr. Shure later.

Mr. Shure caught the early ferry off the island after informing Stonemann personally he would not return until the men were rehired and had agreed to go back to work in the factory.

Without someone on site to sign for the customers, UNICOR was out of business as of the moment Mr. Shure walked, but of course Stonemann was in a position where he couldn't budge. Right where Mother wanted him, too, or so he assured us later that same day.

That evening, around count time, Creech came to the cell and announced we were all going to the hole, charged with "conduct that disrupts the orderly operation of the institution." Mother pointed out that Noid, Fast Eddie, and I did not even work in industries; Creech leered, and replied, "Birds of a feather, Conroy. Remember?"

As we were waiting to be cuffed up for the trip to C-seg, the goon squad rolled in and began trashing the cell. Mother looked over at Creech, smiled, and said, "Gee. This is going to be a real mess to clean up." The statement left both Lieutenant Creech and myself scratching our heads. I mean, if anything was obvious, it was the fact that 3-J-5 was already looking a lot like Hiroshima after the bomb.

A voice echoes up out of the toilet hole, a ghostly modification of Fast Eddie's deep rumble. "We got these mother-fuckers right where we want them now, huh, Flat Store?"

I drop to my knees, put my mouth as close to the hole as I dare, ignore the stale convict's joke, and shout back. "Four days now. We should have gone to I.D.C. yesterday."

Mother's voice joins the conversation. "Patience is a virtue."

"You think they'll see us soon?" Noid shouts.

"Time will tell," Mother answers.

"Okay, ass-hole. Court call," a voice informs my naked ass, which is facing the bars.

Into the pair of coveralls the guard pushes through the door, up through the labyrinth to the I.D.C room, and I find all of the crew is there waiting for me. They usher us in, line us up on one side of the table, and give us the standard admonition to remain silent unless spoken to.

Stonemann leads the committee in, and I can see this isn't going to be a hearing; the judges are grinning like kids at a bachelor party. Stonemann, Creech, Wheeler, and the associate warden, Mr. Lindsay. Wheeler, Creech, and Stonemann were all involved in the "investigation" and therefore technically not supposed to sit on the committee. I figure it doesn't make any difference; this court has everything it needs to live up to its intentions except for a bunch of Australians singing "Waltzing Matilda" and a couple of other trappings of a kangaroo court.

We haven't got a prayer.

Creech opens the hearing with: "You men have been charged with 'conduct that disrupts the orderly operation of the institution.' Have any of you anything to say regarding your culpability in the work stoppage you fostered and abetted at the cable factory?" I'm convinced Creech has taken an instant vocabulary lesson, until I notice he's reading from a notebook.

One look at the faces across the table and I'm ready to plead guilty. Bloodshot eyes, red-rimmed and watery, sagging jowls, and pinched eyebrows tell me these monkeys have been losing a lot of sleep and hitting the bottle on top of it. No way could this debilitated crew run anything. And it's all our fault. *And you love it,* my little voice tells me. True.

Mother raises his hand, gets the nod from Stonemann, and says, "Excuse me, but I'm somewhat confused. What work stoppage? Before we were locked up, the men were exercising extreme diligence in the pursuit of their assigned tasks."

"Shut the fuck up, Conroy. If we say it's a work stoppage, it's a work stoppage. If we say it's a riot, it's a riot. Inciting a riot carries an additional ten years." His voice is raw, hissing hatred. This is the Creech I know, Creech the cobra.

"Illegal imprisonment and malfeasance in office also carry fairly stiff penalties," Mother reminds them gently. Creech leaps to his feet, red-faced and screaming. He knows Mother is making a fool out of him, but all he can do is keep handing him more ammunition. "I'm through with your wise-assed shit, Conroy. Do you hear me? *Fucking through!*"

"That will be enough, Lieutenant Creech," Warden Stonemann says firmly. He turns to Mother and begins to speak in a fatherly tone, which has the hair on the back of my neck trying to jump out of the follicles and off the sinking ship. "It has always been my profound belief, one of the basic tenets of my career in penology, that a convict, any convict, can be rehabilitated if handled properly. That is to say, fairly and firmly. I—"

"You mean beaten and brainwashed until he's a vegetable?" Mother asks innocently.

Stonemann does a thirty-second take, battling with the first-degree murder that's popping out all over his blue-veined face. Finally, he continues as though Mother had not interrupted. "In your case, Mr. Conroy, I have been forced to rethink my previous position and give serious consideration to—"

The warden's secretary literally bursts into the room. She's flushed and out of breath. Stonemann gives her a scorching look and asks, "Yes?"

"It's the director of the Bureau of Prisons, Mr. Allen himself. He told me to get you to the phone immediately, no matter what you were doing. He said to tell you there are some serious problems with the Secretary of Defense, and he's—"

"That will be *enough*, Miss Bates." Stonemann shoots a worried glance at Wheeler and hurries out of the room.

"Score one for Mr. Shure," Mother whispers. His face breaks into a friendly grin, and he turns to a bewildered Lieutenant Creech. "I suppose it's only fair to warn you that one condition of our going back to work in the cable factory will be that you personally supervise the restoration of 3-J-5 to its preshakedown condition. And further, we will reserve the right to give final approval on the quality of the restoration, including, but not limited to, the—"

"You cock sucker! You'll be approving nothing but the ass whipping I'm going to give your mouthy ass when I get you back to C-seg. This is it, Conroy, you arrogant cock sucker. Your ass is mine, and—"

"Lieutenant Creech," the associate warden snaps. "Control yourself!"

Mother and Creech spend the next fifteen long minutes in a silent staring contest while the rest of us exchange sly grins or worried glances, depending on the amount of confidence we have in Mr. Shure and Mother.

The door flies open, and Stonemann is back in the room. His face is twisted into an angry grimace, a boy taking his medicine. "I have been *ordered* to return you men to the general population and your jobs at the cable factory. All reference to this incident will be expunged from your records." He glares at Mother for a full ten seconds, then turns to leave. Mother stops him cold. "If you'll excuse me, Stonemann." I hear Mother mimicking his fatherly tone of voice. "There are certain *conditions* to our leaving here and returning to the factory."

"Conditions?" Stonemann screams. "You want to dictate fucking *conditions?* To me?"

Mr. Lindsay's eyebrows arch, and his mouth falls open. I have the impression he's never heard Stonemann swear before now.

"There you go," Mother says cheerfully, a teacher sharing a discovery with a student.

Now I want to scream—at Mother—not to overplay the hand. Stonemann is approaching a stroke.

Mother ignores Stonemann's fulminating anger, raises his hand in the air, and begins ticking off the conditions on his fingers. "First," he says pleasantly, "there is the matter of an order to Lieutenant Creech and his fine crew of correctional officers to restore our cell to its preshakedown condition." He nods at Creech and winks.

"Do it," Stonemann growls at Creech. Creech sucks in his breath and bites his lower lip. "You're the boss."

"And you'll need to replace the commissary items that were accidentally destroyed in the search: jars of coffee, et cetera," Mother adds.

"Replace anything we've broken," Stonemann says through clenched teeth.

"And, of course, there is the matter of the pay we've lost while awaiting this hearing."

"Pay them," Stonemann barks at Wheeler, and stands up.

Stonemann's humiliation is complete. I know he isn't going to take much more of this, and I give Mother's leg a pinch under the table. Stonemann is about ready to explode.

Mother is definitely not through testing him. "And we'll be needing a couple of *color* television sets installed on the Flats in three/four cell house so the workers can watch the evening news, sort of stay abreast of the flow of society as they plan their . . . *getting back* to the mainstream of the American middle class."

Stonemann's eyes are bouncing from Mother to Creech and wildly on to Wheeler and back to Mother again. Here it comes. What a waste. Mother could have got himself shot asking for something worthwhile, like decent stockings. Hell, I don't watch the evening news when I'm on the street. Same old thing every night: people who don't have anything trying to get something, people who have everything trying to hang on to every bit of it, and every now and then, some spectacular intervention by God . . . just to remind everyone who the material things of this world really belong to. While I'm ruminating, Stonemann has regained control. "Give them two televisions," he orders Creech. "Make them black and white."

Mother allows him the minor victory and nods as if to concede the point. Then he drives him up the wall with: "Well, sir. I know you're a busy man. I have nothing further. You may leave now if you wish."

The dismissal buckles Stonemann's knees. I'm on my feet, pushing Mother out of the room, and the rest of the crew is right on my tail, a gang fleeing a robbery. As I'm shooing Mother down the hall, Stonemann is yelling at the top of his voice. "Wheeler, you ignorant idiot, remember the memo I sent you telling you to keep cutting the corners and I'd handle the Department of Defense if they started complaining about quality? That son of a bitch Shure showed up in Washington, D.C., with a copy of it just three days ago. Conroy has been going through your trash, Wheeler. The director gave me two hours to get this straightened out. I'll tell you one thing ..." and then someone in the room had the presence of mind to close the door.

With his access to Stonemann safely cut off, I stop pushing and give Mother a grin. "Got 'em."

"No doubt about it. We're out of the woods and into the driver's seat."

They let us out of the C-seg gate, and as I'm walking Mother back to the cell I decide to try some of the Smith Brothers' logic on him. "One of these days, Stonemann is going to go under his coat, pull out his pistol, and shoot you ... and he isn't going to care if he does it in front of God and everybody, Mother. You have pushed him as far as he's going to go."

"I think he'll stand a bit more," he tells me, and I catch a flash of the monster in his eyes. This time it doesn't do much for my mood.

The hair on the back of my neck is still doing snap rolls when we reach 3-J-5.

We play with Creech's critters for a while, offering endless suggestions as to how the table wasn't quite in that spot, or the corners on the bed were a wee bit tighter. We have quite a crowd in front of the cell in a matter of minutes. It is the first time in the history of the prison that guards have actually had to clean up after a shakedown.

I'm looking forward to our next stop: a victory tour through the cable factory. We march proudly down the hill like a triumphant army, and into the factory.

They shut the place down, break out the HiHos and hot chocolate, and we have a damn nice victory party. Mother delivers a short talk, which he ends by saying: "And now the ball is squarely in our court. We have taken a position regarding our commitment to quality and told the brass we can make a good finished product *and* complete the contracts on time. In return, we'll get everything we asked for ... but we have to make good on our promises. Can we do it?"

The roar of their agreement lasts for several minutes. The sense of foreboding I have been packing around has disappeared, and I have a feeling of accomplishment, well-being, to take back to the cell with me. We've given a lot of men the opportunity to feel as though they won one. Most of them have never been winners before.

You either, the voice reminds me.

On the way up the hill from the industries area we meet Mr. Shure. He's just come over on the 2:30 ferry. After a few minutes of good-natured kidding, Mr. Shure tells Mother the Pentagon has approved every single item of the in-process inspection system they have developed together over the preceding months. "I did have one problem," he says, frowning up at Mother. "They didn't see the need for the IBM 1360 computer, but they finally accepted your argument about needing it for the statistical quality-control system you want to implement. I expect Stonemann and Wheeler to have a fit"—he stops and grins—"but then, a little additional catharsis doesn't seem to be a bad idea. I'll insist, and you'll get your machine"—he pauses, and looks directly into Mother's eyes—"but for God's sake, Conroy, don't you ever tell me what you're *really* using it for." He tosses us a jaunty wave and is gone, leaving Mother smiling and the rest of us with our jaws bouncing off our chests.

"It's called killing two birds with one stone."

I'm the Tail-end Charlie on the *Return of the Lost Patrol,* and in the relative quiet of my position, I also realize the Pentagon's approval of his comprehensive inspection plan will allow Mother to hire twenty additional inmate inspectors. One of whom will be me.

It won't be long before I'm called to work, and I'll have access to a typewriter. Mary will like that, I'm thinking. Her man is getting ahead in the world.

We have one more surprise for the day. When we get back to the cell, the Giant is waiting!

"Boy howdy! Thut was some slick shit you whupped on Stonemann, Mother. The Doc over at the hospital is still laughing about that one. I wish I had yer talent. Damn me if it don't seem like about all I can do by muhself is git myself fucked up so's you kin save muh country ass." He sprints across the cell, picks up Mother, and gives him a bear hug.

The Giant is such a moving picture of gratitude I can't keep the water from coming to my eyes. From the sounds of snuffles and snorts behind me, I'm not the only one having the problem.

"Hey, you big lug, put me down," Mother pants. "You'll blow out all of your brand-new plumbing."

"Nah," the Giant says, but lowers Mother anyway. "The surgeon at Tacoma General says I'm good as new. Don't even have to take it very easy fer long. 'Bout three more weeks and I can ease back into my old weight-lifting routine. Couple of months of workouts and I'll be able to tell all these suckers to kiss this old country boy's ass."

I don't believe it for a second. The Giant has lost at least seventy-five pounds and aged ten years. His eyes are dull blue marbles perched over huge purple circles under the sockets. His once-lively, lustrous hair is matted to his head, and I see some faint streaks of gray. To tell the truth, the Giant looks as raggedy as a bowl of sauerkraut. If it weren't for the expression of a lost puppy that's found its master, the Giant would look like the walking dead.

"Where'd they cut you?" Noid asks.

The Giant grins and rips off his shirt. Jesus, what a mess. He has enough scars to pass as the assistant in a Polish knife-thrower's act. They have cut him everywhere but the bottoms of his feet. He has so many incision lines he looks like a zipper rack on a notions counter.

"Yup." He grins. "I'm whacked up like a piece of cube steak, but the doc done good, and I feel gooder'n a mother-fucker."

Five weeks away from Mother's English class for wayward convicts hasn't helped the Giant's English much, but what the hell. We're all back together, practically running the prison, and we have everything we need to go horse racing.

Now, if it will only work.

As many times in the last few weeks as I have been forced to leave for work without any stockings, I should be accustomed to the rasping of unfinished leather against my ground pads. Nothing could be further from the truth. This morning's offering, from the Naples numb-nuts whom Greasy Dannie has operating his

22 stocking hustle, resembles a pair of remanufactured dust kitties, woven from the unspun gleanings one might discover under a cathouse cot; forty different colors and a sufficient number of curly black watch-spring-shaped strands to arouse suspicions.

So, despite the seasonal dampness of the March wind lurking somewhere between me and the industries area, I'm off to work with naked feet stuffed into army surplus boondockers.

The wall clock says 7:45, and I'm running a mite late. Halfway down the tier, I run into the Giant; he's coming home from the night fire-watch job Mother has managed to wrangle for him in the cable factory. Giant is puffing a little from the climb to J range, but nothing like he did before his operation. He looks great, too; gained fifteen pounds, and his steady weight-training routine has arranged it in all of the right places.

The fire-watch position isn't much—matter of fact, it's a "nothing" job—but Mother was hard-pressed to place him in a spot where he wouldn't look, and worse, feel, ridiculous. He knows the Giant needs to be a part of the horse-racing project, but there is literally nothing he can do to help. I suspect the Giant knows he's being given busy work, but at least he appears happy, and at every opportunity he's bouncing around Mother like a puppy with an empty dinner bowl. The Giant's eagerness to please has had a very positive effect on Mother, and he is showing us a fun-loving side of his personality that has been under wraps—probably in the same spot where Mother hides the rest of his real self. Whatever, one thing is for certain. Mother and the Giant have become tighter than two ticks in a dog's ear.

"How'd it go last night, Giant?"

"Busy, Flat Store," he replies, pantomiming a man mopping perspiration from his brow. "I moved the *Chart* books and *Daily Racing Forms* into the supply room loft 'n' put all the programmin' notes intuh the middle drawer of the Smith Brothers' desk. Good thing I wuz down there last night; you monks is leavin' all sorts of 'criminatin' stuff layin' 'round. Mother wuz right, sure 'nuff. We needs somebody tuh pick up after y'all."

"Jesus, Giant, that was some good thinking." I decide it won't hurt to stroke him a bit, even though we've finished with the books and forms and are only concerned with feeding our data into the computer at this point. "Anything else going on?"

"Nope." Then his face lights up. "I got two new families of coons visitin'. Made friends with the mom and pop coons, and now they're bringin' thuh kids by fer me tuh meet! Had fifteen of the cutest little buggers you ever saw down last night. Ate damn near every one of muh Snickers bars, too."

"Sounds like you have a talent for working with animals," I say casually, but remind myself to keep an eye on the clock.

"Maybe that's it!" The Giant is beaming now. "Mother says everybody got a talent of sum kind 'er thuh other. Animals might be mine." His eyes add another twenty-five-hundred candle power to his glow. "And yuh know, Flat Store, Mother ain't *never* wrong. If'n he says it is, then yuh kin bet on it."

The P.A. system gives me the excuse I need to end the conversation. "Final work call. All inmates have five minutes to report to their job assignments. Final work call."

"You'd better git, Flat Store. Mother'll be madder 'n hell if'n yer late."

"Right," I agree, and I'm gone.

Busy day today. Good. Three letters from Mary to answer, numbers forty-one, forty-two, and forty-three. True to her word, she's been writing every day, and as she predicted, our relationship has not withered, but continued to grow. Her last letter is one that will stick in my mind for a long time to come. It was simple—a poem, actually—but it covered the past and laid out the future so neatly, I'm going to adopt it into all of my plans. It's still running through my mind as I hit the Flats.

> You've searched the concrete canyons
> beneath the city's glaring lights.
> I've sought self in deepest forests
> and in the river's frothing flights.
>
> The time has come to climb far above
> our pasts of long and lonely nights.
> We've searched all of life's valleys;
> take my hand, we'll seek the heights.

How could I argue with that?

After I answer Mary's letters, the daily tasks begin. Most of the morning will be spent double-checking data already in the computer. While this is more the Smith Brothers' job than it is mine, I have to be available in case there is some question regarding the hieroglyphics I apparently slipped into using when recording the square roots of the elapsed times between the quarter poles in the races at Longacres. I'm also scheduled for Mr. Shure's soldering class. The afternoon is open, so I might do some reading or waste an hour or so daydreaming about getbacks on Stonemann, a pastime Mother encourages, as it tends to diffuse my anger in a way that causes no trouble.

I'm down near the powerhouse before I realize it. In the next instant, the weather turns from a standard Puget Sound drizzle into a bona-fide, frog-strangling cloudburst. In ten seconds, the top of the two-hundred-fifty-foot smokestack is obscured and the Mormon Air Force is walking. I stop to flip the hood of my parka over my head, and while I'm adjusting the drawstrings, Mother and Wheeler stroll by, their gait not at all congruent with the angry words they are exchanging. "You slipped the IBM 1360 in on us, Conroy," Wheeler is saying. "And the information you're putting into it has as little to do with quality control as six or seven of your inspectors."

"Just to set the record straight, Mr. Wheeler," Mother replies, and shifts into his too-smooth tone, which should have Wheeler reaching to protect his wallet, "the computer was on page thirty-four of the in-process inspection system the Department of Defense approved, then *mandated,* for use in this factory. It was a condition to reopening the doors, and Mr. Shure's coming back to work."

"Don't threaten me, Conroy. First, it isn't necessary, and secondly, it won't work. I'm only the nuts-and-bolts man around here. Your real opposition is coming from Stonemann. He *believes* and I *know* you slipped the computer in for reasons of your own. Hell, Shure doesn't know a damn thing about the 1360."

"The depth of Mr. Shure's erudition is not the issue here either," Mother says, and I watch Wheeler's nose follow the red herring right off the track. "The important thing, the *only* important item, is that your factory is back in full production this month and we should double the output of accepted cables by next month. One of the major factors in this continuing success is the 1360. The statistical quality-control program has identified all of the suppliers who are sending us the higher percentage of rejectable components. We're sending them back before they end up causing a failure in a completed cable. Certainly you're not going to argue against the computer on economic grounds."

"I'm not arguing, Conroy," Wheeler says. "Hell, man, I know the factory is running more efficiently, and the 'attaboy' memos are already coming in—with my name on them—but, and I mean a big *but,* if you *are* doing something illegal with the computer and Stonemann finds out, don't expect me to bail you out. I know Stonemann better than any person on this island, and whether or not he gets his evidence, he's going to burn your ass. I don't intend to get caught up in the fire. Believe me. At some point, Stonemann and that computer are going to cause you a lot of trouble."

"Funny thing about an expensive computer," Mother begins; his voice is detached, analytical. "It takes hundreds of people who know each other's thinking well enough to function almost as a single organism a long time to put together the concept of a computer and its programs, at a cost of untold millions. Yet a man, any man, has a brain that is infinitely superior to that of a computer. But the paradox"—he pauses, chuckling—"as evidenced by Warden Stonemann, is that such a marvelous thinking machine as a man can be created in seconds, by unskilled workmen who hardly know each other, and for no more cost than his mother's two-dollar fee."

Wheeler doesn't want to burst out laughing, but he does. Me too.

"So," Mother continues, "don't think for a second I am underestimating the warden, or yourself, for that matter. If you are concerned, have a computer expert come in and go though the memories; then, if you're still suspicious—"

Wheeler cuts him short. "We had a man in last week. He says the 1360 is clean. He can only find Q.C. data. But Stonemann isn't convinced."

"Will he be convinced when your production and orders double and triple?"

"Hold it, Conroy. I'm not going to say I don't admire the way you've turned my factory around. I do. But Stonemann is a vicious S.O.B; vindictive as hell, too. He knows he can't get at you here in the factory, and he's bound to take another shot where you can't hide under Shure's DECAS skirts."

"I fully expect him to. But thanks for the warning."

"That was no warning, Conroy. It's next week's news." With this admonition, Wheeler increases his pace and turns off into the walkway leading to the stairs that go to the back door of his office.

I'm beside Mother before Wheeler has gone ten feet. "Jesus,

Mother," I whisper, "they got into the machine and missed us. What a break!"

"The man from Computer Security Incorporated went into the 1360, hit our access blocks and codes, and was rerouted into the area where all of the inspection data are stored. He didn't miss; we were waiting for him."

"What made you think of putting in access codes?"

"Wheeler. I heard the sneaky son of a gun telling Stonemann they should have an expert check out the computer."

"How in hell did you get up on that conversation?" My mind is spinning from a full-blown attack of Benny's noids.

"Noid Benny has tapped Wheeler's institution phone system and bugged his office." Mother drops the announcement casually and walks off, leaving me with the rain playing a meaty tattoo on my tonsils.

I enter the factory just in time to see Mother slipping into Mr. Shure's office for the daily Q.C. briefing they give each other. I take it upon myself to warn the rest of the crew regarding Stonemann's continuing interest in our operation. My first stop is the input terminal, where Dog and the Smith Brothers are hunched up like three surgeons doing open-heart surgery.

Fred Parker beats me there by half a step. Dog looks up and drops a Q.C. manual over a stack of my notes, then burns the intruder, not saying a word.

"Hi, fellas," Fred says. "What are you up to these days?"

"Fred," Dog answers solemnly. "Under optimal conditions, given prodigious amounts of motivation further endowed by compelling need, you would not perambulate the breadth of a common metropolitan artery to observe a pissant pull a freight train." He pauses, grinning at his quarry as though he'd just paid him a compliment. Fred rewards him with a nervous, confused grin, so Dog continues. "I am therefore more than somewhat in a state of cognitive dissonance regarding your present overtures of camaraderie and your blatant quest to discern the nature of our endeavors. If in fact you are now procrastinating, awaiting an autogenic catharsis that will divulge to you precisely the enumerated goal of our current efforts, I would strongly advise you display the uncommonly profound good judgment to cease and desist."

"Huh?"

Fred is lost, but I notice the Smith Brothers have understood every single word. Me, too, I realize.

"Fuck off," Dog explains in detail.

Fred is gone as quickly as he arrived.

"The head Philistine has sent for the scouts," Dog mutters.

"Well, you got rid of him before he caused any damage. One of your more impressive efforts, I might add."

"Why is it you hardly ever treat us to these demonstrations of your skills with bombast and hyperbole?" Little Smith asks.

Dog shrugs. "You guys have taken all of the fun out of it," he admits, then flicks me an evil grin and adds, *"Veni, vedi, venci."*

I mimic a priest making the sign of the cross and counter with the only Latin I know, having read it on a copy of my indictment. *"Habeas corpus ad prosequendum."* I see from his grin I've guessed wrong. I'd better get something together quick for revenge. I decide to attack Dog in his most vulnerable area. His law work. "I got to admit your Latin's better than mine. But the problem is Fred Parker. Why don't you write him one of your famous writs and get him out of here? The great writ of *Corpus sneakus,* for instance."

The Smiths lend a hand. "That sounds logical," they chirp, and Big adds, "Or the other one, the writ of *Hoppus fencus.*"

"No," I cut in. "Fred's a rat. Dog should give him the one where he takes the guy's cigarettes and tells him he's filing the great writ of *Hocus pocus;* then, when the mark comes back, he tells him the only way he's getting out is to jump through his ass and disappear."

"Comments, derisive comments, regarding my past forays into the field of jurisprudence are not appreciated. What is this mind-boggling news you wish to lay upon us?"

I give them a quick synopsis of Mother and Wheeler's conversation and the news that Noid is into the tapping and bugging business full time. I'm not surprised to learn they don't know about Noid's activities. Mother has us all on a "need to know" system of information sharing. I wonder where he picked that one up. Just as I'm finishing, Odds wanders into the conversation.

"Well, it's pretty damn obvious to me. Stonemann is after my winner's wheel. He accurately perceives it as the real threat."

Jesus. Odds is becoming as self-centered as a fried egg yolk. Everything he hears automatically gets correlated with him and his damn wheel. "I figure your wheel is safe enough, Odds, but the foreman over on line number three is trying to get your attention. You'd better wheel your ass over there."

Odds pouts. "I ain't leaving until I find out what's really going on."

"Let Dog explain it to you, then, shit-head. Mother told us to give the foremen a hand every chance we get, to make them more dependent on us. I'm not going to ignore him just so you can see for sure your four-hundred-dollar piece of shit is safe." I spin and leave Odds with his mouth hanging open.

Mother was right in his approach to dealing with the foremen. They're mostly guards who screwed up in the BOP and got shunted to industries. Not one in ten can read a schematic, so Mother taught us how to make ourselves more valuable and to provide some cover for our other, real functions in horse racing.

As I'm walking across the floor, cussing Odds under my breath for being such a selfish sucker, I happen to glance up at Wheeler's office. Stonemann, Creech, and Wheeler are standing out on the balcony, arguing. While I'm wondering if Noid has the balcony bugged, too, Stonemann starts pointing and gesturing at something on the other side of the plant. I follow his shaking finger and see he has Mother drawn up in his sights. About the same time, Mother looks up, sees him pointing, and gives Stonemann a cheery wave, then walks on down the steps leading away from Mr. Shure's office.

Stonemann's face goes livid, and his knuckles turn white on the railing. He says something to Creech that splits his fat face into an evil grin.

I shoot Mother a worried look, and he smiles back confidently. Whatever is going down, Mother appears to have a handle on it, so I'm off to help out Johnson, the freeman foreman on line three.

I straighten out the problem, a simple interpretation of the number of twists the contract calls for in a wire bundle, then hustle over to my cubbyhole of an office to answer Mary's letter.

Ten minutes pass, and the paper remains as blank as my mind. Something is *wrong*. The hairs on the back of my neck are wriggling around like sun-stroked fish bait.

Dog's and Mother's names are called over the plant's P.A. system, and they're off to the visiting room. I check the calendar. It's Wednesday, all right. Dog's folks come over every Wednesday, because that's the day they'll be picking up the bets for the track, and we decided it would be best to establish the pattern before the opening of Longacres Racecourse. Cynthia Evans comes on Wednesdays because, for some reason or the other, she has taken that as her day off at the paper.

I wish I knew what she was tinkering with that Mother wanted left alone.

It is so quiet in 3-J-5 I can hear the drops of sweat from my forehead as they hit the blotting paper covering the table. Or maybe I hear my heart pumping; I'm too down in the dumps to care. Dog is already in C-segregation, and Mother is in Lieutenant Creech's office receiving the precommitment interrogation, indoctrination, and intimidation routine. He figures to be locked up with Dog before count time.

We have no idea what happened. Something to do with Dog's and Mother's visits. They were going through the postvisit shakedown when the body alarms went off and the goon squad rolled to the Administration Building. That's about all we know.

Everyone is depressed but Odds. He's picked up his winner's wheel and is fumbling with it like a string of rosary beads as he flips through a pile of old *Racing Forms* he brought home from the factory. Finally, the tic-tic-tic of this plastic god Odds is worshiping becomes more than my temperament can deal with. I reach across the table, snatch the wheel from Odds's protesting fingers, and toss it into the waste can.

"What the hell was that for?"

"Every time that thing clicks it reminds me the scam is dead and we're right back where we started. Don't you understand, if Mother and Dog don't get out, there is no way to get the bets to the track, let alone make the selections?"

Odds reaches for the trash can, and I kick it just out of his reach. He's on his feet, fists balled in a split second, as if I'd insulted a member of his family or something. I'm up, ready to go a couple of rounds myself, but Noid is between us. "Why don't you two just chill out?"

"He's driving me nuts with that piece of junk," I complain.

"Junk? Junk, is it? Listen, Flat Store, you'd better start giving this winner's wheel a little more respect. If Mother and Dog don't come out quick, this is the only game in town, or has it slipped your mind that Longacres opens in just thirty-one days?"

"With Dog in the hole, we can't get our bets down."

"I can bankrupt the dago bookies with this baby," Odds replies, patting the wheel, which he's retrieved while my attention was drawn away. "I'll punch a hole in their book you can sail pizza through."

This little bastard. He's hooked on the wheel like Jerry Falwell is on hundreds, and can't see his theory has more holes than a junkie's elbow.

"Thut there piece of shit ain't worth doodly squat," the Giant tells Odds. He's looking at Odds like he can't figure out whether to smash him or the wheel.

The Range Bull walks up, does a quick head count, and eases up close to the bars so the men in the adjoining cells can't hear what he's saying. "Your men got busted with a joint apiece," he whispers. "Creech got them himself."

"Thut move is three days older than jackin' off," Giant protests. "Anything Creech found on them he put on them hisself. Don't expect nobody in 3-J-5 tuh believe they wuz packin' in no smokin' dope. They don't use, neither one, 'n' besides, they'd have had to get it from the reporter lady or Dog's folks, and that won't wash nowheres. Better tell Creech to get his dope back and smoke it hisself."

The Range Bull shrugs, but his eyes are telling the truth. He doesn't believe it either. I sure as hell can't, but my last experience with the Inmate Disciplinary Committee tells me Creech won't have any problem killing both their visits for a year. We're out of business.

Time passes, and I'm not the only one in 3-J-5 who is quietly burying his dreams. Noid has begun pacing up and down the floor, and after a few minutes it becomes a stiff-legged march, the length of his stride growing, and becoming increasingly louder, until he's stomping back and forth across the front of the cell like a caged animal. He stops suddenly and slams a bony fist into his hand. "No! Goddamnit, *no!* I'm not going to give up. I can't just roll over and say, 'That's it; Stonemann wins.' No way."

If he's aware of the even dozen eyeballs that are staring at him, he doesn't show it. "This horse-racing business is the first real chance I've ever had in life, and I'm not going to quit." He pauses and lowers his voice, almost pleading now. "If the situation were reversed and we were racked in the hole, you can bet your butts Mother wouldn't be sitting here with his chin on his chest. He'd be scheming a way around the problem." He pauses, gulps some air to continue, but Little Smith steals the floor before he can crank up again.

"We're a body without a head, Noid. Mother does the thinking in 3-J-5."

"We don't know if that's the only way we can work. Granted, before Mother came we weren't long on thinking, but now, goddamnit, we *can* think for ourselves. I mean, who is going to do our thinking when we get out?" He stops and stares at the semicircle of gaping jaws that are now surrounding him. I don't have anything to add. I have to admit he's figured out what Mother was up to before I did. "Mother has been training us to think for ourselves," Noid whispers.

"There's one other thing, while I'm spouting off, and I might as well get that off my chest too. When Mother brought up the subject of how he was going to make *us* all rich, we dove in, all the way in, every one of us. Now Mother and Dog are in the hole and he can't do the thinking or the work . . . and we're all ready to bail out on him." He takes another break, doesn't see any arguments forming, and continues. "I don't mind living with a bunch of losers. I've been around losers all of my life. I might even be able to handle living with a cellful of quitters. But no way am I going to hang with a bunch of so-called convicts who are in up to their butts for the money but only in up to their lips with their loyalty. I'll be butt-fucked by a gorilla before I'll ever in life accept that kind of shit from my friends." He pauses, and I can't look him in the eye. He's right. "So put the snivels aside. Do we go for it or not?"

"What do you think we should do?" I ask, gladly surrendering command of this light brigade.

"Goddamnit. Think!"

We dive into our think tanks. I reach for one of the westerns we keep on hand; maybe the Sackett Brothers have run into this problem before. The books are gone! Some more of Mother's legacy, I conclude. A minute passes. Then two. Five. Fast snaps his fingers and asks Noid, "You once said you could tap the outside phones in the offices at industries. Is that still possible?"

Noid scratches his head, recalling, I suppose, the night Mother burglarized Stonemann's office. "I was talking about tapping into the institution lines at the time, but it's possible to get into the outside land line too; it's just a bit more difficult. Why?"

"With Dog's and Mother's visits probably gone, it seems like the first problem is how to get our bets out." Fast is onto something, and he presses Noid. "How much trouble would it be?"

"A lot. The lines run under the floor of the factory. That's where we'd need to go in if we wanted unlimited access to a phone. Figure a way to get through ten inches of concrete with five hundred people watching and I can make the tap in thirty seconds."

"How long to get through the floor?" Big Smith asks.

Fast Eddie is the expert on the subject, so he's talking. "With a powered star drill, not more than fifteen minutes . . . maybe as little as five . . . Depends on how much reinforcing rod is in the concrete."

"The factory would have to be empty. Between Stonemann, Creech, and Fred Parker, they must have a couple of dozen sources down there watching us," Fast notes. Then he turns and looks at the Giant . . . he's got the night fire watch! Perfect!

"Not me. I would, but I got no talent fer the star drills 'n' such. I tried to bust intuh a tin cashbox one time. Took me three days. Besides, I got no 'lectricity down there at night, jist the 'mergency lights, 'n' they's runnin' offn batteries. They cuts off all the power tuh avoid fire hazards 'n' such."

"So." Noid is scratching his head again but not showing any sign of giving up. "We need a way to empty the factory in broad daylight, keep it clear for, say, oh, twenty minutes, and yet have someone in there with me who can run a star drill."

"Thut's a tall order," the Giant notes.

Big Smith is on his feet now, pacing right alongside Noid. "Okay. What we need is a way to empty the factory."

"Right," Little Smith agrees as he joins them. "But how?"

Noid stops his pacing and stares at them, and I can't help feeling a moment of panic; then I notice the lights have gone on in Fast Eddie's eyes.

"Coons," he says.

"Huh?" Giant asks.

"We'll get the coons to help us empty the factory," Fast Eddie explains.

"Gee, Fast, it's real nice of you tuh offer to have those other colored boys help out, but whut kin they do?" Giant asks innocently.

"I mean *rac*-coons, mutha-fuckah!" Eddie shouts, but he's grinning, and reaches over and tousles the Giant's hair.

"I don't get it," several of us chorus.

"Try this on for an idea." Fast is on his feet now, drawing pictures in the air. "There must be two–three hundred raccoons inside the compound every night, right?" We nod, and a pair of raccoons scurries by the cell to validate the statement. "They go everywhere in the prison, three/four house, two house, and all the dorms. Any place that has a pipe they can climb or a vent they can squeeze through, right?"

The Giant agrees. "Yup. Had four of 'em in muh room thuh first time I went to thuh hospital. I fed 'em fish patties 'cause they likes 'em better 'n Oreos or Snickers, either one."

"I believe we could lure a batch of them into the supply-room loft in industries, and then, if we turned them all loose first thing one morning . . ."

Giant is shaking his head as Fast is speaking. "Wouldn't scare nobody outa the plant. Most everybody feeds them and them cute little buggers won't bite ya 'lessen ya grab a holt of 'em. They's too lovable to git anybody scairt."

Fast is nodding sadly in agreement when Noid jumps back into the conversation. "They would terrify everyone who was convinced the raccoons on McNeil Island had rabies."

"A bogus news article!" Big Smith shouts. "Something logical . . . say, a group of clam poachers being attacked, bitten, and infected. It could describe the agony of their deaths in detail, too."

Little Smith agrees. "Noid can run off something official-looking, by-lines and everything. I'll write it up, and we'll get News Boy to proof it out."

"But who's going to trick them poor little fellers up tuh the loft?"

"You are, Giant. With your talent in handling animals and a few fish patties lifted from the storeroom, you're a cinch." That's my offering, finally.

"The coons get plenty to eat every night from the cons," Odds adds, and I can see him scrambling in his mind to find a wet blanket. Jesus, he's getting sickening.

Fast is ready for this one. "But remember, Odds, the cons won't be feeding them if they believe they are carrying rabies. And if we raise enough hell about the problem, they'll plug the vents and skylights to keep them out of the housing units."

I help him finish Odds off. "Then the coons will be forced to look outside for their food, find our trail of crumbled fish patties, and follow it right up the ladder and through the skylight, into the loft. We'll have to rig a line so when the time comes, Giant can drop the cover and trap them. Then we're in business."

Noid is beaming. "By God, I think we've got it!"

Fast ignores the theft of the line from *My Fair Lady* and raises a finger for the floor. "One minor embellishment," he says. "We need something very frightening, very visual, some irrefutable evidence of the coons turning into deadly monsters."

"Short Mort!" I shout. "He has that pet of his, Killer, I think he calls him, the one that attacked Mother. He's supposed to be trained to do mock attacks. Maybe we could rent him some night when there's a show in the auditorium."

"Now we're *cooking with gas!*" God, Noid's getting to be more like Mother every minute.

It's time for lights out, and while we still haven't settled on the exact nature of our demonstration, we have kicked around a number of possibilities, divided up the cell into work and action groups, and set the target date for the public demonstration in the auditorium. On Fast's suggestion we settle on two weeks from Friday, when a local country-and-western band will be playing with the convict musicians in a show that guarantees a packed house. We've decided Friday is perfect because it will give us the weekend to train the coons to go up to the loft for their food and water.

The lights go out, and Noid says, "Sorry I went off on you guys."

"Don't be," Big Smith grunts. "We had every bit of it coming."

"Mother is going to be plenty proud of us," Little adds, "but I got to tell you, Noid, I'm even more pleased that no one can ever say we let Dog and Mother down."

"Damn betcha," Giant agrees, " 'n' when they gits out, we's gonna have everythin' tidied up 'n' runnin' smoother'n a motherfucker."

"Smoother than a preacher with a handful of Bibles and a mouth full of gimmee," I agree.

"*If* they get out, and *if* you get the programs debugged, and *if* you can do it before May first, and *if* you can get the information to the Dog's folks, and *if* . . ."

"And *if* you don't shut the fuck up, Odds, I'm gonna put thut there winner's wheel where thuh sun don't shine."

Noid kills the argument and cracks up the cell house with a shout. "Come and get me, copper!"

"*Who's the bastard who said that?*" Arkie Davis screams in agony.

Despite the setbacks of the day, I'm thinking 3-J-5 is almost back to normal. Post-Mother normal, too. But I sure miss Mother lying upstairs, patting out the rhythm of "Camptown Races" on his—"Son of a bitch!"

"What's the matter, Flat Store?" Noid asks.

"I just deciphered it. The little rhythm Mother pats out on his stomach when he's thinking is 'Camptown Races'!"

"So?"

"He's been doing it since his second week in the cell!"

"Yeah," Noid whispers reverently. "How about that? He's been working on the rest of our lives since week two. How about that?"

Son of a bitch.

Watch your language, the little voice reminds me.

I hand Mother another HiHo smothered in peanut butter and strawberry jam. "So when Cynthia's editor called Stonemann and insisted I be given a lie-detector examination because his top investigative reporter was implicated, Stonemann caved in and dropped the charges against me."

"How come thuh Dog didn't git out?" the Giant wonders aloud.

"Reflexes," Mother answers with a note of irritation in his voice. "He saw we were being set up, and instead of keeping quiet, he tried to accept the responsibility for all the contraband. He validated Creech's plant, and now he's stuck with the story; he'll be locked up for two more weeks."

"Thut's terrible." Giant is frowning and shaking his head. "He was jist tryin' tuh be loyal 'n' keep yuh from goin' tuh the hole."

"It would have been better if he'd . . . Oh, well." His face sags into a sad grimace. "The other bad news is that his parents are off his visiting list and we're stuck without someone to take the bets to the track."

"Not really," Noid tells him.

"What do you mean, 'not really,' Noid?"

"I mean, we're not stuck."

"What do you mean, 'we're not stuck,' Noid?"

"We have it worked out." I can see Noid is enjoying the hell out of this role switch.

"*What* do you have worked out?" Mother asks briskly.

"No need to get huffy, Mother," Fast tells him. "We've worked on a way to get the bets out."

"*How?*" Mother is completely out of patience.

"Telephone."

Mother's face breaks into a grin. "You mean you're figured out a way to tap the outside line?"

"Yes," Noid replies proudly. "But we haven't tapped it yet. We're still getting the population worked up about the raccoons."

That does it for Mother. "Hold it! Somebody, anybody, just one of you, preferably, *please* sit down here and explain exactly what is going on."

All eyes turn to Noid; he snags one of Mother's HiHos and begins to fill him in. I get called over to four house to pick up some strawberry jam we had boosted from the officers' mess, and when I return, Noid has Mother almost up-to-date: "So after I had the gaffed news article reproduced and plastered over all the bulletin boards, we started yelling, 'Rabid coon' every time we saw one. It wasn't long before the cops were watching out for them too. No one ever questioned the news article."

"No one ever does," Mother notes. "Go on."

"Within a couple of days the guards' union had petitioned Stonemann to do something about the coons running all over the place, and the crew from Construction One got assigned to plugging up all of their entryways. Once we had them safely out of the cell house, we had—"

"Me," the Giant cuts in, and he's puffed up like a horny toad. "I got the job of trainin' them little guys tuh go up to the loft in the industries fer their chow and water. I'm gittin' 'bout two-fifty up there ever night. I got me sum animal-trainin' talent, huh?"

Mother is grinning like a parent reading a straight-A report card just presented by the heretofore idiot son. "You sure have! This entire scheme is beautiful. What's the next step?" Mother asks eagerly.

"It's jumping off right now," I tell him. "We got to go. Fast?

Giant? It's time for the 3-J-5 players to go onstage. Let's get rolling."

We collect our well wishes and I extract a promise from Mother to be in the audience; then we're off to the auditorium.

When we arrive, I see we're partied it up with Mother a little too long; the houselights are up and the place is packed with convicts who are staring at the stage, waiting to get the first glimpse of the foxy female lead singer from the outside band, a group that plays on KOMO radio all of the time and has a large following in the prison. There is no way we can get up onto that stage and around in back to Mort's mop-closet office.

"Jist wait until the prison band cranks up," Giant suggests. "They's fust, and when they puts them spotlights on, we kin slip 'round the edge of the curtain."

Fast nods, and I agree. We follow the Giant down the side aisle and squat at the base of the stage like we just want to be a bit closer. The joint band comes out; they're suppose to do a song they've written just for this show. We settle in and listen, waiting for the lights to dim and the spots to come on. They don't. As the lead singer rips into the song, there's nothing to do but wait and listen.

> They call her the concrete momma,
> but she's a hooker from the gate.
> They pour you in, she wrings you out,
> through bars of fear and hate.
> She wears a gun-tower girdle
> and her hair is razor wire;
> if you try to flee from her embrace,
> she'll set your ass on fire.
>
> She wants to twist your ego
> with her talons in your brain;
> bringing pain and sorrow
> is how she plays the game.
> When she tucks you in forever
> for a crime you did not do,
> make a haven for your reason, boy,
> or she'll strip it all from you.

If she should take your loved one,
Keep an eye on the evil wench.
She'll play with you and mind-game them;
control is her monkey wrench.
Separating lifelong lovers,
or a mother from her son,
is the game that all the prisons play,
if they split you up, they've won.

They call her the concrete momma,
but she's a mind-devouring beast.
So keep your thoughts close to you
and deny the tramp her feast.
She'll always be the prison
that lives on its own kind.
You can give the bitch your body, boy,
but don't give up your mind.

Just as the song ends, the houselights dip dramatically, and we slip backstage. Short Mort is waiting for us. "You got the smokes?"

Eddie flashes a sleeveful of Camels, and Mort reaches for the stash. "Uh-uh. Not until we see what he can do."

"Yup," Giant agrees, "I'm in charge of the animal trainin', 'n' I needs to see whut we're gittin', 'n' ifn I kin handle him muh-self."

"Killer don't do auditions," Mort complains.

"And 3-J-5 doesn't go for the short con, Mort." I apologize for the reference to his height with, "No offense intended, but either the coon gives us a sample or we walk."

Short Mort looks from the Giant to Eddie and back to me, searching for a glimmer of weakness. He gives up, pats his leg, and says, "Killer! Heel!" In a flash, a seventy-pound raccoon is parked at his instep, and Mort is so confident he doesn't glance down. "What would you like to see?"

"The mock attack," Fast Eddie replies quickly. "Have him lay it on Flat Store and you've got your Camels."

"Hold it! Attack Flat Store? You're the one he's supposed to attack."

"No way, Flat Store. It's my idea, and besides, the brothers would never let me live down the coon-attacks-coon stories. Just stand nice and still, and if he gets out of control, you run like hell." Fast is giving me the full set of ivories, along with the needle.

"Sure I will. Nooooooo problem, Fast. I'm going to start running *now!* You're all the way crazy, Fast, if you think I'm going to let that coon practice on me. I remember what Mother looked like after his session with the beast." Then I get a flash. "How about he practices on *you?* I'll do the stage act if it looks safe."

Fast mulls my offer over for a minute and agrees. "Okay, Mort. What do I do?"

I'm still wiping the sweat off my forehead when Mort replies, with an evil grin on his face, "Nothing. Just stand there and look frightened. Killer? Play!" And he directs a bony finger at Fast Eddie.

Killer charges Eddie. He's growling and snapping like Godzilla with a hangover.

Eddie can't take it, and breaks to the far side of the stage. "Stop running," Mort hisses, "or he'll keep on chasing you."

Eddie doesn't hear a word Mort said. He is jinking from side to side, trying to stay out of Killer's snapping jaws. "Get off me, mutha-fuckah," he screams, and zips around the curtain, out onto the stage.

I peep around my side of the curtain just as Fast Eddie and Killer begin to cut a swath through the band. Drums, electric guitars, microphones, and convicts are scattered about as they plow ahead. Eddie reaches my side of the stage two jumps ahead of Killer, grasps the heavy curtain, and scrambles all the way to the top.

Mort appears at my elbow and mutters, "Dumb son of a bitch is safe up there; I cut Killer's claws. He can't climb anything but a ladder."

I glance back onstage, and Killer is making circle after insane circle just below Fast's sanctuary. Killer's growling and spitting in frustration, and Fast is still screaming. The situation is too good to pass up. I step onstage and yell, *"Jesus! It's one of them rabid coons! Run for your lives!"*

It doesn't take the dumbest convict in the audience long to get the message, and there is an immediate stampede for the doors at the rear of the hall. The theater is empty in less than a minute. Finally, Giant comes onstage and gives Killer a Snickers bar, and he settles down immediately. We only have about five minutes to coax Fast Eddie down so we can get back to the cell before they lock the joint down because of the disturbance. It takes every bit of the time.

I pay Short Mort, the Giant takes possession of Killer and stuffs him under his coat, and we're ready to go. "I *told* you I couldn't deal with any coon-attacks-coon jokes, Flat Store. That was a damn dirty trick."

I have my grin firmly and literally in hand. I slip my palm from my mouth and respond with the first thing that comes to mind. The truth. "It was too good to pass up, Fast. And besides, the cons never would have believed it if we'd stopped the attack and changed actors."

"Worked plumb swell," Giant says in support. "We got 'em scairt good 'n' I got Killer so's I kin do some more trainin'." A ringed black-and-buff tail slips from beneath the Giant's jacket to confirm his possession.

"Where are you going to keep him?" Fast Eddie asks suspiciously.

"In thuh cell, 'course," Giant explains. "We done rented him till Monday night."

Eddie moves over and starts walking on my side, near the wall, but he never gets ahead of the Giant all the way back to 3-J-5.

Mother meets us at the door and gives Fast Eddie the bad news and a worn-out cliché. "The word of a rabid coon attacking a frightened coon has spread through the cell house like wildfire. That was brilliant, Fast. Using people's prejudices against them to deliver your message in a way they'll never forget. A stroke of genius." He grins and shakes Eddie's hand.

The P.A. system comes on to confirm the quality of our ruse.

"Attention in all housing units. Attention in all housing units. A rabid raccoon has been reported on the grounds. Any person seeing a raccoon should notify one of his housing officers at once. Lock-down! Lock-down!"

Fast rolls his eyes to the ceiling and says, "In the words of Martin Luther King when his wife told him she was having triplets: 'I have *over*come.' I'll never live this one down, Flat Store."

"Sure you will," I lie, "soon as the scam goes down."

The lights go out an hour early, killing the celebration we were starting to put together. "Come and get me, coon catcher!" Arkie Davis yells.

"Giant? Do you have that coon in bed with you?" Fast asks.

"Yup," the Giant responds. "He's havin' one hell of a time playin' with the hairs on muh chest."

"Don't let him go on any Easter egg hunts," Fast advises.

"No sweat, Fast. I got him a couple of Snickers bars, and he's all settled down. I got me some talent fer animals, huh, Mother?"

"No doubt about it. The men put the very best person in command of the coon brigade, for certain."

"Damn, it sure feels good tuh know I don't have tuh go through muh life as a no-talent sumbitch."

"There isn't a person in this cell with no talent," Mother says softly. "I've served with groups of men who would give anything to learn the skills you men have developed."

"Yuh means that?"

"You damn betcha, Giant."

" 'N' yer proud of us fer doin' good, too, huh?"

"Sure am."

"Well, yuh got lucky 'n' hooked up with a hell of a crew, 'n' I'm glad we finally got yuh straightened out enough so's yuh could see it. We sorta likes yuh, too, yuh know."

The lights coming through the bars are swimming in front of my eyes. I can't help thinking the Giant has also developed a talent for putting his finger on my emotional button whenever he wants.

And the Giant's right about one other thing. I'm feelin' gooder'n a mother-fucker.

I had to make a trip past News Boy's cell on the way to work. The delay makes me the last one of the crew to leave the cell house. Mother insisted I go by and pick up the original of the *Seattle Times* article the Smith Brothers and Noid Benny put together. Mother is concerned about the piece showing up in News Boy's property inventory on one of his periodic trips to the hole, complete with Noid and the Smith Brothers' fingerprints on the face of the counterfeit clipping.

How Mother has the presence of mind to remember a small item like this is beyond me. With all of the hustle and bustle generated by today's schedule, I forgot to look at the socks I put on! But Mother never forgets anything, and even less often misses an opportunity to improve the chances of our ultimate success. Last Saturday morning was a good example.

The Giant was fiddling around with Killer, teaching him to sit up and beg, roll over, and the whole range of stunts one might be expected to teach a house pet. Killer is a quick study, and it wasn't long before he had the Giant giving up the Snickers bars like a vending machine. Killer was working the Giant as smoothly as any sideshow barker ever worked a crowd of potential marks. Mother watched them for a while, then offered the Giant some advice. "You know, Giant, if you're going to invest your time in Killer, it might be wise to first put him through some of the tricks he will be doing in the scam."

Of course the Giant accepted the message as though it had been delivered from a burning bush or boomed earthward from a dark cloud. In a matter of minutes he had Killer down on the floor, rehearsing for the role they were going to play in the up-coming attempt to clear out the cable factory and tap the outside lines.

First the Giant hopped up on the table, ready to give Killer the instruction to attack. Agonizing protests from the table's legs forced him to relocate his perch to his own bunk. A bounce into the upper and we heard the command. "Play, Killer. Play!"

The raccoon made two laps up and down the floor beside the bunk, then stood on his hind legs, snarling and snapping his teeth. With his upper lip rolled back, Killer was even more con-vincing than he had been in the auditorium. Rows of perfectly pointed teeth seemed to fill the air just beneath the edge of the Giant's bunk. Killer soon realized he wasn't going to get up this way, and scooted down to the edge of the bunk and romped up the rungs of the cross supports. When he reached the top, he charged the Giant. Just when I was certain Killer was going to tear the Giant's throat out, he snuggled up to his neck and began licking the Giant's very embarrassed face.

Mother smiled at Killer's failure to press the mock attack but hid the grin behind his hand as he rubbed his chin, feigning deep thought. "Maybe he might do a little better if you started him out with some basic rules and commands."

The Giant was not only embarrassed by Killer's failure to continue the attack; he was a little pleased by it too, but he didn't let this deter him from following Mother's advice immediately. He picked Killer's seventy-odd pounds up in his ham-sized fists and pressed his nose against the raccoon's muzzle. "Lookie here, Killer. Mother says yuh needs some basic training. You got tuh get yerself some discipline. We got some basic rules 'round here, ya know? Fust off, there's thuh rule 'bout contraband. Ya can't be bringin' nuttin' intuh the cell without ya clears it with Mother." He turned the coon to face Mother, lest Killer misunderstand. "Next, we keeps a clean house. Ya can't be leavin' no tracks like ya wuz out walkin' in the woods, 'n' fer sure, no Snickers wrap-pers alyin' 'round the place." For emphasis, the Giant picked up one of his discarded wrappers and tossed it in the general direction of the waste can. "Then, ya gots tuh try tuh learn sumpthin' new ever day. 'N' ifn ya can't do no 'rithmetic, ya gots tuh try sumpthin' else till ya gets yer talents workin' thuh best they kin." Then he pulled the raccoon down to his chest and stared him in the eye. "But most important, yuh gots to learn tuh trusts us 'n' depend on us, 'cause thuts the way we works."

Giant put Killer aside, slipped off the bunk, and held out his arms. "Jump!"

Killer leaped off the bed, and hit the Giant square in the center of his chest before ricocheting off to the bars. He made another leap up to the first row of crossbars, then climbed the balance of the way to the ceiling, scooting straight up like a steeplejack. He pressed himself into the far corner, then turned, and I'd have sworn he grinned at the Giant. Whatever Killer had in mind at the outset, the payoff was the Snickers bar the Giant finally had to use to coax him down.

Mother's next suggestion was somewhat less subtle than the previous ones. "When he does well, reward him; when he disobeys, ignore him. Otherwise, Killer is going to end up training you."

"I got the hang of it now," the Giant assured us. "Don't worry, come Monday mornin' me and Killer's gonna be a fustclass act, 'n' damn convincin' tuh boot. Doncha worry none, Mother, I'm gonna give him the full benefits of muh animaltrainin' talents."

Giant went to work with Killer and stayed at it all day Saturday. When the yard security officer came to collect the Giant for his midnight fire-watch duty, Giant had Killer safely tucked away underneath his oversized parka. The Giant hadn't been gone more than a second when Mother gave us his evaluation of the Giant's efforts. "The raccoon has him perfectly trained. We'd better work out some sort of backup for Monday in the event Killer refuses to attack until the Giant hangs a Snickers bar out of his mouth." After some discussion and considerable argument, Fast Eddie was given the assignment, based upon his prior, convincing performance.

He's never going to forgive me for that.

The assault of a typical chill, gray McNeil Island morning greets me with all the warmth of the kiss of death and snaps my thoughts back to the present as rudely as the red light in the rear-view mirror when you're both daydreaming and speeding. At least the wind isn't blowing from Tacoma and I won't be treated to the delightful aroma of Tacoma Pulp and Paper before I have my second cup of coffee. Another rarity, I notice. It isn't raining. That should work out well for the scam. In the absence of a cold drizzle and high winds, the cons will milk the rabid-coon scare for all the fresh air they can. Those extra few minutes could be important for Noid and Fast Eddie as they drill the floor and tap the outside line.

The project looks good again, despite a number of second thoughts I had over the weekend. Since the Dog got his thirty days in the slammer on the bogus drug charge, I've been looking over my shoulder at least as often as Noid does, maybe more. But the omens for this morning are all favorable, a feeling of well-being that is shattered when I spot Creech and Stonemann mixed in with the tail-end Charlies straggling down to the cable factory. My first thought is they've figured out the scam, or more likely, Fred Parker has figured it out for them. Experience overrides the fear. If they were coming to arrest someone, they'd have the gooners in tow or already hanging around the area, and there's not another cop in sight. Creech goes over to the back gate a few feet from the edge of the factory and checks the sliding panel that leads out to the prison camp. Satisfied, he returns to where he left Stonemann and leads him down the sidewalk that leads to the stairs up to Wheeler's office.

I'm sprinting for the cons' entrance as soon as they're out of sight. Arms pumping, legs driving, and eyes rolling, I skitter out onto the floor of the plant. I have to find Mother, and damn quick. He needs to know Stonemann and Creech are in the plant, before he is committed to turning the coons loose. Judging by the way the 3-J-5 crew has positioned itself, the scam is set to go at any second: Noid Benny and Fast are standing by the toolroom door; Big Smith is at the base of the stairway leading up to the loft, and he has the rope for the trap door draped around a nail in the wall near his hand. Little Smith and Odds are at opposite corners of the factory, ready to pick up the cry "Rabid coons!" as soon as I do the overture. I can't see Giant or Mother, and I'm about to panic and press the fire alarm, or something, when I catch a flash of the Giant's golden mane through a crack between two shipping cartons. I run around the pile to the shipping area at the back of the factory, and there they are. "I just saw Stonemann and Creech going up to Wheeler's office. They looked as though they were in no hurry, but they saw me, and their disinterest could have been an attempt to put me to sleep."

I rub my chin and add, "As Dog might say, the auguries appear to be adverse. Maybe a short delay until we know what they're up to?"

"I don't think they'll be a problem," Mother says as he's checking the positioning of the crew. "The worst possible scenario would be that they'd come out of the office and walk right into the charge of the coon brigade." But he's smiling, and I can tell he doesn't think that would be such a bad turn of events at all. I have the strange feeling Mother has let his emotions—rather, his hatred—get into his decision-making process, but I don't have a chance to vocalize the thought.

"We'd best go now," Giant whispers to Mother. "I only put three pounds of fish upstairs last night, and a couple of gallons of water. Them little buggers is used tuh twenty times that, and they's already gitting restless. We don't let them out, they's comin' out on their own, sooner or later."

As the Giant is offering his advice, I spot Stonemann, Creech, and Wheeler coming down the steps from Wheeler's office. They're heading straight for us, Creech waddling along in the lead. I tug Mother's fatigue jacket and nod in the direction of the approaching disaster. Mother turns to look, and as he does, I see a marked change in Creech's expression.

Creech's face wrinkles into a puzzled frown, which has the hairs on the back of my neck pleading with my paranoids to cut down on the electricity. I follow Creech's eyes to the hem of the Giant's coat and nearly choke. Killer's tail is hanging out again, swinging back and forth like a warning flag. "The tail, Clyde Beatty! The tail!" I give it all the volume I can for a whisper without having to reclassify the effort as a shout.

I can't tell whether the Giant heard me or not, or whether he heard me but misunderstood the warning; anyway, things start happening so fast it doesn't make any difference.

Giant drops Killer onto the floor and hops up onto the packing table. There is still a slim possibility Creech didn't see the move, but that's no help. The Giant whispers, "Play, Killer! Play!" and I know we're in whether we're ready or not.

"Rabid coons!" I scream. "Rabid coons." As planned, I break into a gallop, heading for the front door of the factory, still screaming at the top of my voice.

Big Smith is right on his job too. Hundreds of coons are spilling out of the stairway coming down from the loft. There is an instant of silence; then pandemonium breaks out as the starved, angry, and frightened coons pour over the factory floor in a rapidly expanding beige-and-black wave.

At the leading edge of the flashing semicircle of snapping teeth are the convicts; running, tripping, and scrabbling over one another to avoid being rolled under by the onrushing wave of swirling madness. Creech is trying to keep Stonemann on his feet as cons and coons wash past, then over, them. They've gone down, and I can't help hoping they've been trampled. I catch a glimpse of Mother's face above the crowd. He's staring at the spot where Creech and Stonemann disappeared, and he's sharing my thoughts; his face twists into an animal rictus of victory just as I'm pushed out the door by a flailing tide of humanity.

My next responsibility is to make sure the men keep moving when they clear the exit, to avoid a pileup, which could turn into something serious. "Head for the top of the hill!" I shout over and over, and as is usually the case in moments of panic, the men follow the first directions they hear. I see Mother and the Smith Brothers have slipped out the rear door, and they join the group of men running up toward the hospital. When they arrive at the crest, they begin working on their other assignment, keeping the men occupied and away from the factory. The faint tap-tap-tap of the star drill won't require much crowd noise to cover, but it will be important to keep the men herded up to produce the minimum hum needed.

The stream of cons is down to a trickle when Odds finally limps past. He has a small cut on his forehead, and his shirt is ripped open. The winner's wheel is clutched in his fist. "Forgot my winner's wheel," he mumbles by way of explanation. Dumb bastard must have run back through the crowd to recover it.

The next two out the door are Creech and Stonemann. The lieutenant has lost his tie, one shoe, and the sleeve is ripped from his jacket. Stonemann's suit coat is split up the back, his face bears the mark of at least one boondocker, and his right eye is starting to puff up; as he passes, I see the outline of several dusty footprints up the back of his white shirt. About halfway up the hill, Stonemann loses a shoe but keeps on going in a lopsided, air-sucking jog that has every man at the top of the rise laughing openly.

A quick peek inside the factory. Except for Noid and Fast, and a couple of hundred raccoons who are still looking for the way out, the place is deserted. I give them the go-ahead signal and turn and trot up the hill. As I pass Stonemann and Creech, Stonemann is saying, "It's Conroy! I can smell it!"

Creech looks up at the rowdy crowd at the top of the hill and hits his body alarm. At that instant, a snarling jet of raccoons spurts out of the factory, and I have to put on some speed to stay out of their way, but it's a waste of energy. The coons turn before they reach me, and head for the back gate. The logical escape route. That's where most of them come through in the evenings. The raccoons are starting to pile up; the ones in front are unable to get through their hole under the fence fast enough to relieve the pressure of the animals behind.

I beat Stonemann and Creech to the top of the hill and turn back to see Stonemann shouting something in Creech's ear.

Creech waddles over to the base of number-three gun tower and yells up at the tower guard. With the noise and confusion, the guard doesn't see or hear Creech, so the lieutenant keys himself through the personnel gate and starts hauling his bowling-ball shape up the outside ladder to the tower.

Stonemann is concentrating on Creech and doesn't see Killer streaking toward him with the Giant in hot pursuit. Killer swerves, and barely misses the warden, but the Giant has to come to a skidding halt to avoid a head-on collision. He bobs his head at Stonemann, and in a flash is off after Killer again. Killer disappears over the lip of the hill, heading for the powerhouse. The Giant is intent on running him down, unaware he's exposing the whole scam with his behavior. "Hold it, Killer," he's yelling as he, too, disappears over the knoll. "Come on, Killer, the show's over."

Stonemann has followed the Giant up the hill, and as he strolls past Mother he says, "Amazing display of courage from your man there. Chasing a rabid raccoon bare-handed."

Stonemann's sarcasm isn't lost on anyone who hears him, but Mother simply ignores the comment and turns back toward the powerhouse. I see Killer scrambling up the rungs that serve as the maintenance ladder for the smokestack. Killer is still playing with the Giant, running a few feet up, then stopping to make sure the Giant is following him. If I didn't already know it's dangerous to assign human attributes to animal behavior, I would swear Killer is laughing at the Giant.

A terrible commotion erupts at the back gate. Creech has tried to open the sliding electric gate, and two raccoons have caught their tails in the apparatus, jamming the chain drive, so the gate will not open. Creech is cursing, and I glance up to the tower. He's slamming the controls back and forth, trying to free the gate so the trapped coons can escape. At last the gate responds and slides swiftly open. The two trapped animals take off with at least two hundred others hot on their tracks.

When I look back up at the smokestack, Killer and the Giant have passed the halfway point. All of the cons on the hill—nearly

five hundred, I estimate—are standing with their faces turned skyward as they track Killer and the Giant up the outside of the
stack. Killer is still climbing easily, but the Giant is beginning to
labor, and I glance over at Mother. He's ignoring everything but
the Giant. Suddenly, his mouth forms a large O, and the other
cons' "ohhhs" and "ahhhhhs" are followed by a deathly still. The
Giant has slipped as he moved from one rung to the next, and he
is barely hanging on by his fingertips. Unexpectedly, he falls another two or three feet before snagging one of the rungs with his
hand. The action spins his feet out away from the ladder and
around the stack, leaving him twisting slowly by one arm as his
feet scratch against the bricks. He has to get turned around and
realign his body with the steel rungs. At last he manages to hook
one of the rungs with his foot and pull himself back to the ladder.
A sigh of relief goes up from the crowd.

A glance at Stonemann reveals him at the end of an exchange
of signals with Creech. Stonemann shrugs, then turns to glare at
Mother.

My eyes snap back to the gun tower just as Creech takes an
M-14 rifle from the rack and slaps a magazine into the bottom of
the weapon. In the silence that follows there is a click as he releases the safety. Jesus, he's going to shoot Killer. I dash over to
Mother, pull at his sleeve, and point just as Creech leans through
the window, braces his elbows on the firing sill, and pulls the
trigger. The *clack!* of the firing pin falling in the empty chamber
echoes down to the yard and turns every head in that direction.

"What is Creech doing?" Mother growls at Stonemann so
loudly most of the cons' attention is refocused on the two of
them.

"I'm not certain," Stonemann replies. "I would imagine he is
going to shoot that rabid animal before he turns and attacks your
friend."

Back in the tower, Creech is struggling with the magazine
and swearing at the weapon. Finally, it feeds. The tower guard
cautions him. "Be careful, Lieutenant Creech. You've set it on
full automatic."

"Mind your fucking business," Creech grumbles in response, then lays the rifle across the firing sill.

I've never heard the staccato bark of automatic weapons fire before, or the supersonic crackle of passing rifle bullets, but I don't have any problem recognizing them right now. Lieutenant Creech has blasted a whole magazine at the top of the smokestack. I force myself to look up; Giant is standing on his tiptoes, stretching to reach the lip of the stack. He turns his head, and a puzzled expression comes over his face. Killer is nowhere to be seen.

Suddenly, Killer's head pops back into view over the rim. The cons start cheering, and the Giant reaches for him. His foot slips, and he quickly drops three rungs, his boondockers twanging off the cold steel. Then he slips two more feet, and his legs slide down between the ladder and the stack itself. With his feet lodged inside the rungs, he suddenly flops over backward like a rag doll. I watch, horrified, as the four bright red dots on his shirt merge into a single crimson splotch.

"Creech shot the Giant!" I hear myself yell in disbelief.

"You *bastard!*" Mother screams at Stonemann, then sprints for the base of the smokestack. I'm rooted in place. First I can't make my legs move, and then they won't hold me up and I see the grass swimming up as I sink to my knees. I'm still muttering, "Creech shot the Giant, Creech shot the Giant," when Big Smith pulls me to my feet.

When I look up, Mother is less than fifty feet from where the Giant is hanging. Bright splashes of blood are hitting Mother's shoulders and back as he climbs, taking the rungs two and three at a time. I can't take my eyes off the scene when I hear another magazine being jammed into the rifle. A con behind me yells, "No more, Creech, you cock sucker. Put that fuckin' gun *down!*" The shout is punctuated by the sound of breaking glass as a missile of some sort hits the gun tower. I snap my head back in time to see Creech duck behind the gun railing as a swarm of rocks strike the tower from three directions.

Fast and Noid arrive, and Big Smith tells them what's happened. "Let's get Stonemann now, before he gets smart and runs for cover," Noid rasps out.

Before we can put Noid's thoughts into action, the goon squad arrives, surrounds Stonemann, and hustles him off in the direction of the Administration Building. Mother's shout pulls my attention back to the stack. "He's still alive. Get the doc. Quick!"

I break for the back door of the hospital and arrive as Cowboy and the doc sprint through the back port. They're carrying the doc's black bag in one of the wire-framed stretchers from the hospital. I grab Doc's arm and point to the top of the stack.

Mother has the Giant over his shoulder already and is working his way rapidly down the ladder when Killer slides down the side rails and perches on Mother's other shoulder. Jesus, I'm thinking, Mother has nearly three hundred pounds on his back and yet he is swinging down the rungs like a spider monkey. We run to the base of the stack and wait. While they are still a few feet above the ground, Killer begins to lick splatters of blood from the Giant's face. He's whimpering pitifully, but all I can think of is killing the furry little bastard.

Mother reaches the ground and eases the Giant off his shoulder, stretches him out, then cradles his head in his lap while the doc starts cutting away at the Giant's shirt. Shreds of flesh and splinters of bone are coming away with the material, and several long, jagged pieces of bone are protruding from the Giant's chest.

Killer snuggles up close to the Giant's neck and begins to lick his face again. The Giant's eyelids flutter, and he says, "We done fucked up thuh works, Killer." Giant is speaking with so much difficulty I'm trying to help by mouthing the words myself. He opens his eyes, rolls them up at Mother, and whispers, "Sorry . . . Ya know sumpthin'? . . . I wuz always afraid I wuz goin' to die a no-talent sumbitch. . . . I didn't want that tuh happen worse than anythin'. . . . Awww, shit."

The deathly still in 3-J-5 has spread over the entire cell house. Even Odds has the decency to put his winner's wheel away. The cell doors rack open quietly, and the Range Bull comes in, nods to everyone, and begins to collect the Giant's property. Mother silently joins him, and while the Range Bull is counting the

 Giant's postage stamps, Mother pens a quick note to the Giant's parents, asking them to drop him a letter because the Giant has some money coming from a business partnership. I take that as an indication Mother is going to go ahead with the horse racing, but don't say anything.

When the Range Bull is finished with the inventory of the Giant's things he asks Mother, "Would you mind stripping the linen off his bed and putting it outside, where the tier-tender can pick it up?" His voice rumbles sadly.

"The bunk is going to stay as it is," Mother replies, and there is a note of finality in his tone that the Range Bull wisely chooses not to challenge. He leaves, and I have the impression he's embarrassed to be wearing his uniform today.

The door slides closed as quietly as it opened. Then the silence is invaded by another sound: the whop-whop-whop of a helicopter coming into the emergency med-evac pad down by the rear gate. I make it for Stonemann trying to put the best possible face on the murder Creech committed in front of five hundred witnesses. He is going to call it an accident and have tons of paper work to prove that the institution spared no expense and did everything possible—everything, that is, except not shooting the Giant in

242

the first place. I have to hand it to Stonemann; he's as slick as a fresh-peeled avocado seed . . . and twice as slimy.

As the helicopter pulls away from the island, I hear a sob behind me. I'm surprised to see it is Odds who has broken down first. Somehow, I've never pictured him as being capable of any emotion not associated with gambling, but there he is, face down on his pillow, his shoulders heaving.

The silence in 3-J-5 stretches beyond the return of the subdued hum of human voices in the cell house. I think I know why none of us is talking; we're all thinking we killed the Giant by involving him in a cockamamie gambling scam. Guilt has smothered our thoughts and even our emotions; only Odds has found a way from beneath the pall, and I'm hoping I can hold on till lights out to take the same route.

Big Smith breaks the daylong silence. "We did that, Mother. You didn't have anything to do with the plan that got the Giant killed. It was our idea, and now it's our fault. I don't want to see you sitting there taking responsibility for—"

Mother reaches over, grabs Big Smith by the collar, and pulls him to his feet; their faces are less than an inch apart when he begins to speak. "We didn't kill the Giant. Creech and Stonemann did. Creech and Stonemann and this crazy system which makes them believe they can get away with anything." He lifts Big Smith completely off his feet and shakes him, a frustrated parent losing patience with a child. "Do you hear me? *We* did *not* kill the Giant. He was murdered!" He sets Big down and continues, talking almost to himself. "Shot down like a dog in the street because the man who pulled the trigger saw him as a dog in the street. No one in this cell is responsible." He looks up and snarls into our faces. "I never want to hear one word about *our* guilt. Stonemann and Creech did it, and if it takes everything I have plus my dying breath, I'm personally going to see them pay."

"Mother," Noid cuts in gently, "this will get whitewashed into oblivion before the day is over. I'd bet the cop who was in the tower with Creech is down in Stonemann's office right now, giving a deposition swearing he dropped the gun this morning and the sights were knocked out of alignment."

"Don't you think I know that?" Mother snaps. "These people never tell the truth about each other's illegal activities. If Cynthia pressed for a congressional inquiry they'd all trot up to Washington, D.C., and perjure themselves." He stares out toward the Administration Building. "I'm not talking about their kind of justice. I'm promising they'll get *my* kind of justice."

"Right." Noid jumps up. "We'll get them alone one at a time and knock them *permanently* out of the box."

"*We* are not going to do anything except mourn the Giant, then get on with the work he helped us begin. If you don't feel you owe this to yourselves, do it for the Giant. The matter of Creech and Stonemann's punishment is something I'll deal with. The rest of you ignore them, avoid confrontations, and don't even say a word they can hear. Do I make myself perfectly clear?" He's the drill instructor impressing the recruits with the breadth of the authority he's assuming over their lives.

"But how are we going to get even for the Giant?" Noid asks.

"I'm going to demonstrate to both Creech and Stonemann, but more importantly to all of you, that there are infinitely worse punishments than simply being locked up for a crime." There is a crafty, cunning look along with the open hatred on his face. I'm convinced he already has a plan.

"Here is your new itinerary." Mother's voice is softer now, and more businesslike. "I want you to say your prayers for the Giant, shed your tears, but be ready to go back to work on the horse racing as soon as Stonemann ends his lock-down. So it's business as usual, no matter how badly you might want to strangle the two of them."

"And while we're waiting, Creech is chuckling in our faces!" Big Smith says. "And I have to tell you, Mother, I'm not sure I can handle much of Lieutenant Creech's walking around breathing air that should have been the Giant's."

"I appreciate your feelings and your honesty, Big. I'll take care of Creech before the lock-down is over, or shortly thereafter."

"But you said they could whitewash the murder." Noid is becoming more and more confused as the conversation goes along.

"True."

I decide to hazard a guess before Mother closes the door on the conversation. "The stuff from Stonemann's safe?"

"I was under the impression I was going to handle this," Mother replies curtly, and that is the end of the discussion.

The Range Bull and several assistants come by, toss in the sack lunches that are the harbingers of a continuing lock-down, and proceed wordlessly down the tier, ducking copious amounts of verbal abuse, questions, and assorted body wastes as they go.

I pick up a book and start turning the pages, and before I know it, the P.A. system is announcing the 9 P.M. count. As soon as the count clears, Killer wriggles through the bars at the front of the cell and captures everyone's attention by standing at the foot of the Giant's bunk and whining pitifully.

"He's gone," Fast Eddie says, and reaches into his locker, grabs a Snickers bar, and rattles the paper as much as he can while stripping it away from the chocolate. Killer trots over, sniffs the offering, and daintily accepts the gift. But instead of devouring the candy on the spot he scurries to the foot of the Giant's bunk and scampers up the crosspieces. He walks over to the pillow, lays the candy bar down gently, and curls up on the blanket.

Several minutes pass as we're all busily removing dust motes and other lachrymose irritants from our eyes. Killer stands up, checks the faces in the cell very carefully, whines at Fast Eddie, then wriggles through the bars and disappears from view.

I walk over to the Giant's bunk, grab the Snickers bar off the pillow, and slam it into the waste can as hard as I'm able. Tears are streaming down my face before I can make it to the pillow.

"Lights out, ten minutes," the P.A. system announces softly.

The next ten minutes are a blur of images and echoes from the past: Giant grinning at Killer the night they met in the auditorium, the look on his face when Mother explained how frightened he'd been when they fought, and the thousand and one times when it was the Giant who placed everything in its proper moral perspective.

The lights flick once, twice, and then they're out. From the corner of four cell house, a strong tenor voice begins to sing: "Rock of ages, blessed for me," and another voice joins in, and another, and another; until all of the men in the prison are at the bars, 3-J-5, too, and we're pouring as much of our pain as we can into the old gospel song.

The last chords of the hymn are still reverberating in the concrete canyon Giant once called home when Arkie Davis expresses the other side of our feelings.

"*I'm coming to get you, copper!*" he screams, and the anger in his voice unleashes an eruption of fulminating negative emotion that lasts until early in the morning.

As the sound dies out, I roll over to see if the sky is getting light; there's Mother's profile, silhouetted against the setting full moon. I'm about to whisper his name when I notice his shoulders are heaving. It's got to be tough, I'm thinking, trying to keep this crew together and never having a place to unload emotions of your own, or a friendly shoulder to cry on. Maybe a good, private cry will help him put the Giant's death in perspective. It worked pretty well for me.

Four days of lock-down. Four days of cold coffee, no showers, and a few dried-out pieces of bread with just enough peanut butter plopped in the middle to make them look like fried eggs that forgot their chromosomal programs. Four days is a considerable amount of lock-down time for the Feds, but as Big Smith remarked: "It's logical. They have much more to cover up this time." I didn't have a comment; Mother simply shot Big a knowing, evil grin.

27

The end of the lock-down comes with: "Work call, work call. All inmates report to your job assignments."

All over the cell house, lockboxes start clacking and clanking and doors begin to rack open. All of the doors, that is, except 3-J-5.

Five minutes after the work call, it is becoming obvious that leaving us locked in was not a simple oversight. We've sent a half dozen of the curious cons who stopped by down to the cell-house desk to tell Range Bull he forgot to open our door. Everyone has come back with the same news: "Someone will be by to talk to you."

"What do you think, Flat Store?" Mother asks.

"Someone will be by to talk to us, all right. Inventory our property for a bus ride. It's that or we're going to segregation on investigation, and they don't have enough staff available during the work call."

"That's the entire range of possibilities?"

I shrug. "This is Stonemann's jail, Mother. He might be holding us in awaiting a NASA shot to Mars. You have to remember, he doesn't need an excuse."

"You ready on that project?" Polaroid asks from the front of the cell.

Mother nods, goes to his locker, and returns with a neatly typed single-page letter of some sort. He drops quickly down to the table, makes a couple of additions with a ball-point, and passes it out to Polaroid.

"You want a copy back?"

"If it wouldn't be too much trouble," Mother tells him. "Can you get it out this morning?"

"The print plant was backed up on orders when Stonemann slammed us. But"—he's studying the paper—"we agreed this could be Xeroxed, right?"

Mother nods.

"Okay. No sweat. I'll run it off and have it back to you before lunch. You still want the same distribution?"

"No change," Mother says.

I'm enjoying this cryptic conversation about as much as a missionary might as he listens to cannibals discussing native recipes in an unintelligible language. As soon as Polaroid is off for the print plant, I'm on Mother like a skin graft. "Okay. What's the real deal?"

"Flat Store, you have no need to know that right now. Better this project unfolds on its own. If something goes wrong, it's one less item you can be hassled over."

I have enough support among the arched eyebrows in 3-J-5 to hold up any demand I might make at the time, but I recall Mother's position on the Stonemann/Creech getbacks and figure this is his first revenge move. "It's your baby. When do we see some results?"

Mother glances at his watch. "Right after lunch."

Range Bull is at the cell door. "Stonemann is going to keep you locked down for the morning. He and Lieutenant Creech will be by to talk with you sometime this afternoon."

"No, they won't," Mother says casually.

"Huh?" Range Bull grunts. "Stonemann just called and told me personally. He said he'd be over with—"

"He'll be over. Creech won't," Mother assures him.

"Hey, Creech is a coward, Conroy. I'll agree with that, but if he doesn't start showing his face around here, he'll never be able to hold on to his job."

"Maybe," Mother agrees. Then a chilling addendum: "We'll see."

I busy myself around the cell, write a long letter to Mary, and before I know it, it's noon and some of the men are coming in from lunch. Polaroid is at the front of the pack. "Got it!" he announces, pushing a sheet of Xerox paper through the bars.

"Distribution?"

"Complete."

"Thanks."

"No sweat. It was a pleasure to be a part of it. If this goes down like you think, cons will be talking about it for the rest of the century."

"Let's make sure they don't start talking about it before it comes down," Mother says as Fred Parker and his roommate Blabbermouth wander by the cell.

Polaroid is gone, and Mother takes a seat at the table, then begins to read the Xerox copy. As he goes through it, I can see his face twisting into a grin. "Two birds with"—he looks up at me and chuckles—"one good idea."

He motions us to join him around the table.

"You might be wondering what I've been up to with Polaroid."

"No shit, Dick Tracy," Fast mutters.

Mother ignores the comment and continues. "I've been working with Polaroid on the Creech getback for some time now. What he did this morning was Xerox this"—he nods at the piece of paper lying face down on the table—"and put a copy on every bulletin board in the prison. You can read it now if you're *interested*." He finishes with a wry grin.

"Is the *National Enquirer* interested in Hollywood gossip?"

Mother turns the copy over and stands up. "Here you go."

I've never had to try and read upside down with a person standing on each foot before, but I find I am a very quick study.

Dear Warden Stonemann:

In the past few months, a series of events have occurred that I feel you should know about. Up until the present, I had assumed Fred Parker was keeping you posted, but the events of the last few days lead me to believe he is no longer your ally. Here are a few of the items Fred should have passed along to you:

1. A few weeks ago, Lieutenant Creech burglarized your offices. You may check his fingerprints against those lifted from your safe for verification.
2. He removed a number of embarrassing records from your safe. They are currently hidden in the paneling behind his desk.

Here are a few more items of interest:

1. The food-service manager is holding out on you.
2. Your bookies are becoming anxious.
3. There is a consensus among the rest of the staff that you should stop mistreating your wife and children.

I hope this letter doesn't prove to be terribly upsetting to you. We don't want to be or sound pushy, but it's time to straighten up your act. We know you are under a lot of pressure, and that is probably what has been causing you to make so many bad judgments lately; but you really should put all my observations aside and start getting as much mileage as you can from your limited mental capacity. The first good thought might be to send Creech out to guard your clam scam—you know, somewhere removed, where he can't cause you any more trouble. Please don't be so ignorant as to fire him; he might take his copies of the information he hid in the wall to the authorities.

That's all for now. Have a nice day.

Very truly yours,

A close friend of Fred Parker

"Jesus, Mother. Stonemann is going to think it's you."

"Ah, but I'm locked down, aren't I?" Mother smiles.

"He's going to *know* it was you. Logic dictates it," Little reminds him.

"Good."

"Good?"

This high-level exchange of intelligence is cut mercifully short by a commotion out in the main corridor. The goon squad is rolling! I wait for them to burst into the cell house, but the sound fades in the direction of the Administration Building.

"Something heavy is coming down out front," Big Smith announces.

"Undoubtedly."

"Creech's office?" Noid asks.

"One would hope," Mother says, and does his no-hander up onto the bunk and lies back, smiling.

We exchange knowing smiles and crowd to the bars, trying to catch a glimpse of Creech's humiliation through the cell-house windows. I'm grinning and waiting, one of a row of expectant kids on the circus-parade route, when something hits the sorting machine doing about Mach 2, causing me to sag against the bars.

Creech's personnel card . . . the Silly Putty–looking potting material . . . the small bottle of machine oil . . . the association with Polaroid in the photoengraving shop at the print plant . . . He's a master photoengraver. . . .The lights go on like million-candlepower searchlights! Mother has lifted Creech's fingerprints off the personnel card by taking a picture of them, then acid-etching it onto a photoengraving plate. After Polaroid developed the plate, Mother pressed the potting material into the etched negative and lifted the prints. Then all he had to do was spread some machine oil over the face of the safe and press the potting material bearing the mold of Creech's print onto the prepared surface. I've heard of crooked cops using the technique to cover up burglaries they've pulled themselves. My next thought was, where did Mother learn the technique? I hesitate to ask—he might say, "Mississippi"—but there is also the paranoid thought that warns he could just as easily say, "The FBI academy, of course."

A couple of hours pass, and Range Bull is in front of the cell, eyeing Mother with an expression somewhere between awe and respect. "You were right. Creech won't be around with the war-

den. He's bringing the new cell-house lieutenant, a Mr. Smith."
He pauses and adds softly, "I'm going to keep your prediction
under my hat." He nods conspiratorially.

"What happened to Creech?" Noid asks.

"He's been busted down to senior officer specialist for 'poor
continuing job performance' and for being overweight," Range
Bull answers gleefully. "But we all figure it was because he shot
your friend . . . and, of course, the note on the bulletin board
didn't help him out much. They took a ton of papers out of the
wall in his office."

"But where is Creech working?" Mother is up, pressing for
information.

"He's been assigned to the midnight-to-eight A.M. island perimeter security detail," Range Bull says, and winks. "It's the
coldest, dirtiest, wettest, most miserable job in the BOP. He'll be
there until he retires in three years."

"*If* he retires in three years," Mother says, and returns Range
Bull's wink. "Creech has a number of very bad habits, and that
job is as well known for its temptations as it is for its discom-
forts."

Big Smith isn't having anything to do with Mother's tête-à-
tête with Creech. "If Stonemann thinks some bullshit little move
like demoting that cock sucker is going to square things for the
Giant's being murdered, he's so full of shit his eyes are brown."

Mother is on Big like a tank top. "Whether it squares it or
not is none of our concern, though, is it?"

Big hangs his head and chokes out, "No. I guess not."

Range Bull nods his approval. "You won't get an unlock if
you show any of your anger to Stonemann."

"Out of the mouth of the opposition comes the truth, more
often than not, however well it may be disguised," I note as
Range Bull leaves.

"Who said that?" Noid asks.

"Me. And I first said it in Washington," I reply, and shoot
Mother a wink.

Less than ten minutes pass, and Stonemann and Lieutenant

Smith are in front of 3-J-5. No question why Stonemann decided to come himself. Mother and Stonemann are staring at each other like two pit bulls when I take it upon myself to remind Mother of his plan to use the intelligent approach. "We heard you sent Creech to the boonies, Warden, and we've been talking it over and decided that while it isn't a fully just punishment for the Giant's death, we also have to give Creech the benefit of the doubt and admit it might have been no more than a stupid accident." I pause, trying to stop my stomach from revealing in detail the difficulty I'm having with this role. "After considering everything, we've decided you did the only fair and honorable thing, even though we would rather have seen Creech fired outright." As I'm speaking, I placate my integrity by telling myself if Mother doesn't fix this bastard good, I'm going to lay a world-class getback on *him.*

"I must say I'm impressed by your reason and logic," Stonemann says, and he actually does seem to be impressed; maybe he's only surprised. "I would, however, like to hear Conroy's thoughts on the matter."

"I think you are a murdering bastard," Mother replies evenly as my chin bounces off my chest. "But there is little I can do about that now, since Creech is safely tucked away where he has no contact with the prison's general population."

Stonemann smiles tightly. "I admire your honesty, Conroy. Stupid statement, but honest."

"Many people, generally the ass-holes of the world, think honesty and stupidity are the same thing. Unfortunately, many of these shit-heads are the so-called leaders of our communities. Bankers and so forth."

I don't know what Mother is up to, but a few seconds ago we were about to get unlocked so we could get back to the racing. Now I don't know. Mother is guilty of one of the oldest mistakes in the con game. It's called "talking past the money."

Big Smith comes to our rescue. "There isn't going to be any trouble from us, Warden Stonemann." I check Big out and wonder where he found the sincere smile he has affixed to his face.

"Admittedly, there were some hard feelings for a couple of days, but we have the matter all sorted out, just as Flat Store said."

Stonemann nods, accepting the explanation, and leaves after giving Mother a full ten seconds of hard stares. My watch cap hits the floor and is promptly pounced upon by both my boots. "That was the best demonstration of idiocy I have ever seen."

"I saw one better," Fast says. "A black guy standing up telling the world how good the Republican party was for black people."

"Really? I can't say I agree with you at all." Mother's face is all innocence. "You see, now Stonemann knows if he wants to take a shot at 3-J-5 there is a single target. Me. I should have left that impression earlier and maybe Dog wouldn't be in the hole, and more importantly, the Giant would still be with us. From now on, Stonemann will know who is gunning for him, and who to gun for."

"You sure that's the way you want it?" Noid asks.

"Just like that."

The conversation is interrupted by the doors racking open. It's the Word Dog. Stonemann has let him out early!

I'm reaching for the HiHos and peanut butter before Mother is two sentences into his recap of the last few weeks.

Greasy Dannie must have given strict instructions to the Trog, his man in the clothing room, to keep us in decent stockings for a month after the Giant's murder, because today is the thirty-first day, and this pair has tops at both ends of the material; great if you're into sweat bands for your calves, but hardly the sort of aberration one should insult a lifelong friend with, and I have grown very attached to my feet. Greasy isn't the only one in the prison who sympathized with us and tried to be supportive. Most of the men on the compound have been working overtime trying to cheer us up. As I'm walking to work, I can see today is no exception, once I discount the socks, of course.

28

Chief, a Sioux Indian, is standing near the paint shack, just a few yards from the entrance to the cable factory. He's gesturing for me to come over to where he has Blabbermouth hooked up in what is obviously another one of his scams. The Chief is a character with a great but well-hidden sense of humor. Being Indian, he has a background that automatically imparts a triple prejudice: First, he's been promoted to Chief solely because most white people see a trip to prison as a status elevation for an Indian, or at least that's how he explains it. Secondly, he's presumed crazy, because Indians have known prisons were insane since their invention, or at least that's the way Chief has it figured. Finally, it is an atavistic, if not genetic, mandate for conquering minions to deem the conquered less intelligent ... my hypothesis. Chief fits none of these prejudicial stereotypes, of course, but uses them, and the

255

system that perpetuates them, as a method of survival and a source of private entertainment. I made him for being the bright, sensitive, well-educated individual he is the first time I spoke with him, but never shared his secret with the rest of the population. The payoff for my discretion is that the Chief often lets me take part in his fun.

The staff has Chief down as driving with one wheel off in the sand, but I know he is really a practical joker upon whom society has bestowed a license to practice; and, unlike doctors and lawyers, Chief has been in practice long enough to get the hang of it.

All Chief lacks to be a complete caricature of an Indian is alcoholism. He's five eight, two-fifty, with bandy legs curving upward into a huge stomach. He has a barrel chest, and his face sports enough chins to be a finalist in an Elizabeth Taylor look-alike contest. Charitably, Chief is as ugly as a bulldog pup.

Right now he's grinning at me and cutting his eyes to Blabbermouth, identifying him as his latest mark. "How! Store of Immense Flatness."

"How, Chief," I reply, and assume the role of second banana by adding, "You have words of wisdom?"

"What he has is some raw bullshit," Blabbermouth interrupts. "He just told me the Booty Bandit is in Atlanta and him and Fred Parker is celled up together. Says they're calling Booty Bandit 'Blow and Tell' and Fred is now known as 'Good Head Fred.' Shit, Fred weren't no homo."

"Well, Fred did get transferred after the note to Stonemann hit the bulletin board. Stonemann thought Fred had joined the opposition, namely, us. So that part of the story is verifiable." I give Chief an inquiring look and ask, "News from the Great Spirit Himself?"

"No. I have spoken with Kawasheega, the Greatest Hunter."

"Well then, Blabbermouth, I expect you'd better believe him. I've never known Kawasheega to lie." I shake my head at the thought of such an unlikely event. "Not once."

"Aw, horse shit, Flat Store, this crazy blanket-ass tells me Fred went out of here on a fuckin' train!" He shakes his head angrily.

"There hasn't been a train run from this island since the railcar ferry sank—that's fifty years ago."

I have to agree with the logic. Aside from the ancient railroad turntable Chief has maneuvered Blabbermouth into, there isn't a sign of a railroad's ever having been on the island. "Well," I respond gravely, "your evidence seems to be pretty strong. I think the fair thing to do is have the Chief check his source again."

Chief nods sagely and begins to spin on his left foot; every time the right foot hits the ground, he says something in a deep voice, rich with mystery, that sounds like "Dumbyokel," because, as Chief explained one day, that is precisely what he is saying. Without warning, the Chief stops, and opens his mouth as if to scream. His neck muscles tense and his eyes roll up into his head, and he says something that sounds like "Yessssss. . . ." Then he throws his face toward the heavens . . . and farts. A couple of beats and he's back into the spinning chant, leaving the audience wondering if he's just received insight or simply made a pit stop.

Blabbermouth wants to flee, but his reputation has been so badly damaged by his past association with Fred Parker, he can't afford to leave. Not many people will talk to Blabbermouth these days.

The Chief stops again, and as I'm edging upwind, he begins to speak in a ghostly voice, "I am Kawasheega, the Greatest Hunter. Many moons ago I stood side by side with the wood spirits and the ghosts of my ancestors to do battle with the moving metal we call the Iron Horse. What a battle it was." He pauses and nods to a tuft of grass growing from under a rail between Blabbermouth's feet and goes on. "Even the grasses trembled from the force of the conflict. In the best tradition of my ancestors, I did not battle with guns; for greater honor, I used only my coup stick to stain the honor of my enemy. Four times I counted coup on the Iron Horse; my dog counted one on a wheel. This consecrated ground"—he frowns at Blabbermouth as though he should move over—"this is where I stood, head to the wind, eyes to the enemy, and feet to the Earth Mother."

Blabbermouth bites. "What happened?"

"The Iron Horse charged, and it came to pass that I came to pass."

"Since you're an old ghost, you're talking about a train being here *years* ago."

"Does the White Eyes interpret the wind? I speak of the passing of an Iron Horse in less than one moon gone."

"Bullshit!"

Chief uncovers the rusted rails of the turntable. "Does the White Eyes propose these tracks were left by water buffalo?"

"Trains don't *leave* tracks, you idiot. They run on them."

"No shit?"

"No shit!"

"Then Kawasheega has wasted your time?"

"Fuckin' right!"

"First time in history Indian ever make an even deal with white man."

Blabbermouth walks away talking to himself, and I find myself chuckling. One of Chief's better efforts.

A bright flash! If they try to put another man in the cell, we could get the Chief! A quick mental inventory is necessary before I make either Chief the offer or the suggestion to the rest of the crew. Let's see: He's doing eighty years for burglary of a K-Mart on a government reservation. The store sold postal money orders, so they tacked on a post-office burglary. The Indian police arrested him sitting at the bottom of a bank of escalators. He had removed every Slinky from the toy department, placed all of them on the top steps of the up escalators, turned the machines on, and spent the greater part of the evening smoking weed and watching the wire coils struggling to reach the bottom. Said it reminded him of trying to change the policies of the Federal government toward Indians.

They took the Chief to trial in Tacoma, Washington, and Chief argued to the jury that he was not burglarizing; he was doing a piece of living art he was going to call *Lifework*. The judge, a man who substituted a perverse sense of humor for common sense on occasion, gave him life under Title 18 of the United States Code, and let him work with that.

His Honor later modified the sentence to only eighty years when the Chief wrote and told the judge he thought it was a bit unfair that his cell partner, a white fur trapper from the Aleutian Islands, was only doing fifteen years, and he had killed and partially devoured his mother-in-law. Now Chief proudly explains his sentence cut as a sterling example of the Federal government's evenhanded justice. Cannibal Charlie, his cellie, usually agrees, unless they're having liver or hamburger that evening; then he's in a trance.

I have one question I have to ask, because I know my cellies will want to know if they're going to consider moving the chief in. "Are you *really* crazy or is this just an act?"

"Flat Store." He is a parent speaking softly but firmly to a child. "I'm doing eighty years for watching Slinkies flop downhill. Who do you think is unbalanced, me or the judge who sentenced me?" He shakes his head and blows me away with this. "I know you're probably thinking about asking me to move into the Giant's spot. I appreciate it, but no, thanks. Who else in the joint would be able to sit in a cell with Cannibal Charlie and watch him eat raw meat? Poor fucker needs the company. I think I'll stay where I'm at." He glances up the hill, and says, "Oops! There's some gooners doing pat-downs, and I've got a pound of the Mexicans' weed under my coat."

Before I can offer any advice as to how he can avoid the shakedown, he's off up the hill, doing his war dance and leering right into the gooners' faces as he stomps by unmolested.

Crazy Indian.

The walk to the factory is made with a huge grin smeared across my face. The sight of what was once my work area erases the smile as rapidly as it has formed. My cubbyhole has been ransacked, and not by an expert, either. I'm looking for one of Attila the Hun's scouts. Papers and notes are strewn everywhere. My first thought is Mary's letters, which I have taken to leaving in my desk drawer. A quick check. They're still where I left them. It occurs to me the letters are undisturbed because Stonemann's already read them. Not so with all of the data in my notebooks, which are missing.

Noid trots over, and I ask, "What the hell happened?"

"Wheeler had the gooners come in early this morning and shake the place down; they took everything related to horse racing. They got us good. Lousy luck. All of the data Mother was going to feed in today is missing." My mind is spinning. Three days before the track opens for the season, we're working like coolies to be ready, and Wheeler gets a bug up his butt to rip us open. It just doesn't figure. Last week his factory won the prime-quality contractor status, which gives him not only the first but an unopposed bid on all high-tech contracts. Production is up over 300 percent, and in general, the cable factory is running more smoothly than a four-wheel drive cloud on a Teflon highway.

Mother, Dog, the Smith Brothers, and Odds have joined my semiprivate wake by the time my sorting machine has coughed up its zeros. "What got into Wheeler?" Big Smith asks. I'm staring at Noid, wondering why he wasn't first with the question. His face tells me he already has the answer.

"Guilt," Mother responds. "He apparently felt Stonemann was becoming mistrustful of him, and decided he'd give the boss something else to think about and rebuild the trust at the same time."

"They wiped us out," Little Smith notes sourly. "Without Flat Store's and Fast Eddie's notebooks, the four million bits of information we already have in the 1360 don't mean a great deal. The notes held all of the important correlation constants."

"I'll get them back from Wheeler right now." Mother is moving toward the office as he makes the promise.

"How in hell is he going to get Wheeler to give them back?" I ask Noid pointedly.

Noid clears his throat, checks the immediate area, and says, "Listen for yourselves." He reaches across my desk and snaps on the light switch for a blueprint reader I never use.

"What is that?" I ask.

"A line to the microphone in Wheeler's office. Shhhhh. Listen."

We hear:

WHEELER: What is it, Conroy? I have a busy morning.

MOTHER: I'm aware of your schedule. I came to pick up the papers your hounds removed from the Q.C. area this morning.

WHEELER: I'll disregard your insolence and return those items required to perform quality-control functions.

MOTHER: I want the papers that are required to compute horse races.

WHEELER: So you admit it?

MOTHER: Sure. Say, do you have any coffee around here?

WHEELER: I don't have time for amenities.

MOTHER: I know. You have a pressing appointment.

WHEELER: What?

MOTHER: An appointment. Here, watch my lips, if it will help. Ap-point-ment.

WHEELER: I'm serious, Conroy. Say what you have to say and get out or you're on your way to the hole.

MOTHER: When?

WHEELER: In about one goddamn minute!

MOTHER: Then I'll beat you there.

WHEELER: What?

MOTHER: I'll be in the hole before you are.

WHEELER: I'm talking about segregation, Conroy.

MOTHER: I'm talking about fornication, Wheeler.

WHEELER: Fornication? What the fuck is this, Conroy, some sort of joke? If it is, you'd best forget it. I've lost my patience with you.

MOTHER: But you haven't lost your patience with the warden's wife? I mean, she's put you off until eleven o'clock tonight. I'd think a man of your single-mindedness wouldn't allow himself to be pushed around like that.

WHEELER: (unintelligible sputters)

MOTHER: Would you like to hear the tape?

WHEELER: You've tapped my phone!

MOTHER: Right again. That's one in a row, Wheeler; you're on a roll.

WHEELER: Okay. What do you want?

MOTHER: Nothing.

WHEELER: Nothing?

MOTHER: There you go! Nothing. No harassment, no more super-sleuthing, no more attempts to give me an informant for the Q.C. crew, no more midnight shakedowns. Nothing. Nothing passes between us that isn't strictly related to our respective jobs in this plant.

WHEELER: Assuming I go for this, how will I convince Stonemann you're not up to something? He's very suspicious of your crew.

MOTHER: Most of his suspicions are ones you've generated, Wheeler, so let's not enter into this new partnership with any more deceptive remarks. What you tell Stonemann is as follows: You convince him we are trying to predict the outcome of horse races with a plastic device called a winner's wheel. You can tell him that's what we're doing with the *Forms* and *Chart* books. You might also tell him we're convinced we have a winning system worked out. That was a fairly complicated dissertation for a man with sex on his mind. Did you get it all?

WHEELER: Okay. I can do it. When do I get the tapes?

MOTHER: What tapes?

WHEELER: The ones you say you have.

MOTHER: I said I had them; I've said nothing about trading them to you. I've decided to tuck them away as sort of a homemade life insurance policy.

WHEELER: You mother-fucker!

MOTHER: That's what the warden's kids should be calling you.

WHEELER: Here's the notes, Conroy. Now, get the fuck out of my office.

MOTHER: Haven't seen any fucks in here. I suggest you try behind the motor pool . . . say, about eleven?

WHEELER: You're a heartless bastard, Conroy.

MOTHER: I've had some great teachers lately.

The sound of the door slamming rattles the speaker. I turn to Odds. His expression is one of agony. It takes me a couple of seconds to match his obvious emotional pain to the hilarious conversation we just overheard. Then I realize Odds doesn't want to see his pet form of mental masturbation going into battle with Stonemann as nothing more than cannon fodder. If Wheeler does put Stonemann on that tack, the wheel isn't going to last much longer.

Little Smith has a reaction that surprises me. "Jesus. Wheeler and the warden's wife threshing about like two suffocating codfish. What would you give to see that?"

"Two Richard Nixon campaign promises and an unidentified

venereal disease." Dog snorts. "Such a union could only come about after a copious exchange of fees. Funny. Stonemann's wife presents the perfect picture of a bureaucrat's wife, too."

"But soft! What light through yonder window breaks?" Fast quotes.

"Not bad, Fast. Shakespeare, isn't it?"

"Right on, Dog. Willie the Shake himself."

"I thought you were a mathematician, not a poet."

"And I," Fast says as he loops his arm around Dog's neck, "always thought you were a redneck."

"You monks need a point man, or is this just a passing affair?" Odds is trying to put a comedic face on his crack, but the tone is caustic.

Before I can say anything to the little creep, Mother strides into the area and asks, "What is this, the world's longest coffee break?" He tosses the notebooks to the Smiths and adds, "Let's get this into the 1360 right away. I want to start debugging tomorrow morning."

At least he didn't say a stitch in time saves nine.

The date window in the watch I bought with part of Mother's money announces Day One of the horse-racing project's testing period. May first on my desk calendar is barely legible, being covered with doodled wreaths, stars, and red overcoating Odds did with his felt-tipped pen. Off in the corner of the same square is a small heart I slipped in when Mother said he believed it would be safe to use the tapped line to call Mary.

29

So sometime this morning, before the phones are tied up out at the main switchboard, I'm going to hear Mary's voice for the first time since Stonemann fired her.

Thus far, the phone tap has worked perfectly. Odds has made eight or nine calls to the Dog's parents without a hitch. My only worry with the arrangement is using Odds. What if his mind got hard from fondling that wheel and he started placing *his* bets instead of ours? I argued for letting the Dog do it instead, but Mother nixed the idea on the grounds that Dog and his folks might start chatting, and increase the chances of accidental exposure either here at the shop or at the switchboard.

The slickness of the telephone hookup has given me a vastly different impression of Noid Benny. He has really found his niche with electronic gadgetry. The tap is a masterpiece of function and simplicity. A line runs up through the floor, enters the cord to my table light, and comes out behind a fourteen-by-twenty-inch quality-control manual. When you open the book to page 156, there is a digital-dialing keyboard imbedded in the left-hand side and a small speaker and microphone likewise set in the right. You simply punch in your number and lean forward as though studying the manual; this position allows you to both hear and speak without the possibility of being overheard. Since this desk has been placed so the person who sits there has his back to the wall, there is virtually no chance for accidental discovery.

The system is foolproof. The tap runs through the main switchboard, and at peak hours the operator might switch to the line we're using. To combat this, Noid has placed a small red warning light above the digital dialer. My task as I call is to watch for the red light and hang up at once if it comes on.

As I'm going over the system, I realize we still haven't solved the communication problem for the weekends. With the Giant gone we don't have anyone in the factory who can make the calls on Friday and Saturday nights.

The lights go on: the Chief! He's perfect. The last person in the world the administration would suspect of being involved with anything more complicated than a Slinky.

I have to find Mother as quickly as I can and share the discovery. I zip out of the factory, heading for the legal library, where he goes occasionally, for the solitude, I suppose. As I'm passing the powerhouse a stray glance at the base of the smokestack reveals Mother, head bowed, a repentant man before the altar. I feel like a peeping Tom. I know he's down there thinking about the Giant, and I don't want him to feel like I've intruded, so I backtrack to the factory entrance to wait until he comes up the hill.

Five minutes later he ambles back down to the factory. "Morning, Flat Store."

"Morning, Mother. Say, I just had a great idea about the problem of phoning out the bets on weekends." Aware of how unreceptive he's been to anyone else's ideas since the Giant's death, I blurt out the entire plan before he can say no.

When I've finished, his face lights up. "Good idea. Chief will be perfect. I've talked with him several times. In my opinion, he's not only trustworthy; he's competent. Do you think you can persuade him to take the fire-watch job?"

"I don't know," I answer honestly. "Let me ask him right now." I'm jogging over to the paint shack, where the Chief picks up his contraband. When I reach the shack, formally the Flammables Storage Facility, I knock on the wall; he pokes his head out and grins. I wipe the grin from his mouth with a tone of voice all Indians have learned to mistrust. "Good morning, Chief. Have I got a deal for you!" Then I run Chief though a quick sell job. Half an hour later I lay Chief's signed request for job change on Mother's desk and smile, a little smugly, I'm afraid.

Mother looks up, takes the paper, reads it, and says, "That was certainly fast."

"Chief's bright, Mother, but he's never been to a carnival."

Mother frowns until he's put all of that together; then he's grinning. "Good job." His eyes cut to the wall clock. "Say, shouldn't you be calling Mary?"

"I'm a little late, but I thought this was more important."

"If you could teach everyone to have the same priorities, I could quit worrying about you men."

"You *do* worry about us, don't you?" I vocalize a sneaking suspicion I've held for several months.

"It goes with the job title. Mother Superior, remember?"

I get Noid to watch out for any of Stonemann's little helpers and go to work. As I'm trying to dial Mary's number I discover a marked advantage of the old, circular dialing system. The dial has a place to hook your fingers when your hands are shaking in anticipation. I finally get all the numbers punched in, and the line buzzes once, twice, and on the third ring a cheery voice says, "Hello?"

"Hi," is all I can sneak past the lump in my throat, which is busily ambushing everything coming its way.

"Hello?"

"Hi, Woman" comes out a bit more easily.

A long silence is punctuated by a squeal. "James!"

"Man."

"Right. Where *are* you?"

"Right where you left me. Listen, honey, we only have a few

seconds, and I can't explain much right now. If the line happens to go dead on my end, don't say anything, and hang up quickly. Okay?"

"Oh, Ja—whatever you say, Man. Just keep talking. You sound wonderful."

"First, get a pencil and paper. I want to give you the Dog's parents' phone number." I'm digging in my shirt pocket for the slip of paper Dog gave me, and I can hear Mary rummaging around for a pencil and paper. Funny how things like that register, even when time is precious. "Ready," Mary says at last.

"Okay, here we go. The Dog's folks are expecting you to call, and they'll explain everything, so be sure to get to them as soon as we're finished. Their number is 206-994-1237. Got it?"

"I have it. James, I can't get over how *good* you sound."

"I'm feeling fine. Listen, are you usually home about this time?"

"I will be."

"I may be able to call a couple of times a week if we don't get too much scrutiny."

"I'll be right here, darling. Every morning at this same time."

Somehow the word *darling* delivers a feeling I never noticed when it came from any other woman. While I'm daydreaming, the red warning light begins to flash. Jesus, I've talked myself right into a jam; I have to snap the book shut to break the connection before I can say good-by. Damn. I hope Mary understood everything.

Dog ambles over, fixes me with his best questioning expression, and asks, "Problem?"

"There was. The switchboard came on, but I got off in time."

"Defeating problems by good planning. I like this style."

"*Veni, vedi, venci.*"

Dog bursts out laughing. "It's *Veni, vidi, vici.*"

"No, I got it right here." I flip open my notebook and flash it on him. "Just like you said it!"

"Ahh, my poor friend. It was a trap!"

Dog walks away, chuckling to himself.

There is nothing to do but accept my defeat and retire to my cubbyhole. I'm barely seated when Mother rushes by, his eyebrows tugging downward at his hairline in what I have come to recognize as his worried expression, as opposed to the angry frown it resembles. I get up and follow Mother to the card-punch and computer-feed stations.

The 1360 is divided into four components. Card punch, card feed, memory storage, and printer. The Smith Brothers have made one modification on the machine and added two additional card punches to speed up the operation.

The warm glow Mary left me with is doused by the next emotion to cross Mother's face. Despair with a tinge of desperation. The Smith Brothers are sending stack after stack of keypunched queries into the machine, and Mother is standing at the printer, ripping the sheets off as they come up; each sheet is scrutinized, attacked with angry slashes of a felt-tipped pen, then discarded. A couple of minutes is all I can take, and I walk away, shaking my head. I don't have to be a Jeane Dixon to tell the future isn't looking very bright right now.

Back at the desk there is nothing to do but worry, so I burrow in and get after it. It might not be a fun way to pass the time, but right now it's the only game in town.

Two hours pass before I see Mother again. His face has become more intense; pinched and hollow. I saw this same expression once on the face of a man who had fallen overboard in freezing water and missed the life preserver. He slipped out of sight a couple of seconds later, and that was the end of the newsreel.

The legs are demanding a stretch, so I take a brisk walk through the area where Mother and the Smiths are working. Every available table has been papered with the blue-and-white print-outs that are supposed to hold the key to our financial futures. Mother and the Smiths have huddled up over one of the pages and are studying it with the intensity of men planning a major invasion in a global conflict ... that, or a television commercial. One glance tells you the fate of mankind is at stake. I don't want to interrupt, but my feet have decided the time has come, and I find myself drifting in Mother's direction. I need to ask them what the prognosis is, but there is also a small voice emanating from just above my paranoid glands that is saying, "If you ask, Mother will straighten up, scratch his head, and say, 'Well, we gave it our best shot, went the extra mile, fought the good fight, and there's nothing here that works. Looks like we'll have to go with Odds's winner's wheel.'" I'm, not ready for that.

The bell sounds warning the workers to turn in tools before lunch, and Mother and company don't appear to have anything worth talking about. Big Smith walks away from the table shaking his head for the tenth time, and before I can control my mouth it asks, "Find anything, Mother?"

"Not yet. We've tried several programs against past performances, and we keep coming up with the wrong horses. There is a problem with either the process or the way we're asking the question." He pauses for a second, then adds sadly, "Or it could be an impossible task. I don't know yet, Flat Store."

The dejection in Mother's voice cancels lunch faster than a handful of diet pills, and when the chow whistle blows, I'm off to the yard to walk the track. I'd rather be running from the Mormon Air Force and dodging parole loads than be sitting in the mess hall staring at seven faces with disaster and disappointment dividing up all of the available territory. I'm off to the yard.

Mount Rainier is as obscured as my future. The thought hangs with me like a bad cold, until it's time to go back to work. Another wasted few minutes won't make much difference on a day like this, I figure, so I take my time and amble back.

My first thought when I return is that I wish I'd hurried. The gnomes are swarming the 1360. Dog and Noid have joined Fast Eddie, running errands and making coffee for Mother and the Smiths. Odds is off in the corner with today's *Racing Form*, flipping through the pages and spinning his winner's wheel.

I go out on the floor and work my way down one of the production lines until I find a problem. The next couple of hours I spend with Mr. Johnson, trying to figure out the composition requirements of a special potting material to waterproof the Trident submarine's power cable. I'm so wrapped up in the work, Odds is practically standing on my feet before I realize he's whispering to me. "Mother wants everyone in the classroom in five minutes."

"What's up?"

"I think we blew it," he answers, and there isn't a single shred of evidence of his being upset. *Shred of evidence?* Mother must be giving me a subliminal course in clichés.

The classroom is quiet as I enter; no one has taken a seat. Maybe they're afraid if they get down any lower, they'll never get back up. I join the crew, lean against the wall, and start inspecting my fingernails.

Mother breezes into the classroom, a wake of quiet efficiency trailing him. "We have some problems I want to brainstorm."

"What kind of problems?" Noid asks.

Big Smith answers the question. "Nothing we've tried so far seems to work. Those kinds of problems."

My heart ricochets off my pelvic bones. "Nothing?"

Fast does a quick double-check. "Nothing at all?"

Mother takes control. "That's not entirely true. We have a couple of hundred punch cards yet to run, but all we've accomplished so far is to eliminate several factors commonly thought to have a bearing on the outcome of horse races."

"Such as?" Odds asks cautiously.

"Minor weight shifts, jockey changes, fast-track post positions, medications lists, prior finishing positions, and one-furlong -or-less variations in race length." He pauses and shakes his head. "About all we've been able to do is prove the winner's wheel doesn't work."

"We'll see," Odds replies calmly . . . too calmly. "The test is at the racetrack, not on some dip-shit digital keyboard."

Mother ignores the cheap shot. "There must be something we've overlooked."

"What about off tracks?" I ask in desperation. It's the only racing term I haven't heard mentioned. It means the track is not posted "fast."

"That's one of the programs waiting to run," Little Smith replies.

"How about variations in track surface on a day-to-day basis?" Fast is scratching his head and beginning to pace.

"We already know there is a massive variation. We just can't get a handle on how to get bettable information out of the machine," Big Smith is saying. "If we could figure that one out, I believe we'd have something to work with."

"You mean a 'fast track,' one that is posted as fast by the track steward and put up on the tote board, might actually be slower than one posted 'good,' 'slow,' 'sloppy,' or 'muddy'?" The questions are stringing out of Noid like hot dogs out of a wienie machine.

"Sure," Little tells him. "Let me give you an example. Bad Sam ran on Sunday and did the six furlongs—that's three-fourths of a mile—in one minute, ten and a half seconds, and won. The track was posted 'fast.' The next week, he ran the six furlongs in one minute, nine seconds flat and came in third against the same quality of horses. The horse that beat him was called Fast Eddie, for example. He'd run the previous Sunday at one-thirteen and one. . . . Same class as Bad Sam, but his race was run three hours later. The only difference? The grounds crew had watered the track. The race was posted 'fast' for both contests, but it was actually several seconds slower when Fast Eddie ran. Now, when Fast Eddie and Bad Sam show up in the same race the next week, Bad Sam should win. Ran the same day, same track, et cetera . . . but he doesn't; Fast Eddie wins by two seconds. So we know that all track postings, the very yardstick by which bettors wager after they read the *Racing Form,* are essentially worthless."

"Jesus, what an edge we'll have if we can get the machine to spit out the information."

"Didn't we make a table of track variants?" I ask. "Seems like I collected enough of them to fill an actuary's hope chest."

"We did them, and the machine has them right now. We're trying to explore some other avenues while we're waiting for the run," Mother explains. "Any more ideas?"

"Well, it's a four-month season, and the track is going to be open for the next twenty years. We don't have to come up with an answer today, do we?" I'm trying to preserve the illusion a bit longer. Mother recognizes that.

"No. We don't need to come up with an answer today, but that's not the problem. We've run out of questions." I hear the printer dinging out another print-out, and Mother hustles out of the room to check the 1360's latest offering.

"What if we come up all the way blank?" Noid asks no one in particular.

He receives no response beyond a derisive grunt from Odds. I get up, jam my watch cap on my head, and start for the door. "Where you going, Flat Store? A good gambler has to learn to take a little pressure. Hang around. Might toughen you up for the gambling game." Odds is gloating, I swear.

"I'm going outside," I snap. "It's starting to smell bad in here. I need breathing room as badly as crotch cricket in Farrah Fawcett's jeans."

"Ah, you can't stand the pressure?" He *is* gloating!

"Yeah, Odds. Too much pressure. And you know why? Because I *care* what happens. We're dealing with our futures, and some of us, including me, don't plan on spending the rest of our lives in some penitentiary trying to outwit a dago bookie, only to discover we have just half the skill we need."

My emotions are hanging out a mile, but I really don't give a damn. "If this fails, Odds, we're stuck in prison wtih the reputations of being burned-out squares. If this doesn't work, none of us, you included, have a place to call home." I have to pause to keep from slapping the grin off his face. "But that's not the worst of it, Odds; if we fail, the dreams are gone, man . . . the dreams are *gone.*"

The driving rain is a welcome feeling as I start for the top of the hill above the factory. I'm about halfway up when Dog calls my name. I turn, and he's frantically waving for me to come back. I break into a jog and hustle back to the factory.

"What's up?" I ask.

"Mother has requested I gather the troops for another meeting," he answers, and shrugs.

Without a word, I join the trickle of 3-J-5 men going into the classroom.

Mother is still studying print-outs when we arrive and take our places along the wall. He looks up, frowns, does a couple of quick calculations on the face of the print-out, then speaks. "There's good news and there's bad news."

"Aw, come on, Mother," Dog complains. "You've got us standin' 'round like a bunch of storks waitin' on a bullfrog, fer chrissakes. Give it to us straight." Mother is staring at the Dog. I guess he's confused Dog's stress-induced west Texan for the Giant's. It *was* a bit like listening to a ghost.

Noid Benny wasn't distracted. "Yeah, what's the bad news?"

"Fuck that. What's the good news?" I cut in.

"The good news is"—and Mother hestitates, allowing his face to wrinkle into a huge grin—"Longacres is a definite go. Apparently there is some sort of drainage problem that produces terrific post-position biases under certain off-track conditions; that is to say, any track that is not posted 'fast.' We now know that when the track is drying rapidly after a heavy rain, the number-one post position is apt to win as many as six races in a row ... without regard to the past performance charts on the horse. When this condition presents itself, we have an 85 percent chance of winning simply by betting the number-one horse. We can also generate some viable bets using the track variants—if we limit our wagers to those horses the computer indicates have a 67 percent or greater chance of winning. There are two such bets this evening."

"Let's get the money *down!*" Odds breathes.

"No, Odds," Mother warns, "we are going to make a dry run first."

"And the bad news?" Noid can't wait for the clouds to form sometimes.

"This." Mother flips open today's copy of the *Daily Racing Form.* The headlines reads:

HORSE OWNERS COMPLAIN LONGACRES RACING
SURFACE NEEDLESS DANGER TO HORSES

Fast Eddie snatches the paper up and reads: "In order to reduce the high incidence of cannon bone fractures at the Longacres Racecourse, the track management announced today it will plow one hundred and fifty tons of sand into the racing surface at the end of the current season."

"That sand will destroy the basis from which we've set up our statistics," Little Smith explains. "It will render all of our prior computations worthless, because the track will run much more slowly. It's like changing racetracks."

"So Longacres is a one-season shot?" I ask. The follow-up is out of my mouth before Noid has even begun to set his lips. "We'll have to do all of the research over again?"

Mother looks to the Smith Brothers and gives the consensus response. "Right. Worse, it will take three years of racing before we'll have enough new stats for another attempt."

"No problem," Dog offers. "We'll load up on the bets *this* year."

"Right," Odds agrees. "*If* it works."

"We'll know after tonight's test run." Mother is looking over the print-out again. "As I said, we have two bets on this evening's race card that fall within the parameters we have agreed upon."

"Who we got?" Odds asks, and I'd swear he's panting.

"Slick Trick, the number-three horse, in the first race, and Suzie's Woozy, the number-eight horse, in the second." Big Smith is reading directly off the print-out.

"Jesus," Odds whispers. "The daily double!"

There is an air of expectancy in 3-J-5 that's been missing since the Giant was murdered. The Smith Brothers are hunched over in one corner, pawing excitedly through a thick stack of print-outs they brought back from the factory. They remind me of two squirrels unearthing a winter cache of nuts. Mother and Dog are in the opposite corner, working out a message to relay to Dog's parents; Mother has put together a notebook of detailed instructions for our banking arrangements, and Dog is translating the information into west Texan. Dog's folks, the Turners, are to set up a central account with the fifteen-thousand-dollar seed money Mother has put up; out of this account they will handle all of the daily transactions, eventually moving the money in equal shares to our individual accounts as Odds tells them to; provided, of course, we actually win. The personal trust accounts were Mother's idea. We can't touch the money while we're in here, a move he made, I'm sure, to keep the money out of some old girlfriend's hands, or, in the case of Odds, some Italian's bookmaking account.

It crosses my mind to lay something on Mother about counting chickens before they hatch, but I decide to spare him the cliché.

Odds has Noid Benny and Fast ensnared with his winner's wheel and today's copy of the *Daily Racing Form*, and is patiently explaining why each of the nine races will be won by a horse the wheel has selected. The wheel has become indistinguishable from the balance of Odds's anatomy by now. Last night Noid caught him working it while he was in the shower. When Noid pointed out that Odds was standing under a stream of water with the wheel in his hand and his soap still in the plastic dish, Odds's only comment was that the wheel was waterproof, so what was Noid worried about?

I have been on my bunk for the last three hours, trying to draft a letter to Mary. What do you say while you're waiting for your future to be decided by twenty-four dumb animals whose only reason for existence is to run around in circles with midgets on their backs? Somehow, this operation suddenly doesn't feel like the cinch it once did.

The electric clock Noid and the Smith Brothers built for the cell says 9:45 P.M. Fifteen minutes before Railbird Ray comes on over KSML radio. Railbird is an amateur handicapper who thinks he's Jimmy the Greek. Every morning at nine he gives the daily scratch report, listing horses who have been withdrawm by either their owners or the track veterinarian. He peppers these hard facts with wild guesses passed off as the result of arduous hours of handicapping the day's program. He claims a winning percentage rate, which is justifiable only if you subtract those horses that he makes excuses for after they lose.

Time is grinding on. The races have all been run, the purses distributed, and the animals back in the barn by now, and we still don't know who won the race that started at four this afternoon. We'll be sitting here like a bunch of ninnies, rooting through Railbird's recaps for selections that are either over the line first or being relisted into the following race. Worse, the future of the operation, and our futures, have already been decided. It's like living on a desert island during a war and not knowing whether you are the conqueror or the conquered until you meet your first human being.

The radio scratches to life. Odds is on his job, tuning the Taiwan tin-tone the prison commissary has elected to call a state-of-the-art digital, transistorized receiver. We gather at the table while Odds turns the volume as low as it will go, then tosses a towel over the radio to further muffle the sound. There is a regulation in the cell house that prohibits the use of radios without earphones after 10:00 P.M. Up until now, I've always thought the rule was a good idea.

"Good evening, ladies and gentlemen," the towel announces, "this is your old equine prognosticator, Railbird Ray, with the results of the opening day of racing from beautiful Longacres Racecourse in friendly Renton, Washington. But before we get to the races, here's a word from Sparky's Auto Parts."

"Every one of his picks this morning was right on with the winner's wheel," Odds says smugly. "I'm betting he had at least eight winners."

Railbird is back, mumbling out from beneath the towel. "And now to the first race. If you caught my morning show—and frankly, race fans, listening should be a law for all serious handicappers—you'll remember I gave you some very solid bets. But, as often happens here at Longacres, today is one of those days when the speed was backing up. My pick in the first was, of course, Mable's Able, and as I predicted, she shot out of the gate and took an early lead. Midway through the back stretch she opened up a five-length advantage, only to be nipped at the wire by the number-three horse, Slick Trick."

"We scored!" Big Smith claps Little Smith on the back.

"Yahoo!" Dog shouts, and earns a cold stare from Mother and the threat of a gag from the rest of the crew. He's forgotten radios are illegal after ten.

"Shit," Odds mutters, and does a quick recalculation on his winner's wheel. "Fucking speed is backing up."

"What does that mumbo jumbo mean?" Noid asks. "I know Railbird uses it to cover up his screw-ups, but—"

"When a *real* horseman says, 'the speed backed up,' he means the front-running horses all ran out of gas early for some reason," Odds replies, and bends back to the wheel.

"So that's a problem of track surface," Little says. "Logical."

Railbird is back from selling his spark plugs. "I knew I was in for a bad day when a maiden claiming horse took an easy lead, then backed up. I don't know what it is about this track, but whoever solves the riddle of these speed variations is going to be a millionaire. Now, one more brief message from one of my loyal sponsors . . ."

"What the hell is a claiming horse? And a maiden claimer?" Noid is asking, and I remember he hasn't been working on racing; he's been bugging everything and everybody for Mother.

"A maiden," Odds explains condescendingly, "is a horse that's never won. A claiming horse is a horse you can buy for the program price by giving the racing secretary a check before the race."

"You mean every time the owner enters his horse, anybody can just walk up to the office and buy him for the price it lists on the program?" Noid is astounded.

"That's it. The owner is bound by the rules to sell," Odds confirms.

"Why would anyone enter a horse in a race where he could be forced to sell it?" Noid presses.

"Half the fun of being an owner is trying to steal other owners' horses while trying to get rid of your own turkeys," Odds explains. "Claiming races are the backbone of the industry."

Railbird is back from Marty's Muffler Shop. "My horse in the second race, Short Date, came into the top of the stretch eleven lengths in front, only to be beaten in the final jumps by the eight horse, Suzie's Woozy." The balance of Railbird's excuses are lost in the cheering Mother is leading.

The Mexicans next door start pounding on the wall and telling us to get on the dummy. We regain sufficient control just in time to hear Railbird announce the payoff on the daily double. Two hundred and seventy-nine dollars! For a two-dollar ticket!

"My God." Odds collapses into his chair. "We had the daily double and two out of two winners . . . and we didn't have a cent down at the track."

"Tomorrow," Mother assures him, but I can see there is a lot of work to be done between now and race time. Mother agrees. "We're going to be busier than . . . how about an old-fashioned Flat Storeism to bail me out?"

"Busier than a two-dollar hooker when the fleet's in and digging it more than the Pope loves Sundays," leaps out of my thoughts and into my mouth with very little encouragement. I'm not that far removed from the old life-style, after all, I guess.

Leopards and spots, the little voice tells me.

We're still laughing and celebrating when the Range Bull comes by and confiscates the radio. "Sorry," he apologizes, "but you're way out of line."

He's right. There's not much to do but wave good-by to the radio. Noid doesn't seem upset by the loss. "We're rich!" he screams.

"Then send me the five packs of smokes you owe me," Arkie Davis yells back.

"Come and get them, Arkie," Noid shouts, and falls down on his bunk laughing. When he sits back up, I'm not certain whether the tears on his cheeks are from happiness or the sudden release of tension.

The lights go out, and I hear Dog chuckling. "Bonanza," he whispers.

"Freedom," echoes back at him. It might have been me who said it.

Without preamble, the Poet gives us the evening's offering, and as happens so often lately, I find my exhilaration is tempered by the reminder of some unfinished business we have with Creech and Stonemann.

Creech is running around the island,
checkin' on the warden's clams.
The head gooner's right behind him,
puttin' boots up 'tween his hams.

You can sign on to work for Stonemann,
but if you make that sucker mad,
he'll send you out at midnight
on the worst job you ever had.

3-J-5 is the only cell that doesn't join in the laughter.

"A whole week, and not a single bet." Noid is shaking his head and talking to himself even though there are five of us in the industries classroom. "Maybe Odds is right. We're being too conservative."

"A watched pot never boils," Mother comments.

31 I want to remain silent and let the conversation work its way back to Odds. He's starting to worry me, but I can't help myself. "Mother, you have a cliché for everything. I *know* you don't use them by accident, and for almost a year now, I've been trying to figure out why you use so many. How about an explanation?"

Mother shrugs and offers me an impish grin. "Sure. Have you considered why a term or phrase becomes a cliché in the first place?"

"An effective mechanism to make a graphic point," Dog joins in, "without placing excessive stress on one's gray matter."

"True," Fast Eddie agrees. "So they invite overuse."

"Because?" Mother has found his assistant in this snow job in the person of Fast Eddie.

"All the clichés I've ever heard are short and sweet, on the money, clear as a bell, and right on target." Fast is leering at me, and I realize I need to investigate yet another conspiracy. "Clichés are consistently accurate and perfectly descriptive. A mental shorthand."

"There you go! A picture-perfect explanation." Mother turns back to me and nods sagely.

280

"Any clichés to cover why we're not getting enough bets out of the computer?" That puts an end to the game, for sure.

Mother appears genuinely perplexed. "I don't know, Flat Store. I've considered Odds's theory of being overcautious and used his hypothesis to run a program against the races run thus far in the season. If we lower the cutoff point to a 60 percent win probability, we would have had three more bets; two of them would have won, but at low payoffs. The bottom line is, we'd have broken about even for our efforts. Too marginal, as far as I'm concerned. The problem is the pressure of this single season. We could have used a bit more luck along with our skills."

"We could go with the wheel," Odds offers.

"If we had bet the wheel's selections, Odds," Mother tells him, "we would have placed fifteen wagers in the last week, all right, but lost 15 percent of our capital."

"Odds and Railbird Ray keep coming up with the same horses!" My statement causes me to spit out a mouthful of coffee, choking and laughing at the same time.

"What's the joke?" Noid asks.

"Odds and Railbird Ray. They're both using the winner's wheel! All his jawboning on the morning scratch report is a smoke screen to disguise his real source of betting tips." As I'm speaking, I know I'm absolutely correct, because Odds sneaks out of the room.

"Odds and Railbird Ray. What a pair to draw on." Mother ends the in-depth analysis.

I'm ready to pursue my concern about Odds calling in the bets, when Fast joins the coffee-klatch-turned-cell-meeting. "Anything for today?"

Mother is shaking his head. "Not yet. The Smiths are running a new program, trying to identify horses that might do well on the 'slow' track forecast for this afternoon."

On cue, the computer begins dinging out a message, and Mother sprints out of the classroom before the subject of Odds can be brought up again. Odds slips through the door a second later, and he's crowing about last night's results as though he'd won something. "How about Railbird's picks yesterday? He's right on with my wheel again. He had four winners."

"Railbird is using the wheel," I inform him once more.

"Bullshit. He's a scratch handicapper, and a darn good one."

"He picks his horses with the winner's wheel, I'm telling you; then he lies his way to the same conclusion."

Mother sticks his head in the classroom and ends the conversation. "Odds, get out here and go to work with the winner's wheel."

Odds's face lights up, and he heads for the door. "We going to try it tonight?"

"No. Stonemann is in the factory, and I want him to see you with the wheel and some *Daily Racing Forms.* Get on it!" Mother disappears, and Odds hesitates for a second. I can tell he wants to resist.

"Get moving, Odds. It's time for the wheel to pay for itself for real," I snap. Odds snatches his plastic mistress, a couple of forms, and leaves in a huff.

A peek out the window of the classroom reveals Stonemann standing near the computer. Odds rushes by, drops a racing form practically at his feet, and retires to his cubicle. By the time Stonemann strolls by, Odds is so engrossed in the wheel, his intensity is no longer an act.

Big Smith bursts into the classroom, and he's grinning. "We've got three bets for tonight! Miss Muffin in the second, Sherry's Cuzy in the fifth, and Dancing Navajo in the sixth." He looks around and asks, "Where's Mother?"

"Out leading Stonemann on a chase through the other end of the factory. Better get the information to Odds so he can check them against Railbird's scratch report to make certain they're still in the race." Damn reflexes. I've sent Big Smith off to Odds as though I trusted the little vermin. I should have talked with Mother first.

After Big Smith has disappeared, I'm called away to the NASA soldering room.

It takes about five minutes to get into the sterile coveralls, mask, and gloves, and go through the negative pressure lock into the area where we do the NASA quality soldering. "Clean Room" is no misnomer anymore. The place is spotless. At first, Wheeler resisted upgrading the area to military/space-agency standards, but the payoff has been remarkable. As has happened with each improvement Mother fought him for, the quality and production have both increased, but more importantly, the men who have worked there are finding employment easily when they are released. One has even been promoted to night-shift foreman at North American Rockwell.

When I return to the Q.C. area, Odds is speaking on the subject he knows something about, the operation of racetracks and some of the built-in problems facing the average bettor.

". . . so Irish Billy and Macaroni Junior were fixing races in the northeastern fair circuit. They were working the county fair in Brockton, Massachusetts, getting ready to stop some horses—"

"Stop horses?" Mother asks.

"A term for doping an animal to keep him from running up to his potential. They would drug the favorites with a tranquilizer called Acepromazine to take away the horses' competitive edge and make them run more slowly than normal."

"Wouldn't drug testing bust them?"

"No way. Most small tracks only test the first three finishers, and then to see if they've been speeded up. Irish Billy and Junior were slowing horses down."

"Ah! A beauty," Dog comments.

Odds gets up and begins rubbing his hands together as he speaks. "So, anyway, Irish Billy and Junior have a redheaded trainer who needs money to keep fifteen redheaded kids in groceries and himself in Muscatel. Bugger Red, they called him. Since Bugger Red was a licensed trainer, he had free access to the stalls at the backside of the track. It was no problem for him to shoot the horses up with the trank just before they were called out for saddling."

"I don't think you should be blowing this story around," Noid warns. "Aren't you afraid you'll get somebody busted?"

"No. The statute of limitations has run out, and besides, the story is already famous throughout the horse-racing circles." He pauses, arranging his thoughts. "Where was I? Oh, yeah, well, the race Irish Billy and Junior want to rig is the fifth, and they need to stop nine horses so they can bet a ticket where you pick the first, second, and third place horses in order. It's called a trifecta. They only work trifecta and other gimmick betting races so a lot of money dumped into the windows won't show up on the tote board and tip their hand."

"Smart," I offer.

"Irish Billy was the brains of the outfit and the man in charge of the doping. He gives Bugger Red nine needles and a 50 cc bottle of Acepromazine, telling him to give each horse 2 cc's of the drug. Of course, Bugger Red is drunk, and passes the task—dope and needles—to his oldest son. This kid had a date with a hotwalker in the hayloft, so he passes it down to the next-youngest kid." Odds stops, grinning. "Ends up that four children between eight and twelve are giving the shots, and, like most youngsters would, they figure if 2 cc's was good, 4 cc's would be better."

"Jesus, must have knocked the horses out," Fast notes.

"No. But you're close. Bugger Red was saddling two for this race, and the story has it he was punching the horses in the nose to keep them awake long enough to make the call to the post."

"Didn't the other trainers know something was up?" Mother is intent as he asks the question.

"Trainers with entries in twenty-five-hundred-dollar claiming races are happy as hell if their horses can get to the gate without falling down when they're *not* drugged."

"I see," Mother says.

"When the post call came, the Acepromazine demonstrated another of its side effects. The doped horses' penises began slipping out of their sheaths in varying degrees, from a foot or so, to way down and dragging in the dirt."

Odds takes a sip of coffee while we set the picture in our minds. "Oddly enough, very few people in the stands said anything. I mean, what do you say to your date in that spot? Don't bet number seven, darling, his dick is in the dirt?" Odds shows me the first real smile I've seen on his face in months. "The track handlers finally get the horses in the gate and started. When the field swings into the homestretch, they're *really* swinging into the homestretch. What the crowd sees is three bright-eyed claimers thundering down the stretch in front, followed by nine other horses trotting along, eyes at half mast and three feet of cock flailing from side to side."

"Who won?" Noid asks.

"The clean horses, naturally."

"No one got busted?"

"No. Everyone at the track who was with it knew something was wrong and laid off the race."

Noid is suspicious. "Is that race in the *Chart* books?"

"Yes. Fifth race, Brockton Fair, 1972 . . . but everyone in the world of racing calls it the Swinging-Dick Derby."

"You say they only fixed the cheap claiming races?" Big Smith is leaning forward, frowning.

"Yes."

"All three of tonight's bets are twenty-five-hundred-dollar claimers," Little Smith reminds us. "Real cheapies."

"Oh, shit, *no!*" Odds hits his forehead, and hustles away.

The hair on the back of my neck is trying to get under my skin.

What now?

It's eight-thirty. Half an hour until Railbird comes on. The bets are down, won or lost, and we're killing time, exploring new theories of ways to increase the number of viable bets.

"So," Little Smith is saying, "if Big's theory is correct, we could greatly increase our accuracy and also the number of bets if we had the precise condition of the track shortly *before* race time."

"How close to race time?" Dog is scratching his ear and frowning.

"Two in the afternoon would be fine, provided it wasn't raining," Big answers.

"How can we get that information?" Mother is right on top of the conversation.

"Someone would have to go out on the surface itself to make the evaluation," Little Smith replies.

Dog is talking to himself, mumbling. ". . . What did they call that thing . . . used it to figure out density . . . A soil tester! We used them back on the farm to see how deep we'd have to plow to loosen the ground up enough to be self-aerating. If I remember correctly, you can borrow soil testers from any County Extension agent."

"How does it work?" Mother's interest perks up my own.

"A lot like a Rockwell hardness tester. It's mounted on a long handle, like a mine detector. A trigger drives a spring-loaded peg into the ground, and the hardness of the earth is measured on a dial located on the handle."

"Sounds perfect!" Big Smith is definitely excited now.

"Could Dog's folks go out onto the track and use it?" I'm asking.

Odds is into the problem now. "The only people allowed on the racing surface before race time are the grounds crew, the owners, trainers, and jockeys."

"Are we talking about buying a racehorse, then?" Mother gets right to the point.

"Well, we could claim a cheap one"—Odds is mulling the problem over in his mind—"but even if we claimed one for the bottom price, we're talking twenty-five hundred dollars, and that's just for openers. Racehorses are expensive critters to keep, very expensive."

"True," Dog agrees. "While they bear the *nom de guerre* of hay burners, these particular quadruped herbivores tend to metabolize another verdant comestible, namely, your fuckin' dough!"

Odds agrees with Dog. "True. Claiming a cheap horse is the worst investment on earth."

Mother is rubbing a spot red on his chin. "But we're not after a money-making investment. We want access to the track surface. How do you go about claiming a horse?"

"No problem. The person who wants to buy the animal gives the racing secretary a check before the race starts. Ownership is transferred after the race is run."

"Who gets the purse if the horse wins?" Noid asks.

"The prior owner."

"And what happens if the horse breaks a leg *during* the race?"

"Then the new owner takes possession anyway," Odds tells him.

"Sounds like one hell of a deal," I snort.

"It gets worse. An old horse eats more, needs more medical attention, and doesn't win as much as a younger animal. Probably lose a grand a month even if he wins one race in five."

"Money isn't the object," Mother reminds him.

"Right, Odds, think of it as gambling. All outlay, no returns. Like a bet with the dago bookies." Odds is squirming; and the guiltier he looks, the more nervous I become.

Mother interrupts the string of other insinuations I'm prepared to hit Odds with. He takes out a note pad, does a quick calculation, and says, "Okay, we're going to buy a racehorse. Now, which one?"

The Smith Brothers are a chorus. "Dancing Navajo."

"Why?"

"We've already researched him, for one."

"And?"

Big gives Little the floor. "He's a horse that could be running distance races, eight furlongs or more, but his owners have never entered him in anything longer than six furlongs. In short, he's a miler plus, and he's only been run in three-quarter-mile races. Every chart we ran on him shows him accelerating throughout the entire three-quarters of a mile. It figures, and the computer agrees, that he should do much better in a longer race. Matter of fact, that's why the computer picked him in tonight's six and a half furlongs ... that's thirteen-sixteenths of a mile."

"Is he healthy?" Mother is asking all the right questions.

"Never been on the injured or medications lists," Big replies, "and he's a five-year-old gelding. I'd say the worst we'd do with him is break even; even if he didn't make any money, he'd be paying his way by giving us access to the racing surface."

"Odds? I want you to prepare to explain the claiming process to Dog's parents when you call. Tell them to take the money out of the general account and claim Dancing Navajo the next time he runs."

Odds glowers at him from his winner's wheel, and snaps, "Dancing Navajo is the worst dog on the track. If we're going to buy a cheap claiming horse, we should go for Sid's Last Bet. He's in the race with this turkey Dancing Navajo tonight. The wheel says he'll cream Dancing Navajo for sure."

"Whose side are you on, Odds?" I'm hot. This beady-eyed excuse for a human being has worn me out. "We've got serious money bet on Dancing Navajo. The least you could do is root for him."

"Gamblers don't get sentimental, Flat Store."

"Gamblers don't bet with dago bookies, either," I shoot back.

From the look on his face I know I've struck home. Now's the time to get it all out in the open. I *know* he's going to be trouble if we leave him in control of the betting.

Railbird Ray cuts me off: "Well, race fans, if you caught my morning show and scratch report, the maintenance people out at Longacres should be putting your name up over the owner's box about now."

"Yeah then why isn't yours up there?" Fast says grumpily.

The radio the Smith Brothers and Noid have put together sounds better than the one the commissary sells, but it hasn't altered Railbird's auto-part-selling habit, and he breaks right into a commercial.

Dog turns to the Smith Brothers and asks, "Could you figure out a way of wiring a generator to his jaw? We could put Puget Sound Power and Light out of business. Just give him a chance to tell the world how slick he is a couple of times a day, and he'd put out megawatts."

"Let him rave, Dog. He won't stop talking until he makes himself sick, no matter what we say or think." Mother is trying to calm Dog down. I've noticed myself he's much more tense than usual. Dog is worried about his folks handling things properly. *I'm* worried about Odds giving the Turners *his* horses instead of *our* horses.

Railbird is back. "In the first race, just as your old Railbird explained on the morning show, Molly's John jumped out of the gate on top, led the field through the backstretch, and won going away by seven lengths."

Mother is frowning. "Where did the 1360 have that horse finishing?"

"Second from last," Big replies, reading from the print-out. "The computer liked Trundle the Bed, but she was only a 37 percent possibility, so we passed on the race."

"Good thinking," Mother agrees absently, but his frown deepens.

"The wheel had the winner . . . of course." Odds is puffed up like a TV preacher's opinion of himself.

Suddenly the hair on the back of my neck leaps to attention. I run my hand down the nape, and it feels like I've been given a crew cut. I hold my breath until Railbird comes back on. This is the first race we've bet on.

"Well, folks, the second one was for the books. They came out of the gate four wide. Miss Muffin on the inside, Tight Promise next to her and Salley's Alley, with Misty's Easy jammed up tight against them, and that's the way they ran clear through the backstretch."

Noid is so excited, he's forgotten who we bet on. "Who we got?"

"Miss Muffin," Little Smith whispers.

Railbird returns. "Coming into the top of the homestretch, their tails came up, and they started drifting and bumping each other. Near the final eighth pole, Miss Muffin got her second wind and began what appeared to be a respectable stretch drive, then ... and get this, folks, out of the pack comes Earned My Mink, passes Miss Muffin like she was parked, and went on to win by five lengths! It was the most amazing finish I've seen so far this season."

Stunned silence. The first race we bet and the machine is wrong by five lengths! "How much did we invest on Miss Muffin?" Mother asks calmly.

"Forty-two hundred," Odds answers matter-of-factly. I'm thinking he's the picture of serenity when he's losing. He's losing? Hell, *I'm* losing!

"Why did you bet so much?" Fast Eddie asks.

"I thought we agreed to load up because of the short season," Odds reminds him. He's right; no one challenged him during the meeting. Maybe that's what has my hair doing cartwheels.

Mother turns to the Smith Brothers. "Any ideas on what may have gone wrong?"

The Smith Brothers are into their print-outs, grunting the peculiar language they've developed from their computer study. Railbird must have missed badly also, because he's still making excuses. "Well, folks, you figure it out. Either they got hooked up and burned each other out, they were all equally overtrained and a setup for Earned My Mink, or the speed of the race simply backed up once more."

"Or you hiccoughed while you were spinning your winner's wheel," I add uncharitably.

The Smith Brothers report back to Mother. Big delivers the blow. He looks frightened. "Everything checks out."

"Any variable you might have missed?" Fast Eddie beats Noid to the question. I can't recall ever seeing him look so desperate.

Little Smith takes over the bad-news department. "We're not absolutely positive about the variant we're using for this surface, but with the variant's range of possible error factored in, the 1360 still gave us all three of our bets tonight as 67 percent or greater possibilities."

"Sixty-seven percent isn't one hundred percent," Mother reminds us, "but if we've erred in the track variant, we may lose a lot tonight." He pauses, and I can see the wheels turning as he totals up his losses thus far. "Odds? What did we bet in the fifth?"

"Ninety-six hundred to win on Sherry's Cuzy," Odds announces.

"So much?" Mother asks.

"Hey, I don't want to go through this on every race. We agreed to load up. I loaded up."

He's right. No one put any restraints on him. I should have spoken up, I tell myself for the second time. What the hell, at least he's betting the computer's horses . . . so far, anyway.

Odds brightens up. "Might not be the 1360's error after all. The wheel missed that one too. Might be a series of Swinging-Dick derbies."

Leave it to Odds to brighten up a rainstorm by starting a hurricane.

The third and fourth races are repetitions of the first two. The 1360 passed on both races, but its best-of-the-lot computations came in dead last every single time. God, this is depressing.

An eternity passes before Railbird announces his recap of

the fifth race. "You'll remember from the morning show," he begins with the pat phrase I have come to dislike as much as the nasal tone that delivers it. "I told you there was an overlay in the fifth . . ."

"What's an overlay?" Noid whispers.

"A horse that's underbet. Goes off at eight to one instead of the three to one his record indicates the odds should be." Odds may not know how to gamble, but I've never heard him wrong on a gambling definition.

Railbird returns from his latest hubcap-selling foray. "Out of the gate it was Sherry's Cuzy," and I find myself cheering with the rest of the crew. Sherry's Cuzy is *our* horse and she's in front! We miss the next three calls, then hear: "Good-by Innocence closed on the leaders at the eighth pole but lacked a final kick, her tail came up, and for a moment it looked as though she'd lost her pace. Six-French-Nine made a move on Sherry's Cuzy at the sixteenth pole, but got blown off . . ."

We're cheering and pounding each other on the back. A ninety-six-hundred-dollar miss right now would have put one hell of a dent in the bankroll. Odds is shushing us. "Let me get the prices, or we won't know how much we've won."

Railbird is right on his job. "The winner, Smooth-In-Satin, paid nine-sixty to win, four-eighty to place, and two-forty to show. Six-French-Nine paid five-forty to place and three-twenty to show. Good-by Innocence paid four-sixty to show. The fifth- and sixth-place finishers, Sherry's Cuzy and Hot To Trot, were claimed."

Several seconds pass before Mother encapsulates our feelings in a single and insufficiently profane word. "Shucks!"

"It has to be a problem with the track variant." Big Smith is looking at Little. "We need the track condition before post time."

"We've already bet the money," Little reminds him—and the rest of us.

"What did we bet on Dancing Navajo?" Mother is studying Odds, maybe seeing the real him for the first time.

"The rest of the bankroll," Odds answers. The more we lose, the calmer he becomes. Jesus, what a habit.

"How does it look for our horse?" Noid expresses my concern as well.

"He wasn't our best bet," Big Smith admits. "He's in a six-and-a-half-furlong race and he's never gone over six, but he has done well in the mud. The track is posted 'good' now, but running very slowly. The machine believes the extra distance will be to his advantage, and if that's true, he will also benefit from the slower track."

And there it is. If Dancing Navajo doesn't win, the bankroll is gone, we're out of business, and all we have to show for our effort is enough scrap paper to wipe every butt in China fifty times. I don't know any Indian prayers to help Dancing Navajo, so I offer one up in tent-show carny. "Lord? Let it rain all you want, but please don't blow the canvas down."

Railbird jumps right into the call of the sixth race. Our race. Maybe our *last* race.

"The first long sprint of the evening has a field of ten going the six and a half furlongs. Mud Slinger broke on top, followed to the first eighth pole by Kid Gaitor, Mr. Packard, Eddie On The Line, Whirling Mister, and the rest of the field."

"We didn't get a call, did we?" Noid groans.

"My wheel's picks are one, two, three." Odds is giving me a malicious grin.

"Odds." Dog has him by the shirt front before anyone can separate them. "No one in the room gives a big Texas rat's ass how your winner's wheel did. I suggest you can that shit before everyone in the cell loses interest in whether you're breathing in and out properly." He drops Odds and turns back to the radio.

Big Smith is the picture of confidence. "Dancing Navajo is right on schedule. The 1360 said he would be dead last for the first half-mile."

"Big deal. A machine that follows horses who follow horses. Now it's thinking we should buy this nag." Odds must have a life-insurance policy no one knows about, I'm thinking.

Railbird is back on his job in time to save Odds from a punch between his running lights. "At the five-eighths pole, Mud Slinger began to fade and Kid Gaitor moved into first place, leaving Mr. Mustard, Mr. Packard, Whirling Mister, Eddie On The Line, and Sid's Last Bet fighting it out for second. One horse came from the back of the field and began to close on the outside at the eleven-sixteenths point. But now, how about a word from the Speed Shop Auto Parts?"

I inspect my shoes, find they are polished up better than my mood, and risk a glance at Mother. He's beaming up from a print-out Little Smith has pushed under his nose. "If Railbird ever finishes this commercial, we should have our first winner."

"Are you on drugs? Mother, we aren't even in the race." Noid is up on the balls of his feet, shooting wild looks around the room like a trapped animal.

"Mother's right," Fast Eddie double-checks the sheet as he agrees.

Big Smith concurs. "Indeed he is. Obviously the track surface is even slower than we thought. They did the first half in a slow fifty-one seconds! These horses are tiring as though they were running a mile or more. Dancing Navajo should soon appear, flying like Pegasus."

Big nods. "He's going to pass them like they were embalmed."

"A sixteenth of a mile from the finish." I detect a tone of excitement in Railbird's voice I haven't heard before. Maybe he gets high selling distributor caps. "Dancing Navajo shot out of the pack and put on a finish you wouldn't believe! He came from dead last to win by an eleven-length lead. When he hit the finish line, he wasn't even breathing hard."

"That's the horse the computer wants to buy, Odds. How'd Sid's Last Bet do?" I can't help myself. Before I start cheering, I have to slip the little rumpkin the needle.

Railbird is back on, giving Odds a chance to escape a couple of more jewels of wisdom I'm saving for him. "Dancing Navajo has to be the mystery horse of the season, folks. He was thirty-five to one on the morning line, but he only paid a little over two to one. Six-twenty, three-eighty, and two-twenty. Boy, would I like to see the saliva test on this horse. Somebody bet a bundle!"

A cop ambles by, and Noid tosses a blanket over the radio and pulls the plug.

We're laughing and pounding one another on the back, but Mother looks completely puzzled. He turns to Odds and asks, "What happened?" He holds up his calculator. "We only get back eighteen thousand dollars. We should have made a hundred thousand."

I do a quick mental computation and discover after we deduct for the first two losers, we've made less than three thousand dollars for the night. I'm interested in Odds's answer too. He stares at Mother; his face blanks, then turns white. He claps his hand to his forehead and falls backward onto his bunk. "The pools. I forgot about the fucking pari-mutuel pools."

"What about them?" Mother is on the bunk beside him.

"Mother, we bet too much money." He pauses and scans the rest of us, then apologizes. "My fault. A claiming race like this only has 100K in the entire pool. Take out the track's 18 percent and deduct half for the Show and Place money, and there's only about 40K left to shoot at. Our nine-thousand-odd dollars knocked the bottom right out of the pool. We had one third of the winning tickets!"

"My folks got the money down okay. At least we know that for sure."

"Right, Dog; they did a good job."

While Dog is beaming and accepting congratulations for the Turners, and I'm scaling down my future to reflect this new piece of bad news, Mother and the Smith Brothers go into conference. I start figuring, and come up with the best-possible-scenario prediction of only netting around 20K as my share for the whole season. Not the sort of money to take care of a wife on, for sure.

Mother calls the dwindling celebration back to order. "Don't let this put you down in the dumps. We made some mistakes, but we didn't hurt ourselves, and after we claim Dancing Navajo, we'll have more bets at greater payoffs. I think you might safely elevate my original estimate of 25K per year up to better than

100K. We have to take smaller bites out of the pool, but we'll be able to take more of them."

Big Smith stands up, taps on the table for our attention, and begins speed-rapping us. "We need to get some things organized. Mother, I'd like you and the Dog to get together with Odds and figure out how you're going to explain the process of claiming Dancing Navajo to the Turners. Fast and Flat Store? I'll need the two of you to rehash the square roots with an eye toward incorporating a track variant based on the surface density just before the race begins. And I want an adjusted time between the quarter poles, with the variant figured into the final print-out."

Big Smith is giving orders like he was born to it! Or is it just that he's been trained to leadership? I check Mother out, and he's grinning, a father at graduation time. Son of a gun is at it again.

When the lights go out, I again experience the familiar sensation of watching square roots dancing before my eyelids like drunken dust motes, but it's a good feeling. We're on our way, the system is working, and I'm already laying out the living room for Mary's Gingerbread House.

Funny, with our newfound wealth, I haven't heard a word mentioned about vacations, Cadillacs, hard bellies, Hickey Freeman suits, or Rolex watches. No, not funny; weird, I conclude. Convicts with money are supposed to be like children in candy stores. 3-J-5 is growing up.

"Come and get me, copper!" Arkie Davis yells. He doesn't get a chuckle. Worse, some new fish screams up from the Flats, "Somebody shut that old bastard up so we can get some sleep."

Fame is ephemeral in prison, and legends like Arkie sometimes die slow but living deaths. I don't believe we'll ever hear his lights-out cry again. What the hell, things have to change.

Don't they, though? A person with your faith should know that . . . right?

Mother is just back from a visit with Cynthia Evans. According to Cowboy, they had a knockdown, drag-out argument because she had gone to Idaho, interviewed some of his relatives and some man she kept referring to as "the colonel." Mother was furious, Cowboy said, and for a time he thought Mother was going to walk out on her, but as usually happens when they fight—nearly every visit, as I figure it—they ended up snuggled in a corner of the visiting room.

33

As soon as the count clears, Mother calls a meeting, and while we're getting ourselves arranged I'm wondering if he's finally decided to share the secret of Cynthia Evans with us.

Wrong.

"Tonight is the first time Dancing Navajo will run since we claimed him two weeks ago. He's in the last race, as you all know, a five-thousand-dollar claiming race. Mr. Turner entered him two classes above his prior outing, but he's still worried the horse might be claimed at this price. The computer agrees, because Dancing Navajo can run against much better animals. Any idea how we can avoid a claim?"

"Nobody but the computer would buy that five-year-old, swaybacked hay burner," Odds grumps, as he looks up from his wheel. "He got lucky the last time out."

"Whether or not you agree with the computer is not at issue." Mother is close to losing his temper with Odds. "What I want to know is how to prevent our losing him by being claimed."

"The only cinch way to avoid claims is to enter him in an allowance race, one for a much higher purse, where the horses are not automatically for sale. But"—Odds's lips twist into a sneer—"Dancing Navajo would get laughed off the track in those classes. You could enter him, though, if you don't mind embarrassing the Turners."

Mother ignores Odds's continuing obnoxious attitude. "Then we're in business. Odds? Tell the Turners to enter him in the next allowance race. Better call them tomorrow."

"Tomorrow is Saturday. If you want them to get the information before Monday, you'd better tell the Chief to call them when he's on fire watch at the factory," Big Smith reminds Mother.

"Right. The Chief has turned out to be a real lifesaver, hasn't he? We need to do something for him." Mother takes out his notebook and makes an entry. Something tells me the Chief is going to get one hell of a payoff ... maybe it's the grin on Mother's face.

"Odds? Did you get it straight with the Turners on how to bet this evening?" Little Smith is asking the question, but I'm the most interested person in 3-J-5.

Odds blows out his breath like an angered sperm whale, then replies. "Little, for the *tenth* and *last* time, I told them if the track is posted from 'slow' up to 'good,' to bet every horse in the number-one post position until the track is uprated to 'fast.' If the track has already dried enough to open as 'fast,' their only bet is Dancing Navajo." He glances at Mother, then at me. "I have to tell you I think betting by post position is the dumbest move since we bought Dancing Navajo, and I don't care if a thousand computers disagree. It just isn't handicapping."

"For the last time, Odds, 3-J-5 is going with the computer, and the 1360 says the inside post position will win with today's fast drying conditions." Little Smith has run out of patience with Railbird Ray's clone too. I can't suppress my grin, and I really don't want to. Not one bit.

"Did your computer tell you why this micracle occurs?" Odds is back to his superior, know-it-all tone of voice.

"All it indicates is that each time these conditions exist, the number-one post position wins 85 percent of the time, regardless of the relative quality of the horses. But to answer your question, I have figured out the relationship between the weather and the track."

"Please elucidate for this mere mortal," Odds replies.

"It rains a great deal at Longacres—"

"Ahhhh," Odds interrupts. "A stunning revelation."

Little ignores the sarcasm. "When the track is 'slow,' 'muddy,' or 'sloppy,' there is water standing along the rail, and the jockeys avoid that strip of the track. Several days of racing their horses on the outside churns up the earth, making the track deeper and slower. Now"—Little leans forward, and I find myself leaning right along with him—"when the track starts to dry from the sun and wind, the standing water evaporates quickly, leaving a hard, undisturbed racing surface right next to the rail." He pauses, and adds, "Ever notice a mud puddle when it dries up? Like concrete; and this is the type of surface the number-one horse runs on, while the others are struggling in ground so churned it's like loose sand. Matter of fact, that's a good analogy. Two men are racing on the beach. One is at the surf line, where the sand is packed, and the other is away from the water, where the sand is loose. Who wins?"

I can see the man next to the water romping away with the prize, and Odds's face says he sees it too. First his eyes light up when he recognizes the truth, and then his cheeks take on a greenish pallor, telling me he's made some sort of very bad mistake.

"Yeah," Odds admits, "well, whatever, the wheel says Slip Willie is going to eat Dancing Navajo's ass."

Little comes back as smooth as you please. "From their relative positions at the finish, he should logically accomplish that with ease." Odds walks out the door pouting.

"We can watch the eighth and ninth races on KOMO-TV. They have a sports report on television that recaps the last two races. If you guys would like to go down and see your horse run, we can afford the time off this once." Mother pauses, then adds, "Besides, since we now own a horse, I'd like to see the track he's running on."

"Sure, Mother," Big Smith says. "Purely professional interest."

I don't need any persuasion. I'm out the door before Mother has his shoes on. Halfway down the stairwell I realize the television set we are about to watch was one of the payoffs Mother asked for when we had the factory shut down; seems like a million years ago. . . . Damn, Mother's done it again. I'd swear he could stand flat-footed and see all the way to China.

When I reach the Flats I slide by Greasy Dannie and put twenty-five packs of Camels down on Dancing Navajo to win. He grins like a successful bank robber, takes the bet, and I'm off to find a place to watch the race. I end up with the rest of 3-J-5, leaning against the radiators on the wall. Odds goes right to the first row of chairs and plops down on the floor in front of the television, props his head on his elbow, and stretches out. He's only been there a second or two when his legs start twitching; Odds is a junkie, third in line to the spoon.

The feature race of the program, the eighth, comes on, and the first thing I notice is the track condition posted at the corner of the tote board: GOOD, the three-foot-high neon letters announce. As the 1360 predicted, the number-one horse, a twelve-to-one shot, romps home the winner without breaking a sweat. If the track has been in the same condition throughout the previous seven races, and the machine was correct regarding the post-position bias toward the number-one gate, this horse was our eighth winner in a row! Unfortunately, we won't know that until Railbird Ray gives the recaps at ten-thirty on the radio.

The screen flashes a brief clip of the horses coming out for the ninth race, and we get our first look at the colors the Turners have chosen for 3-J-5 Stables: Red-on-white, convict's stripes. I suck my breath in; Jesus, what a dumb move. I glance at Mother; he smiles and nods. He knew. Damn, it was probably his idea.

Dancing Navajo turns out to be a big gelding, spotted in a

pattern that generates a quip from Fast Eddie. "Must have been an Appaloosa in the woodpile."

The next film clip shows the horses at the post, and the 3-J-5 crew is giving unnatural attention to the horses' waterworks in a search for evidence of another Swinging-Dick Derby. Dancing Navajo appears to be in good shape.

"Who's the favorite, Odds?" one of the cons in the back row asks.

"Slip Willie is a mortal lock," Odds answers without taking his eyes from the screen. "He's going to devour these other feed-bag-sucking nags."

So much for my lecture on loyalty.

I check the tote board, and the track has dried out; the posting is moved up from 'good' to 'fast,' so our bets are down on the Chief. Good.

The horses break cleanly, and Dancing Navajo immediately disappears off the left side of the screen. The other horses have left him out of the picture. The computer has figured he runs best in the rear of the pack for the first six furlongs. Having to watch my horse trail the field for three-quarters of a mile is a chore that stretches my faith, but, true to the machine's evaluation, the Turners have instructed the jockey to hold him back; "off the pace," they call it. The entire technique is called "rating" the horse, according to Odds, but it appears as though the jockey is trying to dump the race.

Slip Willie has broken out on top and stayed there. As they pass the grandstand for the first time, he is five lengths ahead, and doesn't appear to be working very hard to maintain the lead. In the middle of the backstretch, a horse called Long Odds catches him, and they enter the top of the homestretch neck and neck. I'm wondering how Odds managed to lay off a namesake bet, when Dancing Navajo begins to make his move. Odds jumps to his feet, blocking the screen, and starts screaming for his horse, Slip Willie.

Mother handles this complete defection from our camp with a shake of his head. He looks to Noid, who makes a face; then he turns to me. "Odds is nuts," I explain.

"Sit down, you stupid cock sucker," someone shouts, reminding us that Odds is blocking the view of at least fifty certified killers.

"Somebody stick something in his ass," comes a more ominous suggestion.

Suddenly, Odds all but disappears in a shower of butt cans, wadded newspapers, and one well-placed boondocker, which bounces off the back of his head and into the television. Fortunately, the screen doesn't break. Unfortunately, neither does Odds's head. Odds doesn't even blink. His face is an inch from the screen now, and he's screaming for Slip Willie at the top of his voice.

The only way we know the race is over is the audio, and the expression on Odds's face as he turns away from the television. It doesn't take a Sherlock Holmes to see his horse has lost; the problem is, we don't know who won.

"What happened?" one of the men in the first row asks.

Odds glares at his questioner for a moment; then his face lights up and I know he's unearthed his best and most plausible excuse. "Damn jockey went to the whip at the final quarter pole, blew the horse out, and had nothing left for the finish."

I can't help smiling. Railbird Ray has trained him well.

"I didn't ask why you *lost*, ass-hole, I want to know who won."

"Ask Flat Store," Odds says, and slinks away, heading for the three-house stairwell.

"Dancing Navajo," I answer the sea of inquiring faces. "Best horse from off the pace at Longacres." God, now *I'm* sounding like Railbird. I have a vicious need to follow Odds up the cell and rub it in a bit—no, rub it in a *lot*—but first a very pleasurable task. Collecting my bet from Greasy Dannie. I amble over to where he is holding court with his fellow Sons of Italy and give him my best winning-sucker grin.

"Hi, Pinocchio. Looks like I hit one."

"My name is Puntacelli," Greasy corrects me.

"Yeah, sure. Look, *dago*, where do *I go* to collect?"

"Get 'em from Odds," he replies, and turns his back on me.

I grab his arm and spin him around without thinking. Several of his soldiers come to their feet and start over our way, but I'm in too deep to back out now. Greasy stares down at my hand on his arm as though I am committing some sort of sacrilege. He can't believe this is happening to him.

Mother is on the scene before Dannie gets his thoughts organized. "Mr. Puntacelli," he says respectfully.

"Evening, Mr. Conroy," Dannie says, returning the insult by dropping the joint handle. It occurs to me that Mother may not be as interested in placating him as it first appears.

"What's the problem?" Mother asks, ignoring the counter-insult.

"No problem if your man keeps his fuckin' arm off me." He looks down as Mother tugs my hand free. "Flat Store won ten cartons at four to one. I told him to pick up his winnings from Odds, who also bet ten cartons at even money. Odds went with Slip Willie, and he owes me the ten. Flat Store is supposed to collect from Odds. Routine. Saves me from placin' one of my boys on front street, luggin' cigarettes around the joint."

The logic is impeccable. The cops will confiscate any cigarettes you have on you that exceed the two-pack limit. I knew that. I didn't know Odds had lost. Even if I had known, I wouldn't have surrendered the personal satisfaction I got by telling Dannie *he* owed *me*; and besides, as far as I know, Odds doesn't have a whole package of Camels to his name.

It strikes me how far out of line I've gotten. I have a quick flash of Flat Store going through the safety screen, and a cold sweat pops out on my back. Jesus, what am I trying to do, get killed? The next thought is, why hasn't something happened already? That question gets answered with a quick check of the area; we're surrounded by the crew from 3-J-5. I suppose if I were honest, I'd admit I was counting on their support, at least subconsciously. I don't feel real good about myself right now, I conclude.

Unanimous, my conscience agrees.

"Flat Store?" Mother is speaking firmly. "You get your cigarettes from Odds, as Mr. Puntacelli suggested." He nods at Greasy. "Sorry for the misunderstanding."

"People have been sorrier," Greasy mutters for the benefit of his audience. "Your man puts his hand on me again, *Mr. Conroy,* and we got serious troubles ... and by the way, the name is Greasy."

Mother grasps my elbow and steers me away from the knot of cons drawn up around us. When we reach the stairwell I tell him, "Thanks, Mother. I guess I lost my head."

"Nearly," he agrees with a dry smile.

In the cell, Odds has a pitiful seventeen packs of cigarettes laid out on his bunk. He points to them and says, "I'm eighty-three packs short. I'll hustle them up for you in the morning."

The entire crew is following the conversation. Dog is fuming. "You idiot, Odds. What were you doing betting with Greasy Dannie? We agreed, we made a gentleman's *a-g-r-e-e-m-e-n-t,* not to become involved with anything that might endanger the horse-racing scam." He turns his anger on me. "And you're included in this, Flat Store. We're supposed to be keeping a low profile, and the next thing I know, you're as much as calling Greasy Dannie 'Fettuccini Face.' You *fuck-head.* You, of all people, should know that's war talk with the Italian clique."

Odds has sense enough to keep his mouth shut, but I open mine out of reflex. "Look, Dog, it was just—"

He cuts me off. "I don't want to hear some bullshit excuse. You fucked up, Flat Store, and that's all there is to it."

Now Mother jumps on me. "No, that's not all. I have a few additional comments." His voice is the sad, flat tone of the executioner as he reads the death warrant aloud. "If we had become involved with the minor riot that was setting up with the Italians, we'd have been out of business, even if we'd won the war. We can't run the computer from C-seg." He's shaking his head sadly. "If you can't do anything constructive, Flat Store, please remember you're not the only person affected by your actions anymore. And, aside from those of us in the cell, there are the Turners, who also have a large investment in this project in terms of their time ... and the fact that they've disrupted their lives to help us with this." Now Dog's anger makes a lot of sense.

Need I mention Mary? the little voice reminds me.

While I'm trying to come up with an apology, Mother continues, broadening the scope of this tail-chewing session. "So let's deal with this now. From this moment on, and this goes for everyone in the cell, no more tokes behind the dumpster at the factory, green money in your shoes, and absolutely no more personal bets ... anywhere. It's time to grow up and begin thinking of the future. Right or wrong?"

We're nodding, our heads sunflowers in a windstorm, eager to see the end of this blast before it turns into something more dangerous.

Mother isn't finished with us yet. "I want this project to work, more than any of you can imagine. But I also have hopes it will demonstrate a simple truth. Anything worth having is not only worth working for, but, once the goal is attained, it is certainly worth protecting. You all need to learn to exercise enough common sense to hang on to what you've earned." He pauses, scans the cell in a search for disagreement, and, finding none, continues. "Money or property earned legitimately has a value, or should have a value, different from the money you've gained by other means in the past. You've earned this. There's no need to endanger your gains out of guilt or toss it away on a whim. Can you all see the logic of what I'm trying to tell you?"

Nodding sunflowers.

"Let me tell you what really caused the problem with Greasy. I don't for a minute believe Flat Store set out to create a situation with the Italians. What happened was a result of his penitentiary-grown reflexes. Unconscious habits he's picked up in prison that limited him to a single course of action: reflexes, deadly reflexes."

No one is arguing the point. Mother's dead right again.

He's up on his feet now, totally engrossed in driving home his points. I have the feeling I'm getting a glimpse of a part of Mother I've never seen before. "Reflexes," he says, jabbing his fingers into the air like a man punching buttons on a control panel. "Reflexes. Have you ever noticed when a convict escapes from jail, he's invariably caught at home? When the vice squad wants to fatten up its arrest records, how is it they always know exactly where to find the pimps and whores? When a parole officer wants to bust you, how does he know which bar to go to and when?" He pauses and picks up my blue watch cap.

"Have you ever wondered how every beat cop in America can spot an ex-con who's been recently released from prison?" He waves the cap in the air. "These caps. A prison habit. A symbol of a way of life. A reflex." He stares directly at me. "I have a long list of things I've noticed. If you want to survive when you get out, you'll need to begin trying to shed the habits that will identify you as a cons . . . or lead you into blind alleys in your decision making."

He reaches across the table and snatches the winner's wheel from Odds. "I did you a disservice with this. I'm going to make certain the administration confiscates it soon; I want you to be absolutely positive they don't find any of the other project materials in your possession."

That's the end of that pain in the butt, I'm thinking; the wheel's days are numbered . . . but the hairs on the back of my neck are sending out telegraph messages saying we haven't seen the end of Odds's gambling troubles.

"Anyone figure up how we did on the Dancing Navajo race?" Mother asks, to end the lecture.

"They didn't give the prices on television," Little says. "Something about off-track betting information. It's against the law in this state to broadcast the information until it's at least two hours old."

"Then we'll have to wait on Railbird," Mother says, and does his no-hands leap up into his bunk. He rolls over, facing the wall, and sighs softly.

Jesus, I'm thinking; first a big fight with Cynthia Evans and then the poor guy has to come in here and deal with a cellful of self-destructive cretins.

Three hours pass, and when we add up the totals and I see we've made over eleven thousand dollars apiece for the day, it all seems worthwhile.

For you, at least, huh, Mr. Thoughtful?

I'm struggling into a pair of socks crafted for a Budweiser Clydesdale by a seizure-prone tarantula when I realize there is no sense in my becoming paranoid because Mother insists in leaving Odds in control of our money. It's a simple solution. Stop worrying. Mother said he'd handle it.

34

While I have confidence in Mother's ability to control Odds, I'm starting to wonder if the power extends to Cynthia Evans. She's stepped up the frequency of her visits, and from my visiting-room sources, I gather her attacks are becoming more strident. She is still trying to push Mother into doing something he is obviously dead set against. The romance seems to be flourishing, despite twice-a-week battles, but the upshot of the affair with Miss Evans is turning Mother into a grouch . . . and an attorney. He's spending most of every morning in the legal library, doing God only knows what. I've tried to figure it out by watching him at work, but come away every time with the impression that I've seen nothing more than a lost soul wandering through dusty old law books.

One day I asked Mother if he needed some help with his legal work. I was planning on having Word Dog dust off his attorney's talents and give him a hand. Mother assured me he was thoroughly capable of handling the research himself, and when I asked him where he'd received his legal training, he snapped, "Minnesota." And that, of course, was the end of the conversation.

Since then, I've tried to curb my curiosity. Mother, after all, deserves some privacy, and if I want to tell myself the truth, it has been a pretty one-sided friendship, even if I just isolate the financial aspects. I don't have a precise breakdown, but I believe I have around fifty thousand dollars in the bank. I can't get an exact figure at the present because the time on the phone with the Turners has become extremely limited, thanks to some more of Stonemann's little helpers being assigned to the factory. BOP regulations prohibit a private, unmonitored bank account, since you aren't supposed to run a business in prison. Correspondence with the First National Bank of Washington might cause some suspicions in the mailroom, particularly if I started receiving monthly statements. Though 50K is a ballpark figure, I like the shape of the ballpark. If I can get out, Mary and I are very close to a substantial down payment on a home.

Time to get to work. I'm out of the cell, heading down the hill, when Blabbermouth stops me. "Your horse, Dancing Navajo, won again last night, huh?"

"For the hundredth time, Blabbermouth, Dancing Navajo is *not* my horse. I bet on him once, that's all."

"Sure, Flat Store, whatever you say. And the owners aren't Dog's parents, either." He shoots me a knowing smile, and leaves before I can come up with anything to shut off his rumor machine.

Blabbermouth is right about one thing. Dancing Navajo is burning up the track as an allowance horse, despite Odds's dire predictions. He won the first time out in the higher class, was second in his next outing, but only because he threw a shoe in the homestretch, and last night he won again. Since the race crowd has become aware of him, the prices on Dancing Navajo have been shorter, but he has also managed to bring home 25K in purse money, more than offsetting his training fees and stable costs. Dancing Navajo has become a major portion of my fantasy.

As I near the factory, I turn off the dream machine and start addressing the problems of the morning. No call to Mary today, but I have several problems in the Clean Room that I need to work out with the foreman and convict lead man. After that, there's another special soldering class, and of course the daily problem of correlating the print-outs, Railbird's scratch reports, and the track-surface information from the Turners.

When I reach the factory I go straight to my desk and turn the page on the calendar. Twenty-ninth of June. The season is nearly half over. Despite the slow start, I figure we still have the potential to reach 150K apiece for the year. Not bad, I'm thinking as I open my desk drawer. There is a note from Chief attached to a *National Geographic* magazine.

Flat Store:
Kawasheega found this last night in the officers' coffee mess. You might notice the article on the Puyallup Indians on page 87.

Chief

I open the magazine, scan the article, and can't make head or tail of it. A fleet of Indians in motorized canoes are dropping gill nets into the waters of Puget Sound. I check the picture more closely and see they are just offshore from the prison's honor camp.

Now what?

The bit of mystery adds a hint of spice to the morning but doesn't help my day's schedule, which is gradually starting to fall apart.

Mr. Wheeler comes by looking for Mother. Mr. Burr, the cable-assembly foreman, gave Mother a pass to the legal library an hour ago, but I suppress the impulse to tell Wheeler. He hustles off. Within a few minutes he's stirred up the whole 3-J-5 crew and they are gathered around my desk, all wanting to know where Mother got off to and why. A gaggle of goslings standing at the edge of a pond couldn't appear more pitifully lost.

I put up with the bombardment for as long as I can, and tell them. "Look, it's no big deal. He's up in the legal library."

Noid Benny is suspicious. "Doing what?"

"I don't know; working on his case, maybe." That was a serious error. I'm suddenly surrounded by the worried faces in a hospital waiting room.

"He said he wasn't going to appeal," Odds reminds us. "He's probably decided to bail out on us," he adds in disgust.

Panic brings out cowardice sometimes, but this is the first time I've seen fear arouse anger against a true friend. Dog points out our lack of trust. "At the outset of this noble venture we all swore an intimate fealty to one another. Now, are we prepared to leap to the wildest and most damning conclusion on the advice of a man who cannot outwit a piece of plastic?" He glowers at Odds. "Have you not considered he might be aligning the thunderous power of jurisprudence to avenge the slaying of the Giant? Is it not possible we are as yet unaware of the impact that foul deed has had upon Mother?"

"Hell, Dog, we're all upset about the Giant, but Mother is acting like it might have been his fault," Fast says, tapping one finger to his temple.

"I can tell you one thing," Noid says. "He's acting guilty as hell about *something*." In a heartbeat, Noid is into an advanced stage of his disease.

Unfortunately, Odds has a good grip on something negative, and he can't or won't let go. "Mother is up there right now trying to figure a way out through the courts. He wants to get himself out. Big deal."

"The 'big deal' is being created right here," Fast replies. "If Mother *were* working on his early release, he'd let us know. He's secretive, but he wouldn't leave us high and dry."

Odds can't agree with anybody anymore. "That's crap. Mother is no different from me or anyone else. Get what you can and run with it." I have a fleeting image of Odds sprinting for an airplane with *my* bank account, and the hairs on the back of my neck are standing tall, an honor guard for passing royalty.

"So, Odds. You think Mother is using us?" Big Smith's tone is menacing, then softens as he continues. "If he left us today, he's already given us something we couldn't buy for *any* amount of money. Something we would never have gained on our own."

"Yeah? Like what? A broken-down racehouse and a computer

that's had a run of dumb luck; or is it the few dollars you have in the bank?"

"None of those, Odds," Big Smith says firmly. "He's given us—some of us—back our self-respect."

There is a moment of silence in the room that comes about when a stunning, clear truth hits a muddy disagreement. Little Smith picks up the thread of Big's reasoning. "In your case, Odds, I believe Mother has failed. You're the only person in 3-J-5 who hasn't changed remarkably for the better." Little's statement is followed by another telling silence.

Little is dead right. I'm thinking even Odds can see the truth by now. He doesn't. The winner's wheel is back in his hands like a security blanket.

"You know where Mother let you down, Odds?" I'm back in the conversation. "He overlooked a bit of information I once gave him regarding Lieutenant Creech that applies to you perfectly."

"Yeah, get it over with."

"No matter how fine the emery paper and diligent the worker, there is just no way to polish shit."

The crew is still laughing and giving Odds the needle when I leave. Somebody has to find out exactly what Mother is doing— not that I've come to mistrust him, of course—but just to be, as he might say, "on the safe side."

I meet Mother at the door of the factory. He has a starving lamprey eel affixed to his arm, in the person of Good Ears Kelly. Mother motions toward the classroom and tells me, "Circle the wagons; we've developed a major problem."

I zip back to my area, give the crew a coded emergency whistle, and in less than a minute we are all gathered in the classroom. "Good Ears has some news for us." Mother spits out the words, and I know Good Ears is going to deliver some Bad News.

Good Ears steps to the center of the floor and begins without hesitation. "I got this straight. Greasy Dannie, the Frog, Sid the Squid, and Ballbats Benny are going to hit one of you this evening."

"Who?" I ask, but I already know it isn't me, because the hairs on the back of my neck are taking a nap.

"Odds," Good Ears answers, glancing quickly in the victim's direction.

Noid is right to the point. "Who put out the contract?"

"No contract. A gambling debt Dannie has taken personal, like."

"How large a debt?" Mother inquires calmly, and I'm inventorying my Camels again.

"Four hundred cartons of Camels," Odds answers defiantly. "But this is my problem, and I want all of you to stay out of it."

I'm thinking, sure you do, you little welcher, when a double check of his eyes reveals an incredible agony. . . . My evil thoughts are erased in a micro-second. Now the hairs on the back of my neck wake up, announcing that I'm going to be involved, like it or not. I want to think Odds has faked the pain in his face. Then I realize the tough-guy expression I've been seeing for the last six months was the act. I'm looking through that now, seeing a man so miserable he is probably thinking about suicide. As my sorting machine is making this revelation, another thought surfaces: The reason Odds has been grating on my nerves is because of the misery he has been covering up with less-revealing traits . . . like being a pain in the ass.

Mother pats Good Ears on the back. "Thanks for the information. We'll handle it from here." Good Ears accepts the dismissal and turns to leave.

Fast stops him with a firm hand on his arm. "Don't tell the dagos we're hip to them."

Good Ears is insulted. "I got no truck with the wops. I brought you this because I don't want to see some good guys get ambushed. And if you're smart, now you won't." He shrugs. "The only advice I have is to be careful; they're thirty sets of hands being run by one ass-hole, and he's the one with his reputation on the line. Greasy can't let this slide."

Good Ears leaves, and Mother sends Noid to check the door.

"Clean?" Mother asks.

"Hound's tooth," Noid answers.

Jesus, now they're doing Laurel and Hardy with clichés.

Mother turns to Odds, frowns, and lets out a sigh. The smile that follows belongs to a father who has a son with a preggers girlfriend. "How much did you say you owe Greasy?"

"Four fucking hundred cartons of fucking Camels!" His voice is somewhere between anger and anguish. "And it's *my* fucking business."

"Not true," Mother tells him firmly. "We're all in this, be-cause—"

"Because we're a family, Odds, and even if one of our brothers is a stupid, hardheaded rumpkin, he's still our brother." Little has summed the matter up neatly.

"It's my debt, and I'll get it straight," Odds tells him, but I can see Little's speech has choked him up. "You guys just stay out; I'm telling you I'll get it straight."

Noid is on him. "No, you knucklehead, you can't. If you could have, you would have by now. There aren't four hundred unattached cartons of Camels in this entire prison, and you can't get at the money in the bank. Even if we could find the smokes or get enough green money brought in to cover you, Greasy couldn't accept that. The word's out you're going to get hit for a bad debt; if you don't get hit, Dannie is out of business. Bookies have to collect, Odds, you know that. If they let one man slide, the rest of their clients won't pay up. Most bookies need a small murder every now and then to keep operating." He stops, lowers his voice, and adds, "No two ways about it, Odds, they have to make the hit tonight."

Suddenly, I'm watching the war movie where everything is falling apart at the front and the Pentagon's ace, number-one gen-eral comes into the command post and takes over. Mother even begins with the proper lines for our hero. "Okay, somebody give me the tactical situation. How, when, and where will they attack, what will they have for weaponry, and what is the strength of their reserves?"

I can answer those questions better than anyone. "They'll send someone, a messenger, who will try and lure Odds out of the cell and down onto the Flats. My guess would be the cleaning-equipment storage closet. Once the messenger has him in place,

Greasy will slip around the corner and stick Odds. Frog, Squid, and Ballbat will then pipe him a few times each for good measure."

"Somebody would hear the commotion," Mother objects.

"In the first place, there won't be any commotion. Zip, biff, bam, whack. It's like Batman comics, but just in case, they'll have some other guys in the clique stage a fight at the opposite end of the cell house to draw off the cops. When the gooners roll on the fake fight, Greasy will send a couple more men by where he dropped Odds, and they'll slit his throat and hang around until he bleeds out on the tiles."

Mother is grimacing, so I add, "It won't be very pretty, but it will certainly be effective."

Mother answers so quickly I now know he wasn't upset by the pictures I've been drawing in blood and gore. "I was thinking it is unnecessarily complex."

"Where'd you become an expert on hits?" Noid asks, confirming my suspicions.

"Laos," Mother replies absently. "Anyone have any suggestions?"

Big Smith offers a solution. "I could get Blabbermouth to make a few bombs out of diesel fuel and the ammonium-nitrate fertilizer the grounds crew uses on the warden's lawns. We'll slip one in each of the dago tip's cells and blast them around count time."

Mother grimaces. "You can't kill thirty people just because you happen to be angry with a few. This must be an intelligent, surgical response."

Even Odds doesn't like the idea. "Yeah, man, we can't take thirty lives just like that; there are some good dudes in the Italian clique."

Dog sides with Big Smith. "Big Smith is right. Odds might be, too, but myself, I can't tell them apart. I vote we kill them all and let God sort them out."

"Yeah," Fast agrees. "They all smell alike to me."

Now I can see what's happening. This isn't a planned put-on, but a reflexive way cons release tension—by using sick humor.

"I can't believe this; you have to be the most nearsighted, hardheaded, habit-run, tradition-fueled, reflex-operated bunch since the KKK. We're not going to kill a soul and no one is going to kill Odds." Mother is getting angry, no doubt about it.

"What are we going to do?" Noid is definitely interested; all of the logical solutions have been jokingly covered. Basically the most workable ones, too.

Mother's answer is caustic. "Why don't we try this? Think! We've been training for months to handle situations just like this. Let's sit down, outline the problem, and come up with a solution." He scans the semicircle of shamefaced bumpkins and continues. "Do any of you seriously doubt your ability to out-think these cretins? We have the best weapons in the prison—our minds; now let's get to work and use them."

Dog clears his throat. "We were just funning a little to get rid of the cotton in our mouths, Mother, but I can tell you right now, no matter how much we think on the subject, the only way to deal with Greasy Dannie is to load up and get off first. He's far too stupid to trick."

Dog has expressed my feelings perfectly.

"Mother isn't going to try any tricks and nobody is going after Greasy Dannie but me. I dug this hole, and I'm going to get out of it by myself." Odds looks like he means it, too.

Dog is on his feet, glowering. "Odds, my dear departed pater was the sole proprietor of a dairy farm for the preponderance of his stay on this verdant orb. He labored himself into an early grave, wasting his God-given energy and paper-thin slice of eternity extracting the precious pristine fluid from a bevy of capricious bovines. Dad maintained the only creature in all of the Almighty's creation more ignorant than these simple animals were the the poor misguided souls who caressed their udders for a livelihood." Dog pauses for effect, plucks an imaginary leftover from his beard, and continues. "Now ... I've come to know the heartbreak I presently suffer, which forces me to reevaluate your cerebral capacity and its obvious dysfunctions in the light of your most recent statement." His voice drops to a sorrowful tone as he continues. "It tears at the depths of my immortal soul to discover through the questionable vehicle of a shrimp-faced little artifact like yourself, Odds, that my dear father was in error. *You* are the dumbest animal in all of the known universe. Mary, Mother of Jesus, Odds. If you became embroiled in a three-way debate with a rock and a fence post, you'd come in *fifth!*"

"What did I do?" Odds whines.

"Do? You've done *nothing* yet, but you have, without question, from Alpha to Omega, start to finish, prologue to epilogue, by your asinine show of false bravery, demonstrated less mental acumen than one might reasonably expect from a loose-leaf cabbage." Dog drives a cantaloupe-sized fist into his palm. Sounds like a young cannon going off.

Mother has a forced smile on his face, but he isn't buying any of this. He stands up, white knuckles pushing into his hips, and I'm looking at the drill instructor once again. What follows is a page from Patton's book: a study in planning, mobility and firepower . . . with one small deviation. As Mother lays out his plan of attack, I can see the firepower is all intellectual, but when he's finished, there is absolutely no doubt in my mind he's in for an earthshaking surprise.

I offer my honest evaluation of his plan. "Mother? That scheme is weaker than well water and twice as transparent. No way is Dannie going to get *talked* out of this, even if, as you plan, he's going to be too embarrassed to go after Odds when you've finished with him. Dannie is a killer, and he understands killing; that's it—no frills—just stick something in your problems and they go away."

"I'll be the judge of the strengths and weaknesses of the operation." Mother's tone is out of character. Authoritarian. "If anyone doesn't want to do his part, I'll need to know right now. Anyone want out?" We're all shaking our heads, but I know I've told Mother the truth. This is going to be a Chinese fire drill or there isn't a hawk in the Pentagon. Mother wants to do a modified rehash of his victory over the Booty Bandit, and it just isn't going to work.

"Okay," Mother begins in a soft voice, "listen closely while I go over our roles. As soon as we come in from work, I go to Greasy's cell and tell him I've got the cigarettes for Odds. I'll tell him to meet me after count." He pauses and looks at us, and I'm put in mind of a pitchman I once watched with a pyramid sales scheme. All nods, smiles, and assurances. "Flat Store will then send a message right after count telling the Frog he wants to meet him in the yard and that *he* has the cigarettes. Now, Fast Eddie sends a similar message to Squid to meet him in the gym, saying that *he* has the cigarettes, and so on down the line of Dannie's aides. Now—"

Odds can't take it anymore. "No! Listen, guys, I really appreciate this, but Mother, this plan . . . well, it just *sucks*, and I'm not going to let the bunch of you get involved. Even if this scheme does go down right, you'll still be up against thirty killers for the rest of the time you're here; I can't let that happen because I've been a jerk, an ass-hole who can't keep his word to his friends . . . or even to himself."

"It would have helped if you'd gone ahead and kicked your habit," Little Smith agrees.

"I can tell you one thing, Little. If I live through this, I'll never place another bet in my life."

I have to add: "And Walt Disney will start making porn flicks next month."

"I mean it," Odds replies softly to no one in particular. For a split second, I believe him.

The moment passes.

"It is a nice thought," Little Smith says wistfully.

"If we're finished?" Mother cuts the conversation off. "There is still the matter of using our intellect to make this plan work. Let's go over it one last time and get it right."

"I'm thinking we should be looking for someone to do the last rites," Big Smith quips.

I agree.

I don't remember a phalanx *à la* Alexander the Great's being a portion of Mother's plan, but it is the formation we adopt when we head to the cell house at quitting time. Odds is in the center, with the rest of us loosely grouped around him in the vanguard. Noid Benny is in the lead, and the Dog is at the rear. We must be

35

motivated to military formations by the martial tone of Mother's voice as he drilled the plan into our heads during the last six hours.

I do have to give Odds credit for one thing. He has been arguing against our involvement throughout the meetings. By this time, I can't tell whether he really wants to get himself killed or he actually has some character buried beneath his gambling habit.

When we reach the corridor just before entering the cell house, Noid waves us off to one side. "They're shaking down. Is everyone clean?"

We nod and take a place along the wall as Fast Eddie explains this change in the situation to Mother. "One of Greasy's sleazy moves. He's had a crony drop a note to the cell-house lieutenant saying there's some serious trouble coming down in the cell house and the crew from the cable factory is going to bring in weapons when they return from work. This way, Greasy is assured that his opponents, namely us, are going to be coming onto the battlefield unarmed."

"But we're all in the same boat. Dannie can't get his knives and pipes in either," Mother points out.

"He doesn't drop the note until he has all of his weapons brought in from their stashes on the yard. It's so neat and tidy for

Dannie; he's dead certain anyone coming through this shakedown is going to be unarmed right after the count clears."

"Then he must know Good Ears told us. Makes Good Ears a potential victim, too, doesn't it?" Mother asks.

"I don't think so. This is a routine move when Dannie is getting ready to make a hit. Like all of these so-called penitentiary tough guys, he only wants to play aces, straights, and cinches." I know I'm right. Greasy Dannie is a Santayana character; even his future is reruns.

The cop at the door motions us forward and we're moving though the gauntlet of officers. The conversation dies as we reach the metal detectors and proceed on to the individual pat-down, part of the routine the cops go through just in case someone has brought in a wooden or plastic weapon.

I have never been able to adjust to someone running his hands over my body, and this time is no different. I swear, one of these days I'm going to leave this country and move to one that is so small they don't have to fold the road maps . . . that, or I'm going to have to go straight.

As I clear the last gooner in the line, I glance upward and see Greasy and his hit team standing at the top of the stairwell. I nudge Mother. "Up there."

"Okay, I'm going to go and get the first portion of the diversionary story implanted," Mother says out of the corner of his mouth. I'm wondering if it is this stress that has him affecting the speaking habits of convicts. "You go up to the cell and run the men through the plan one more time."

"Mother, I wish you wouldn't. They're liable to jump you."

"Intellect," he says, tapping the side of his head with his forefinger. "Intellect conquers all."

"The best-laid plans of mice and men . . ." I begin, but he's gone, loping up the stairs to where Dannie lives: a four-man cell he shares with Frog, the Squid, and Ballbats Benny.

I go up the three-house side, mulling over the plan again as I climb. By the time I reach the top range, I have decided this plan doesn't have one chance in a thousand. I'm the last man in the cell, and signal for the others to gather around the table. "Okay,"

I whisper, "Mother wants me to talk everyone through their roles one more time. As soon as he gets back, he's going to start asking questions. Detailed questions."

They nod, but sour faces send much clearer messages. I'm not alone in my distaste for the plan of intellectual assault on bared and sharpened weapons. "Okay, Fast," I begin dutifully, "what's your first detail when the doors rack open after count?"

"I go with you to Greasy's cell and send my messenger, Blabbermouth, in to tell Squid I have the smokes and need to speak with him." He shakes his head. "If he goes for that, he'll go for fried ice cream."

"Look, Fast, I don't believe this will work, either, but Mother's never missed yet."

"Mother is not going to *miss*." Dog is shaking his head sadly. "At best, he's going to get arrested. He meets Dannie right out in the open, like he's planning, and no amount of finesse in the world will prevent someone from seeing the action and telling on him, because he's going to have to get *physical*, as opposed to metaphysical. And even if Greasy does go for the scam about getting paid off, he's still going to have three armed thugs with him."

"Hold everything," Odds says. "There isn't going to be any problem between Mother, Greasy, and the rest of you guys." He pulls a sawed-off baseball bat from beneath his mattress, reaches back in, and extracts a short length of pipe. "I brought these up at noon after Mother laid his dumb-assed plan on us. As soon as the count clears, I'm going straight to Dannie's cell, jump inside, and get this over with one way or another. Win, Place, Show, or rained out, I'll have settled my own business and the rest of you are in the clear—and, more importantly, safe."

Fast opens his mouth to disagree, then turns away. Odds's solution is not only the most logical; it's the only classy way out for him. I fight off a twinge of admiration and start warming up to give him another piece of my mind, when Big Smith hops into the conversation. "Odds, you can't do it. There are four of them, and you won't have a prayer. If we go Mother's route, at least we'll probably all survive."

Noid is poking his hand mirror through the bars, flashing the range. "Mother's coming. Looks like the first part went down okay."

Mother is through the door a second before Range Bull begins rattling the door to announce the 4 P.M. lockup for count. I'm eyeballing a large manila envelope and a copy of the *National Geographic* he has tucked under one arm. Funny, I didn't notice them before; he must have had them hidden in his shirt. "All set for the briefing?" He's smiling as though he still expects this nutty plan to work and prevent the coming of World War III, which, I realize, is no more than half an hour away.

"We've got our parts down, Mother, but"—Fast tips his head in Odds's direction—"he really doesn't want us involved. I think we owe him a chance to explain his idea. It's as dumb as yours, but there'll be a lot fewer casualties."

"Man down, 4-J-1," a voice screams from the other part of the cell house. A split second later: *"Men* down, 4-J-1." I hear the whistle of an officer's body alarm, then the thunder of the goon squad, rolling into the cell house.

I glance at Mother. He's wearing a sad, Mona Lisa smile, but his eyes are dancing Irish jigs on either side of his nose. The *National Geographic* catches my eye again—rather, the bits of hair and faint spots of blood on one edge do—then I lock eyes with Mother. "Greasy?"

He confirms my growing suspicion. "Greasy, Frog, Squid, and Ballbats Benny."

Noid has picked up on the interchange, and his eyes are bouncing back and forth between Mother and myself, two balls in an arcade machine gone amok. "What happened?"

"Early on in the preoperation planning process I discovered a fatal flaw in the plan of attack. A minor adjustment was necessary, and to avoid having you men sitting around with nothing to do but worry while I worked out an alternative, I"—his face splits into a grin—"conned you."

"You what?" Noid asks.

"Conned you. When it became apparent I could not win on

an intellectual level, I took the leaf from Patton's book and got there 'fustus with the mostus'; I think it worked."

Dog is incredulous. "You killed them?"

"Of course not. I did, however, separate three clavicles, fracture several fibulae and tibiae, then toss in a sprinkling of broken ribs. I'm out of training," he admits shyly; "I'm afraid I knocked them out in the process."

"What happened with the bullshit about outwitting cretins?"

"Yeah, polished minds over gleaming metal and all that."

"Wait one fat-assed Texas minute here. What happened to all of the noble philosophy about using our brains instead of violence?"

Mother shrugs. "Sometimes, the only viable cure for a mad dog is to shoot it or otherwise put it out of its misery." He grins boyishy. "Mission accomplished."

"Jesus. This means war with the dagos," I sputter.

Mother disagrees. "I don't believe so. Greasy and his hit squad will require medical services on the mainland. They'll be med-evac'd out shortly. Besides, they'll be unable to identify their attacker." He pulls my watch cap out of the manila envelope and tosses it to me. I stretch it open and see a pair of slanted eyeholes peering back up at me. "If I understand the research I did in the law library, the BOP policy statement says these men have to be transferred unless their attacker is identified and apprehended. A rule to prevent such ongoing feuds, I suppose."

Dog is grinning. Me too. Mother has laid this out perfectly and executed the only possible plan that would solve every one of Odds's problems. And I now know he made his decision in the first hour of this morning's meeting, too.

"You'll still get a roust. Greasy knows who hit him. Stevie Wonder could figure that one out," Fast tells him.

"I disagree. How could Greasy ever admit it was one man, armed with a *National Geographic*, who took him and three bodyguards? Not hardly, Fast. They'd get laughed out of the system. It's over and done with, and you have a new lease on life." Mother gives him a double cliché as punishment.

We swarm over Mother, shaking his hand and passing out the well-deserved compliments. Odds pushes next to Mother and hands him the winner's wheel. "Take it. I can't think of a better way to say thanks . . . to all of you. I'm never going to gamble again. Here, Mother, take this damn thing. I swear I won't need it."

Mother pushes the wheel back into his hand. "Hang on to it. We still might need it for Stonemann."

I can't keep quiet. I want to nail something down. "Odds? Did I hear you right? You're through betting?"

"Swear to God, Flat Store, no more bets, except the ones you give me to phone out."

"Okay," I tell him, "I'll buy that, but I need to ask you something else, and I want a straight answer. Have you given the Turners any bets we weren't aware of, or . . . had any money sent anywhere but to our bank accounts?"

Odds denies the indictment. "Nope on both counts, but I can understand your mistrust. I vote we put someone else in charge of the bets and money from now on."

"No." Mother is emphatic. "You have a job in this operation, and we expect you to keep on doing it."

I find myself nodding in agreement with the others.

Range Bull is in front of the cell. "Let's see the hands. Somebody beat all the dog shit out of Greasy Dannie and his three sidekicks." He's staring at Mother, and ignores our knuckles as we present them for inspection. "Conroy?" He asks for Mother's hands, and I'm thinking, uh-oh. Here it comes.

"Yes, sir?" Mother lifts his hands to eye level and rolls them from side to side.

"Conroy, if you never went over to four house just before the count, I sure as hell didn't see you coming back." He grins broadly and walks away whistling. The whop-whop-whop of the helicopter blades provide an interesting rhythmic counterpoint to Range Bull's tune. "Camptown Races"!

It's becoming extremely difficult to identify the enemy around here.

I can't go to sleep. A conversation I had with Mother six weeks ago is bothering me. I slip the sorter into past/reference, and relive the day again.

For nearly an hour now I have been sitting in the bleachers, nothing to do but dodge parole loads from the circling gulls and fight off the attacks of a mosquito who apparently attempted a sex act with a heavy canvas punching bag and bent his tools out of shape. These two annoyances, coupled with Mother's uncharacteristic tardiness, are beginning to irritate me. Fortunately, the weather is nice, and the gulls, harbor seals, and a pod of passing orcas are having fun, playing in this rarest of all things, a sunny day on Puget Sound.

While Mount Rainier surveys this peaceful scene with appropriate majesty and calm, I'm becoming worried to the point of nausea. Up to now, Mother has had some sort of private business with everyone in the cell. Except me. This morning he made an appointment to meet me here, and now he's late, and I'm worried.

There are times when the depth of your faith astounds me.

Before I can reply to my conscience, Mother appears, jogging across the yard in the peculiar military gait he affects when something serious needs to be dealt with. Before I can work my concerns into a full-blown attack of terror, he has reached the bleachers. An effortless sprint to the top and he arrives at the same time that the hairs on the back of my neck begin the second movement of an African voodoo dance. "Sorry, James, I'm a bit late."

"James?"

"Flat Store seems to stick in my throat lately," he says innocently.

"The only person on earth who calls me James is Mary," I remind him.

"Ahhhh, yes. Mary." Now his innocence is staged to the point of being laughable. He's tricked me into bringing Mary into the conversation. "Just by coincidence," he continues, "I want to discuss something with you that involves Mary."

The cold knot in my stomach allows me a raspy, "It's your nickel."

"I want you to start giving Mary a couple of bets each week." He pauses, recording the flight of my eyebrows toward my retreating hairline. "No more than three bets a week at the most."

"Why?" I can hear the anguish in my voice. I see the distrustful tone of my response register in his eyes.

"Well ..." He pauses, and right now I need very badly to hear him say we are not going to cut the others out with some side bets. I don't hear it. "I have reasons I can't share with you, James, but believe me, it is important you give Mary the bets and keep it our secret."

"I'll have to work through Odds."

"No. Nothing by telephone. I want you to send her the bets by letter."

The next question is sticking in my throat. "How much does she bet?"

"Two dollars on each one you give her," he tells me, and I catch a hint of a smile tugging at the corners of his mouth.

"I'll do it, but have you forgotten Stonemann is reading my mail? With the winner's wheel getting to be a joke, I don't think we'll be confusing him very much."

"If you brag about the wheel and he checks it against the results—and he should; he's going to Longacres every afternoon now—he just might be convinced the wheel is producing all the right answers." The hairs on the back of my neck are calling him a liar, but I dutifully go for the story. If it is a story. Who the hell can tell with this gentleman?

"Okay. I'll do whatever you say."

"And keep it our secret? You, Mary, and me?"

"You got it."

I don't have to run this transaction through the sorting machine to determine Mother is up to something very different this time. My staring makes him uncomfortable. If *I* were a gentleman, I'd drop the subject, trust him, and do as I am told. I discover something about myself when my mouth flies open and I say: "Look, this involves Mary. I want to be sure there are no repercussions for her down the line."

His pained expression is all the chastisement I need. "Please, James. Don't even consider that I might do something that would endanger Mary. It would be out of the realm of possibility."

I apologize with: "When do I start?"

"This afternoon. Write Mary and tell her to bet the money on Mark's Man in the seventh race the day after tomorrow. Don't mention how much; you can tell her it's only a two-dollar bet on the phone."

I don't understand why I can't do the whole thing over the phone, but I've used up my interrogation rights already. "Mark's Man is a cinch. The 1360 had him down for less than a three-dollar payoff. We aren't even going to bet him."

"I know. The perfect horse for my plan. None of the horses I give you will be doing much better." He looks into my face, apologizing. "You'll do it, then? This afternoon for certain?" The plea in his tone affirms my evaluation: This is important, personal.

"Don't worry; the letter will be in the box by the 4 P.M. count."

He sighs in relief and turns to face the Sound. We're both watching as a sea gull swoops down, has a minor squabble with another gull over an unattached oyster, wrests it away, and struggles into the air. He climbs above the tarmac road that runs around the perimeter fence. A couple of hundred feet up now, he drops it, and the shellfish explodes when it hits the road. Before the bird who dropped it can swoop down and claim his prize, another gull dives and begins trying to gobble down the succulent meat. The owner attacks, and their features blur into a swirl of grays and whites; they're doing battle, climbing in the convection currents of an updraft. Up and up they go, each seeking a height advantage over the other. As they continue to climb, a third gull flutters down and daintily consumes the oyster.

"It's so easy to become lost in the struggle, you lose sight of the goal," Mother mutters absently; then he's gone, jogging down the steps and across the yard.

Reliving the conversation with Mother has passed most of the night, I notice. My watch gives me the good news. Five minutes to six. The lights will go on at any moment and we'll have the cell meeting Mother announced as the lights went out last night. I couldn't detect any reason for the meeting, or anything in his tone that should have made me worry the night away, but nevertheless I've been awake, trying to sort out what his next move might be.

I'm hoping it has something to do with the notes I'm sending Mary, because I'm starting to feel like I'm doing something dishonorable to the rest of the crew with those outside bets. True to his word, Mother has only given me two or three bets a week, and on the cheapest horses, but each time, the hairs do their number.

The lights flick on, and I'm immediately struck by the change in 3-J-5 from a year ago. As opposed to the generally predictable grunting, groaning, scratching, and farting, plus the lethargic, almost posthibernational stirring of the denizens, 3-J-5 is awake, and instantly the scene of organized, meaningful activity. Everyone is up, cleaning his area and moving smoothly through the rotation of dress, bathroom, and cell cleaning that have become the hallmark of our programmed day. I know we'll be in place for the meeting in ten minutes and it's time for me to get moving. I'm next at the toilet, and my bladder is telling me the timing is exquisite.

Odds catches my eye as I'm washing up. His personality has undergone a complete metamorphosis. He's become a likable, calm, and incredibly methodical, thoughtful person. Sagittarius to Virgo without changing his birthday. When he lost his winner's wheel to the gooners a few days back, he was the picture of tranquility. Mother had to remind him to put up a bit of an argument when they took his plastic mistress. While I'm sure Odds has had some stressful moments since the Greasy incident, he's definitely kicked the habit, as near as I can tell. Now instead of twirling the wheel at count time, he takes a nap . . . and his face is beatific.

Odds calls the meeting to order, but I can see Mother has already established its direction. An inventory of the men reveals as many confused faces as one would expect, so I can write off a mass conspiracy as the reason for the early assembly.

Odds does an overstaged nose count and grins. "Good. We didn't lose anyone." He clears his throat nervously and continues. "Mother has asked me to chair this meeting, and I suppose, for all intents and purposes, it is going to be a treasurer's report."

Uh-oh, I tell myself, but there is no movement among the others, and the hair at the back of my neck is still dozing. Good news from Odds?

"Ahh, the melodic sound of tinkling coins." Fast is wringing his hands and doing a passable imitation of a venal moneylender. It strikes me that I busted him watching *The Merchant of Venice* on PBS last week. His pose completes the connection. Fast has become a bit greedy. I wonder what he's going to do with his money. He interrupts my analysis with: "M-o-n-e-y, the optimal method of gaining my undivided attention."

Odds grins self-consciously and opens a yellow legal pad. "It has been two months since our last financial meeting, so Mother has suggested I bring you up-to-date."

No comments. Odds plucks a pencil from behind his ear and aims it at the notebook. "I don't have anything of earthshaking importance to say, but I thought you emerging tycoons might be interested in knowing the money-market accounts I put your funds into have issued the quarterly interest payment. Better than 15 percent!"

"Surely our bounty is secure. Might not that high rate of interest amount to a high-risk venture?" I know Dog's lost. Me too.

I make a mental note to start learning something about the world of finance.

"Your money is better than secure. We have each accrued $3,825 in interest!"

"For doing nothing?" This is a new one on Noid.

"So what's my balance?" Big Smith asks.

"You don't know?" Odds is stunned.

"Same as Little's, I imagine." He turns to Little Smith.

"Don't ask me." Little throws up his hands. "I haven't the slightest."

"Noid?" Odds asks.

"Beats me, man. Taking care of the money is your job."

I try a couple of quick computations and put my balance at around 125K.

Odds is deathly pale. "No one has been double-checking me?" The question ends with a squeak, which announces the lump in Odds's throat.

"You gave us your word, Odds," Fast Eddie reminds him. "If you aren't gambling, there's no need to keep tabs on you. Hell, man, you're one of us. We trust you."

The unexpected vote of confidence has Odds's eyes watering, and he has to turn away from us. Mother picks up the pad. "There is $168,925 in each account."

"That much." Noid Benny whistles.

"Allllll right, Odds," Fast says, and claps him on the back.

That *is* all right, I'm thinking . . . and maybe Odds is too.

The doors rack open for chow, and we troop off, leaving Odds alone with his thoughts.

After breakfast, Mother and I walk down to the factory, and I try not to notice the hitch in his step as we pass the smokestack. The brief slumping of his shoulders is harder to pass over. Mother sighs, and we walk the rest of the way to work in silence.

The tinny-sounding P.A. speakers are rattling as we enter the factory. "All immates and foremen assemble in the number-two packaging area."

I glance at Mother, and he answers the unspoken question.

"We're going to get an 'attaboy' speech from Warden Stonemann."

He's right. As we're gathering around the packing and shipping tables, Stonemann and Wheeler are already pushing their way through the crowd. They mount the table via a stepstool, and I'm wishing I'd known they were coming, so I could have sawed through at least one of the legs.

Wheeler introduces Stonemann as though we loyal subjects had never met the king or visited his dungeons. He is so lavish in his praise during the introduction of the warden, I'm wondering if Stonemann can see through him as easily as I do. Here is a man having an affair with the boss's wife; and they're trysting in a closet with cellophane doors. Wheeler gets away with the introduction without laughing out loud, and now Stonemann is telling us what a fine fellow Wheeler is for winning the Bureau of Prisons/UNICOR quarterly award for outstanding quality control and production. Our factory had the lowest customer-rejection rate of any factory working Department of Defense contracts, convict or civilian!

Wheeler accepts the plaque with an open, almost adoring smile. What an actor. What a cold-blooded son of a bitch. What a typical bureaucrat.

After the standard banal congratualtory speeches that Stonemann has prepared with a thesaurus and a crossword dictionary so he can astound the natives, Wheeler leads him down off the table, heading for Wheeler's office.

As Stonemann passes Mother, he tosses him the winner's wheel. "Nice try, ass-hole."

"Nice try, yourself, Mr. Warden, sir." Mother is grinning, but the tone is vicious.

Stonemann stops and stares into Mother's face. "You're an ass-hole, Conroy. An arrogant fucking ass-hole."

Mother grins, and replies, "My, such language."

Stonemann is quivering with rage. "Listen, you arrogant bastard, you watch your fucking mouth!" He is starting to gulp air, but I'm watching his hand edge toward the bulge in his jacket.

"You're an ass-hole." The voice is near a scream, and the other cons are starting to stare.

"Redundant. Profane." Mother is shaking his head, a disapproving schoolmaster in the old western movie. "You've been hanging around Longacres' backside too much. You sound just like a stable hand."

"Who told you I go to Longacres?"

"Fred Parker," Mother shoots back.

Stonemann sputters, and I see a struggle going on for a last grip on sanity. Wheeler tugs at his sleeve, and Stonemann turns and follows him away in a stiff-legged shuffle.

I let out my breath and turn to Mother. Before I can get out either a word of caution or an angry admonishment, he begins whistling "Camptown Races." Stonemann stops in mid-shuffle, takes another huge gulp of air, and hurries off like a man with a broom handle hidden in his nether regions.

"Why are you agitating the Philistines?" Dog asks.

"Was I agitating?" Mother's tone is mischievous.

"Was I agitating?" Dog mimics him in a childlike voice. "One of these days, Stonemann is going to blow all the fuses, Mother. He's lost his ability to deal with you. *Please,* don't push him any more."

"I don't need to push him," Mother assures Dog. "He's ready to jump all by himself." Mother spins and walks away, whistling "Camptown Races" again.

I have to break into a trot to catch up with him. "Do you want me to cancel the letter to Mary with the bets for the week?"

"No. Just for the fun of it, let's keep sending her the cheap horses. At least for a couple of weeks."

"But we have the wheel back and there're only two weeks left in the season. Besides, Stonemann didn't buy any part of that wheel business."

"He bought everything I needed him to, lock, stock, and barrel." His fingers curl into a tight fist. "Stonemann's mine, Flat Store. Mine and the Giant's."

Poor Stonemann, I find myself thinking. If he did figure out what we're actually doing, he wouldn't believe that either. What the heck; as Mother says, it couldn't hurt to carry his scheme through. Whatever it is.

I sit down and begin the letter.

Dear Woman,
There are some horses you might want to bet on: Mad Mike in the sixth race, day after tomorrow; then . . .

Mother's agitated, excited state over our next bet has begun to worry even Odds. Three days left in the season, and suddenly, Mr. Conservative is lobbying to put down one hundred thousand dollars on a single race! The horse Mother is salivating over is Suzie's Sister. She's running tonight in the last stakes race of the season. I had a brief argument with Mother over the amount of the bet, taking the position that a wager of this size would depress the pari-mutuel pools to the point where there would be practically no return on the investment, even if we win. Mother countered with an article from the *Daily Racing Form* that estimates the handle for this, the last big race of the season, will exceed three hundred thousand, which would give us a return on the wager of nearly two to one, even after we bet the horse down from the thirty-five-to-one price it carries on the morning odds line. Apparently no one but Mother and the computer think this horse has a prayer.

As Mother explained the strategy, I gradually became convinced; but since then, I have been having flashbacks to a film out of the 1940s where a noble band of thieves decides to go for the Last Big Score, even though the group's already amassed enough money for retirement. Even the hairs on the back of my neck remember what happened to those guys, and they couldn't even see the screen at the time.

I look up at the clock. Nine-fifteen A.M. Right on schedule, Odds comes in from outside, where he has been listening to Railbird Ray's scratch report on a hand-held radio. Odds is wearing a frown that, if his new attitude toward betting is unchanged, means Suzie's Sister is in the race, and so is our hundred thou.

Mother and Odds have a brief discussion; then Mother sends Odds to watch for the gooners. Mother sits down at the desk and opens up the telephone. The responsibility for phoning out the bets mysteriously changed hands last Wednesday. We never asked for an explanation, and, judging by Mother's ever-increasing proclivity for secrecy, we wouldn't have received an illuminating answer anyway. I've decided Mother has discovered that one of Stonemann's informants is watching, and so he has decided to handle the sensitive operation himself.

Mother completes the call, snaps the book shut, and stands up wearing a very satisfied smile. The Cheshire cat on payday.

Mr. Johnson, the Clean Room foreman, is motioning for me to come over; I open the desk drawer to gather up my micrometer and gauges and discover an Inmate Request Form attached to a note for Mother. I can't help reading the note:

> Mother,
> Here is the transfer request to the prison camp you asked me to fill out. I asked Kawasheega for *His* impression of the idea, and He told me, "If the White Eyes warden is foolish enough to send you out where you will have free contact with the brother Puyallup Indians and their delightfully fast motorized canoes, you would be terribly remiss if you stayed around to complete the balance of your eighty-year sentence."
>
> As you will note, Kawasheega has been studying English at the Celestial Mission School and has attained Great Wisdom. While I do not believe your plan to get me out to the camp has a peace treaty's chance in Washington, D.C., of succeeding, I am nevertheless pleased you are thinking of me. Let's give it a shot.
>
> Thanks, Mr. Conroy. The Earth Mother must be proud to share your name.
>
> Chief

I fold the mysterious note and request for transfer and carry them over to Mother. "You got a wire from the Chief."

Mother opens the folded papers, scans them and tucks the

note into his shirt pocket and attaches the request to his clip-board. "Looking to pull off a miracle?" I ask.

"Nope. Trying to mind my own business." He's grinning and I'm blushing. I keep forgetting I taught him that line.

"Mother!" Noid's voice slices into our exchange. "We have a serious problem."

"Stonemann has been listening in on our tap?" Mother asks calmly.

Noid blanches. "How did you know?"

"Wheeler told me last Tuesday. Stonemann brought in an ex-pert and figured out a way to beat your warning system." Mother sounds bored.

"Why didn't you tell me—Wait a minute, you say Wheeler told you?"

"Right. He's still trying to get the tapes of his conversations with the warden's wife. He thought he could make a trade. I told him, sure, he could, and he coughed up the news about the tap."

"Did you give him the tapes?"

"Copies. He didn't ask for the originals until it was too late."

Noid is biting his lip, about one more quiver away from a pout. "Why didn't you tell me? I could have beaten the expert's counter-tap with a cutout."

"No need to go through the trouble. It's so late in the season I decided Stonemann's worst move would be to shut us down; we'd only have lost a few days." Mother has to be the worst liar I've ever seen.

"We should have protected ourselves. We're committing *fel-onies* here. Wiretap alone is worth ten years." Noid is dancing on one foot to the Latin rhythm of his clicking eyeballs. "Felonies, Mother."

"Isn't murder a felony? How about fraudulent use of govern-ment funds? Even his clam scam has to be a gross misdemeanor. Relax, Noid. We have him by the . . ." He turns to me for assis-tance.

"Short and curlies."

Noid is pressing him. "Does he know we've tapped the lines *in his office?*"

"Wheeler didn't mention it." Mother yawns and stretches. "Quit worrying. Stonemann certainly isn't acting as though he knows, is he? He's been burning up the lines to his bookie."

I can't help staring. Stonemann is betting the horses I've been giving Mary! Now he is obviously taking the rest of our bets also. "He must be doing pretty damn well," I grumble.

"Fair," Mother admits as he rocks one hand from side to side. "He bets everything he wins copying us right back into losing horses. He makes a bet on each and every race."

"He's taking our winners and still losing?" Noid asks excitedly.

Mother grins. "He's worse off than he was a year ago. Stonemann is flat broke, overextended on credit, and the bookies are riding his tail."

"He's going to get well with the thirty-five-to-one shot he just heard you phone out," Noid comments.

"I don't believe so." Mother replies. "Remember, our hundred thousand will drive the price down near two to one. Stonemann will be thinking he has a chance to make enough to get out of debt . . . then our money will hit the pools and he'll be watching the bottom go out of the price on his horse. The shock may kill him. He'll do well to double his money, and that won't get him anywhere. . . . He'll have to plunge some more, and I don't have to tell you what will happen then. He'll be wiped out." Mother's smile is threatening to turn sadistic. "But for a few tantalizing moments, Stonemann is going to be a happy man, like a farmer who just got a loan, and then the roof will cave in on him."

"Christ, I'd like to be there when he sees the thirty-five-to-one on the tote board start sinking out of sight. He'll flip out completely."

"I hope so," Mother comments.

"He won't be able to handle it, Mother. This could get serious."

"I hope so."

Without my noticing, Odds has joined us. "As long as Stonemann thinks he's made a little, all he's going to have on his mind is the next race," he says. "Believe me, I know gamblers." He shakes his head sadly. "Sick monks."

We're in the cell, hunched over the radio as if it were a witches' boiling caldron. "One Hundred Thousand Dollars." Fast Eddie is capitalizing the letters as he spits them out through clenched teeth. "I know I can afford to lose an eighth of that amount, but Jesus, I can't bear the thought."

Odds offers some advice. "We've made a calculated wager based upon the best information available, a process that has worked well for the entire summer. Relax, Fast. The 1360 says we have an 87 percent chance of winning."

"Yes, Fast." Noid tells him. "The worst we can do is lose. If *we* lose, *Stonemann* will get zapped. He's on Suzie's Sister too."

Mother is musing, a da Vinci–quality smile reflecting his thoughts.

Odds continues. "According to what we heard on the tap today, Stonemann has borrowed every nickel he can lay his hands on, browbeat the credit-union manager out of forty-five hundred dollars over his limit, and taken a second mortgage on his home in California."

"Yeah, with thirty-five-to-one on the tote board, Stonemann must be approaching orgasm." Dog grins.

"I can't wait till our hundred thousand hits the pool. He's going to have a heart attack when Suzie's Sister hits even money."

"It's already happened," I remind them. "The race was run a couple of hours ago."

Railbird Ray scratches his way through the static, and I notice Mother has joined the cluster around the card table for the first time since early May. Even the two minutes Railbird takes to tell us what a great day of handicapping he's had, how the auto shops he advertises are the best in all creation, and, in general, how fortunate we are to be able to listen to a nifty son of a gun like he is—none of this seems to take the edge off Mother's interest.

Mercifully, Railbird doesn't take much extra time to tell the world how handsome he is, and he's back at the track with the call for the seventh race, *our* race.

"Come on, Suzie's Sister," Mother whispers.

Railbird is in rare form, I'm thinking as he begins. He may have discovered a nasal spray that overcomes his allergy to humility. At least he doesn't sound like he's talking through an iron pipe tonight. "In this, the feature race of the evening, six and one half furlongs for a field of ten three- and four-year-old fillies and mares, Railbird gave you Morning Star as his first pick. Unfortunately, she was a late scratch by the track veterinarian. Apparently, Morning Star has a hairline fracture of her left cannon bone, and the vet, Dr. Ford, whom you will remember . . ." and Railbird is off into one of his endless and meaningless digressions.

"What size shoes was the vet wearing, you oaf?" Dog is furious. "Give us the result, you dingbat."

The radio responds. "The old Railbird's second pick, Millie's Friend, had a jockey switch at the last minute. Now, fans, you know how the Railbird feels about those eleventh-hour changes. I remember the time, and I'm sure all of you do, too, back in '66, it was—I think—a horse called Gray Pappa . . . gee, no, that was in '67—" Railbird is off the air.

Worried glances are put to rest by Fast Eddie. "Just the producer telling him to get on with it."

Fast must be right. Railbird is back on his job. "Out of the gate it was all Honey Blaze with an easy lead. Millie's Friend and Queen City shared second, three lengths back. At the first quarter pole, Honey Blaze stood off an early challenge by Millie's Friend as Queen City began to close rapidly, with Suzie's Sister right behind her."

Fast is singing. "Get up, Little Suzie. Get *up!*"

"At the top of the stretch the horses are four wide in a cavalry charge to the finish. As they come down to the wire, Suzie's Sister moves up between horses on the rail and Honey Blaze duplicates her move in the center of the track. At the wire, they're neck and neck for the photo finish." Railbird pauses.

"Who won?" Mother rasps out.

"And now a word from Harry's Transmissions . . . no? Very well, the producer is waving at me, folks, so here's the winner. Suzie's Sister, paying $72.20, $38.40, and $16.20. Boy! Could the old Railbird use a handful of those tickets."

"Christ." Odds's hands are shaking as he tries to punch the figures into his calculator. "Let me get this straight. I'm not going to believe it until I see the numbers."

Mother reaches across the table and places his hand gently on Odds's arm. "Put it away, Odds. I didn't get the bet down."

"What!" I sound strangled. I am! I *saw* Mother phone our bet out to the Turners.

"I'm sorry. I didn't get the bet placed," Mother reiterates to the circle of shocked faces.

I don't like the first thought into my head. Mother just made his attorney money on Suzie's Sister and froze us out. But why? Any one of us would have given him our whole share. When in doubt, find out. Mother gave me that advice more than once. "I'd swear I saw you phone the Suzie's Sister bet out."

"No." Mother is slowly shaking his head. "You saw me make a call to Willie's Arco station, where I undoubtedly left a very confused attendant talking to himself. Stonemann is the only one who got to the track with the bet."

"You gave Stonemann Suzie's Sister? He got down and we didn't?" Noid is furious. "If he bet and *we* didn't . . . ahhh, shit. That's what *did* happen. The horse paid over thirty-five-to-one. Stonemann is rich!"

Mother answers the pinched sets of eyebrows and beady eyes with: "You're jumping to conclusions again. What the warden heard me say is the following. 'Put it all on Queen City. She's a cinch.' Then I immediately hung up." He pauses as we assimilate the information. Grins of realization are spreading around the table when Mother adds a sobering addendum. "Get ready for a rip-up shakedown. The race was over nearly three hours ago, and by now Warden Stonemann is back, probably drunk, and certainly madder than hell. I expect the goon squad here in less than ten minutes."

"Why?" Dog is shaking his head. "Stonemann will have to believe we took a bath right along with him."

"No. Not really." Mother is pensive, but his eyes are glittering again. "After he left for the track, I had the institution's mail runner slip a note under the door to his office. He'll discover it when he stops by to put his pistol in the safe." Mother's lips are struggling against a grin and losing.

Noid has recovered. "What did the note say?"

Mother leans back and closes his eyes, and we watch him savoring each syllable as he reads the note from the inside of his eyelids.

Dear Mr. Warden Stonemann, sir:
Queen City, my ass, you ignorant piece of offal. The computer you were kind enough to buy me picked *Suzie's Sister!*
Have a nice evening.

Mother

"Whew!" Big Smith whistles. The echo of the sound is unnaturally loud as it bounces back off the cell-house wall.

"Hold it down, Big," I whisper; then I realize the problem is not Big's volume level, it is the cell house itself. Graveyard still.

The quiet doesn't last more than a second. "I don't care what *you* think, Lieutenant. I'm the fucking *warden* of this shit heap and I want that cock sucker Conroy down here right fucking *now!*" Even in the slurred falsetto I recognize Stonemann's voice.

We're all at the bars, straining to hear the lieutenant's response, when Mother says calmly, "Get up on your bunks and stay out of this."

Mother is on his feet, zipping up his field jacket, looking for all the world like a man about to take an evening stroll in the park.

"Stay out of what?" Noid asks.

"Up on your bunks ... now ... please," Mother responds.

Feet are pounding up the metal steps of the three/four cell-house stairwell. Mother is following their progress, his lips keeping mute count as shoes slap on the concrete of the landings.

A mumbled rush of conversation, the jangle of keys, the clink of metal against metal; then the key box at the end of the range bangs open. Mother hurries to the front of the cell, finger to his lips. "Stonemann," he whispers.

The warden skids to a stop in front of the cell, stares in at Mother, and makes a visible effort to regain his composure. The reek of whiskey wafts into the room as Stonemann gasps for breath. His face is a dusky purple over the bright red of his throat. His eyes begin to flick from side to side, and I notice flecks of spittle in the corners of his mouth.

"Good evening, Warden Stonemann, sir," Mother greets him.

"Too much, Conroy. That was too fucking much." His hand is clawing beneath his coat. It reappears, clutching a snub-nosed .38 police special.

"Nice little peashooter you have there." Mother snickers. "Be careful you don't shoot yourself in the foot."

"*Warden Stonemann.*" Lieutenant Smith's voice is a pistol shot.

Stonemann's eyes do not waver from the center of Mother's chest as the pistol begins an upward arc.

I can't help myself; I'm on my feet trying to pull Mother away from the cell door. He gives me a sharp jab in the ribs that takes my breath away, and I stumble backward onto my bunk.

Mother begins to chuckle; the soft, clucking sound grows into a bemused laugh. "Little anger there, huh, Warden? Tell you what . . . you don't let the rest of the world know how stupid you've been, and I won't tell anyone how abysmally ignorant you really are."

Stonemann isn't going to take much more of this. He's frozen in place; only his eyes are moving . . . snapping back and forth between the tip of the gun barrel and Mother's chest. For a moment it seems he's regained control. He lowers the weapon and begins turning it slowly in his hand, an archaeologist inspecting an unnamed artifact.

"Give it here," Lieutenant Smith says softly from Stonemann's elbow. "It's over."

Mother won't let it be. "Confused, Warden? . . . Feel as though you've lost everything?" Lieutenant Smith is gesturing wildly for Mother to keep quiet, but Mother has Stonemann's attention again, and he isn't letting go. His voice becomes one of a psychiatrist, empathizing with a patient. "I've suffered some losses myself. Of course, I didn't lose everything, as you have. I still have my self-respect . . . and I don't have a brother in a loony bin . . . and *my* staff isn't laughing at *me*. . . ."

"Shut up, Conroy!" Lieutenant Smith commands.

"Let him talk," Stonemann says, his voice nearly a whisper. I see a new light in the warden's eyes. Insanity.

Mother signs on to play out the scene. "Must be tough, sort of like being impotent, I suppose. . . . Or maybe you really can't get it up. Is that the reason your wife is sleeping with your employees?"

"You know it all, don't you, Conroy?" Stonemann says sadly. "There isn't a thing on earth you won't stick your nose into . . . nothing is private or sacred with you, is it?"

"Good man! Now you know exactly what it's like on this side of the bars. . . ." Mother pauses, glancing at the gun hanging loosely in Stonemann's fingers. "You don't have the guts to kill me, do you? . . . No, you need an intermediary, someone like Creech, to get the blood on his hands . . . but you've sent Creech out to supervise the clam digging, remember? . . . the ones you steal and sell to the Indians? . . . Maybe you could send me over on the truck to the Auburn sales yard and shoot me for stealing the beef *you've* been lining your bookies' pockets with. Not much left, is there, Stonemann? You're just a pathetic old man, and all the power in the world can't help you get it up. . . ." He nods to the gun in Stonemann's hand.

The dam breaks. "You shut the fuck up, Conroy!"

Dog's voice is a strained whisper from offstage. "Leave it be, Mother."

Mother edges closer to the bars, taunting Stonemann. "Shoot, you damn coward. Shoot!"

The .38 comes up and steadies. Stonemann's fingers are white on the grip. A flash of army fatigues and Big Smith pushes Mother aside.

"*Pop!*" A spurt of flame touches Big's shirt, and I see a puff of smoke from the material; then the bullet clips through the vent screen over my head.

The door pops open, and Lieutenant Smith screams, "Run, Conroy! Get the hell out of there."

Mother lunges at Stonemann before the door has stopped jiggling. *Pop!* ... *Pop!* ... *Pop!* ... Three shots, close together. Mother doubles over and staggers past Stonemann. The doors bang closed as suddenly as they opened, trapping us inside.

Stonemann is still standing in front of the cell, staring curiously at the smoking pistol in his hand. Lieutenant Smith runs up, takes the weapon from Stonemann's unprotesting fingers, and propels him down the range and out of sight.

Water splashes against the back of my neck, and I turn as Little is refilling his cup from the tap. The web of material under Big's armpit is smouldering, but I don't see any blood.

"Your shirt's still smoking." Little turns and pours the water under Big's arm.

"What happened to Mother?" I ask.

"He got hit," Noid answers. "Bad. Real bad."

The uproar in the cell house drowns out even the scratching of the radios and whistles of body alarms for a half minute; then Dog yells down to the Flats. "Hey, Blabbermouth, what's happening with Mother?"

"Don't know," Blabbermouth shouts back. "But he's hurt. They're loading him into a stretcher basket."

Blabbermouth's announcement quiets the cell house, and a thousand pairs of ears strain against the bars. "Somebody get the associate warden on the phone." Lieutenant Smith, I think.

"Better get the United States marshals. We got a murder on our hands," Range Bull bellows.

Lieutenant Smith again. "Call the doc and have him set up a med-evac."

"Too late for that." Range Bull's voice is a soft, rolling thunder. "Looks like he's gone."

"Do it!" Smith again.

A shuffle of feet, crackle of radio static, and then the cell-house doors clang shut and there is silence. Cold, ominous silence. Deathly silence.

"He killed Mother," Odds 'whispers.

"Mother committed suicide," I reply without thinking.

"But why?" Little Smith asks. "For God's sake, why?"

The question hangs in the air for the rest of the evening as the crew from 3-J-5 tries to sort out what has happened and why. I don't participate. I want to scream, beat the bars, start a riot . . . something . . . anything. It just can't end like this.

The night becomes a surrealistic dream. Saucer-eyed cell mates, alternately choking back sobs and ventilating anger . . . the beastlike red and green eyes of speedboats skittering back and forth between the prison and the Steilacoom dock like frenetic waterbugs . . . the *whop, whop, whop* of helicopter blades and the *flop, flop, flop* of guards' shoes . . . lights on . . . lights off . . . flashes of light . . . and flashlights . . . flashbulbs flashing crime scenes . . . and through it all, flashes of insight where I could have said or done just one thing and changed the course of the evening are rolling across my mind like advertising worms at the bottom of a television screen. Then darkness . . . total darkness . . . soul darkness . . . future darkness . . . darkness of my thoughts, and finally, near morning, darkness darkness.

And the silence.

Anger and fear grow well in the dark; mushrooms of anguish in the dank cellar of a mind twisted by grief, fear and hate . . . fertilized by anxiety, watered by sorrow, and warmed in the twin hellfires of guilt and thoughts of revenge, the fungus grows and grows and grows in my mind.

And I like it. I need it. I want it. I want to hang on to this hate for all the rest of my life.

The voice offers something to kill the pain. *We need a getback.*

The day begins with the announcement of an institution-wide lock-down. The news is delivered in the form of a brown paper bag stuffed with hastily prepared peanut butter sandwiches and dispensed by silent guards who are unable to look you in the eye.

I toss my sack into the waste can and hop back up onto my bunk, still trying to figure out why Mother steered himself right into the fatal wreck with Stonemann. I know when the final part of his plan began: the letters to Mary. The bets he had me include were there only to whet Stonemann's appetite. He took Odds off the telephone so he could carry out the final phase of his getback, but the open hole in the unsolved mystery is the relationship he developed with the Chief and the mysterious request to transfer to the prison camp, even though Chief wasn't even remotely eligible. Chief has as much chance of getting that transfer as we have of making parole. I have five years left, and I'm the first man in 3-J-5 scheduled for release.

I can't think. I can't sleep; might as well have a cup of coffee. Off with the blanket and over to the tap for some water. I glance at my watch. The time for work call has come and passed without notice. 3-J-5 is right back into its continuous pre-Mother depression.

I look around for confirmation. Mother's death has had the same effect on everyone; not a head is showing from beneath the covers. They are all in bed; not a chance they're sleeping. Lost in thought, red-eyed, tight-lipped . . . wondering how to get even for Mother.

It's after 9 A.M. when Range Bull appears at the door. "I need to get Mr. Conroy's property," he says apologetically.

"Then you'd better get Stonemann to come up here with a fucking army," Dog growls as he throws back his covers. "Somebody's ass is going to pay."

"Stonemann is in plenty of trouble," Range Bull assures us. "They've got him out at the Administration Building right now. FBI and everything. Serve the fucker right if he gets charged. Mr. Conroy was an all-right guy with me."

"How long we going to be locked down?" I ask casually.

"Probably unlock in a few minutes," Range Bull answers. "Acting Warden McMuff wants to get back to normal operations as soon as possible."

"You talking about the same McMuff who wears the bearskin cap winter and summer?" Noid asks.

Range Bull confirms Noid's suspicions. "That's him. A real by-the-book S.O.B."

I know him too. McMuff is a cold-blooded career man who would slit his mother's throat for a one-step pay increase. This joint's heading downhill in a hurry.

"Work call, work call," the P.A. blasts. "All inmates report to their work assignments."

Every eye in the cell is out in the open, staring at me. I know the question. I surprise myself with the answer. "We go. Business as usual until we figure out a way to get Stonemann. We'll do like Mother always did. Put them to sleep and then . . . catch them with their pants down." The cliché hopped out of my mouth on its own, leaving a trail of goose bumps down the back of my neck.

"Come on. Let's hit it." I'm out the door and down on the Flats. There are a couple of questions I want to ask Blabbermouth before I go to work.

I spend ten minutes trying to get a clear picture of how Mother looked when he went out, but Blabbermouth still doesn't know which side of the fence he wants to land on, and it's a dry run.

The walk down to the factory is an opportunity to reflect on everything that's happened in my life since Mother came through it like a whirlwind. Before the sorting machine even begins to get organized, the con who drives the ambulance shoots out of the hospital and falls in beside me. "Mother was still alive when I put him in the chopper, Flat Store. Didn't look to me like he was in shock or anything, and he was wide awake. Touchy as hell, though; wouldn't let anyone lay a hand on him. I think he has a good shot at making it."

I want to grab this straw and hang on for all I'm worth. "Yeah? It's kind of strange they unlocked us so quick. You have a chance to talk with the doc yet?"

"Nope. Doc went over with the chopper. Seems to me if Mother had died, Doc would have been back by now."

The logic mixed with my hope is a heady, irresistible concoction. I take a deep drink and start running toward the factory.

Word Dog is waiting for me at the door with a fifty-thousand-candle-power smile. "Stonemann can't pick a horse, hold on to his wife, or shoot straight! Mother's going to be okay, Flat Store. Mr. Shure just told me. He made it!"

The rest of the crew straggles down and joins us. We're laughing and slapping each other on the back like a tribe of drunken aborigines. The men going past stop, add some words of congratulations, and go on. "Stonemann is a finished product," Mr. Johnson, the Clean Room foreman, says. "Best job this factory ever shipped out of here."

Our collective laughter turns into a gasp as we enter the factory. The shop is fully qualified for federal disaster aid. The computer is gone; ditto the *Chart* books and *Racing Forms*. All of our notes, print-outs, and notebooks, too. The Q.C. manual that held the telephone is conspicuous by its absence, and my work area in particular appears to have been overrun by an unfriendly gaggle of gremlins.

I notice Wheeler is standing in front of his office, so he has survived the initial blast; but, judging by the paranoia rampant on his face, it doesn't appear as though he thinks he'll be around much longer. We gather at my desk, and for the next few hours we are musk oxen, waiting for the wolf pack.

Chief comes into the factory at about a quarter to eleven. "How!" I greet him.

"Can it, Flat Store. This is serious business." By reflex I lean my head closer as he adds, "The custody lieutenant just called me in and told me to pack up. I've been approved for the honor camp. I leave in the morning."

Alarms are going off in the sorting machine. I feel my eyes cross and uncross, and say the first thing that falls into my mouth. "Looks like Mother knew what he was doing."

Chief is grinning now. "Sure did. When he gets back, tell him I send my regards . . . from wherever."

I offer him my hand and a piece of advice. "Good luck, but keep your next move to yourself, Chief. Very few people go to camp if the administration doesn't have some reason to trust them."

"Kawasheega is aware of the dangers of the eavesdropped smoke signal." He pumps my hand again. "You be sure and tell Mother thanks."

"No sweat."

The P.A. cuts the parting sentiments short: "Inmates Barker, Burns, McCoy, Smith, J., and Smith, R., Hargrove, and Osgood report to Mr. Wheeler's office immediately."

"Gotta go, Chief. This might be the train to Atlanta."

"No way. Kawasheega knows."

"The call to judgment," Dog reminds me, and the 3-J-5 crew forms into a loose line of condemned men following Word Dog up to Wheeler's aerie.

Wheeler is waiting at the door with his passbook in his hand. "You men are wanted at classification and parole. Here are your passes." He gives us each a slip of paper and waves us away.

We're back at my desk, and I'm putting on my jacket, before Noid works up the nerve to ask, "I wonder what this is about?"

"Routine. They're going to ask us where we want to be transferred to, then send us to the opposite end of the country."

"I don't think so," Big Smith is saying.

"Okay." I'm off into my Perry Mason bit. "You must be the one he told. What's going on?"

"I don't know." Big pleads ignorance.

"Bull. Mother knew he was going to be shot. He must have told one of us what to expect."

Blank, innocent faces.

"You think Mother *knew* Stonemann was going to shoot him?"

"Has Mother *ever* had an accident?" I counter Noid's question with one of my own.

"We did warn him about Stonemann and his gun."

Little agrees with Big. "He knew Stonemann carried it every time he came inside the prison."

"You men get moving!" Wheeler shouts from his balcony. "They just called for you again."

"What for?" Noid yells back.

"Don't tell me you sleazy bastards don't know," Wheeler snaps, and slams the door to his office.

"Bum rap," Dog shouts after him. "Come on. Let's go find out what the Philistines have on their minds." We follow Dog out of the factory and up the hill to the Administration Building. Inside, we present our passes to the guard at the C&P desk.

The guard checks a sheet of paper and says: "Barker? Inside. The rest of you have a seat." He motions me toward the office door of the chief of classification and parole, and the others to some chairs along the wall.

I knock on the door and open it without waiting for an answer. No sense letting them know I'm frightened to death. Inside I see a typical prison office. A large desk with a hard wooden chair on my side and a huge, slightly higher, overstuffed swivel chair on the other. A picture of the President of the United States on the left wall is facing an even larger picture of Delbert Allen, director of the Bureau of Prisons, on the right. The President is smiling; Mr. Allen isn't. Small wonder; despite the effort to increase his stature, he still appears as the short, squat, bulbous-nosed Munchkin he is in real life. A cigarette-burned carpet and the odor of depression and antipathy complete the ambience reigned over by the head of C&P, Mr. Donald Chatterton.

Mr. Chatterton has two guests, dour-faced individuals in wrinkled linen suits more appropriate for September in California. A tape recorder is spinning away on the desk top, and I'm thinking if this isn't a couple of displaced FBI agents, there isn't a Mafioso left in the Vatican bank. The hairs on my neck disagree.

"Mr. Barker?" the chubbier of the two asks.

"Barker, Humbert James. 36136-136." Name, rank, and serial number.

"Mr. Barker, my name is R. Redford Tapette. I'm a member of the United States Parole Commission. I'm here today with Mr. Tony Maricone"—he nods at his effeminate-looking partner—"for the purpose of affirming your new parole date."

"New parole date?"

"Yes." He pushes a paper across the desk. It *is* an application for parole. Every square is filled in except the place for my signature.

My fingers grab the pen and sign before my mind has an opportunity to muck up the miracle. "When do I go?"

"One week from today. Provided, of course, you execute a document that will be delivered to you the day before your release."

"What kind of document?" Noid would be proud of me, I'm thinking.

"Better the man who delivers it explain in person." He makes a sour face, as though he were taking some very bitter medicine.

"Do you have any questions?" Mr. Chatterton asks.

"None I could get answered here," I reply, feeling cocky.

"Right. Would you send Mr. Burns in, please?"

I step outside and do a successful job of masking an explosion of joy, until Dog asks, "What's goin' on in there?"

"We're going home, Dog. We're all going home!"

"Come on, Dog. Let's go get this last jailhouse breakfast." I'm trying to tug Dog away from the mirror.

"Okay. Okay, man. I'm telling you, they still have food on the outside. Why the big push to eat more of this crap?"

"Because I never want to forget the taste," I tell him honestly.

39 "And when we leave tomorrow morning, I don't want the taste in my mouth." We're off to the chow hall.

Inside, the usual lines of bleary-eyed men are waiting in two long, silent columns down either side of the huge hall. Just in front of us are two old-timers; not really *old*-timers, maybe a half-dozen years older than Dog and me. One of them is asking the other, "What did the menu say we got for soup at lunch?"

"Soup de jour," the other answers, pronouncing it "d'ja-hour."

"They got that fuckin' shit *again?*"

"Yup."

"Mother-fuckers must have a warehouse fulla that shit. Seems like we get it nearly ever' day."

Dog turns to me and whispers, "We've come a long way, baby."

I wink my heartfelt agreement. We've come so far it's been hard to look back and see ourselves, until just now.

Breakfast is greasy chipped beef on burnt toast, cold coffee, powdered milk on Rice Krispies, and an unidentifiable Russian-steppes fungus being served as a fruit. We pick our way through the meal like a patrol through a minefield.

"I'm glad you dragged me down here," Dog admits as we're dumping our trays. "If I ever in life have to eat in another prison mess hall, I will have been unjustly accused, tried, and convicted."

My sentiments precisely.

Back in the cell I have another chore to attend to. I glance at my watch, figure I have an hour or so for the task, and sit down at the table, select a felt-tipped pen from the coffee mug/pencil holder, and remove my right shoe. A piece of clean white typing paper under my friend the foot and I'm committing the outline to the paper. I have promised myself over and over that one day I would send the drawing to the company who manufactures our stockings, on the hypothesis that they obviously have never seen a human foot, and have no idea of its form or dimensions.

I'm completing the task as Mother comes through the door an hour early and unannounced. There is a moment of stunned silence; then it's mail call in Army basic, Red Cross package time in the POW camp, or, possibly, the second coming of Christ. We mob him.

"Back away, varlets," Dog yells. "The man is wounded."

Fast does the apologizing. "Sorry, man. Hope we didn't hurt you."

"Nothing to hurt. I was healed up by the third day." Mother pulls up his T-shirt, exposing three black-and-blue indentations over his heart. You could cover all three of them with a dollar bill. He grins.

Noid verbalizes my own amazement. "Barely broke the skin!"

"Three shots in the heart? We thought you were dead or dying." Big is shaking his head in disbelief.

"So did Lieutenant Smith." Mother is wearing the mischievous grin once more. "It's a wonder they put me on the chopper." He winks.

No one responds. It's difficult to form and articulate a question when your lower lip and your navel are roughly on the same level. Mother realizes we are going to demand an explanation. "When Stonemann fired, I fell and rolled up into a fetal position. I told the doc there was a staff conspiracy to kill me, and refused to let them examine me until I got to a civilian hospital."

Little Smith points out the logic of that: "You were in a good spot to dictate."

Noid comes out of his trance. "But you don't look shot. I mean, what stopped the bullets?"

"Remember when I broke into Stonemann's safe?" We're nodding, so he continues. "I took the bullets out of his gun, removed most of the propellant charge, and hand loaded them with just enough powder to produce a passable-sounding gunshot."

"Where did you learn hand loading?" Noid's reflexes are back to normal.

"Georgia," Mother replies. "When I replaced the pistol, I knew all I had to do was provoke him sufficiently."

Jesus Christ! He's been planning this for months. Every move, every enticement, all leading to capitalizing on Stonemann's gambling habit and mental instability.

Noid is scratching his head. "But how could Stonemann hope to get away with it?"

"He was so angry, I doubt if he considered the consequences. But if he did, he had plenty of reason to believe he could cover it up, just like he did with Giant ... but I drove him around the bend, and it wasn't really something he *could* stop and think about." He pauses, and I can see he is not really enjoying the moment. "Stonemann is finished. Financially, socially, and careerwise."

"We heard he was promoted to assistant to the regional director. He's at the regional office in Burlingame right now," Odds informs Mother.

"He's also in a psychiatric and alcoholism dry-out hospital," Mother corrects him. "If he can straighten himself out, they might give him a swan-song shot at some metropolitan correctional center or another nothing post. His dream of becoming the director is dead."

"What a getback."

"A superior getback."

Little caps off the progression of group thought. "A mother superior's getback."

"Not bad, but I'm not through with him or Creech yet. I

have the ultimate getback cooking." Mother's comment provides the hairs on the back of my neck with some needed exercise.

"How did you talk the parole board out of the paroles?" Noid is in good form.

"I struck a deal. You sign some papers, and thereby agree to remain silent about the incident."

"The rest of the deal?" Noid asks.

"I agreed not to press charges for attempted murder."

"Who did you deal with?" Noid is becoming more suspicious.

"The regional director himself. Grossenberger. It's tight," Mother assures us.

"You should have called in more lawyers than a producer hires to change a light bulb on a movie set," I warn him.

"I did. Top firm in Seattle."

"When are you leaving?" I ask.

"I'm not included in the deal."

Shocked silence. Noid to the rescue. "How come?"

"There are other, overriding considerations and circumstances," Mother says, evading the question gracefully. I want to tell him the sidestep is as obvious as a Mount Rushmore nose, but decide to let him finish. "You will all be leaving tomorrow, and I'm sure you have a lot to do. Are you ready to sign?"

Nods.

He tosses a stack of forms on the table. "If you'll sign these releases, I'll take them up to Mr. Chatterton and get back to the hospital."

"Hold it!" Noid is clutching Mother's arm. "Why did you get the job of making us sign? And why can't you just stay here? And . . . and . . ."

Mother takes pity on him—and me. "I wanted to hand-carry the papers to you so if there were questions you would have a source you could trust. And, of course, I wanted to make sure what you signed was airtight." He pauses, and I see a twinge of sorrow at the corners of his mouth. "I have to stay in the hospital because I've raised the issue of staff conspiracy to kill me, and I think the doc believes me. He insisted I remain in his care . . . and go to work for him as an aide. So"—he spreads his hands in the air—"if you'll get those signed, please?"

We fall to the task, and in a matter of a minute or so, Mother has gathered up the release papers, promised to meet us at Receiving and Discharge in the morning, and turned to go.

"Wait a minute." I'm desperate; I don't want him to leave just yet, but don't have a good excuse to prolong the moment. For a change, the sorting machine comes to my rescue. "I have a message for you from the Chief. He wanted me to be sure and thank you for helping him get out. He said he'd drop you a note from the camp."

"Chief escaped yesterday." Mother smiles. "The U.S. Marshal's office in Tacoma is trying to get a warrant to search every Indian reservation in the state. They won't be able to, of course. I believe if Chief stays put on the reservation, we could safely say that Kawasheega has been returned to his people for as long as the rivers flow and the grass is green." Mother pauses, smiling wistfully. "Those Puyallups do have some delightfully fast canoes, don't they?"

"Hold it just a goddamn minute!" Dog pulls Mother back into the cell and firmly pushes him to a seat at the table. "What is happening in *your* case?"

"Nothing."

Noid gives him both barrels. "You mean you're really stuck here? How long?"

"I don't really know."

"Who does?"

Mother shrugs. "In the final analysis, that may very well be up to the crew from 3-J-5." His grin is somewhere between evil and bemused.

I'm seeing pictures of rubber rafts, helicopters, motorized canoes, fence cutters, and Creech, up to his ass in a swamp with a handful of frustrated bloodhounds. I like the picture, and add my knowing smile to those around the table.

Mother is on his feet again. "Look, if I don't get these papers up to Chatterton, I'm going to be looking at you monkeys for the next five or ten years. Please, spare me that." He turns at the door, and adds: "Do me one favor? Get out there and do yourself a favor . . . and go straight. Believe me, it will be easy for you. In case you haven't noticed, you're all rehabilitated." Now the grin is broad, warm, and toothy.

I can't help myself. *"I knew it!* You were sent here by the BOP to turn us into squares. You've been at it since the day you arrived. A sneaky, insidious attempt to alter the socioeconomic patterns and status of the men in 3-J-5. A test run on a new BOP program! Did Delbert Allen send you on this mission personally?"

Mother is laughing so hard the tears are streaming down his cheeks. Makes a good excuse for the rest of us, too. I decide to put some icing on his cake. "You made us over, changed our values, twisted us around, and made us think like *citizens.* Damn your eyes, Mother, you made *me, the Flat Store, King Kong of the short con,* go for an ill-disguised rehabilitation project. You turned me into a square!"

"But Flat Store, I'm a square," he replies. Every square millimeter of his face is innocent . . . but his eyes are flashing mischief.

"Awwwwww, Mother." Dog's anguish may or may not be feigned. "Don't tell me no shit like that. You're a world-class bank robber. Our hero."

"Sorry, but it's true. I've never once stolen a nickel from its rightful owner."

That sentence sounds like it has something suspiciously extra in it, but the sorter is on strike because of the high water levels in my eyes.

Mother nods, trying to nail down this whopper he just laid on us. "Never stole a nickel."

There it is. Now, what to do with a pronouncement like that? I can't punch him, even though I know he's only bruised and I wouldn't hurt him; problem is, I'd get *my* ass kicked. I pick up my pillow and whop him over the head with it. In a flash, I'm joined by the rest of the crew.

Range Bull comes loping down the tier a few seconds later,

and arrives in time to discover a cellful of ex-convicts rolling on the floor amidst a snowstorm of feathers.

"This a private party?" He grins.

"Yup," Mother says proudly. "And a private club."

Who would want to argue with that?

We spend the rest of the day going from department to department on what the cons call "the merry-go-round." Good name. While it's difficult to say good-by to many of our acquaintances, we have the knowledge that their day will come eventually. Not so with Mother, and every time I spot him as we're moving around the grounds I get a pain something between guilt and sorrow.

Most of the men in the population have figured out why and how we got parole, although the old cons never mention it, but no one has the foggiest why Mother didn't try and ride out with us. Me included.

On the way down to the factory to sign off our jobs and turn in our gauges and tools, we pass the smokestack. Mother is standing at its base, his hands clasped behind his back. Staring at the spot on the ground where the Giant died in his arms, he isn't moving. Just once he raises his eyes to the top of the obscene red monstrosity; his shoulders slump and the picture blurs. I nudge Dog and Fast Eddie, and we walk quietly away.

Damn, it's a heartbreaker to see a friend in so much pain.

Late evening now, and Mother stops by for some hot chocolate, HiHos, and peanut butter. He brings jam, so I know it was no accident. He remembers the getting-out party, all right.

We pass the evening making small talk and discussing what we're going to try to do when we get released. I hear some surprising plans, but what the hell, I'm going straight myself . . . if they let me.

I get the only chuckle of the evening with: "When I see Mary, the second thing I'm going to do is take my hat!"

I'm in bed, waiting for lights out, when Arkie Davis is back on the line, after a four-month absence. "Go and get them, 3-J-5!"

I fall asleep thinking we, damn sure will.

Morning comes, and I'm slipping on the civilian stockings they gave me yesterday in Receiving and Discharge. After the stockings, the "dress-out shoes"; in this instance a pair of green tennis sneakers. I don't get the rest of my freedom issue until I get to R&D. Thank God. They've given me a plaid shirt to go with my striped pants, chartreuse tennis shoes, and red socks. I figure the Tacoma City police will arrest me the second they see the outfit. Why not? An easy vagrancy score for them, and just enough of a fine to wipe out my release money.

"Let's go, Flat Store." Noid Benny is already outside on the tier.

"We'll miss the boat, man," Fast adds.

"I'm coming. I'm coming." I hustle to the door and stop, looking back inside. Except for the Giant's bunk, which is still made up, 3-J-5 is cleaned out. Empty mattresses and vacant lockers. I hope the next poor sucker does as well here as I believe I have.

"Don't tell me you're not leaving," Big Smith jokes.

"No. But to tell the truth, a part of me wants to stay," I admit.

They get behind me and push me to the stairwell. The legs get the message at the first step. This is the last time they will make *this* journey. We're off to R&D.

By the time Mother arrives to help us carry our things down to the dock, we're decked out like a group of Howdy Doody look-alikes, in plaids and baggy stripes only partially hidden beneath plastic windbreakers. I go by the cashier's office, sign for my fifty dollars release money, and wonder how in hell a man dressed like this with fifty bucks in his pocket could ever do anything *but* come back to prison. Must be part of Allen's program, I think as I'm tucking the money away; keeps the budget growing.

We're out through the gates, pick up the two shotgun guards

the prison assigns so one of your friends can walk you to the dock, and we're off down the quarter-mile hill to the ferry landing.

There isn't much conversation. Dog is chewing on his lips and shooting sad glances at Mother.

Mother is struggling to put the best possible face on the morning. The Smith Brothers are cavorting around at the rear of the group, alternately rushing ahead and falling back. They remind me of a couple of farm kids on the way to the schoolbus who don't have their homework done. They don't want to leave and they don't want to stay home and do more chores.

I could get a part in their play, I'm thinking.

"I feel as though I'm being deported to another planet," Fast Eddie remarks to no one in particular. "I've never tried to make it out there on the square. It's pretty damn scary."

Mother grabs his shoulder and waves the rest of us to a halt. "You can do it. You all have money in the bank, marketable job skills, and friends you can count on." He pauses and grins. "And you'd better make it in business, too, because when I come out, I may be hunting for a job." Then he tosses us a hand grenade. "Or I might even need some help to leave here," he whispers.

"You got whatever you need, Mother. I'm speaking for all of us," Dog says.

When we reach the dock I give Mother a hug and hustle onto the boat while I can still see the gangplank through the blur my eyes are causing. Mother waits until we are all aboard, then turns and begins walking slowly back to the prison, the two shotgun guards trailing along behind him. It begins to rain, and we press our noses against the glass of the passenger compartment. By the time the ferry is underway, Mother is only a smudge of movement against the gray backdrop of the prison.

"Who was that?" Noid whispers. "Really?"

The question is left unanswered; only the soft throbbing of the engines beneath our feet offers a break in the silence.

The ferry touches the dock on the Steilacoom side, and I sprint up the ramp and scoop Mary off her feet. While we're holding each other, I feel something pressing through my shirt pocket. I put her down and pull out an envelope. Mother must have tucked it in when he hugged me.

Flat Store:
Save the Fall City police report for me in case I need it for evidence. Open the envelope when you feel the time has come to make a very difficult decision regarding helping me with a problem.
  Good luck to both of you,
            Mother

"What is it?" Mary asks.

"I don't know for sure." I answer truthfully, turning the envelope over and over in my hands.

"Where on earth did you get it?"

I explain in detail. "Washington. Where did you park the car?"

Mary's hand is feather-light on my shoulder. "Ready for lunch?"

"Now?"

"It's past twelve, James," she informs me gently.

"I was thinking about fixing this fish." I tilt my head toward the perch dozing in the live-catch box.

40

Mary chuckles softly. "No, you weren't. You've caught the fish twenty times or more. You've been thinking about Mr. Conroy."

"Guilty, Your Honor, on all counts." I lift the screened front of the box, tickle the perch awake with my finger, and he escapes into the lake. "You'll never learn, will you?" I inquire of his departing wake.

"On the contrary, James. He has learned. Anytime he needs a respite from the pressures of the wild, he has only to grab hold of your hook, and presto! He's housed, fed, and protected from worrying about bass, carp, ospreys, and eagles."

"You know your fish, Woman."

"I had a big sucker for a teacher." Suddenly she's hugging me, and I feel tears wet against my face. "Oh, James. What does it mean? Is he ready to escape?"

"I haven't figured it out. I'd better call Noid Bennie."

"His telegram didn't give you a hint?"

"No. But I'm sure Mother needs some help."

"I thought so." She's nibbling her lower lip. "Mr. Conroy was a good friend, wasn't he?"

"The best," I answer, realizing at once the reply is inadequate.

"He's responsible for all my happiness. You, freedom, 3-J-5 Stables. I owe him a lot."

"I don't believe he expected to be repaid, James."

"Of course not. That's what makes the debt so heavy."

"You'd do anything for him, wouldn't you? Even"—she's choosing her words carefully now—"risk going back to prison?"

The answer doesn't require any thought, but Mother's training forces me to consider the question before I respond. "I suppose I would."

Mary clutches me more tightly and pats me gently on the back. "That's my man. Let's go find out what we're supposed to do."

I can't help the chuckle. "I knew there was something more to you than a foxy little strut."

The walk to our gingerbread cottage is passed in silence, two teenagers holding on to each other against the uncertainty of the future. Inside I go to the phone. Mary picks up her notebook and settles on the footstool at my feet.

"Super Security Services, Inc. May I help you?" The voice is warm as it echoes out over the speaker.

"This is James Barker. I have a wire instructing me to call."

"Just a moment." The speaker scratches, falls silent, then comes back to life with: "Flat Store?"

"Yup."

"I'm in my car. Go to scramble seven twenty-one."

I punch in the code on the scrambling device Noid installed for all of us when the probation department decided we should no longer associate with one another. A short whistle indicates the call is now being scrambled and is unmonitored. "What's happening?" I ask.

"Mother needs some help."

"Okay. I'm in. How do we break him out?"

"We don't. He wants us to testify for the United States attorney as witnesses against him."

Before the entire message is processed, my sorting machine serves up a conclusion. "He got his reversal? And a new trial?"

"Did you hear what I said? He wants us to appear as witnesses for the *prosecution*," Noid says.

"Your aren't serious."

"I have a note from Cynthia Evans I'm supposed to read to you. Here goes. 'Tell Flat Store to read the instructions I gave him.' That's it."

"Okay. Anything else?"

"You have an appointment with Dr. Freidling tomorrow morning at 10 A.M. in Spokane, Washington. The address is"—and Mary is ready, pencil poised over the paper—"Suite 232, Professional Building, 181 Riverside."

"He's expecting me for what?"

"He's a hypnotist. No questions on that one, please."

"I don't even have a subpoena," I note, as Mary confirms she has the address.

"You will before the day's over," he says confidently. "The trial begins the day after tomorrow in Fall City."

"Same judge?"

"And prosecutor. Mother is up against a stacked deck," Noid says, confirming my suspicion.

"See you there." As usual, Noid hangs up without a good-by.

I switch off the speaker and scrambler, drop into my recliner, and whisper, "Mother got a retrial."

"Thank God," Mary says, and snuggles into my lap. "I don't know if I'd have been much help with an escape."

"If it were an escape, you weren't going to go."

I can't see her face, but the mischievous grin comes through in her voice. "But James, I've already packed the car!"

I'm astounded. "When did you make that decision?"

"From the first day you were out. I knew you were going to help however you could."

"How on earth could you put that together?"

"The hairs on the back of my neck were doing the Watusi." She giggles, and I know I'm never in life going to get any more out of her on the subject.

"Better read the note," she suggests. "It might shed some light—"

"—on the subject. Don't you start doing clichés on me, Woman."

I tug the plastic packet out of my pocket, and together we read:

Flat Store,
Let your conscience be your guide. . . . The truth will set me free.
Donald R. Conroy
A.K.A. "Mother"

"The son of a gun can stand flatfooted and see the day after the end of the world," I mutter.

"Why the hypnotist?" Mary wonders aloud.

"Who knows? But one thing is for sure, the appointment won't be a waste of time." As I speak I'm remembering the logo on Noid Benny's business card. "You aren't paranoid; someone *is* watching you."

The Federal Building in beautiful downtown Fall City, Idaho, was built in the 1930s and named after an obscure United States senator in honor of his having spent his entire life as a politician and never once becoming involved in a scandal. The architecture is Neo-American Confused, the materials expensive/imported, and the workmanship obvious WPA. Huge columns of European granite form the entryway, through which you pass into a main lobby that is a study in long flights of polished Italian marble stairways lined with Philippine mahogany banisters. Overhead, at the apex of the rotunda, three stories up, is a Belgian chandelier with enough bulbs to light the homes of fifty welfare families. The crystals glisten down on a bank of Swedish elevators, each sporting an "out of order" sign.

"Judge Logan's courtroom is on the fifth floor," Mary informs me.

"Figures. This five-story monument to FDR's New Deal couldn't possibly be arranged logically." I survey the lobby once more. "Seems like he tried to bail out every country in the world.

The only American products they used are mortar, wax, and sweat."

"Don't be so cynical, James." She touches my arm. "Isn't that Miss Evans over there?" She points to the opposite side of the rotunda.

"That's her."

"She looks exactly like her picture in the *Times*," Mary notes.

Cynthia is the same model-thin, Bonwit Teller–chic woman I saw in the prison's visiting yard nearly five years ago. She sees us, and begins waving. She can't possibly recognize me, I'm thinking, when I hear Noid's voice behind me. "Flat Store." I turn, and he has the rest of the 3-J-5 gang in tow.

It's a class reunion for the next few minutes, because we haven't visited since my wedding. The next time we tried to get together, our respective parole officers raided the party, and we nearly went back to McNeil Island for associating with ex-felons. According to them, we were in violation of policy statement such-and-such, which specifically precludes us from meeting socially because of the potential for our being a "bad influence" on one another! I've been seeing Dog on occasion in the office we share as the owners of 3-J-5 Stables, but we are not allowed to go outside the office together, even for a cup of coffee.

Cynthia joins the group, and as she is being introduced around by Noid Benny, whom she apparently knows quite well, I notice a look of disapproval in her eyes. Mary does, too, and I feel her tensing against my arm.

"Miss Evans? Is something wrong?" Mary has beat me to the punch.

"Yes," she says, and smiles sweetly—and sincerely, too, I decide. "The men look too respectable."

"Too respectable?" I ask.

Noid jumps into the conversation, and I notice he's vintage Noid Benny again. Shaggy hair, scruffy shoes, a couple of days' growth of beard. His checked shirt and striped pants sketch the picture of an ex-con, but the blue watch cap is the telling detail. "The reason Mr. Kroeger is calling us to testify against Mother is fairly devious. He's going to ask us if Mother ever admitted robbing the bank, and figures when the jury sees the collection of reprobates Mother has for friends, they will turn against him, transforming our denials into affirmations."

"It would help if you'd clean up a little," Fast Eddie says.

"You miss the point. If I appear too clean, Mr. Kroeger, the AUSA, won't put me on the stand, and Mother needs us desperately."

I do a quick scan of the group. If Noid is right, we're definitely not dressed for the parts. The Smith Brothers are a pair of models from the cover of *Esquire,* the quality and style of their clothes reflecting their status as the owners of a nationwide computer dating service. Fast Eddie and his petite wife are also the picture of success. Fast Eddie's Hot Roofing Company is nailing down every large contract in the city of Seattle, and he's dressing the part of an affluent businessman, in a three-piece suit, close-cropped hair, and an air of confidence he wears as well as his clothing. Odds, now the premier sportswriter for the *Seattle Times* with his *Odds On* column, he's wearing the Hickey Freeman suit he purchased when his daily evaluations of important sporting events went into national syndication. With Dog and me decked out as the successful horse owners we are, we present an overwhelming impression of solid citizenry.

"I have to see the AUSA Kroeger in ten minutes," I say, glancing at my watch. "No time to change."

Mary looks me over critically and says, "I can fix that." She musses my hair, removes my string tie and puts my collar outside my jacket, pulls the shirttails out slightly, and says, "Now, slouch a little, and be sure to stuff your hands in your pockets when you enter his office."

While the rest of the crew is making what alterations they can, I ask Noid, "How can you be so sure of Kroeger's strategy? Most AUSAs are cagey enough not to publish their intentions."

Mary interrupts with: "What's an AUSA?"

"An assistant United States attorney. Usually people recently out of law school who want to build local reputations as hotshot attorneys. The government hires them for peanuts and allows them to hunt scalps to add to their vitae so when the time comes, they can land a job in a large law firm."

"It sounds like an awful practice."

"AUSAs are to law what proctologists are to medicine," I explain, "but back to my question, Noid. How can you be sure what the prosecutor is after?"

Noid grins, and a sudden realization causes cold chills to romp unencumbered down my spinal column. "You've bugged the offices?"

Noid nods. "And the judge's chambers," he admits. He sees my eyebrows pull together, so he continues. "No problem with the law, Flat Store; Super Securities Services, Inc. has the contract for this building. I've therefore taken the precaution of having some listening devices installed to catch anyone who might attempt to sneak in at night and plant one of his own." He's grinning. "It's routine."

"Mother can see the end of creation," I mutter as I think back to how smoothly he led Noid into this profession.

Cynthia calls the group to order. "Now. At Donald's request, I have some items to check off. Did everyone see the hypnotist?" Noid pulls her aside, whispers something, and she nods in agreement. "Very well, I suppose there's nothing left for the present but to go for your interviews with Mr. Kroeger."

We make the climb to the fifth floor. When we reach the top landing, the first things I notice are the numerous signs protruding out into the hallway. Courtroom, Clerk's Office, FBI Office, DEA Office, Immigration Office, IRS Office, and the United States Attorney's Office snuggled up next to one marked Judge's Chambers. Jammed together as they are, I see the possibility for some incestuous abuses and unfairness, when one considers the fact that the public defender's office is fifteen blocks away, in a cubbyhole that still has a bare wire sticking out of the wall where there was once a pay phone.

At the far end of the hallway, the panel of prospective jurors is milling around waiting to be called. They are in full view of a pair of metal detectors, and for a moment I place myself in the mind of one of the citizens on the panel: If the marshal is taking such severe precautions, I'm going to be hearing a case involving an extremely dangerous character.

Mr. Kroeger, the AUSA, certainly hasn't missed a bet thus far in his efforts to stack the deck. A well-armed deputy marshal asks us if we are jurors, spectators, or witnesses. He's a huge, glowering individual who puts me in mind of the Giant on a morning when he was badly hung over. The ladies tell him they are spectators, and he nods curtly toward the courtroom. When Fast Eddie informs him we are *prosecution* witnesses, there is a Jekyll-and-Hyde transformation, and we're personally escorted to a room marked Government Witnesses.

Inside is the VIP lounge at United Airlines, complete with the attractive young lady offering coffee, tea, milk, and a selection of hot rolls.

"Mother is in some serious trouble here," I whisper to the Dog.

A loud "Ohhhhhh" from the crowd in the corridor pulls us back outside. Six deputy marshals armed with shotguns and M-16s are escorting Mother down the hall, past the jury panel. Mother is the picture of a mad-dog killer. His hands are shackled with a device that makes even small movements of the fingers painful. The "black box" is hooked to a chain that runs up and around the back of his neck and then down to a pair of leg irons, reducing his once-proud stride to a pathetic shuffle. In truth, the hardware is standard equipment routinely used for transporting a federal prisoner, particularly *if* the marshal in charge also has the standard issue of sadistic tendencies. To the jurors, Mother looks as though he is the type of person requiring massive restraint to prevent him from disemboweling a Boy Scout on the way to court.

He's been dressed in an inexpensive polyester suit, and the chains are clinched so tightly I know the jury will still be able to see the wrinkles they've left at the close of today's sessions. A planned, not very subtle reminder of the animal they are about to pass judgment upon.

Dog is watching the scene over my shoulder. "This isn't going to be a trial; we're about to witness a crucifixion."

I whisper my agreement as Mother shuffles by. "He hasn't a prayer." I offer Mother a weak smile, but he pretends not to see me. Part of his overall plan, I suppose.

"Mr. Barker?" The stewardess type is smiling sweetly. "Mr. Kroeger can see you now."

I hand her the coffee and Dog the uneaten roll and step into the office. Inside it's Federal Waste-the-Taxpayer's-Money Posh: lots of leather and dark-grained wood—and Mr. Kroeger, the AUSA. He's about five eight, maybe one forty-five if he had a decent breakfast, and is dressed as though his taste is all in his mouth: a blue suit with a red-and-white striped tie; red, white, and blue suspenders are backgrounded by a wrinkled white shirt. He has miniatures of the American flag in both lapels and a John Birch Society pin as a tie tack. "Mr. Humbert James Barker?" He smiles up at me.

"Right. But if you lay that dumb-assed moniker on me in public I won't answer yer ass. Name's Flat Store."

"You prefer Flat Store?"

"Bet yer ass."

"I see. Very well, Mr. Flat Store, do you know Donald R. Conroy, the defendant in the bank-robbery case?" I can see he is having difficulty holding back a smirk, obviously extrapolating this interchange to the witness stand.

"Me 'n' the monk was cribbed up for a long singleton."

"Is that a yes or no?" He asks innocently.

"You got hearin' problems, or is you just a dummy?" Damn, this is fun!

He ignores the question. "Did the defendant, Mr. Conroy, ever admit he had robbed the bank of Fall City?"

"Hell, no! Mother's way too slick fer some shit like that. Monk's gibbs is jammed so tight you couldn't get a flax seed outa his mouth with a pile driver in his throat. Him makin' a mistake like blowin' his story on some bullshit jailhouse rap session is all the way outta the question." If his rapid breathing is any indicator, Mr. Kroeger is more than thoroughly pleased with my response.

"Let me rephrase the question. In your considered opinion as a lifelong confidence man and racketeer, did Mr. Conroy commit the robbery of the Fall City National Bank?"

"If he did, he's smart enough to lie around it. Hell, man, he's the King Kong of convicts. Anybody ever tell you Mother copped out on hisself, you tell they're so fulla shit their eyes are brown."

"Well"—he offers me a staged sigh—"I think your testimony will be truthful, even if it falls short of supporting the government's case. My oath of office mandates I put you on the stand so the jurors will hear all of the facts. One small item. There are ladies and gentlemen on the jury, so I would appreciate it if you would make some effort to clean up your language."

"No sweat, Kroeger. I'll clean it up at lot."

I wink at the rest of the crew as I come out and return to the hallway. Mary, Cynthia, and Fast Eddie's wife, Alecia, are standing outside the courtroom. Cynthia is being interviewed by a couple of artsy-looking youngsters in their late twenties. One is holding the microphone, the other a video recording camera. By the time they've finished taping the segment, the jury has lost interest in the group, and I join them.

"Who were the television people?"

Cynthia smiles. "From our affiliate here in Fall City. Since the *Times* bought KING-TV we've expanded our news-gathering and reporting capabilities quite a bit."

"Don't tell me." I pause, feigning a mystic's pretrance concentration: hand to my forehead and eyes squinched shut. "They are doing a story on Mother that will air sometime this evening. Say, right after the jury has had enough time to go home, eat dinner, and be ready for the special local news report?"

"Perfect," Cynthia makes an OK sign with her fingers. "You met Kroeger. Now you know why Mother says we have to fight fire—"

"—with fire. He got you, too, huh?"

The conversation is cut short by the bailiff's calling the jury panel for examination. We tag along with the crowd.

Inside, the courtroom has the dusty-mausoleum smell of all courtrooms. The judge's bench is on a raised platform in the right corner of the room; the jury box is on the left. Two tables, separated by a lectern, are centered between them, directly in front of the witness box. As we enter the bailiff says, "All rise," and I get my first look at Judge Logan. He's tall, thin, obviously intelligent-looking individual with iron-gray hair and bushy white eyebrows. A long, sharp nose and glittering eyes give the fleeting impression of a hunting eagle. He offers the courtroom a warm, fatherly smile, which quickly wipes away the bird-of-prey image.

One can easily predict the quality of justice a judge is about to dispense in a federal criminal prosecution by the amount of time he takes to pick the jury. Judge Logan has his selected, sworn, and seated in fifteen minutes flat. As soon as they are comfortable, he begins an explanation of their duties. It's delivered in a paternal tone. Civics 101 with him as the professor emeritus.

Judge Logan opens by pushing his glasses down his nose and staring over them at the jury. A flex of the eyebrows, and his classroom stills. "Ladies and gentlemen. You have been selected, sworn, and seated in a criminal prosecution of a most heinous crime: a bank robbery involving the mental torture of the primary victim. You have undertaken a grave task. I'm aware that some of you might consider jury duty an inconvenience; for others this fulfillment of a primary duty of citizenship may have caused major upsets in your lives, missed appointments, loss of work time, unmet deadlines. For you, this court offers no apology; for jury duty is imposed upon us all by the same Constitution that has made this nation the most civilized nation on the face of the earth." Logan and the AUSA exchange glances, and I see a message pass between them. The hairs on the back of my neck snap to rigid attention.

"Along with your sacred duty, the Founding Fathers of this great country have also conferred a solemn responsibility. Soon you must weigh the right of a community, your community, to protect itself from marauding outlaws, against the rights of a human being to be fairly treated in a court of law. I expect you to discharge your duties with the wisdom of a Solomon and the patience of a Job, considering only the facts of the case." He pauses and gives them another demonstration of his ability to articulate his eyebrows individually. "On matters of law, I am the sole judge. I decide what is admissible for your consideration and what is not. The decisions I reach on these points of law are not to be interpreted as implying either guilt or innocence, so please do not let them color your judgment. And one more item. Do not let my facial expressions or other reactions to testimony affect your decision. I might very well think a specific witness's testimony is false, for instance, and so react, but you must evaluate the information you will hear, according to your own feelings."

I lean over and whisper in Mary's ear. "That's like telling the jury not to think of a blue horse. Logan has guaranteed himself control of the trial and verdict by the use of his eyebrows alone."

Mother doesn't bat an eyelid as the jury is charged. He hasn't turned to the audience, either. He's sitting there, staring holes through Judge Logan, and while I can only see one side of Mother's face I can recognize an expression I last saw when he was talking with Warden Stonemann.

"Will we invoke the exclusionary rule?" Logan asks Mother and Kroeger.

Kroeger shakes his head, and Mother replies, "I have no problem with the government's witnesses hearing one another's testimony. In fact, it might serve to clear up some very murky areas in this case."

Mother's openness has made a point with two members of the jury, I conclude. Logan and Kroeger must agree. They're frowning. *Two on our side*, I write on a note to Cynthia. Might as well put my people-reading skills to work. . . . Hell, that's what I'm here for, I remember.

"Very well." Logan's voice is deep, well modulated. "Are the respective counsels present and ready to proceed?"

"C. James Kroeger for the government, Your Honor."

"Donald R. Conroy, in *pro per,* for the defense, Your Honor."

"Ahhhh yes, Mr. Conroy; once again you insist on defending yourself?"

"Yes, Your Honor." Mother is as respectful as a Marine private addressing the President of the United States.

"You are aware that the Constitution affords you the right to professional counsel, and in the event that you are unable to afford such counsel, one will be provided at the expense of the government?"

Judge Logan is playing his paternal, protective role too perfectly. I get the impression from at least one juror that I'm not the only person who has detected the sarcastic note in Logan's speech; I point him out to Cynthia.

"I prefer to represent myself, Your Honor."

"Ever the cavalier, eh, Mr. Conroy? Very well. Mr. Kroeger, are you ready for opening remarks?" Kroeger nods. "Proceed."

Kroeger positions himself in front of the jury box and delivers an hour-long lecture explaining how this despicable Donald R. Conroy person robbed a pillar of the community by trickery and deceit, gleefully removed an astronomical sum from the vault, and in the process caused the mental collapse of one of Fall City's more honored citizens. He tells them he will prove the defendant Conroy is the culpable party by eyewitness, fingerprints, and an FBI lab expert. He also promises to give the jury an opportunity to evaluate the people Mr. Conroy has chosen to associate himself with; these people, he promises, will either implicate Mr. Conroy in the crime or perjure themselves in an attempt to save their friend.

By the time he's finished, the entire jury is frowning and shuffling in the box, shooting hard glances in Mother's direction, and it's clear to me a vote at this moment would produce a guilty vote of twelve to zero.

"Opening remarks, Mr. Conroy?" Judge Logan asks.

"I will reserve the right until after the prosecution rests," Mother answers calmly.

"Very well. Mr. Kroeger, call your first witness."

"The government calls Mr. Ephraim Collier, chief of accounting, Amalgamated Banks, parent company of the Fall City National Bank."

As a bookish, tweedy gentleman rises and proceeds toward the witness stand, Cynthia leans over and whispers, "Have you noticed how few spectators there are?"

"Thank God," I reply. "Mother isn't doing too well."

"He's going to pack the house before it's over," Cynthia whispers, and I glance at Noid Benny. He's also grinning. Mother has a contagious virus that turns people into walking cryptograms, I'm thinking. Judge Logan is frowning at us, so I settle back and listen as Mr. Kroeger takes the accountant through his paces. He establishes that the bank is insured by the Federal Deposit Insurance Corporation through the Prudential, that there was in fact a cash shortage after the robbery, and how much money was missing, all the details necessary to underpin the basis for a federal criminal prosecution. Kroeger is thorough.

Mother declines to cross-examine but asks Logan to put the witness on call for later direct examination by the defense.

The request raises Logan's eyebrows. Mine too. I can see no reason for the tactic, and conclude Mother is simply trying to appear competent.

Kroeger's next witness is Frank Pierce, one of the bank's security guards. Kroeger has him sworn in, then very carefully establishes the witness as a God-fearing Christian, a hardworking retired police officer, a scout leader, and generally so red, white, and blue he wouldn't say *communism* if he had a mouthful. Then Kroeger gets to the meat of the testimony. The inevitable "night in question."

"On the evening of the robbery," Pierce begins, "I was called to Mr. Everett Stonemann's office at around 3 P.M. He informed me I would be working overtime, as a large cash deposit was coming in and he would be keeping the main vault open. I remember it clearly because I had to cancel a Boy Scout meeting, call my wife, ask her to hold dinner, and make arrangements to have my daughter picked up from her music lesson." He's smiling at the jury, emphasizing his solid Protestant values. "At about 5 P.M.—excuse me—around 6:05 P.M.—no, excuse me . . ." He reaches into his pocket, removes a sheet of paper, and begins to read. "At exactly 6:00."

"Objection to this testimony, Your Honor." Mother is on his feet.

"What's the problem, Mr. Conroy?" Judge Logan sighs as though this sort of interruption has already happened several times and he's becoming weary from it.

"I would like to review the form he is reading."

"It's a standard FBI 302 Field Report, Your Honor," Kroeger breaks in. "Perfectly acceptable. Witnesses are allowed to review their statements for the purpose of refreshing their memories." He doesn't cite any case law, but I'm convinced he's right. Kroeger is smoother than I expected.

"Objection overruled. You may proceed, Mr. Pierce."

"It was exactly a quarter after six." He's reading directly from the paper, despite Kroeger's definition of the rule. "A rap at the front door drew my attention. Since the bank had been closed for an hour, I thought it was probably the mysterious depositor."

"Mysterious?" Kroeger asks.

"Yes. It was unusual for us to accept a late deposit, but what made it appear more mysterious was the fact that the person rapping on the door was dressed as a nun."

"Do you see that person in the courtroom?"

Mr. Pierce makes an obviously practiced and careful study of the faces in front of him, then finally points at Mother. "That's him. Mr. Conroy."

I glance toward the jury, and they are scowling at Mother. He's ignoring them.

"What happened then?" Kroeger's voice is soft and sympathetic.

"On Mr. Stonemann's instructions, I went to the door, opened it, and proceeded to go outside to help the nun carry in the money. When we got to the car, the nun, Mr. Conroy, went to the front door, opened it, and handed me the keys, indicating I should open the trunk. While the other guard, Mr. Waterman, held the flashlight, I inserted the key into the lock and popped the trunk open." He pauses, closing his eyes, and I see perspiration forming on his forehead. "The trunk was filled with green garbage bags. I was unable to dislodge any of them, and while the nun held the flashlight, Mr. Waterman came to my assistance. We tugged and tugged until the top sack came free. There was a puff of air or smoke against my face, and that's all I remember."

"No further questions, Your Honor." Kroeger is savoring the anger written on the face of the jury.

"Cross, Mr. Conroy?" Logan's tone is bordering on the sarcastic, as if to say, "What are you going to do with this?"

"Yes, Your Honor. A couple of questions. Mr. Pierce. If you knew it was me trying to disguise myself as a nun, why didn't you tell Mr. Stonemann something like, 'Hey, Mr. Conroy is out here dressed up like a nun?' I mean, since we know each other, wouldn't you have said something to that effect?"

Mother's question stirs several of the jurors. It's a damm good one.

"Well, I didn't recognize you right off. Wasn't till the next day. I only remember that the face under the hood was somehow familiar, that's all."

Dog leans over and whispers, "Look at the jury. They bought that lie. Mother is digging himself a hole with this witness."

I have to agree.

Mother apparently doesn't. "What is the date on the FBI Field Report you've been reading from?"

"March 16, 1976."

"And the robbery occurred when, again?"

"December 7th, 1975. Pearl Harbor day."

"No further questions at this time. I would like the witness ordered to remain available for recall and direct examination by the defense," Mother says, and begins shuffling some papers on the counsel table.

"Very well. You have that right. The witness is so instructed."

Mr. Pierce smiles at the jury and leaves the stand as Kroeger is calling his next witness. "The prosecution calls Officer Pete Dolan of the Fall City Police Department."

Officer Dolan takes the stand and reads the police report into the record. I take my copy of it and give it to Big Smith, who pushes it over the railing to Mother. When Officer Dolan reaches the portion of the report that describes the assault by a giant penguin, nine jurors are smiling, two are frowning, and one is examining the ceiling. I figure the religious makeup of the jury is nine Protestants, two Catholics, and one Jew.

Officer Dolan explains again the scene when he opened the vault and found Stonemann with his wet pants and covered with garden snakes wearing baby rattles. I see two jurors hiding smiles. Probably ex–bank customers who have had dealings with Stonemann in the past.

As Dolan approaches the portion of the report covering the thumbprint, I see Mother tensing, ready to spring to his feet. As soon as Kroeger finishes, Mother goes right after Dolan. "Didn't this thumbprint have a red circle drawn around it?"

"Yes, sir, it did."

"Would you say it is unusual for a robber to leave his prints, then blatantly draw attention to the location?"

"Yes."

"No further questions, Your Honor." Everyone on the jury is frowning now. Bells are ringing in my sorting machine, but before I can get a handle on the source, Judge Logan speaks. "The witness may step down. I'm sure the jury must be as eager for lunch as I am. Let's adjourn until one P.M."

"All rise."

And the first session is completed.

Outside the courtroom we gather into a compact group at the head of the stairs. Cynthia takes charge. "I have to spend some time with Noid," she says, "and then I'd like to meet with all of you. The Red Lion Inn, just down the street. Why don't you go ahead, and we'll be along in a few minutes."

We agree, and we're off down the stairs. "How does it look to you," I ask Mary.

"Bad, James. The prosecutor is a very efficient man."

I concur, and all the way to the restaurant we're silent. We park and go inside, to find the rest of the group waiting. It has more the appearance of a wake than of a continuation of the morning's reunion. We find a table, and I sign a blank government voucher, "Flat Store, government witness." I give the waitress the ticket and a five-dollar bill and tell her to fill in the blanks. I just don't want her to think we're some cheap Feds, or something.

Cynthia comes in as we're getting settled, and reaches the same conclusion I have. "My, what a sad-looking bunch."

"You bring some good news and I'll celebrate till the cows come home," Dog tells her.

"Well," she says softly, and we lean toward the center of the huge table we've taken. "There's good news and . . . there's great news!"

"Run the program," Little Smith insists.

"My investigators have been doing some digging. Everett Stonemann, the bank's president, apparently pulled the same land-loan swindle he used with Donald's aunt and uncle on at least twenty-five other families in this area. We have a local TV crew out interviewing them right now."

"Is Noid with them?" Little Smith asks.

"No. He's monitoring the judge's chambers. He just heard that Logan is on the board of directors of the parent company of the Fall City National Bank."

"He should excuse himself," Dog says, suddenly the joint attorney once more. "If he has a vested interest in the trial, it's a flagrant breach of ethics for him to sit."

"Logan's involvement is deeper than suspected," Cynthia replies. "I'm sorry, I can't share the why with you just now. Mother's orders," she adds, to preclude further questioning on the subject.

"We're going to break the story on the six o'clock news, along with the information that Everett Stonemann, the warden's brother, is faking his mental illness to avoid prosecution in the land swindles."

"Jesus, I hope Warden Stonemann is watching the six o'clock news."

"If he is, there's another interesting item," she says, digging in her handbag. "I meant to show this to you this morning." She lays a piece of copy out on the table. "I just got this from the home office on the wire. Frederick Ralton Creech, a senior officer specialist of the Bureau of Prisons, was arrested today by wildlife agents as he completed a sale of clams illegally taken from the Federal Game Preserve at McNeil Island. As he was taken into custody he claimed he was operating under the instruction of former warden Clifford J. Stonemann, who is presently the special assistant to the western regional director of the Bureau of Prisons, Mr. Samuel S. Grossenberger. Mr. Creech has agreed to testify against the ex-warden in a federal criminal prosecution . . . in exchange for immunity."

"They nailed them!" Big shouts, and several customers turn in our direction, shake their heads, and return to their conversations.

"Who did they say Creech sold the clams to?" I ask suspiciously.

"An Indian. He gave his name as Kawasheega," Cynthia answers me matter-of-factly. "He was not detained, as the Indians have the treaty right to buy or sell shellfish year round. Mother thought you in particular would be interested in the story, Flat Store."

"Damn, but Mother has mastered the art of the getback!" Dog beams.

"I think it would be better if he'd mastered the art of self-defense," Mary reminds us. "He still has to get through this trial."

The thought stays with me all the way back to the court-house.

We're a few seconds late, and the trial is already underway as we return to our seats. Kroeger has the Fall City Police Department's fingerprint expert on the stand. Detective Albert Stonemann. "And so, after you lifted the print, you—By the way, did you lift the print from the vault personally?"

"Yes, sir. *Personally*. I took the lift to the lab, and then compared it to prints on file belonging to Mr. Donald R. Conroy, that gentleman seated right over there at the defense table. The prints were identical."

"A perfect match?"

"No question about it."

"You may cross-examine," Kroeger says pointedly.

Mother rises to his feet, his shoulders slump, and he ambles to the stand. "Are you related to the president of the Fall City National Bank?"

"Yes, sir," the witness answers proudly. "Everett Horton Stonemann is one of my uncles."

"I see. Do you do any other types of fingerprint work, by the way, such as identifying corpses?"

"Yes, sir." He looks puzzled. So does everyone else in the courtroom.

"Did you have occasion to identify one Karl W. Conroy's body after he blew his—"

"Objection, Your Honor. Irrelevant."

Mother edges in front of the jury as he speaks rapidly to the judge. "I'm simply trying to establish whether or not he's ever taken a fingerprint before, Your Honor. The prosecution has introduced him as an expert witness without laying the proper foundation for his expertise. I have a right to establish his credentials."

Logan is scowling at the prosecutor. Obviously the fair-haired boy of the court has committed a major blunder. "The witness shall answer."

"Yes. I identified the body."

"Did the prints on the corpse match those on file?"

"Yes, sir."

Mother makes a show of considering his next question, then tells the court, "I would concede that this witness is qualified as an expert, Your Honor."

"Note the qualification for the record," Logan says dryly. He's staring daggers at Kroeger, though. One juror has noted the interchange.

"Now, then, Detective Stonemann. Were my prints the first

ones you checked in your files after you lifted the print *personally* from the vault?"

"No. We checked many."

"Isn't it a fact that the very first one you checked was that of the deceased's son, also named Karl W. Conroy?"

"Yes, as a matter of fact, I believe that's correct."

"The reason you checked those particular prints first, please?"

"Well ..." Detective Stonemann is shifting in his seat, his eyes shooting nervous glances at AUSA Kroeger. Kroeger is busy whispering back and forth with an assistant. "He was the prime suspect," Detective Stonemann blurts out. "After both his parents killed themselves because they felt they had been cheated out of their land by my uncle, we assumed—"

"*Objection!*" Kroeger screams.

"Ahhh, Mr. Kroeger. I see you're back with us. The objection?"

"Your Honor," Mother cuts in quickly. "Since the bank all but murdered the boy's parents, it's only logical that—"

Wham! Wham! Wham! Logan's gavel is crashing on the block. "You are entirely out of order, Mr. Conroy."

Mother has done his job. The jury is awake, alert, and paying very close attention. The juror who has been following the silent messages between Kroeger and Logan is whispering to the jurors on either side.

"I will tolerate no more questions outside the field of expertise of this witness, whom you have taken such care to identify as an expert in fingerprinting." He glowers at Mother, then shifts his gaze to Kroeger and frowns. "Your next question, please."

"No further questions, Your Honor," Kroeger blurts out.

"Mr. Kroeger, I was speaking to Mr. Conroy. It's his cross."

"No further cross," Mother says, and beams at the judge.

Kroeger calls an FBI expert from the fingerprint and identification lab. Special agent Bruce Ell. For the next twenty minutes the AUSA works very meticulously to establish this agent's credentials. He has the agent give the jury a short course in the identification process used, and allows Agent Ell to establish himself in the jury's mind as an unchallengeable authority.

Mother does not object throughout the lengthy buildup.

Kroeger is into the heart of the agent's testimony. He passes him a yellowed five-by-eight card. "I show you the government's exhibit A. Are those your initials on the back of the fingerprint card?"

Agent Ell studies the lettering carefully, and replies, "Yes, sir, those are most definitely my initials. You see, as the lifts come in, I very carefully date and initial each card so as to preclude the possibility of a mix-up."

"And this is the lift of a print taken from the vault door of the Fall City National Bank by one Detective Stonemann?"

"Yes, sir. I have been able to independently establish that fact."

"And this print. It's a thumbprint, isn't it?"

"Yes. The left thumb."

"Is this print or is it not the exact configuration of the print you have on file for Mr. Donald R. Conroy, the man sitting over there?" He points accusingly at Mother, who gives the agent a friendly wave.

"The same configuration exactly."

"No doubt about it?"

"None."

"Your witness, Mr. Conroy." Kroeger is talking to Mother but staring at the jury. I can't blame him. They're all nodding in full agreement.

Mother appears defeated as he takes his place in front of the lectern. "Did you file the standard report form on the submitted print?"

"Yes. It's routine with the Bureau."

"Do you have a copy of the report with you?"

"No, sir, I do not."

Mother slumps visibly. "No further questions. Please instruct the witness to remain available for direct examination."

"Done. The court will recess for ten minutes. I would like to see Mr. Kroeger in chambers with his proposed jury instructions. Mr. Conroy? We'll cover yours in the morning."

Judge Logan is glaring at Kroeger. Three members of the jury are studying the interchange as Kroeger scurries toward the entrance to His Honor's chambers. "Looks like Kroeger is in trouble with the judge," Little Smith whispers.

"I thought the judge was supposed to be impartial." Mary's dry comment evokes smiles from the rest of the crew.

Noid comes in from the corridor and whispers, "Judge Logan is chewing Kroeger out for letting Mother get in the information regarding the suicides." He notices a U.S. marshal staring in our direction, and lowers his voice further. "He's also very concerned about the fingerprint report. He believes Mother might have a copy and is setting up the FBI agent for a perjury charge."

"Does Mother have a copy?" Odds asks.

"Of course," Cynthia replies. "I came by an uncensored version."

"Where did you get that?" Odds presses.

"Washington, D.C.," she explains. I recognize the tone and nearly burst out laughing.

"All rise," the bailiff commands. "The court of the Honorable Francis W. Logan is back in session."

Kroeger's composure has returned. "The prosecution calls Mr. Humbert James Barker, also known as Flat Store." He receives a few chuckles from the jury box for his witty little introduction. The son of a gun will pay for that, I'm thinking as I'm sworn in.

"State your name for the record," Kroeger says, smirking.

"Humbert James Barker. That's H-u-m-b-e-r-t James Barker," I say proudly.

"Aren't you also known as Flat Store . . . F-l-a-t S-t-o-r-e?" he says, attempting to mimic my voice.

"At one time I did respond to the name, but I have since shed my prison nickname as a part of my rehabilitation." He looks stunned at the switch-up, and for the first time I see him take note that I'm respectably dressed.

"So you now prefer to conceal the fact you were once called Flat Store?"

"No, I prefer to think I have shed the name much as a cater-pillar divests itself of its ugly cocoon to become a butterfly."

Kroeger's jaw drops, and I turn to Judge Logan and smile in-nocently. The judge has obviously been led to expect something besides what he's hearing, too. The jury members haven't batted an eye. They never met Flat Store.

Kroeger has lost his train of thought. "Ahhh, I see.... Did the defendant—that man over there"—he points an accusing fin-ger at Mother—"did he ever tell you . . . Strike the question. Are you or are you not the friend of Mr. Conroy?"

"Yes, sir. Mr. Conroy is my closest friend."

"Did he ever tell you how he robbed the bank of Fall City?"

"During the period of time I was incarcerated with Mr. Conroy, the subject of the Fall City bank robbery did arise. Since he was convicted of the crime, it was only natural that the subject surface in our conversations. I developed a bona fide curiosity about the . . ."

"Bona fide, Mr. Barker?" He's grinning. The cat in the cage with the feathers in his mouth.

"B-o-n-a f-i-d-e . . . excuse me, it's Latin. The literal translation is commonly held to imply that something is true or correct. It—"

"*I know what bona fide means!*" Kroeger shouts.

"Then why did you ask?" The jury is smiling at me for the first time.

Judge Logan comes to his rescue. "It might help, Mr. Kroeger, if you simply asked the questions and listened to the an-swers."

"We were discussing the bank robbery," I offer helpfully. "Would you like me to continue?"

"Yessss," he hisses. "Continue."

"Throughout our conversations regarding the robbery, Mr. Conroy never once alluded to the possibility that he might have been the perpetrator."

"The what?"

"Perpetrator. P—"

"That's *enough!*" Kroeger sits down.

Judge Logan finishes the job for him. "Any cross, Mr. Conroy?"

Mother steps to the lectern and stares at me for a moment, and I can see he is having the same trouble I am. Maintaining a straight face. "Did you receive any communication from me regarding your testimony here today?"

"Yes, I did. You told me to tell the truth, that the truth would set you free."

"Have you told the truth?"

"Yes, sir."

"No further questions."

When I look up, Kroeger is studying the rest of the crew from 3-J-5, trying to find someone he can handle. His ingrained prejudice directs his eyes to Fast Eddie.

"I call Edward Wilson McCoy."

Fast goes to the stand and is sworn in as I'm returning to my seat next to Mary. She tickles me gently in the ribs as I join her. "You were magnificent!"

"Yup."

Kroeger goes to work on Fast. "Did you have a nickname in prison?"

"How could one not?"

"What was it?" Kroeger snaps. I believe he realizes he's been had by now, and can't find a way out, so he's elected to be intimidating.

"I was once known by the somewhat dubious but descriptive appellation of Fast Eddie. While I decline to feel pride over my prior prison experience, I have incorporated the name into my modest roofing business, where it is both appropriate and illuminating."

"So, you're a businessman?" Kroeger is trying to help the jury see this obvious half-truth.

"As I said, a modest one. I have fewer than one hundred people in my employ." Fast Eddie's tone is almost apologetic. Kroeger is nearly apoplectic.

"Did Mr. Conroy list *you* in his circle of friends?"

"I don't know what category he might place me in, but I would certainly *hope* he considered me a friend. He is one of the finest gentlemen it has ever been my pleasure to meet. He found me at the bottom of the social ladder and guided me to a decent life in the mainstream of American society. Certainly, he merits my friendship for life." Fast's wife, Alecia, is glowing.

Kroeger is tongue-tied, shuffling his notes and moving aimlessly back and forth between the prosecution table and the lectern. After an embarrassing silence, Judge Logan asks. "Have you considered proceeding with your direct, Mr. Kroeger?" Logan puts his face in his hand. The jurors are nodding and whispering amongst themselves.

"No further questions, Your Honor."

Mother is on his feet. "Mr. McCoy. Did I ever tell you I had robbed the bank of Fall City?"

"No, you did not."

"Did the prosecutor attempt to elicit this information from you in private before the trial started?"

"*Objection.* Beyond the scope of the direct." Kroeger shouts.

"Affirmed." Logan's expression is raw rage.

"Procedurally, he's right," Dog whispers. "But Mother got it in anyway. Neat bit of work."

Kroeger is too deeply committed and too confused to attempt to cut his losses. He calls Noid Benny to the stand, attempts to swear him in himself, is corrected by the clerk, and finally begins his questioning. "Did Mr. Conroy ever tell you he robbed the Fall City Bank?"

"No. He never told anyone in 3-J-5 he robbed anything."

Kroeger believes he's on to something. He arches an eyebrow for the jury and asks, "How can you be certain of that statement? Were you with him all of the time? Were you privy to every conversation he had?"

"Of course not. I know he didn't tell anyone he robbed the bank because every man who lived in the cell was examined by a trained hypnotist just yesterday. Dr. Freidling, in Spokane, Washington. A certified expert witness on hypnotism. You used him yourself in *U.S.* v. *Martin.* I have the transcripts of those examinations right here—" Noid is reaching into his briefcase.

"That will be enough!" Kroeger shouts, cutting him off.

"—in my briefcase." Noid slips a huge stack of papers up onto the railing of the witness box . . . on the jury side, of course.

The jury is staring at the papers, and Kroeger is doing imitations of the ovulating guppy we kept in the cell. Judge Logan can't take his eyes off the transcripts, and neither can the members of the jury.

Kroeger grabs at a straw. "Possibly the hypnotist could tell the jury just how Mr. Conroy's fingerprints came to be found on the vault door."

"Objection." Mother is on his feet.

"Reason?"

"I don't object to the question, Your Honor; certainly someone should look into how my fingerprints came to be lifted from the safe. What I do object to is the disservice the prosecutor is showing to the sacred office he holds by trying to substantiate previously admitted evidence during colloquy with an unrelated witness. It borders on the unethical."

"Sustained," Logan whispers.

"No further questions, Your Honor," Kroeger croaks.

"All rise," the bailiff says, and Logan is out of the courtroom before half the people in the audience get to their feet.

Mother turns and winks.

I find myself wishing I knew how in hell he was going to get around his thumbprint on the door of the vault and the eyewitness testimony that accompanied it. Mother's been cute, we've all done our part, but it is not a working substitute for something to destroy the damning evidence against him.

My conscience points out the obvious. *The problem is we're letting them do all the lying.*

The dining room of the Red Lion Inn is crowded. We have managed to secure the same large circular table we had at lunch, and consequently have a fairly decent view of the television screen at the end of the bar.

Cynthia comes in looking as though she's been rode hard and put up wet, as our trainer might say. She's a tuckered young lady.

"Busy evening?" Mary asks sympathetically.

"Wait until you see the news," Cynthia replies, perking up. "You aren't going to believe the can of worms Mother's trial has opened." She glances at her watch. "Where's the television?"

"Over there." Odds points.

Cynthia turns in her chair and settles back just as the local station goes from the network feed to its own programming. The sequence opens with an establishing shot of the federal courthouse. A voice-over says: "Evidence of possible wrongdoing by members of the board of directors of Amalgamated Banks, parent company of the Fall City National Bank, emerged today from a source close to Judge Francis W. Logan, himself a member of the board. Judge Logan is currently sitting on the trial of Mr. Donald R. Conroy, a sometime resident of Fall City and the subject of our feature story this evening."

"Source close to Judge Logan?" I ask.

"Right in his telephone." Noid beams.

"Amid rising civic concerns regarding the bank's possible misconduct in certain loan matters, questions arose today in the case of the *United States* v. *Donald Conroy* that appear to link alle-

389

gations of perjury in the trial to a rapidly spreading panorama of malfeasance throughout the civic hierarchy of the entire county. What began as a simple criminal prosecution for bank robbery has also become the focus of the investigations of several well-known investigative reporters."

Cynthia is glowing with pride. "A little something I slipped into the segment to keep Mr. Kroeger, Judge Logan, and the government's witnesses from sleeping too soundly tonight." Her eyes are dancing!

"At the center of this unfolding drama is Donald R. Conroy, the defendant in the Fall City National Bank robbery case." The screen blanks momentarily, then opens on a young woman holding a microphone. She is standing in front of an aging, run-down farmhouse that is struggling to keep from being overgrown by ivy. A number of wild-looking chickens are scratching in the yard, and sounds of lowing cattle are recognizable from somewhere off-camera. "Good evening. This is Elaine Garcia with a personalized report on the man who has once again managed to stir the surface of this seemingly placid community. Donald R. Conroy's life began here, in this simple farmhouse, on a note of tragedy. Shortly after birth, both of his natural parents were killed in an automobile accident. At the age of six months, he was adopted by his aunt and uncle, Louise and Karl Conroy. From this point on, Mr. Conroy enjoyed a normal childhood." The station cuts to a fading Kodak print of a freckled-faced boy proudly showing off a string of trout to a smiling couple in their mid-twenties. Despite his youth and the missing front teeth, it is clearly a picture of Mother. "Donald Conroy graduated from Coolidge High School, matriculated at the University of Idaho, and after graduation, entered the United States Army through the ROTC program." A montage of shots shows Mother in cap and gown, then standing with the same couple in front of the U of I administration building; he's wearing the uniform and insignia of a second lieutenant in the infantry. The final shot in the series has a graying version of the same couple pinning a major's oak leaves onto a pair of combat fatigues that are embellished with a parachutist's wings and a ranger patch. "Mr. Conroy was a member of the cadre that trained the Cuban expeditionary force for the ill-fated Bay of Pigs invasion . . ."

Odds leans forward and whispers, "Georgia, Alabama, California, Florida, and Mississippi! They have Army training bases in all those spots. Mother learned everything he knows about burglary, robbery, and forgery in Army training schools!"

"After the Bay of Pigs fiasco, Major Conroy"—the picture cuts from the young woman reporter to Mother standing waist-deep in a group of Asiatic-looking pygmies—"was posted to Laos to train friendly Meo tribesmen in ambush tactics along the Ho Chi Minh Trail." The camera returns to the reporter. "Major Conroy's experiences in Southeast Asia led to a period of disillusionment with our government's policy. He abhorred the inhuman use and eventual slaughter of these essentially trusting Stone Age peoples, complained to his superiors, and finally, in frustration, filed a suit in the federal district court in Columbus, Georgia, to protest the actions. The filing resulted in a court-martial, in which he was acquitted. He nevertheless resigned his commission and returned here to take up farming with his adoptive parents, Karl and Louise Conroy."

I'm starting to get a tight knot in the pit of my stomach. The reporter takes my mind off the thought for a moment. "Back home, Mr. Conroy quickly established himself as a quixotic advocate of various protest and consumer-advocacy groups, filing suits in the local federal court on such issues as migrant-worker housing, welfare disputes, and abuses of Native Americans. Whether or not he has also become the bank-robbing criminal whom FBI and local law-enforcement officials insist he is, will be a matter settled tomorrow in Judge Logan's court. Back to you, Bill."

"Mother was telling us the truth all along. He's a dyed-in-the-wool do-gooder. I *knew* he was a square at the beginning," Little Smith says.

"At the beginning, you were a vegetable," Dog reminds him.

I want to argue, but the knot is back in my stomach. The television shows a commercial, and then I see the face of the young man with the camera Cynthia was talking to earlier. "Sources in the offices of the Federal Land Bank in Boise announced today they are launching an investigation into the practices of the Fall City National Bank during the stewardship of Everett Horton Stonemann. Our information indicates that as many as fifty local families, possibly a much higher number, may have been swindled out of their property. You might remember the double suicide of Karl and Louise Conroy some years back. It was . . ."

"Jesus." I can't hold it anymore.

"What is it?" Noid asks.

"I just woke up! Mother's aunt and uncle. They were the only parents he'd ever known. It's just as if the bank drove his mother and father to suicide. His entire family has been wiped out by the bank. Jesus."

"He took it hard," Cynthia confirms. "I've talked to people who said he wandered around in a daze for a week or more after it happened." She pauses, considering her next words. "But you're wrong about one thing. He has other family. His brother . . . actually his cousin, but they were raised as brothers. Donald became very angry with me when I tracked him down—"

"That's what you two were always arguing about in the visiting room?"

"That's part of it. Shortly after the robbery, young Conroy went to South America."

I watch her mental brakes go on. End of discourse.

Mary is frowning. "How does this affect the trial? I mean, the exposé."

"It can't hurt Mother's case at all." Big Smith is grinning. "I wish we could develop a program that would predict the behavior of juries, though."

"I make it eight to five against the government," Odds puts in.

"I thought you'd quit betting," Mary says playfully.

"I did. Three years ago. I haven't bet a dime since I learned a lesson about friendship and trust that will last me for the rest of my life."

An uncomfortable moment of silence is broken by Noid. "Eight to five isn't good enough. They still have the eyewitness and the damn print."

Now the other light goes on in my head. "They haven't got a damn thing." I don't elaborate, and everyone takes the outburst for anger. I let them have the impression, because I don't want to ruin their fun tomorrow.

I try to sign the tab as a government witness, and the waitress tells me Mr. Kroeger has cut off our expenses. His idea of a getback, I suppose. He'll see what one is really supposed to look like in the morning, because now it's Mother's turn.

I'm still rubbing the sleep out of my eyes when we reach the courthouse. Noid is waiting for us just outside the courtroom. "Judge Logan has been giving it to Kroeger for twenty minutes. The newscast last night has him plenty scared."

Noid removes the earplug from his ear, and I see an almost-invisible wire leading down through his collar to a lump in his jacket. He's mastered his trade, for sure. "Judge Logan also told Kroeger if the case falls apart he's not going to be able to bail him out. His Honor is worried about being indicted himself."

"We'd better find some seats." Mary is tugging at my sleeve. "Look at the crowd."

She's right. People are streaming through the metal detectors. Mostly simple-looking folks in housedresses and bib overalls, but I see a sprinkling of journalistic chic, tropical worsted shirts and slacks, in sufficient quantity to realize the trial is getting national coverage starting today. A familiar profile catches my eye. "There's Warden Stonemann!"

Cynthia studies him for a second and smiles. "No. That's *Senator* Stonemann. The uncle of the warden and the president of the bank. He's responsible for Logan's and Kroeger's appointments through the Senate justice committee. He's come to survey his own political damage." She's smiling, wicked to the gum line.

Mary pulls me into the courtroom, and we take our seats just as Mother is being brought in by the marshals. He smiles, waves, and goes immediately to the defense table and begins rearranging his papers.

Kroeger comes in, and he looks as though he's been out all

night with a nymphomaniac on a speeding motorcycle. The members of the jury follow him with their eyes, and I notice every one of them is casting glances in Mother's direction as Kroeger opens his briefcase. Most of them are smiling.

"All rise. The court of the Honorable Francis W. Logan is now in session."

"Your Honor? The government rests," Kroeger announces.

"Very well. Mr. Conroy? Do you exercise your privilege?"

"Yes, Your Honor. I have a brief opening statement to make." Mother begins, and once again his tone is deceptively professional. "Ladies and gentlemen of the jury. Counsel for the government has presented an interesting and seemingly compelling case, the substance of which centers around three witnesses. I will recall these three today and prove that the eyewitness testimony of Mr. Pierce, the bank guard, is tainted beyond the point that a reasonable person would accept. We will also hear that the thumbprint upon which the prosecution has placed so much emphasis is a pure and simple forgery." There is a stirring of surprise in the spectators' section and, more importantly, in the jury box. "But first I will recall the chief of accounting, Amalgamated Banks, parent company of the Fall City National Bank. He possesses some interesting information, which he was, I'm sure, hesitant to divulge to you yesterday." Mother positions himself in front of the jury box and stares directly into their faces. "When I have finished today, you will be able to conclude beyond any doubt that the case presented against me is not only woven out of whole cloth, but the tapestry it forms is tinted with the green of greed, the red of malice, and the black of foul perjury. Thank you."

The overcrowded courtroom is full of "Ohhh"s and "Ahhh"s. A subtle shifting in their seats indicates the jury is leaning the same way. Our way. Mother's way.

"The defense calls Ephraim Collier."

The accountant takes the stand, and Judge Logan reminds him he is still under oath. It doesn't take a Mike Hammer to see they know each other.

Mother begins to question him. "Would you please tell the

jury if the stolen money, or any portion thereof, was ever returned directly to the board of directors of the bank's parent company?"

"Pardon me?" The accountant is stalling, and I can see perspiration breaking out on his forehead. The jurors are leaning forward, and Judge Logan has turned his face to the wall.

"Did you or did you not get the money back?"

"No, sir. Well, not exactly."

"Could you please explain 'not exactly'?"

"We did receive a package that we believed might contain at least a portion of the stolen funds."

"I see. And could you describe the contents of this package?"

The accountant is looking to Kroeger for some help. Kroeger shrugs. "We sent it all to the FBI crime lab, and they confirmed our belief."

"Which was?" Mother asks patiently.

"That the package contained the ashes of marked bills taken during the robbery and a large quantity of . . . ah . . . mule manure."

The jury is tittering, the farmers in the audience are guffawing loudly, and our crew is laughing so hard tears are streaming down their faces.

"Isn't it a bit unusual for a bank to receive stolen money back in such a manner?"

"Of course it's unusual," Collier snaps. "It was downright preposterous."

Logan frowns, and I double-check the jury. They are laughing openly now.

"Did it occur to you at the time, based upon the bizarre incident with the mule sh—ah . . . droppings, that the robber might have had some motive other than simple greed?"

"Objection. Calls for a conclusion on the part of the witness."

"Ahh, Mr. Kroeger. Good morning to you, sir," Logan growls.

Mother interrupts as Logan is preparing to speak. "Your Honor? Murder by fraud calls for a conclusion on the part of humanity itself."

"Shut up! . . . Mr. Conroy," Logan shouts, then takes a moment to recompose himself. He turns to the jury and says, "The jury is instructed to disregard Mr. Conroy's outburst." He looks back to Mother, and I see the face of the eagle once more. "Mr. Conroy. You have long been a thorn in the side of this court. While I may not be able to regulate your impulsive behavior outside this courtroom, I can assure you I will demand and receive proper respect during the balance of this trial."

"Of course, Your Honor. I would not wish to do anything to further disillusion the public about the quality of justice found here." He faces the jury and bobs his head. "Ladies and gentlemen, I apologize for my ill-timed statement."

"If you would just get on with it, Mr. Conroy."

"Certainly, Your Honor. No further questions about the mule manure for Mr. Collier. Thank you, sir."

Kroeger wants the odor of the mule manure out of the courtroom as quickly as possible. So does Logan. "No cross, Your Honor."

"Thank you. Call your next witness, Mr. Conroy," Logan commands.

Mother faces the audience and says, "The defense calls Karl W. Conroy."

A big, rawboned youngster steps away from the back wall of the courtroom and proceeds to the bar, where the bailiff lets him through. The court clerk swears him in.

"He looks enough like Mother to be his brother," Mary notes.

Mother takes a few seconds, then asks softly, "Karl? We're relatives, are we not?

"Yes. We're first cousins."

"Have we discussed the testimony you are about to give?"

"We haven't seen each other in nearly five years."

"Are you the son of—"

"Objection. Irrelevant." Kroeger doesn't want another version of the Conroys' double suicide in the record, and the judge obviously doesn't either.

Dog leans over and tells me, "He has to let this in to establish the relationship with the defendant."

Right on cue, Judge Logan rules, "Overruled. The witness may answer."

"Are you the son of Karl and Louise Conroy?"

"They were my parents," the boy offers softly.

"Were?" The question falls gently on the silent courtroom.

"They committed suicide after Everett Stonemann swindled them out of our farm."

There is a rumbling in the courtroom that has the hairs on the back of my neck trundling about and the marshals glancing nervously at their shotguns.

"Did you ever tell me you wanted to kill Mr. Stonemann?"

"Yes. Several times."

"Would I, then, have reason to believe you might have robbed the Fall City National Bank, and do you think I'd have allowed myself to be convicted of the crime?"

"Objection. Calls for a conclusion."

"*Overruled,* Mr. Kroeger."

"Logan is bailing out on the prosecutor," Dog notes. "The objection is perfectly legitimate."

Young Conroy is smiling sadly at Mother. "Yes. I think you'd have ample reason to believe I'd committed the crime. The police, too . . . and certainly you'd allow yourself to be convicted in my place. I suppose I'd do the same for you."

Everyone in the courtroom takes a breath. We know what the next question will be. "Did you rob the bank, son?" The voice is cotton-ball-soft.

"No. I've even passed a lie-detector test on the question. I was at my girlfriend's home with her father. They were trying to talk me out of going to South America. I didn't have enough hate left to rob Stonemann, and I didn't even know the bank had been robbed, until a few months ago, when Miss Evans of the *Seattle Times* tracked me down."

"Do you have any evidence that I robbed the bank of Fall City?"

Logan lets Mother get away with the question. You don't have to be a federal judge to see the mood of the people in the courtroom.

"No, but I wish one of us had!" He pauses and smiles. "Still, I don't think we'd have been as delightfully inventive as the man who did!"

The courtroom erupts in laughter. Mother's next words sober us all.

"I missed seeing you, Karl," Mother adds softly.

"Me too," he replies, and his hands beat my own to the handkerchief by half a tick. All members of the jury are dabbing at their eyes and shooting hard looks at Kroeger and the Judge.

"No further questions," Mother says. "I'm sorry, Karl."

"No cross," Kroeger mumbles, without rising.

"Call Mr. Frank Pierce." Mother's voice is husky.

For the first time, I notice a new, stronger, and more ugly undercurrent in the courtroom. It's the spectators mulling over the latest testimony and comparing what they've heard with last evening's newscast. Logan raps for order. "I expect quiet in my court. If I don't get it I will have the marshals clear the room of spectators."

The angry hum subsides, and Mother moves back to the lectern and begins his interrogation of Frank Pierce, the bank guard. Logan holds up a hand until he reminds Pierce of his oath, then Mother goes right after him. "Mr. Pierce. You previously testified that the bank was robbed on December seventh, 1975, but you did not sign the FBI 302 Field Report until March sixteenth, 1976. Is that correct?"

Pierce is already beginning to perspire. He looks to Kroeger for support.

"Objection!"

"Grounds?"

"Ahhh . . . repetitious questioning?"

Logan considers the question for a moment, and Dog gives me his opinion. "He has to let it in. Mother has the right to ask whatever he wants on direct examination. Pierce is *his* witness now."

"Overruled. The witness shall answer."

"Yes, sir. I did. That's what I said."

Mother turns to the jury. "Did you answer 'Yes'?" He's smiling the same smile he was wearing the first time I saw him up close, just before he whipped the Giant. The trap is about to spring.

"Yes." Pierce is sweating profusely now.

"Let me get one more thing straight in my mind. You were drugged senseless on the seventh of December, gave the FBI an oral report the following day, then waited until March before you actually signed the statement?"

"Yes."

"The report—did it reflect your exact words, or was it not in fact the FBI agent's interpretation of what you told him?"

"It wasn't quite word for word."

"Did you notice any glaring errors?"

Now I know what Mother's up to. It's standard FBI procedure to leave all the statements in note form until after the investigation is complete. Then all statements can be adjusted to dovetail so the AUSA who gets the case doesn't have any embarrassing inconsistencies to deal with. Most witnesses accept the minor deviations in their stories, and by the time the case actually goes to trial, the FBI 302 has replaced their real memory of the events, and they testify to the contents of the report. The courts tolerate the process even though it is the culprit in most of the miscarriages of justice that occur.

Pierce wants to be cute with his answer. "In substance, the report was perfectly accurate."

"In substance?"

"In substance. It's right dead on the money." Pierce is regaining his confidence. The jury senses it, too.

Mother strolls back to the counsel table, selects a single sheet of paper, and returns to his position between the jury box and Mr. Pierce.

"That's the unexpurgated 302 I dug up for him," Cynthia says proudly.

"I have a copy of that report, Mr. Pierce." Mother lays it on the rail of the jury box. Judge Logan's eyes snap to Kroeger, and the AUSA blanches. Even from the spectators' section I can see it is not the half-blanked-out version the FBI usually surrenders to the defense.

"You know, Mr. Pierce, what I can't understand after reading this report and comparing it to your testimony is the fact that not once, never, did you mention *my name* as the person who robbed the bank!"

Pierce relaxes. He's prepared for this one. "Well, that's very easy to explain."

"Please do."

"I told the Fall City police officers it was you, and forgot to mention it to the federal agent when he interviewed me."

"I see. And once again, please, when did you give this information to Detective Stonemann."

"When ..." I see a crafty look come over Pierce's face. "When," he continues, "Detective Stonemann absolutely and positively identified your print on the vault face. A few days after the robbery."

"Oh, I see." Mother is rubbing his jaw as though this bald-faced lie makes perfect sense to him. "You got robbed. Knew it was me—and didn't tell anyone for approximately a week? ... But wait, didn't you say you reported it the very next day?"

Frank Pierce has the gall to blush. The kid with his hand in the cookie jar.

"You're a liar, Mr. Pierce," Mother says softly.

"An' you are one of those damn Conroys that was always causin' trouble fer the bank. You're worse than a liar," he shouts as the last vestiges of civilization begin to fall away. "You're some kinda damn troublemaker who don't have no respect fer quality people like Mr. Stonemann."

"That I am, Mr. Pierce. That ... I ... am." He glares at him for a moment, then shakes his head sadly. "No further questions of this government ... witness."

"No cross," Kroeger mumbles.

"Call Bruce Ell, special agent, Federal Bureau of Investigation."

The agent is recalled, reminded of his oath, and Mother starts to work. "Did you tell this court you didn't have a copy of the fingerprint report you filed in this case?"

"No, sir. I said I didn't have one with me." Agent Ell is trying to reproduce the assured, pedantic tone of his prior appearance, and I have to admit he's not doing too badly.

Mother turns to the counsel table, picks up several papers, and walks slowly back to the witness box. He stacks the pile next to the agent's arm. "Did you tell this jury the submitted print matched mine exactly?"

Agent Ell squirms in his seat, and for a moment then I see him discover the back door out of the trap, and he needs one desperately. Agents are taught that a lie or deliberately planted false impression is okay, but if they get caught, their butts are off to Billings, Montana, to search the sagebrush for subversive jackrabbits. The agent elects for his career. "What I told you and this fine jury, Mr. Conroy, was that the *configuration* of the print was precisely the same as yours."

Mother spits out the next question. "Was . . . that . . . my . . . print?"

"No." The agent pauses and offers apologetic looks to the judge and the prosecutor; then he bails out of the smoking aircraft. "As a matter of fact, it was a rather clever fake, a copy of your print, but its slightly larger size was a dead giveaway."

"A *dead* giveaway?"

"Certainly. I noticed it the second the print came in."

A scuffle at the rear of the courtroom, and I turn in time to see Detective Stonemann pushing his way through the standing crowd, trying to get to the door. He makes it, but a roar of protest comes from the spectators, forcing Judge Logan to repeatedly rap for order. Mother faces the crowd and raises his hands for quiet, and there follows an insistent, expectant silence. He nods this thanks and returns to the FBI agent. "Is the thumbprint—the one lifted from the face of the vault by Detective Stonemann *personally,* the one signed, dated, and recorded by yourself—is that *my* thumbprint?"

"No, sir." The agent is quietly respectful. "Someone skilled in fingerprinting made a photoengraving of your print, fashioned a replica in some soft material, and pressed it into the lightly oiled surface of the vault door."

"Someone skilled in fingerprinting, who also had access to the door of the vault?"

The agent nods, shifts uncomfortably, and whispers, "Yes, sir."

"Why didn't you explain this in my first trial?"

"You never asked."

Dog is laughing and shaking his head. "Boy, does that process ever sound familiar. The warden's office wasn't a creation. It was a rehash!"

"A rehash of what the detective did to him!" Odds grins. "What a getback."

Mother is in front of the bench, staring up at Judge Logan. "Your Honor, based upon the perjured and deliberately misleading testimony presented by the government, I move for a directed verdict of acquittal."

The spectator section erupts. Logan is banging for order, and finally several United States marshals burst through the doors and begin herding everyone outside. We are ejected with the rest of the audience. As I'm being pushed out the door, I catch a glimpse of Mother. He's moved over to the corner of the first row and is staring angrily down into the face of Senator Stonemann. The hairs on the back of my neck are waltzing to the tune of "Here I Go Again."

Noid is off to one side with Cynthia when I extricate Mary from the crush. We work our way through a crowd of grumbling citizens and join them in a relatively quiet corner.

"Logan and Kroeger are trying to find a way around the motion for a directed verdict." Cynthia motions to Noid, who is listening intently on his earplug radio.

"He's going to send the case to the jury!" Noid is incredulous.

"But that's ridiculous," Mary complains. "No jury in the world would convict on perjured testimony."

"Judge Logan has a golfing partner on the jury," Noid answers, tapping the earplug. "He thinks there is some possibility he might hang the jury with a single vote for conviction."

"And put his friend Logan through this publicity again? I don't think so." Mary is shaking her head.

The bailiff raps on the wall for our attention, and shouts, "Judge Logan is going to reopen the courtroom in five minutes. He advises, any more demonstrations and he will close the courtroom and seal it to the public."

"He oughta close it permanent," an older man in bib overalls shouts back. "Afore he gets hisself run outa town on a rail."

The bailiff glances nervously at the marshals and scurries back inside.

"Mother's finest hour." Big Smith is grinning as he joins us. "What a getback!"

The doors to the courtroom swing open, and we are swept back inside by the angry and ominously silent crowd.

Inside I break all of the rules and go to the bar. "You're killing them, Mother," I say proudly.

He smiles back sadly. "I just didn't get the job done soon enough." And his eyes cut to where Karl Conroy is sitting. The younger Conroy gives Mother a thumbs-up sign and smiles.

"All rise. The court of the Honorable Francis W. Logan is back in session."

"Mr. Conroy?" Judge Logan's tone is tight.

"Your Honor."

"I have decided to let this case go to the jury. The prosecution will now make its closing argument." Amid the surprised muttering in the courtroom and the incredulous expressions of the jury members, Mr. Kroeger rises and begins his summation. "Ladies and gentlemen of the jury. You have had the opportunity to hear the evidence. And I admit it was imperfect evidence, but there are many considerations in a criminal trial, the first of which is the right of a community to protect itself against the marauders . . ." and I realize I'm hearing the same speech the judge gave at the beginning of the trial. Kroeger has decided not to sum up the facts; he's in the process of summing up the indictment. As he speaks, I'm able to identify Judge Logan's golfing partner. He's a sharp-featured man in a gray pinstripe sitting in the last seat of the first row. Damn! It's the traditional foreman's seat!

"Mr. Conroy. Your summation, please." Logan's voice brings me back to the business at hand.

Mother gives Kroeger a look I would classify as sympathetic, and begins his summation. "Ladies and gentlemen of the jury, you have heard the government's case, seen that same case dissected, and learned two possible motives for the robbery: greed or revenge. Revenge against a blight on this community, the Fall City National Bank, a cancerous institution that threatens the financial stability of the area, and, as you have heard for yourselves, corrupted the moral fiber of those you depend upon to keep the peace."

He is staring at the judge and prosecutor alternately as he speaks, completely ignoring the jury. The jurors are looking over his shoulder as he chastises the guilty parties.

"Yes, a crime has been committed in Fall City. Many crimes. Crimes where lands were stolen, lives ruined and . . . snuffed out. I am not on trial here. Fall City is, and I expect you to retire to the jury room, reach a verdict of not guilty, and return in less than five minutes. In this way, and *only* in this way, you can deliver your clear and unmistakable message. Enough is enough! We will not support these frauds any longer. Thank you."

Judge Logan charges the jury members. They are fidgeting in the box, eager to get to the deliberation room. Even Judge Logan's buddy looks like he wants to kill something, or somebody . . . possibly Judge Logan, from the way he's glaring at him.

The jury is out and back in four minutes flat. The foreman hands its verdict to the court clerk, who opens it, makes a notation, then hands it up to Judge Logan. He reads it, and I have to hand it to him: There isn't a quiver of emotion on his face. He writes himself a brief note that I'd give 10K to read, then hands the decision back to the clerk to be read.

"The jury finds the defendant, Donald R. Conroy, not guilty on all c—"

The courtroom erupts. People are cheering, men are slapping

one another on the back, and some farmers are holding their children up above the crowd to let them see what has to become a major event in the history of Fall City. The noise is deafening.

And 3-J-5 isn't doing much to lower the noise level. Dog, the Smiths, and Fast Eddie are doing something akin to an Irish jig, while Mary, Cynthia, and Alecia are hugging one another and generally trying to raise the local water table to the fifth floor with their tears.

"I'll stay here while Mother gets his things," I shout to Mary over the cheering as the marshals hustle Mother out of the courtroom. "We'll meet at the Red Lion as soon as I can get him out of here."

Cynthia is sobbing, and can't speak. I nod to Noid, and he leads her away. "Go along with Fast and Alecia," I tell Mary.

I cut through the back door of the courtroom and down to the marshal's office. Mother is just signing for a small package as I enter. I can't help myself; I hug him. "You got 'em."

"They got themselves," he says, and he sounds tired, withdrawn.

"But they're out of business. The detective, Kroeger, Logan, probably even the bank!"

"Not a very good trade," he says, and looks up at Karl Jr., who has just come into the office.

I'm in the way. "I'll be waiting for you outside on the steps." As I leave, they're hugging each other and exchanging pats on the back.

Outside, the crowd is gradually dissipating into angry knots of people. My prediction was right. The Fall City National Bank is in for some very close scrutiny. Scrutiny that it cannot survive.

By the time Mother comes down the steps I'm alone.

"Where's your cousin?"

"He's down at the Federal Land Bank office, filing papers to recover the farm."

"He'll win that one."

"Yeah." Mother allows himself a smile. "I suppose he will."

I know where I want to take this conversation; I just don't know where to start. Sound the bugles. Charge. "Who in hell really robbed the bank? We've got it figured it was the detectives working with the bank president."

"I robbed the bank, James."

When I find my voice I mutter, "The fake fingerprints—same deal you pulled on Creech?"

"Of course. Remember I told you I learned the technique in Idaho?"

"But why did you wait so long to—"

"After I robbed the bank I went by young Karl's and discovered he'd left for South America. His note said he needed some time to himself to sort out what he wanted to do with his life. I knew if I did as I had intended, proved the print a fake at the first trial, he would have been extradited immediately, then tried and convicted in Logan's court."

"Cynthia found young Karl and brought him back?"

"Yes. She also dug up two solid alibi witnesses. His girlfriend and her father were trying to talk him out of leaving at the time the bank was being robbed." He pauses and sighs. "He had a perfect alibi. The best-laid plans . . ."

"God. You wasted five years of your life in prison."

"Wasted?" He's smiling and shaking his head. "I don't think so. I certainly don't consider the men from 3-J-5 a waste."

"You son of a bitch."

"Your language." He chuckles. "Well, I suppose that's about it." He shakes my hand and walks off down the steps. I'm so choked up I can't speak.

"Hey. The celebration," I finally manage to say.

"That's your victory party, Flat Store. You and the rest. You've beaten the system by staying out." And he's off again.

"Is the trial over?" A young woman is at my elbow, notebook in hands, and out of breath.

"Yes," I say as I watch Mother reach the bottom of the steps and head toward the corner.

"That man you were talking to—wasn't he . . . I mean, I'm supposed to be covering this story, and I'm late. Oh, shit! Who was that man?"

Mother is crossing the street now, his image wavering in the heat bouncing up from the pavement. A truck passes between us, and when it's gone, Mother is too.

"I said, who was that man you were talking to?"

"I don't know, young lady. I really don't know."

Epilogue

Déjà vu. I'm fishing again. Another unopened telegram waits confidently in my lap.

I'm thinking back to the last day of Mother's trial.

Dog and Big Smith always did have more sense than I did. They'd expected Mother to try a disappearing act, and they were waiting for him. Big grabbed him right off the street, and he and the Dog bundled Mother into the back of Dog's pickup and brought him to the party at the Red Lion.

It was a great celebration: HiHo crackers, peanut butter, and jam, along with several gallons of hot chocolate.

I took a lot of ribbing about letting Mother get away. Dog said I'd lost all of my criminal instincts. The conversation went downhill from there. It took Mother a while to loosen up, but by the end of the party he was laughing and telling jokes with us and whispering to Cynthia as she snuggled up under his arm. The arrangement was starting to look permanent, but it hasn't worked out that way as yet.

Cynthia won her Pulitzer for the exposé on the Fall City National Bank, and the last time I talked with Mother, he was starting after Senator Stonemann. When I heard that, all the hairs on the back of my neck took a quick lap to the top, peered into the future, and skittered back home, shaky as a Democrat's morals at a beach party.

But things have worked out well, I tell myself, eyeing the telegram suspiciously. Cynthia with her prize, Mary and me happier than the law allows, the rest of the crew in varying stages of Fat City, and Mother and young Karl with the family farm in full production.

I'm still trying to educate this perch. Have been since the trial ended six months ago. Even now he's playing games with the bait, sort of pushing it around with his nose, trying to put some thrills and meaning back into his life, I imagine. Risky business.

Dumb fish. He'll never learn.

That's three of us ... Let's read the telegram and find out when we're going to work.